ONLY WHEN IT'S US

Bergman Brothers (#1)

CHLOE LIESE

Cover Art by
JENNIE ROSE DENTON OF LAMPLIGHT CREATIVE

Only When It's Us

A Bergman Brothers Novel (#1)

Chloe Liese

Copyright © 2020, 2021 Chloe Liese

Published by Chloe Liese

All rights reserved.

REVISED AND EXPANDED 2021 EDITION

As of August 21, 2021, this title has been revised, expanded, and republished to improve representational authenticity and content quality. As of December 7, 2021, the audiobook reflecting this version is now sold everywhere, and the previous version has been unpublished.

Please note, some libraries may retain earlier versions of both print and audiobook; to be sure you have the latest edition, check that their publication year is 2021 and that the description includes this heading: "Revised and Expanded 2021 Edition."

CONTENT NOTES

INCLUDES SPOILERS

This is an open door romance that portrays on-page consensual sexual intimacy. This story includes terminal illness of a parent due to cancer. Parental death occurs but is not portrayed on-page. As someone who has lost loved ones in this way, I know this topic is difficult and tender for many. This story also includes a main character who is late-deafened. As of this book's revision, expansion, and republication on August 21, 2021, its portrayal has been informed by the consulted experience and critique of a late-deafened authenticity reader. I hope I have given these subjects the respect, care, and sensitivity they deserve.

PLAYLIST NOTE

At the beginning of each chapter, a song and artist is provided as another optional means of emotional connection to the story. It isn't a necessity—for some it may be a distraction or for others, inaccessible—nor are the lyrics literally about the chapter. Listen before or while you read for a soundtrack experience. If you enjoy playlists, rather than individually searching each song as you read, you can directly access these songs on a Spotify Playlist by logging onto your Spotify account and entering "Only When It's Us (BB #1)" into the search browser.

For every woman who fought bravely
and for those who loved her through it.

"Is not general incivility the very essence of love?"
  – Jane Austen, *Pride and Prejudice*

CONTENTS

WILLA

Playlist: "Hurricane," Bridgit Mendler

I'VE BEEN TOLD I HAVE A TEMPER.

I prefer to be called *tempestuous*. Big word for a soccer jock, I know, but work in a bookstore as many summers as I have, and you can't help but broaden your vocabulary.

Tempestuous: "typified by strong, turbulent or conflicting emotion."

For better or for worse, that's me, Willa Rose Sutter, to a T.

Is my fuse a little short? Sure. Are my responses occasionally disproportional? Sometimes. I could learn to simmer down here and there, but I refuse to subdue the storm inside myself. Because inextricably knotted with my tempestuousness is the force of nature that is my drive. I'm competitive. And *that* is an advantageous personality trait. I'm an aspiring professional athlete, set on becoming the world's best in my sport. To be the best, you need raw skill, but even more so, you have to be hungry. You have to want it more than anybody else. That's how far-off dreams become reality.

So, yes. Sometimes, I'm a little feisty. I'm scrappy and

hardworking, and I like to win. I don't settle. I won't give up. *Nothing* gets in my way.

Which is why I seriously need to get my shit together, because something *is* about to get in my way. My eligibility for next week's match against our biggest rival hangs by a thread, thanks to the Business Mathematics course and professor from hell.

I'm late to class, trying not to limp because of how much my muscles ache after a brutal practice. As I scurry down the ramp in the massive lecture hall, it takes everything in me not to say *ouch-ouch-ouch-ouch* with every single step I take.

The room's packed, only a few stray seats remaining in the very first row.

A groan leaves me. Great. I get to show up late and make that super obvious by sitting front and center. As quietly as I can manage with muscles that are screaming for ibuprofen and a hot bath, I slip into an empty spot and silently extract my notebook.

Professor MacCormack continues scribbling equations on the board. Maybe my late entrance went undetected.

"Miss Sutter." He drops the chalk and spins, dusting off his hands. "Good of you to join us."

Dammit.

"Sorry, Professor."

"Get caught up from Ryder." Completely sidestepping my apology, MacCormack spins back to the board and throws a thumb over his shoulder to the right of me. "He has my notes."

My jaw drops. I've asked Mac for notes three times so far this semester when I had to miss for traveling games. He'd shrugged, then said I needed to "problem solve and figure out my priorities." This Ryder guy just *gets* them?

That temper of mine turns my cheeks red. The tips of my

ears grow hot, and if flames could burst out of my head, they would.

Finally, I turn to where Mac gestured, sickly curious to see this guy that my professor favors with lecture notes while I'm left scrambling to catch up with no help whatsoever. And I really need that help. I'm barely holding a C minus that's about to become a D, unless God looks with favor on his lowly maiden, Willa Rose Sutter, and does her a solid on our upcoming midterm.

Rage is a whole-body experience for me. My breathing accelerates. From the neck up, I turn into a hot tamale. My heart beats so thunderously, my pulse points bang like drums. I am *livid*. And it's with that full-body anger coursing through my veins that I lay my eyes on the favored one. Ryder, Keeper of Notes.

He wears a ball cap tugged low over shaggy dark-blond hair. A mangy beard that's not terribly long still obscures his face enough that I don't really know what he looks like, not that I care. His eyes are down on the lecture notes, tracking left–right, so I can't see what they look like. He has a long nose that's annoyingly perfect and which sniffs absently, as if he's completely clueless that I'm both watching him and that he's supposed to be sharing those lecture notes. The notes that I could have used to avoid failing the last two pop quizzes and our first writing assignment.

My eyes flick back up to MacCormack, who has the audacity to smirk at me over his shoulder. I shut my eyes, summoning calm that I don't have. It's that or tackle my professor in a blind rage.

Eyes on the prize, Willa.

I need to pass this class to stay eligible to play. I need to stay eligible to play because I need to play every game, both to maximize my team's chances for success, and because

Murphy's Law states that scouts come to games you miss. Well, really it just states that if something can go wrong when it's real inconvenient, it will. The scout scenario is my version of it.

The point is I need the damn notes, and in order to get them, I'm going to have to swallow my pride and explicitly petition this jerk who's ignoring me. I clear my throat. *Loudly*. Ryder sniffs again and flips the page, his eyes glancing up to the equations on the board, then back down. Does he turn? Acknowledge me? Say, *Hi, how can I help you*?

Of course not.

MacCormack prattles on, his notes both on the chalkboard and the projector screen, where his words unfurl as captioned text in large, clear font. The next slide pops up before I got it all written down, and I grow angrier by the minute. It's like Mac *wants* me to fail.

Taking another steadying breath, I whisper to Ryder, "Excuse me?"

Ryder blinks. His brow furrows. I have the faintest hope he's heard me and is about to turn my way, but instead, he flicks to a previous page of the printout and scribbles a note.

I sit dumbfounded for minutes before I slowly face the board, fury shaking my limbs. My fingers curl around my pen. My hand whips open my notebook so violently, I almost rip off the cover. I want to scream with frustration, but the fact is that all I have control over is the here and now. So I bite my tongue and start writing madly.

After twenty minutes, MacCormack drops his chalk, then turns and addresses the class. In the haze of my wrath, I vaguely hear him field questions. Students raise their hands and answer, because they've actually followed this lecture, because, unlike me, most of them probably don't have two lives pulling them apart. Athlete and student, woman and daughter.

Because they have leeway, wiggle room, which I don't. I *have* to be excellent, and the problem is that this pressure is instead turning me into an absolute failure. Well, except for soccer. Over my dead body will I fail at that. Everything else, though, is going to shit. I'm a scattered friend, an absent daughter, a lackluster student. And if this professor would just cut me a damn break, I'd have a chance of at least scratching one of those failures off my list.

MacCormack must feel my eyes burning holes into him, because after he accepts the last answer, he turns, looks at me again, and smirks.

"Professor MacCormack," I say between clenched teeth.

"Why, yes, Miss Sutter?"

"Is this some kind of joke?"

"I'm sorry, no, that is not the correct formula for calculating compound interest." Turning back to everyone, he offers them a smile I have yet to see. "Class dismissed!"

I sit, stupefied that I've been swept aside by my professor yet again. It's the cherry on top when Ryder rises from his seat, slides those precious notes into a worn leather crossbody bag, and throws it over his shoulder. As he secures the flap on his bag, his eyes dart up, then finally meet mine. They widen, then take me in with a quick trail over my body.

Ryder's eyes are deep green, and damn him, that's my favorite color, the precise shade of a pristine soccer field. That's all I have time to notice before my resentment blocks me from appreciating any more of his features. When his gaze returns from my sneakers and sweatpants ensemble, our eyes meet, his narrowing as he processes whatever terrifying expression I wear. I am enraged. I'm sure I look murderous.

Now he acknowledges my existence, after so thoroughly ignoring me?

Rolling his shoulders back, he straightens fully. All I can think is, *Wow, that's not just an asshole. That's a tall asshole.*

I shoot out of my seat, sweeping my notebook off the desk. Jamming my pen into the giant messy bun on top of my head, I give him a death glare. Ryder's gaze widens as I take a step closer and meet those nauseatingly perfect green eyes.

A long, intense stare-down ensues. Ryder's eyes narrow. Mine do, too. They water, begging me to blink. I refuse to.

Slowly, the corner of his mouth tugs up. He's smirking at me, the asshole.

And just like that, my eyes drag down to his mouth, which is hidden under all that gnarly facial hair. I blink.

Shit. I hate losing. I *hate* losing.

I'm about to open my mouth and ask just what's so damn funny when Ryder backs away and pivots smoothly, then jogs up the ramp of the lecture hall. I stand, shaking with rage, pissed at this jerk and his odd, dismissive behavior, until the room is virtually empty.

"Cheer up, Miss Sutter." MacCormack switches off the lights, bathing the lecture hall in gray shadows and faint morning sun that streams through the windows.

"I don't really know how to be cheery when I'm about to fail your class and I can't afford to do that, Professor."

For a moment, his mask of detached amusement slips, but it's back before I can even be sure it ever left. "You'll figure out what to do. Have a nice day."

When the door falls shut and I'm left alone, I sink into my seat once again, the whisper of failure echoing in the room.

———

"HE REALLY JUST WALKED OFF?" ROONEY—MY TEAMMATE and roommate—stares at me in disbelief.

"Yup." I'd say more, but I'm too angry and winded. We're doing technical drills, and while I'm in the best shape of my life, ladders always kick my butt.

"Wow." Rooney, on the other hand, isn't winded one bit. I've decided she's a mutant, because I have never heard that woman short of breath, and it's not for lack of trying. Our coach is a clinically verified sadist. "What a dick."

Rooney looks like a life-size Barbie. Classic SoCal girl— legs for miles, glowing skin and faint freckles, a sheet of platinum-blonde hair that's forever in a long, smooth ponytail. She stands and drinks her water, looking like a beach model as the sun lowers in the sky. I, on the other hand, look like Dolores Umbridge after the centaurs got her. My wiry hair puffs madly from my ponytail, my cheeks are dark pink with exertion, and my muscular soccer quads are shaking from effort. Rooney and I could not be more opposite, not just when it comes to looks, but also personality, and that's perhaps what makes us such good friends.

"No doubt, he's a dick," I confirm. "But he's the dick who has what I need: past lecture notes and the ones I'll miss when I'm gone for two more classes during away games."

We both jog toward the next section of the field to start one-touch drills. I run backward first, Rooney flicking the ball into the air before she lofts it my way. I head it back, she volleys it to me, I head it back. We'll do this until we switch directions, then it's her turn.

Rooney serves me the ball, and I head it down to her feet. "So if that guy won't give you the notes, what are you going to do?"

"I don't *know* what to do. That's my problem. I see no solution for a guy who downright ignores me. I know I can be a little prickly, but I was polite. Whereas he was just…rude. I don't get why. And I really need those notes."

Switching directions, I scoop the ball onto my foot and softly kick it into the air, right to Rooney's forehead.

"Honestly," Rooney says as she returns my pass with a header, "I'd say the issue is with your professor. He's obligated by our student contract to accommodate your schedule, and this behavior is overtly hostile to your efforts as a student athlete. If I were you, I'd print out our agreement, head to office hours, and remind that jerk that he's ethically and legally bound to support your learning while you earn his college more publicity and money than his pathetic academic papers have *ever* contributed."

Yeah. Rooney looks like Barbie, but she's got stuff between her ears. She'll make a great lawyer one day.

"Maybe. But this guy's a hard-ass, Roo. I think he'll just make my life even more miserable if I do that."

Rooney frowns, heading the ball back again. "Okay, so show him the contract, but do it nicely. Kill him with kindness. Do whatever it takes to be sure you're eligible to play next week. We need you, and honestly, Willa, I think if you don't play, you'll internally combust."

As we finish our drill, the ball drops to my feet, and I stare down at its familiar shape. It's a view I've seen a thousand times—that black and white ball set against bright green grass, my cleats on either side of it. Soccer is the one constant in my life when everything else has been unpredictable. I live and breathe this sport, not only because I want to be the best, but because it's the only thing that's kept me going sometimes.

Rooney's right. I can't miss, I can't be ineligible. I'm going to have to suck it up and do whatever it takes to pass this class.

"Come on," she says, throwing an arm over my shoulder. "My turn to cook tonight."

I fake a dry heave, earning her rough shove that sends me stumbling sideways. "Great. I needed a good cleanse anyway."

2

WILLA

Playlist: "Might Not Like Me," Brynn Elliott

MY REPUTATION AS A HOTHEAD IS WELL-KNOWN ACROSS campus. I've had a few altercations on the soccer field, as well as one episode freshman year, when some chick went off on Rooney in the cafeteria, accusing her of stealing her boyfriend. I'd already climbed the table with the intent to knock that liar on the ground and finish her off with a good, WWE-style elbow drop, when Rooney thankfully grabbed me by the collar before I could get myself expelled. Nevertheless, the incident earned me a reputation I've done nothing to disabuse people of. It's kept almost everyone either afraid of me or allowing me a healthy distance. That suits me just fine.

But the truth is, as much as I spring to the defense of the people I love, as ready as I am to lean in a shoulder, to shove and struggle for possession every moment I'm on the field, I do *not* like verbal conflict. I think I'm actually allergic to verbal disagreements and uncomfortable conversations. Every time they happen, I break out in hives.

Which is why angry, itchy spots pop up along my neck and chest as I sit at Professor MacCormack's desk and watch him read my student athlete agreement.

"Hm." Flipping over the last page, he spins the document on his desk and slides it back my way. "Listen, Sutter. Believe it or not, I like and respect you."

My eyebrows shoot up. "Could have fooled me."

Mac's smirk is back. I have to sit on my hands so I don't accidentally slap it off.

"I'm not handing this class to you. You chose to be a student athlete, and with that comes a responsibility to manage your time. You didn't tell me ahead of the class when you'd be missing, or that you'd need notes. You didn't communicate until the day of class you missed and then the second time, *afterward*. That tells me this class isn't a priority, and frankly, I think it needs to be. This is a foundational course if you want to be prepared for any kind of business management down the line."

I shift in my seat. I knew I'd be missing classes for games, but asking him ahead of time was daunting. I would have had to meet with him separately, ask for those considerations. It felt...well, it felt uncomfortable, and as I've said, I don't do verbal confrontation well.

"Which leads me to believe," he continues, "that you're one of those athletes who thinks she doesn't *need* an education, who's just punching in and out, going through the motions. That doesn't fly in my class."

I open my mouth to tell him that's really unfair, that I love learning what I need to know for business management. That I truly want to do well in this class and my other major-related courses, because I know I won't be a professional athlete forever. When I'm retired, I hope to use my platform for philanthropic work, and I want to ensure I run it myself and do a damn good job of it. I should tell him all of that, but nothing comes out. My jaw clamps shut, and my stomach knots sharply.

MacCormack leans in, elbows on his desk. Nerdy black frames obscure ocean-blue eyes. His near-black hair is stylishly messy, he has a constant five-o'clock shadow, and if he weren't such a giant sabotaging jerkface who was at least ten years older than me, I'd probably think he was cute. Right now, all I can think is that he's the guy who's going to ruin my soccer career.

"You look upset," he says quietly.

I take a jagged inhale as hot tears prick my eyes. *No crying, Sutter. Never show them your weak spot.*

"I'm sorry," I manage around the lump in my throat. "I'm not...I don't talk well when..." Swallowing, I pinch the bridge of my nose and breathe deeply. When I exhale, I'm somewhat together, and I find my courage. "I care about this class. I realize I haven't shown you that very well. I should have asked you before the semester started, but I've never had to do that before. In the past, professors have automatically held notes for me and sent me what I needed."

Mac sits back in his seat, brow furrowed. "Well, I'm not one of those professors, and if you're going to make it as a professional female athlete, I've got news for you—you have to learn how to start sticking up for yourself."

I reel. "Yeah, so, I'm aware of the prejudices and double standards female athletes face, and I'm prepared for them. But thanks for the lecture anyway."

"Fine." He throws his hands up. "My point is, I'm not impeding your success in this class. I've been here, available to you, and there's a sea of people in that room you could ask for notes. I handed you Ryder on a silver platter—"

"A silver platter?" I slap my hands on his desk and lean in. "He ignored me entirely."

"Maybe you didn't do enough to make yourself heard." Mac shrugs, standing and sweeping a pile of papers and his laptop into his arms. He looks at his wristwatch, then at me. "Either way, your success is not my responsibility. I've given you a solution to your problem. I'm not holding your hand to get there. Figure it out. Talk to him. Don't just whisper once, then give up and throw him a death glare."

My eyes widen. "Do you have surveillance in that room?"

That damn smirk widens to a grin. "Just eyes in the back of my head. What professor doesn't? Come on, Sutter. Time for class."

———

THIS TIME I'M NOT THE ONLY ONE WHO'S LATE. MacCormack strides briskly ahead of me, dropping his pile of papers onto the desk with a *thwack*, hooking up his laptop to the projector and a small microphone to his dress-shirt collar, then immediately jumping into the lecture. Once again, the place is packed, and once again, the only remaining seat is next to the tall asshole, Ryder, Keeper of Notes.

While I was too angry to really process his appearance last time, I recognize in retrospect that he's wearing essentially the same thing, a uniform of sorts: frayed dark-blue ball cap, another soft-looking flannel loose over his torso, and faded jeans. His long legs stretch out from his seat, and his eyes are down, scanning this class's lecture notes. Once again, he completely ignores me. I drop into my seat, huffing as I whip open my notebook.

At least this time I'll be able to follow the lecture in its entirety. No thanks to *him.*

As MacCormack lectures, I'm sucked into the class material because, like I nearly chickened out on telling him, I really do love learning about business management. My concentration is unflappable. I'm making notes left and right.

I even raise my hand and ask Mac a question that earns his surprised, approving smile. I'm getting back on track. I still have to figure out how to get notes for the remaining coursework I'll miss, but for today, Willa Rose Sutter is on her game—

My arm's bumped, and my writing hand flies diagonally, sending a slash of black pen across my notes. I whip to the right, meeting eyes with Ryder. His are annoyingly, startlingly green like last time, and once again they're wide, as if I surprised him by existing.

I glance down from my page, then back to him. "What the hell was that?" I hiss.

His mouth drops open, and for a second, I'm oddly distracted by that. With his startled expression, that haphazard hair and scraggly beard, the blue-and-green plaid flannel he's wearing, he looks like a lumberjack interrupted mid-swing. My gaze lowers from his eyes, searching his face. So much is hidden behind that blond scruff. Cheekbones, lips, a jawline.

What does he look like underneath all that?

Snapping myself out of those bizarre thoughts, I lock eyes with him again, my gaze widening with expectation. I'm waiting for an apology, an explanation, *anything* that accounts for why he just threw an elbow into my arm and made me screw up my notes.

But nothing comes. His jaw clamps shut, his eyes narrow, and then he spins forward, his focus back on the chalkboard. Mac changes the slide on the projector, earning a groan from roughly one-third of the class who wasn't writing fast enough. That would include me, thanks to the asshole lumberjack, who distracted me from reading and recording the last few minutes.

"You'll remember," Mac says to the class, "that the format of this course is the first six weeks are dedicated to drilling into you the foundation of Business Mathematics. I'm teaching you theory, and I'm cramming it down your throat. I realize you're probably overwhelmed at this point."

A collective sigh followed by a wave of mumbles and whispers indicates MacCormack might be a formidable instructor, but at least knows his audience.

"Now we are at the point in our course in which you are assigned a collaborative partner for the remainder of the semester. This is for two reasons. One, because of the size of this class," Mac says. "Unlike many instructors, I'm not passing you off to TAs. You get me, all semester, all office hours, and the trade-off is I halve the number of papers and projects I have to keep up on grading when I pair you up. Two, because anybody who wants a career in business needs to develop core skills of collaboration, negotiation, and compromise. Knowing numbers and economic theory is useless if you can't talk with your teammates, listen to their ideas, and synthesize your insights into a practical, successful application.

"While the major focus of your teamwork is your final project and test, midterms are right around the corner. I suggest you begin sooner rather than later familiarizing your-self with your partner and supporting each other's learning. Study together, quiz each other. Get used to each other. Even though we aren't even halfway through the semester, start working on your project concept as soon as you're paired off. Your final project and examination account for fifty percent of your grade, so for those of you who are struggling thus far…" His eyes dance across the room, and he makes a point of lifting his eyebrows when he looks at me. "I suggest you take this quite seriously. It can make or break your grade."

Another collective groan echoes around the lecture hall.

Mac smirks, hands in his pockets. "Pairs will be announced . next class. Have a great day, everybody!"

Before I can even put the cap on my pen, Ryder's out of his seat. Tossing his bag over his shoulder, he storms out of the room, weaving and pressing his way through the slowly exiting throng.

I turn back slowly, stunned at this guy's level of douchery. I mean, it takes *work* to be that big of a dick.

"But he's kind of a cute dick," a voice says.

I jump and spin to my left. "Sorry. I didn't know I was thinking out loud."

She shrugs and smiles. "No worries. I could tell. I'm Emily."

"Willa." Standing, I fold my notebook shut and stuff it into my bookbag.

Her smile widens. "Oh, I love that name. Like the novelist, Willa Cather?"

I nod as pain pinches my chest and I think of Mama. "Yep."

I should ask Emily if she takes thorough notes and if I could impose on her to copy them. But once again, my tongue-tied fear of asking anyone for anything—or worse, having my request be rejected—silences me.

"Well, have a nice day!" she says brightly.

I have mountains of schoolwork, practice to prepare for the game against one of our toughest competitors, and I'm heading to the hospital to hear how my mom's latest biopsy went. *Nice* isn't what I expect this day to be.

"Thanks," I manage. "You too."

———

I'M USED TO THE HOSPITAL ROUTINE BY NOW. THE SMELLS, the sounds. The whoosh and ping of elevators arriving, sneakers squeaking on linoleum. The din of fluorescents and the mixed smell of antiseptic and urine. Oddly enough, I don't hate it. It's the place that's been home to Mama this past month, and wherever she is, that's where I want to be.

"Willa Rose!" Mama sets down her book and opens her thin arms wide for me.

"Hi, Mama." I blow her a kiss, then tug off my hoodie and wash my hands diligently. Mama's immunosuppressed, and college kids are petri dishes, Dr. B said, so I scrub up to my elbows, followed by a few squirts of hand sanitizer for good measure.

Finally, I can lean over and accept her hug. It's strong and long-lasting. She clasps her fingers together behind my back like always and gives me a good squeeze.

"How was your day, honey?" she asks.

Mama sits back, and her eyes meet mine. When I look at my mother, I'm always grateful for the reminder that, but for my crazy hair, I'm nearly her duplicate. It lets me pretend that I just came from Mama, that I'm all hers.

"Not too bad." I sit gently on the edge of her bed and eyeball her uneaten tray of food.

She waves her hand. "It tastes like garbage."

"But, Mama, if you don't eat, you won't have energy. And you need your energy."

Sighing, she clasps my fingers. "I know. Barbara from that church outreach program is bringing me homemade chicken soup later on."

God bless that church program because it picks up my slack. *I* should be cooking my mom homemade meals, not some sweet Lutheran lady named Barbara, but I'll take it. It nourishes Mama, and she usually gets a nice visit with a stranger. Unlike me, my mother doesn't totally stick her foot in her mouth when she converses with others, and actually enjoys small talk.

Mama and I are all alone, and I don't see that as a bad thing, just how it is. We've traveled too much over the years to pick up any lasting friendships, and we're both fairly solitary women. My family has only ever been Grandma Rose and Mama. Grandma Rose died when I was in high school, and I still miss her. She was a real firecracker who loved her vegetable and flower gardens, always won at Trivial Pursuit, chain-smoked, and swore like a sailor. Apparently, I inherited her temper.

"Okay." I pull out an orange and start peeling it. Once I tug all the fine fibers off of the segments, Mama and I will split it. It's our routine. "What's the news?" My eyes are on the orange as I tear the peel and send a spray of zest into the air. I'm worried I'm going to see that look in Mama's eyes when she has to tell me bad news.

"What news?" she asks.

My eyes snap up to her. "Don't play dumb, Joy Sutter."

She smiles, and it makes her eyes twinkle. "Biopsy wasn't great, but Dr. B's got a game plan for me. He's my triple threat—brains, balls, and beauty."

I jerk my head back, making sure no one is at the door.

Mama chuckles. "He knows I'm joking. But I do think the world of him, and he totally uses it to his advantage, getting me to do things like eat my meals and walk around the halls."

"Smart man," I mutter. "Tall, ginger, and handsome was always your speed."

"I like what I like. Gingers don't get enough love in this world. Now, talk to me about life, school, the team." Mama shifts in her bed and tries to hide a grimace. "I feel like I have no clue what's going on these days."

I tell her about the pad thai that Rooney tried to make the other night, how it made the whole apartment smell like a rotten fish carcass and the noodles were so hard when I took a bite, I was positive I'd cracked a molar.

Mama laughs until it turns into a coughing fit. A nurse stops in, giving my mom some oxygen while giving me a look that says, *Simmer down, Sutter.*

Deciding I'll try not to make her laugh like that anymore for the night, I tell Mama about the upcoming match, the strategy we're taking to be more offensive than usual. We've been playing me as the lone striker, so if they're smart, our opposition will try to double-team me. We'll set Rooney on top with me as a fellow forward, rather than her typical spot in midfield. If Rooney's up there, pulling their defense, hopefully she and I can string together a couple of goals.

"That sounds great," Mama says. She pops an orange segment in her mouth and smiles. "Scouts will be coming around soon, keeping their eye on you, right?"

I throw back an orange segment, too. "Yep," I say around my bite. "If I can stay eligible."

Mama's faint eyebrows shoot up. "I'm sorry, Willa Rose, have I missed something? You are a hardworking, dependable student. Your grades have never been in jeopardy before."

Groaning, I drop sideways until my head is in her lap. Mama's hands wander to my hair, trying to make order out of chaos. "Tell me, honey."

It tumbles out. How I naively expected Professor MacCormack to act like every other instructor I've had, and when I realized he wasn't going to, how nervous I got to ask him for what I needed. I don't get to tell her about the asshole lumberjack before Mama *tsks* and shakes her head.

"You never have been good at having the tough conversations." Mama sighs. "Don't know where you got that. If someone paid me to argue for a living, I would."

Her hands are so soothing, I let my eyes slide shut and savor the sensation of her fingers, rhythmically sliding through my hair. Once she's done, my wild hair won't be half as tangled, but it will be twice as puffy. I don't mind, though. "You'd have made a great lawyer, Mama. Between you and Rooney, I'm surrounded by pugnacious personalities—"

"That's it!" Mom reaches for her crossword puzzle, tongue stuck out as she writes in the letters. "Pug-na-cious. Oh, Willa, thank you. Now I can rub it in Dr. B's face when he next stops in."

I pick up my head and meet her eyes. "So it's Dr. B who put you up to crosswords?" She's been obsessed with them for a few weeks now, texting me all hours of the day and night, when she wants to see if Rooney or I know a word she's looking for.

"Well, he said if I ate my meals and didn't drop any more weight on him, he'd let me out for your championship game."

"Mama, we have to make it through qualifiers and playoffs—"

"Ah. Ah. Ah." Mama holds up her hand, commanding silence. "What have I taught you?"

I sigh. "I can do anything I set my heart and mind to."

"That's right. You want that championship game, Willa, you'll get it. As I was saying, if I keep my weight up, I get to come, but if I do the *New York Times* crossword in one day, he'll take me himself in his fancy sports car."

I sit upright, abruptly. "But it's in San Jose this year. Isn't that dangerous? I mean, the travel will take it out of you, and the outside world is a germ-fest, and—"

"Willa." Mama interlaces her fingers with mine and smiles reassuringly. "It's fine. He's a doctor, he knows."

My shoulders are pinched, worry twisting my stomach. I hate that Mama's sick enough to need to be in the hospital, but I love that here, I know she's safe and taken care of. As far as I'm concerned, I want her here, getting the care she needs, for as long as necessary. Thankfully, Grandma Rose left us decent life savings, and Mama's military pension helps. That's where virtually all of our finances go—her cancer treatment, so she can get better as soon as possible.

Given that, I'm pretty much financially on my own, which I don't mind. For years each summer, I've worked at a local bookstore—that's where I learn words like *tempestuous* and *pugnacious* to add to my vocabulary. An indie bookseller that also serves coffee and baked goods, it experiences a great boost to business during touristy summer months, so I make nice tips, on top of a decent hourly wage. Whatever I earn during the summer is my disposable income for the school year. With my full ride thanks to academic and athletic scholarships, on top of careful budgeting, I squeak by for monthly expenses of groceries and utilities in the apartment I share with Rooney.

The last couple of months, though, Rooney's "accidentally" paid the rent and full utility bills rather than letting me write a check for half and mailing it off with hers like we used to. I have a nagging suspicion that's because Rooney's family is loaded—her dad's a big-time producer in Hollywood—so it's nothing to her, and she knows I'm on a shoestring budget. She'd deny it until the day she died, but I'm onto her.

"Willa, you're getting that far-off look that has no business being on a twenty-one-year-old woman's face." Mama's hand is cold and painfully slim, but I still lean my cheek into her touch. This isn't her first rodeo with cancer, and I know better than to take any moment with her for granted. Life is fragile, and while I'm hopeful Mama can beat this, I never pass up the chance to slow down and savor that she's here.

"You don't need to worry, honey," she whispers. "I'm taking care. Dr. B's doing everything he can for me and worries enough for the both of us, okay?" Her hand drops and squeezes mine. "You need to live your life. All you do is exercise, go to class, practice, and play, then sit here in the hospital, watching your mom lose her hair again."

"Stop it." Tears prick my eyes. "I love you. I want to be with you."

"But you need to *live*, Willa. To thrive, not just survive. Go out with Rooney. Wear a short dress, show off those killer soccer legs. Kiss a boy, screw him six ways to Sunday—using protection of course—"

"Mother!" My cheeks turn bright red. "You know I don't date."

"I didn't tell you to date. I told you to get laid."

"*Motherrrr*," I groan.

"I've been sick off and on for a while now, but you know what, Willa? I don't feel like I'm missing too much. I *lived* as a young woman. I went to wild concerts and backpacked. I hung out with weirdo beat poets and read fat novels and hitchhiked. Smoked dope and stared at the sky while I rode in truck beds. I had fun and worked hard, enlisted, traveled the world as a nurse. Got to see new places, have exotic lovers and a few sexy soldiers—"

"Mama." I shake my head. My mom's pretty, even with her hair gone and a soft turban around her head. Her eyes are a rich brown like mine and wide set. Her cheekbones pop, and her lips are full. I've seen pictures. Mama was a babe when she was younger. I just really don't like to think about her boinking.

"You know what I'm saying, Willa. Life doesn't live itself

for you, and nothing is promised to us. You have a lot to offer, so much to experience. I don't want you to miss it because of me."

I want to tell her that I'd miss everything life had to offer if it meant I got to keep her always. I want to tell her I'm scared she's sicker than she lets on, that I'll hate myself for spending nights doing what regular college kids do when I could have been spending those fleeting moments with her.

But I'm me. I don't talk about uncomfortable things like that. So, instead, I squeeze her hand in reassurance and say, "Okay, Mama. I will."

RYDER

Playlist: "Elephant Gun," Beirut

PRECISELY TWO YEARS AGO, I REALIZED MY LIFE WAS NEVER going to turn out how I thought it would. Denial's a powerful coping mechanism. After I got sick, my psyche held on to denial as long as it could. But, eventually, the thick pragmatic streak that runs in my family came knocking on my mind's door and demanded I face reality.

I'm not your stereotypical Cali guy. I don't *hang ten* or say *gnarly*. I grew up in Olympia, Washington, and I wish I still lived there, but Dad got an offer he couldn't refuse from Ronald Reagan UCLA Medical Center—RRMC, as most people call it—so here we are.

I miss the feeling of fall. I miss wet leaves smashed into a slippery carpet beneath my feet. I miss the cold turning my nose pink and burning my lungs on long, snowy runs. I miss darkness, as weird as that might sound. I miss candles and hearth fires and hunkering down with a book once the sun set at dinnertime.

And I miss soccer. I miss the game I was so sure would direct and fulfill my adult life.

So, of course, on the anniversary of all my dreams going

down the shitter, Willa Sutter, women's soccer's rising star, dropped herself in the seat next to me in Business Mathematics. It felt like the universe was kicking me right where it counts.

Didn't help that she seemed to inexplicably hate my guts. As class ended, she gave me the death glare and shoved a pen in her hair like she wished it was a shiv spearing my heart. Rage tinged her amber irises coppery red, and violent energy practically radiated off of her. The woman whose future was once mine looked like she wanted to kill me, then do it again, just for kicks. Sticking around to watch her try to melt me with her eyes when I had no idea what I'd done to earn such hatred might have been entertaining another time, but not that day.

Next class was just as bad. Once again, she dropped into the seat beside me, making me intensely aware of her body nearly brushing against mine. I'm an over-average-sized guy. I have broad shoulders, long legs. I don't *fit* in those desks. So, it wasn't necessarily surprising when I shifted in my seat and accidentally elbowed her, earning her evil eyes again.

What *was* surprising was that when she glared at me, demanding an explanation, I actually wanted to answer her. And that's really saying something because I haven't spoken a word in two years.

"Ry." I hear it like I'm underwater, faint and warped. That's what life sounds like with moderate and severe hearing loss, in the right and left ears, respectively. Bacterial meningitis came out of nowhere just a few cruel weeks before preseason at UCLA began. I got horribly sick, fast, and the next time I woke up, I was in the hospital, hearing my mom's voice as a tinny, garbled sound I barely recognized. Meningitis damaged my inner ear, and the antibiotics did their fair share, too.

There are Deaf soccer players at every level of play. I recognize what's possible, and I'm happy for those who are Deaf or have hearing loss and who've pursued that path. It just doesn't mean that path is for me. I hung up my cleats, forwent my athletic scholarship, and moved on. Now I'm not Ryder Bergman, solid left-back, freshman starter destined for greatness. Not anymore. I'll always love the game, and maybe someday I'll find my way back to it in a setting that I'm comfortable with. I'm just not there yet.

"Ry," Ren tries again. I mean, maybe he said my nickname. My brother could have just as easily said my full name and I simply failed to catch most of it. I try not to care about details like that anymore, to wonder and worry about what I'm missing. Some days that's easier than others.

I swivel in my desk chair and face my brother Ren. Like me, he's tall, broad-shouldered and built, but his blond hair is tinged russet, his eyes, pale blue-gray just like Mom's.

Ren's a professional hockey player who was massively anxious about the draft, convinced he'd get shipped away from us to the other side of the country. To his immense relief, he managed to get signed with LA, though despite working and living nearby, he's rarely home during the season. When he is, he's usually up my ass.

I tip my head to the side and give him a look he knows by now. *Can I help you?*

With a roll of his eyes, Ren yanks his phone out of his pocket and wiggles it side to side in the air, which after two years, is code for, *Get your phone out, asshole, and actually talk to me.*

Sighing, I pull out my cell and open up our text message thread.

I know what day it is, he writes. *Come on, I'm taking you out.*

Don't you have a game to play? I type.

Off day, he writes. *Next game's tomorrow. Now let's go.*

I meet his eyes as I hit send. *No.*

Ren leans his shoulder against the doorframe, crossing his arms. A stare-down ensues.

Freya threatened to drag you out if you don't come willingly, he writes.

I throw my hands up, then text, *What the fuck?*

Ren shrugs as he types, *She's tired of your bullshit. Says she knows a spot with a good burger that's not loud, so it won't give you a headache.*

A sigh leaves me. *And if I don't?*

Ren texts back, *She's your sister, too. You know what will happen.*

Freya's the oldest. She makes my brand of stubborn look like childish willfulness by comparison. It's better to let her have her way. And maybe I wouldn't entirely mind hanging in a quiet place with a few of my siblings, having a meal with them after a long, shitty day.

Standing, I yank off my hoodie and run a hand through my hair, looking around for my ball cap. Ren takes my wardrobe change for the sign that it is and whoops in victory, a rare-pitched sound I can still hear, even without my hearing aids. I want to say I'm grateful that I can hear him, but I'd be lying. All I think about when I hear something like that is everything I don't. The counselor my parents made me see after everything happened told me it takes a while to see life as glass half full again.

Glass half full is a far way off.

———

To the outside observer, we look like a sadly asocial bunch, with our noses buried in our phones, but it's just the way we can all talk. Our group chat unfurls in conversational texts, Ren beside me, my sister Freya and her husband, Aiden, across from us.

Aiden sips his beer and sets it down, then types, *Someone ask Ry about his new friend in my class*.

My eyes narrow at him. Yes, Aiden is Professor MacCormack. My brother-in-law is also my instructor, which I was concerned would be a conflict of interest. Business Mathematics is a prerequisite for a class I'm dying to take next semester that only comes around once in a blue moon, and Aiden's class was the only one with openings. He told me we'd be fine, and I believed him. If anyone's a big enough asshole to compartmentalize *and* enjoy making class a nightmare for me, it's him.

Freya perks up and texts, *New friend? Spill.*

She's Mom's twin, and I have the uncanny feeling of my mother poking me to talk about girlfriends, how she used to back in high school. Freya's blonde hair is cut in a choppy pixie, her icy-blue eyes sharp as ever, and she has a new piercing I hadn't noticed.

I make a *y* with my fingers and bring my thumb to my temple.

Freya's eyes narrow at me. "What?"

I smirk, typing in group chat, *Bull. Your new piercing makes you look like a bull.*

Ren snorts and tries to hide it with a cough, while Aiden chokes on his beer. Nobody fucks with Freya. Except me.

You little shit, she types, then she leans across the table and makes a vain attempt to twist my nipple. Settling back into her seat, Freya delicately adjusts her septum piercing, then picks up her phone again. *I look distinguished.*

More snorts and laughs take up the table. I hide mine behind a fist, letting my shoulders shake.

Suddenly the laughter dies off when I faintly hear Aiden's voice and watch his lips saying, "Dammit."

Freya's head turns in the direction Aiden's looking, as does Ren's. Willa Sutter walks in the door, but I have no idea what they're saying about her. In a rare moment, they forget either to make sure I can read their lips or to use their phones.

I clap my hands twice, earning their attention and three different facial expressions of guilt.

Sorry, Ry, Ren texts.

Aiden writes, *Sutter's here. It's not going to look good.*

Freya types, *Who? Why?*

I throw up my hands, then point to Aiden. *Look at him.*

Aiden sighs and writes, *Willa Sutter is her name, a student of mine. I might have been a bit hard on her. But entitled D-1 athletes are my Achilles' heel. I figured I'd make it up to her by telling her to ask Ry for notes.*

How would she ask him? Ren texts, *Does she know he's functionally deaf and texts to talk?*

Aiden lowers his eyes. Guilty.

A huff of anger leaves my chest. I bang the table, pointing a finger in his face. *You asshole.*

That must be why she hates me, I type. *She probably asked me for notes and I didn't hear her because she sat on my left side, the ear I can't hear shit out of. I bet she thought I was being some dick, ignoring her. Now she's going to see us together and think we're best friends who are out to ruin her GPA.*

Slow down, Freya types. *Why would she think you're best friends?*

Because Aiden gives me the notes for lecture. The lecture's captioned on a projector, but it's still a lot to keep track of, so I get the full lecture notes to help me follow along in class and to refer to later. My thumbs fly, anger building as I realize what a mess he got us into. *Aiden's not doing me favors—he's legally required to make the course accessible —but she doesn't know that's why I have them.*

Ren types, *So she thinks he's doing you a favor and screwing her since you won't share.*

I nod again, throwing down my phone.

Ren gives Aiden a disbelieving look as he types, *You're still not over this campaign?*

Aiden scowls into his beer and doesn't say anything.

Aiden doesn't want to see me treated differently for my hearing loss, and he's worried about how much I've withdrawn since it happened. So he periodically throws people in my path in the hopes that I'll magically open up to them, even with my hearing aid frustration and my discomfort with speaking. Keeping to texting only, not always wearing my hearing aids, has made my social circle small, but it's honestly all I've had the capacity for. I know Aiden loves me and he means well, but he's just too damn pushy on this point.

I'd like to remind the committee, I type, *that this is not the first time Aiden's stuck a woman on me and conveniently forgotten to tell her I can't hear for shit.*

Freya spins and slaps Aiden upside the head. "I told you to stop that."

"I did it one other time!" he pleads.

He doesn't need a yenta, Freya types. *Look at him. He'll get laid the moment he wants to.*

All three of us men shudder for various reasons. I don't want my sister talking about me getting laid, Ren doesn't want to hear about his brother getting laid, and Aiden definitely doesn't want to hear his wife acknowledging her brother's sex appeal.

Before I can say anything further on the matter, my peripheral vision, which I've relied on more than ever in the past few years, changes, making me turn to the left.

Willa stands a few feet away, a disbelieving look tightening her face. "Professor MacCormack?" She says it softly, I think, judging that it's almost inaudible to me, but watching her lips fills in the gaps.

God, her lips. They look bee-stung, impossibly soft. I hate that to understand her, I have to stare at that full mouth, especially now that I know she doesn't hate my guts for no good reason, which would make hating her back so much easier. She hates my guts because she thinks I was being a prick and ignoring her.

Much, much harder to hate now.

"Willa, hey!" Aiden half-stands, but Freya's pinning him inside the booth and giving him a death glare. Slowly, he sinks back into his seat.

Willa's gaze dances between us. "Wow."

"This isn't what it looks like," Aiden says, angling himself so I can read his lips—at least, I think that's what he says—but lipreading is hard to begin with, even when combined with what I'm able to hear, and he's speaking closer to conversational speed, not slow, like I need. It's too difficult to follow. I glance at Freya and shake my head. She picks up her phone and transcribes for me in our private text what Aiden's saying: *Listen, Willa, I know I gave you a hard time about the notes, and I understand why you're confused as to why Ryder gets them, when I didn't give them to you, but the thing is—*

Willa's hand flies up, interrupting him, and Freya transcribes what she says next: *I'll pass on the excuse. You've made it clear that while this guy has earned special treat-ment, I need to fend for myself.*

A leggy blonde stands behind Willa, her brow pinched in disapproval, eyes on Aiden, as she says something I'm pretty sure involves the phrase "piece of shit." Her mouth starts flying, so I can't follow her anymore. Ren signals Freya that he's aware of this, and pulls out his phone, taking over tran-scribing what's being said:

You don't think female athletes have a hard enough time? Every professor of ours provides what we need rather than making us beg. I was under the impression it's not that hard to be a decent human being, but here you are, proving me wrong. Fuck you and good night.

Before either of us can even begin to explain, the tall blonde yanks Willa by the arm and turns them right around, then out the door.

Ren drops his phone, genuinely impressed, and claps as they go. "Wow."

Aiden rubs his face.

Freya takes his beer and finishes it, then wipes a hand across her mouth before she writes, *I've said it before, and I'll say it again: men are idiots. Remind me, why'd I marry you?*

Aiden drops his head to the table but manages to type his answer in our group chat. *Good question.*

MY LEG BOUNCES WITH NERVES AS CLASS STARTS. IT'S almost comical at this point, but the only seat I can see that's vacant is next to me, *again*. Aiden's yammering on about some formula I already got the hang of when I prepped for class last night, as Willa comes bounding down the ramp, bookbag jostling almost as much as her wild hair that can't seem to make up its mind between waves or curls.

She wears sweats that completely drown her body, and she looks winded, which means she must have been sprinting the whole way here, given she's obviously in incredible shape. Slowly, she comes to a stop at the vacant seat next to me, while Aiden lectures and pointedly ignores her late arrival.

Her eyes, fueled with loathing, meet mine. Those amber irises once again turn an angry copper. If she could erupt in flames, she would.

She's fiery and pissed. I find it much more delightful than I should.

When I lost most of my hearing, I pulled away from the things that I no longer knew how to relate to—playing music, competitive soccer, rowdy nights out with friends. My social life has narrowed to a few buddies who stuck around and my family. In my free time, I work out, spend time in nature, and do schoolwork. For the past two years, that's been what I needed, what I could manage. But lately I've felt this… nagging tug, an edginess simmering beneath my skin. I'm not sure what it means, if I'm bored, if I want more than I once did, if I've turned some corner since my life changed. And if so…what now?

I don't have easy answers to those complicated, daunting questions. What I *do* have is a welcome distraction in Willa Sutter, the wild-haired firecracker in class beside me who's shockingly easy to provoke. I'm the smack-dab middle child in a brood of seven, so I know a thing or two about provoking. It's my area of expertise, actually.

I stare at her, making sure to add a touch of smirk to my expression. Just enough to piss her off.

If the curl of her lip is any indication, she growls at me as she drops into her seat and slaps her notebook on the desk. Then she whips back the cover and slams her pen on its surface, too. I hear only some of it, but I feel the intensity in all her movements.

I *almost* feel bad that she's frustrated, until I remind myself she didn't give either Aiden or me a chance the other night to set the record straight, not that I really would have been able to.

Not that she knows that.

If I were Willa, as desperate for those notes as Aiden told me she is, I would have calmed down enough to hear out my professor. I'd have been sensible enough to realize that was the only way I could get to the bottom of what was going on, and get what I needed. But I'm a practical, level-headed person. Willa Sutter clearly is not. If her hotheaded temper keeps her making shitty assumptions and seeing the worst in a person, that's her problem, not mine.

My empathy for her went far enough that when we parted ways in the parking lot after dinner, I told Aiden he needed to explain the situation to Willa. He's the one who created this confusion in the first place. His guilt did not extend that far.

You have methods of communication at your disposal, Ryder, he texted me. *Use them.*

Asshole.

I steal a glance at Willa, who seems to have buckled down, her eyes flicking repeatedly from the board to her notebook. Halfway through class, she raises her hand, looking both defiant and like it's the last thing she wants to do. Aiden uses live remote captioning, meaning he wears a microphone that a captioner listens to and then transcribes whatever they hear right as it's spoken. Repeating what Willa said so that it's captioned too, Aiden then answers, the words unfurling on the projector. *The answer to that question is a formula that I broke down in class two weeks ago, Willa. I suggest taking notes when you're here so you can refer back to them.*

Which of course puts Willa's focus once again on me, gifted recipient of the notes. I'm going to murder my brother-in-law. Freya might miss Aiden for a while, but she'll get over him.

Slowly, Willa's eyes drift toward me. I can't help but glance up and meet them. If looks could kill, hers would. Flames burst in her irises. Her cheeks are blotched with pink. She's the portrait of *pissed*. I, on the other hand, am as placid as a lake. Calm, cool, still. I hold her gaze as long as she holds mine. For the second time, she blinks away first, then turns to the front of the room.

The first strike happens five minutes later, when a pointy elbow nails my ribs. Wind rushes out of me as I spin instinctively toward her. Willa's composed, eyes on her notebook, jotting down Aiden's words furiously.

Ohhh, Sutter. Two can play this game.

I feign stretching my legs and kick her foot, flipping her leg off from being crossed over the other. She tips sideways, nearly thrown off her chair from the impact. When I feel her livid gaze on me, I'm scouring my notes, eyes down.

Suddenly an arm comes toward me and smacks my ball cap clean away. I reach behind my seat immediately and scoop it up. Raking back my hair, I tug my hat low over my eyes. Ball cap back in place, I turn toward her and give her an icy stare.

"Oops," she says with those damn pouty lips. Her arms lower from her feigned stretching position. "My bad."

I'm done pretending I'm not giving her hell right back. Leaning slowly her way, I watch her eyes widen, her mouth pop open in surprise. Closer, closer until our noses are only a few inches apart. While I have her eyes, I reach up, find a nice thick chunk of that wild hair, and give it a hefty tug.

"Ouch!" her mouth says, but I catch a faint din of noise. Considering how fucked my ears are, that means she had to have screeched.

Aiden whips around, eyes darting between both of us. I'm an experienced middle child. I know how to get away with way worse than this, so I'm already innocently jotting something down in the margins of my class notes.

My eyes cheat a glance from underneath the brim of my ball cap, as I watch Aiden's words appear on the projector: *Miss Sutter, everything all right?*

Willa's sputtering, her hand still clasping her hair, but it seems she's speechless.

All right, then. Aiden returns his focus to the class, his words captioned on the screen above him. *We'll stop there. Now, time to talk about the final. Two things. Anyone who did their homework before they registered for my class read in the course description that this final is unique. It's actually what I'm most proud of in this class. Successful businesses are inherently collaborative. They require teamwork, compromise, and unity of message and purpose. So, this class final involves working with your partner both to create a comprehensive business model and budget plan, as well as to test jointly—*

A massive groan interrupts him.

Aiden unleashes his sinister grin. The man takes way too much delight in torturing students. *That'll teach you not to skip the course description again. And don't try to get out of it. Legally, it's watertight. You signed up and in doing so consented to this class's terms.*

Willa scrubs her face, leading me to think she might be

one of those unlucky ducks who did *not* read the course description.

Your partner takes a written test. You take a complimentary other half. Together, you two complete your final. Aiden's eyes dance around the room. *I've heard from past students that they were pleasantly surprised by the natural byproduct of this pairing. It incentivized them to work better together and study extensively, both for the midterm and the final tests. So, without further ado, I have collaborative pairs assigned, which I'll put on the projector in just a second.* Leaning, Aiden presses a button on his laptop, changing the image on the projector to a tidy row chart with names in two columns. Immediately, my eyes begin scouring it, as dread fills my stomach.

He wouldn't. He wouldn't *dare.*

Hands in pockets, Aiden smiles out at the sea of students. *Good luck, everyone!*

Finally, I find it. Ryder Bergman. In the adjacent column, Willa Sutter.

Mother. Fucker.

WILLA

Playlist: "Written in The Water," Gin Wigmore

In middle school, I broke my ankle during a game and managed to play straight through overtime. Obviously, I have a high pain threshold, a tolerance for suffering. This, however, is pushing it.

"You've *got* to be kidding me," I mutter.

There we are, Ryder and I, paired up for the final. Not only do we have to collaborate for the remainder of the semester, but we also have to agree on a project idea, work together, and test cumulatively well enough to ensure I pass. Impossible is the understatement of the century.

Ryder sighs and scrubs his face.

"Listen," I tell him. "I'm not thrilled either."

He doesn't respond. It's almost as if he doesn't even hear me. In fact, it seems like he's *never* heard me. I've been friends with Rooney long enough to know that's her major complaint with men: "*They just don't listen, Willa! They don't try to understand.*"

Ryder so far seems completely typical in this aspect.

"Hey." I poke his arm and earn his abrupt attention. Well, hi there, muscles upon muscles. Damn.

He straightens in his seat, turning to look at me. Even in the shadow of his ball cap, his eyes are an unfairly striking shade of grass green.

"What's your deal?" I ask.

His gaze drifts to my mouth, then down to my hands, where I'm spinning my phone across my desk. Suddenly, his hand lands heavy over mine, stilling my fidgety movement. Breath surges out of my lungs. His grip is warm, his fingers long, his palm calloused. He's closer, and I get the faintest whiff of evergreens and soft, clean soap.

His fingers curl gently around my phone before Ryder swipes it and holds it to my face, assuming correctly that I use Face ID to unlock it. Once it's open, he creates a new blank message sent to a number I don't recognize. I stare down, watching those three bubbles, then glance up to him, as his thumbs fly over the keys.

I'm deaf, the message reads. *This is how I can talk to you.*

I gape. He can't hear. That would explain...well, so much. But still, even if he's deaf, there's no defense for him kicking me and pulling my hair.

You started it, says the voice of reason in my head, making a surprise appearance.

Fine, I started it. Because he was being a jerk.

He wasn't being a jerk, it points out. You're *the jerk. He couldn't hear you, and you assumed the worst and treated him like garbage.*

I groan, blowing a puff of air from my cheeks. Then, I pick up my phone. I'm about to text when his hand lands heavy on mine again. I glance up, and my heart does a weird flip-flop. The dude's got an intensity to him. He swallows up the chair he's sitting in, his legs stretch out long past the desk. He leans an elbow on its surface, and his lumberjack bicep has its own zip code. He's actually a little intimidating. Well, he would be. If I were the intimidated type.

Ryder points to his eye, then sets a finger right outside my mouth. I shiver at the brush of his fingertip tracing my cheek.

"You can read lips?"

He nods, but with his spare hand, he gestures how people do when they want you to *slow down.* Then he pinches two fingers close, leaving only a sliver of space between them.

"Slowly. If I speak slowly. And just a little?"

He nods.

"But you don't talk?"

He shakes his head. My shoulders slump. How the heck are we going to communicate? I only know a little American Sign Language, because one summer, every evening after my shift at the bookstore, I nannied a seven-year-old named Lola, who was Deaf. Mom taught me some ASL that she'd learned in her nursing years, and I memorized quite a bit to take care of Lola, but you know how it goes—use it or lose it—and it's been years. I lost it. Actually, I do remember one key expression, one that Lola and I used regularly.

I'm sorry, I sign, making a fist and circling my hand over my heart. *I didn't know*, I text him. *I thought you were just an asshole lumberjack.*

His mouth twitches with amusement. Glancing down to his phone, he types, *Lumberjack? What, because I wear flannel?*

And a beard. And boots, I write. *You're in Los Angeles, Brawny, not the Pacific Northwest. How are you not roasting?*

He tips his head down, and if I'm not mistaken, I almost made the asshole smile.

It's thin, he types. *I wear nothing under it.*

My cheeks heat. The lumberjack seems muscly. It's not

hard to imagine the six-pack and pecs of steel hidden beneath soft, threadbare plaid. I teased him about it, but the man can wear flannel. It clings to the curve of his rounded shoulders, the swell of his bicep, yet leaves enough of his shape to the imagination that I've just spent thirty seconds stupidly ogling him and wondering what kind of heat he's packing beneath that woodsman-wear.

I snap out of staring, then, to hide my blush, bend over my phone and type, *Well, at any rate. I'm sorry about the misunderstanding.*

His reply is stunningly fast, but I guess if that was the only way I communicated, I'd get pretty quick at it, too. *It's okay. An understandable misunderstanding. And speaking of, at the restaurant, that was a family dinner. We aren't friends—MacCormack's my brother-in-law. I'm about to throttle him because this situation is entirely his fault.*

I look up and gape at Ryder. "Seriously?"

He nods, then types, *Yep. Blame The Nutty Professor.*

That makes a snort of laughter sneak out. I cover my mouth, trying to hide how funny I found it.

Also, I don't sign much, he writes. *This is…newer.*

I read his text, then glance up at him. "You mean you haven't always been deaf?"

He frowns and taps my lips with his finger, leaving my skin burning from his touch. Turning to his phone again, he types, *Open your mouth. Slow down. You mumble worse than my brother. Like your jaw's wired shut.*

The lumberjack is bossy. Blunt. It's supremely annoying. Irritation barrels through me, a hot flush staining my cheeks. Sweeping up my phone, I type, *Sorry I skipped my elocution lesson this morning, Professor Higgins. I wasn't expecting to be accosted by a bossy hard-of-hearing lumberjack.*

His eyebrows shoot up as his thumbs fly over the phone. *Excellent. A mumbler *and* a shaming ableist.*

Gasping, I slap the desk and turn toward him. "Am not!"

My phone dings. *Simmer your sweatpants. I was teasing.*

I'm only slightly relieved he wasn't actually accusing me of shaming him for being deaf. I scowl as I write, *Are you always this much of a jerk?*

Are you always this much of a hothead? he fires back.

Our eyes meet as both phones clatter to our desks.

Taking a long, centering breath, I decide to rise above the petty insults and get down to business. *How are we going to do this?* I ask in our text thread.

Ryder shrugs, then picks up his phone. *Do you have a Mac laptop?*

I nod.

Good, he types. *Bring it to our first work session. We can sit across from each other and text our conversation in Messenger. It's odd at first, but you'll get used to it. Unless you want to request a different partner. I get that it's not an ideal pairing.*

Something knots in my chest as I read those words. It's like he *expects* to be discarded because someone might find him inconvenient.

I don't mind, if you don't, I write.

The ghost of a smile tugs at his mouth as he reads it, before it's wiped away with a stoic expression. When his eyes meet mine, he shrugs again.

My phone dings with a new message.

Works for me.

———

"You mean that asshole's coming *here*?" Rooney shrieks.

I wiggle a finger in my ringing ear. "Yes, Roo. It was a big misunderstanding. I mean, I still find him infuriating, but there's a reason he didn't give me the notes. He couldn't hear me."

Rooney's eyebrows shoot up. "What?"

"He's deaf. MacCormack just didn't seem to find that important to tell me when he referred me to Ryder. Ryder told me it's MacCormack's trip. In his mind, good people figure it out by being open-mindedly diligent, and bad people fail because they get butthurt the moment Ryder doesn't respond. I failed. I assumed he was ignoring me and pretty much devolved to wrestling him in class."

"Wait, what?" Rooney drops down at the dining room table while I sauté shrimp, garlic, and shallots in butter. Thick linguine rests in the neighboring pan, tossed in olive oil and some Parmesan. The whole place smells like Mama's and my favorite Italian restaurant, Squisito.

My heart sinks a little. It's been so long since we were there. Maybe I'll pick up Squisito takeout and bring it to the hospital when I visit tomorrow. But then I picture Mama trying to eat all that rich, heavy food she can't stomach, just to placate me, picking limply at her chicken Parmesan and forcing bite after bite.

Maybe I won't pick up Squisito.

"Willa?"

I snap out of it. "Right. So…I elbowed him. I was so pissed he wasn't giving me the notes. So I elbowed him, he kicked my foot, I knocked off his ball cap, and he tugged my hair."

Rooney rolls her eyes. "You should have just talked to him."

"I tried!"

Not really, that annoyingly rational voice says. *You did the minimal amount of talking—per usual—then assumed the worst.*

Also typical of me. But you try having a sperm-donor dad who never bothered to know you, and a disappointing string of short-term boyfriends, then see where it gets you in your opinion of men.

Rooney opens her mouth, probably to call bullshit, but a knock on the door interrupts us.

"Ack!" she yelps. "That's him."

I return my attention to the cooking shrimp. "Yes, Captain Obvious, it is. Now go answer the door, please. I'm covered in garlic, and I have to add the white wine right now."

Rooney slinks off the chair and strolls to the door, squealing when she looks through the peephole. "You know, I was a little too enraged last time to notice, but he's kind of cute. At least his eyes are. I can't really see the rest of him."

"Nobody can. He's incapable of shaving his face or wearing anything besides a scowl, a ball cap, and flannel. Now open the door already."

Rooney yanks it open, and time suspends as I wait. What will this be like, for Ryder to be in my apartment, sitting across the table from me as we work together? He's brusque and surly, and he still hasn't offered me the notes, but even so, he's possibly not as terrible as I thought, considering he really just didn't hear me. Still, it's hard. It's hard to look back on his response and not be angry, even if there's an explanation that makes my anger irrational.

Maybe it's because I sense that Ryder likes getting under my skin and pissing me off. Maybe it's because I have an inkling that even if he weren't deaf, he may well have pretended not to hear me when I asked him. Ryder's a teaser, an antagonist, a pain in the ass. Like me. I know when I see one of my kind.

He walks in, crossbody bag over his shoulder and ball cap pulled low. Once again, I'm reminded he's not just an asshole. He's a tall asshole. Broad shoulders, long legs. It feels like his presence takes up half the apartment. His head tips up when he turns toward me. Quickly his eyes drift up my body, then to my right, as he notices pans cluttering the range.

Our eyes meet. His are dark and intense as they lock on mine. It's unsettling.

"What?" I ask.

He pauses, seeming to deliberate before waving a hand toward his nose, miming savoring a delicious aroma. Then, his fingertips tap his chin before dropping down. I know that one, and I put them together.

"Smells good?"

His lips barely tip in a grin, and he nods.

Rooney looks between us, mystified that we aren't tearing out each other's jugulars. There's time for that still. "So we don't hate him anymore?"

My head swivels to hers, and Ryder's follows suit. His eyes narrow. He missed what she said.

"You can't talk around him, Roo. Say it again."

Her eyes widen. "Seriously?"

Ryder nods.

"I said—" Rooney clears her throat, her cheeks turning pink. "I said, 'So we don't hate him anymore?'"

Ryder smirks, then shrugs, gesturing toward me, as if to say, *It's up to her.*

Rooney laughs nervously. "Okay, I'm just gonna…" She dashes out of the room. "Call me when dinner's ready!"

I scowl at Ryder, then turn back toward the pasta, adding

a final splash of white wine and watching it cook off. Up to me, is it? As if *I'm* the one who created all this frustration. Sure, it's mostly Mac's fault—he set us up for one big misunderstanding—but you're telling me when you're deaf, you don't maybe give your desk-mate a heads-up about that?

Does he owe anyone who ever sits next to him his life story? that voice chides. *Plus, you gave him death eyes. The first time he saw you,* that's *how you were looking at him.*

The sound of a photo being taken jars me. Ryder leans his phone my way, showing me a picture of my profile. My eyes are narrowed, my focus on the food while I know secretly my thoughts were spinning about the jerk-turned-stealth-photographer. My hair's a giant puffball on my head. Loose curls gather at my neck, ears, and temple.

"What the hell?"

I smack his shoulder, but he waves his hand, as if to say, *No, no you don't get it.* Pointing first to the pan where I'm cooking, then the photo, specifically, the half of it taken up by my hair, Ryder then sets his phone on the counter, frames his hands around his head and makes the mind-blown gesture.

Heat crawls up my neck as I white-knuckle my phone and type, *The humidity from cooking tends to make my hair get bigger, yes, you butthead.*

He cocks an eyebrow and smirks as his thumbs fly over his phone. My phone dings.

Does wonders for it.

I growl, shoving his phone into his chest, then typing, *Delete it. Didn't your mother teach you not to take a lady's photo without her consent?*

My phone dings almost immediately.

Didn't know I was dealing with a lady.

"Out of my kitchen, Bergman." I throw a hand in the direction of the dining room table as I type with the other.

And let me be clear that if you were not my obligatory partner for this class, and my GPA wasn't resting on our working together, I'd have kicked your ass to the curb five minutes ago.

My phone dings.

Duly noted.

Turning back to the food, I roughly toss the pasta, shrimp, and some sauce, perhaps with more force than necessary, but I need something to channel my fury. My hair is a sore subject. I'm constantly exercising and showering, so while everything I read about taming thick, curly waves like mine says I need to wash less and condition more, that's just not practical for how active I am. I also hate that my unruly hair obviously came from the sperm donor, since Mama's hair is poker straight. Every day, my hair is a reminder of the guy who fucked and trucked my mom, who wanted nothing to do with me. Ryder doesn't know any of that, but it doesn't matter. He teased me about it, and now he's going to pay.

I glance at the container of cayenne sitting in the spice rack. Quickly, I add some to a bowl, pour sauce into it, then whisk it around and set it aside for Ryder's serving. Just enough to get his tongue sweating, then make him shit fire in a few hours.

Behind me, I hear Ryder unpacking at the table, the click of his laptop on the hardwood surface, the dance of his fingers across the keys. My phone dings.

I'm assuming most of that's for me.

I let out a humorless laugh. The audacity of this guy. *Assumptive of you,* I type.

A soft sound leaves him, almost like a huff of laughter. Chills run up my spine. *It's quite rude to cook in front of someone and not offer to feed them.*

I roll my eyes. *Well, as you said, you're not dealing with a lady. Rude is my specialty.* I start a new message, typing, *I was planning on feeding you, Lumberjack. Counting on it making you less grumpy.*

He turns, frozen in profile. Ryder's mouth opens, and he looks as if he's about to say something to me, rather than type it. I stare at the outline of his thick lashes, his long, straight nose, waiting. But he turns back to his computer and types, *I'm not grumpy.*

You're grumpy, I text back. Right as I'm about to tell her dinner's ready, Rooney all but skips back into the room.

She has a guilty flush to her cheeks, and she keeps nervously glancing over at Ryder. She's a transparent soul, so I always enjoy needling her when I know for a fact, she can't lie to save her own ass.

"How interesting," I tell her. "You just knew instinctively when to come back for food. It's almost like you were watching us through that tiny crack in the door from your room to the dining room."

"I'm like a puppy," Rooney says, flipping her hair over her shoulder and avoiding my eyes. "I have a keen sniffer, and I know exactly when food's ready, then come running."

"Sure, Roo." Turning off the dial beneath the pan, I scoop pasta onto three separate plates, taking care to pour Ryder's sauce over his plate. Handing Rooney hers, I pat her cheek. "Run along, Peeping Tom."

Rooney's face falls. "Okay, I watched. But it was like a hot silent film—all these loaded gazes and sultry body language." She fans herself. "You guys are better entertainment than a sweaty, silent tennis match. Well, I guess it's silent except for all that grunting they do."

The idea of a grunting, sweaty anything with Ryder bizarrely sends a jolt of heat between my legs. I could slap myself.

"Stop talking like that." I tug Rooney's ponytail. "Be gone."

"Fine," she says primly, spinning with her pasta. When she's at the threshold of her bedroom door, she turns back, waving to Ryder. "Bye!" she practically yells.

Ryder winces, then gives her a reluctant wave.

I set down his plate, then circle the table and sit with mine. "No shellfish allergy?" I ask.

He shakes his head.

"Damn."

Ryder's eyes narrow. It almost looks like he's biting back a smile. He takes off his hat, a surprisingly polite, gentlemanly gesture. After he combs all that thick, shaggy blond back and secures it with a hair tie, he dips his fork into the pasta.

I watch him with grinch-like glee. But after two bites, he's acting completely unaffected. He should be squirming in his mountain-man britches by now.

He takes another bite and chews thoughtfully. No discomfort. Nothing.

Dammit. Of course, the lumberjack is one of those freaks with virtually no capsaicin receptors. My luck.

Ryder's eyes are on his plate. I could tap the table, but I'm not sure if he finds that helpful or offensive. Same with waving, not that it would work while his eyes are shut as he chews a bite of pasta. Tentatively, I slide my foot under the table until our toes touch.

His eyes snap open, then meet mine.

"Taste okay?" I ask.

He frowns, setting down his fork. Lifting one hand, he wiggles it side to side, the universal gesture for *so-so*.

Heat rises in my cheeks. As my temperature skyrockets,

his smirk deepens. Suddenly, he turns toward his computer, quickly followed by a ding from Messenger on my laptop.

You're fun to tease.

I scowl at the laptop as I type, *And you're a pain in my ass.*

Another soft sound leaves him as he turns toward his pasta. I spend the majority of my meal glaring at the crown of his head, barely tasting my food.

———

THAT'S A BAD IDEA, HE TYPES.

No, it's a great idea, I write back.

Our eyes dance from our laptops to each other, our positions mirror images of stubborn intractability across the table. It's ten o'clock. We finished dinner two hours ago, and we have yet to agree on a business project.

Nonprofits for children with additional support needs are chronically under-resourced, I write. *Nonprofits geared toward outdoor and sports activity for those kids are even rarer and less well funded. This model relies on not only outside donors but also athletic and outdoors competition fundraisers, as well as internal sales that market the kids' creativity—crafts, artwork, baked goods.*

No one pays ten dollars for a dozen campfire cookies, he types. *And this is kid art, not a Monet at auction.*

Okay, I write, *so maybe that part of the budget's a stretch.*

Stretch? It's delusional. I'm with you on a business geared toward sportswear and outdoorsmanship, and sure, gear and training for different needs and abilities. But this nonprofit idea is a waste of time.

My eyes snap up to his as I shut my laptop forcefully. "You're being obstinate."

He rips off his ball cap, raking both hands through his hair.

An odd feeling comes over me, watching those long fingers scrape through his dirty-blond locks, tugging, combing repeatedly. Tendons in his arms pop, and the bulk of his bicep presses against his shirtsleeves. With one hand, he sweeps up his phone and types faster than I could ever dream of doing.

My phone dings.

I'm not being obstinate. I'm being practical. You need to be, too. You know how little the NWSL pays. You're going to have to support yourself with sponsorships and savvy business agreements. You're talking like business isn't entirely about shrewd negotiation and profit. That's *all* it's about, Willa.

A growl leaves me as I type, *You're great at shutting down ideas, Ryder, but you know what you suck at? Offering good ones.*

Storming away, I sweep both of our plates off the table and toss them in the sink so roughly, I might have just cracked one.

His snide criticism highlighting my weak spot is the last thing I needed to hear. I hate that he's right, that the National Women's Soccer League, while not paying ideally, is going to open doors for me, doors that will require I do what I'm terrible at—tough negotiations, having uncomfortable, aggressive talks about payment and percentages that make me head-to-toe hive and freak out. I *am* nervous about how I'm going to succeed and support myself while playing, but I am trying to learn. Ryder's needling just hit that tender, insecure part of my plans for my future.

Maybe he said it, like almost everything else he does,

teasingly, merely to get under my skin, but he doesn't know how thin my skin is, how breakable I feel most of the time.

Standing slowly, Ryder swipes his phone off the table and pockets it, then walks from the dining table into the kitchen area. He pauses, dragging a fist over his heart, just how I did earlier. *I'm sorry.*

I glare at him. I'm hurt and pissed, annoyed that for every nice thing he has to say, he has twice as many zingers. I'm tired and ready for bed after an exhausting day. *Whatever, Ryder*, I text. *Come up with an idea, and let's meet next week.*

His jaw ticks as he reads my message, before that cool mask he wore in class descends over his features. A hefty shrug is all I get before he spins, sweeps up his laptop, and shoves it into his bag. I'm well trained to expect disappointment in men. I'm positive he's about to walk out that door without another word. But instead, he returns to the kitchen and sidesteps me to the sink.

I move to block him, but his hand grips my elbow. With very little effort on his part, Ryder drags me toward the other end of the room. A palm comes up. *Stay.*

Frowning, I cross my arms and stare at him. He turns away before I can say anything else, quickly running the water on the plates, scraping them clean, and using the in-sink garbage disposal. Ryder bends to open the dishwasher door and sets our plates and silverware inside, then tugs it shut. I watch him bring the pans, utensils, and bowls I used into the sink, squirt soap on them, and wash, then rinse, them. Once he's set everything to dry on the rack, he wipes my work area clean, folds the dish towel with military precision, and sets it on the counter, exactly parallel to the edge.

"Neat freak," I mutter, realizing guiltily what I've just done. My frustratingly bad habit of mumbling my thoughts aloud is always embarrassing, but it's downright humiliating on the occasions that I don't even realize I've done it until someone points it out. At the moment, it's horrifying—it's inconsiderate to mumble around someone who doesn't hear well. Even if he is an *asshole* who doesn't hear well.

Ryder turns my way and wipes his damp hands on his jeans.

Our eyes meet as he walks up to me, making me once again very aware that he's a very tall, muscly, green-eyed asshole lumberjack. One who I now know has a neurotic need for a clean kitchen and towels folded into crisp ninety-degree angles.

Thank you, he signs.

Then he slips around me and leaves me alone in my kitchen, but for the faintest ghost of his scent—clean soap and pine forests.

Eau de asshole lumberjack, don't you forget that.

As if I could. God, this is going to be a long semester.

5

RYDER

Playlist: "Roma Fade," Andrew Bird

I SPOKE TOO HARSHLY TO HER. I DO THAT SOMETIMES. I'M blunt and honest to a fault. I say what I mean when I'm in an analytical conversation that deserves practical conclusions. But that doesn't seem to be the wisest tactic with Willa. I pissed her off when I told her to get real about what's feasible in a business model's budget, but I sent her off the deep end when I suggested the success of her soccer career rested not only on her raw skill at the game, but on significantly greater pragmatism.

I don't feel too bad, since she took her opportunity for a prompt revenge after I teased her about her hair. I knew the pasta tasted a little spicy, but I have a high threshold for heat, at least my mouth does. My ass, on the other hand, is as sensitive as everyone else's, so I'm careful in general not to eat incredibly spicy food. Judging by the fact that it's only this morning that I stopped wincing when I sit down, Willa dumped enough cayenne in my pasta to make the toughest hot-sauce lover weep.

At first, I was tempted to get her back, but the fact is that my unflappable responses seem to needle her to no end. Just keeping my mouth shut and letting her think that pepper never got to me is revenge enough.

"You're quiet." Aiden's on my right side, and I'm wearing the hearing aid on that ear. He's had enough practice that he knows how loud, briefly, and in what environments to speak so I can understand him. We're running on a trail hidden in shade, not a soul around, so I have a chance of hearing him decently out of the right ear, which handles the hearing aid better. The other has so far proved a lost cause, riddled with tinnitus and hypersensitivity to what sounds it *can* hear that makes it so frustratingly uncomfortable, I've basically given up on it.

Even now, wearing the one on my right ear, it's work to parse the sound and follow as he speaks, and that's what people don't understand—how much *work* it is, even with hearing aids. They just see anything that makes me more like them as "good." But it's not that simple.

I appreciate the spirit of Aiden's unwavering belief in continuing to treat me like he always has, but sometimes that feels less like trying to include me and more like wanting me to be who I was before hearing loss. And while I want to say I'm the same guy I was before all this happened, I'm not. I'm different, and no, I never want pity or special treatment, but I wouldn't mind simply being allowed to be changed. Because I am. Deafness changed me, and I'll never be able to give him back the carefree nineteen-year-old who used to bullshit while playing video games, who arrogantly taunted him and schooled his ass playing pickup soccer in the backyard.

I know he's trying to amuse me, telling me I'm "quiet," but I don't find it funny today. I'm twisted up about this situation with Willa, confused by how quickly she snaps, how readily she dishes out shit but can barely take it. I want to confide in Aiden because historically, he's been good for advice. But with this situation, Aiden's the last person I want to talk to about Willa. He's already too invested in us.

I can feel his gaze on me, so I give him a shrug and keep my eyes on the path. After that, Aiden doesn't talk while we finish the second half of our distance.

I savor the peaceful silence while we run, which might sound odd, but when you're deaf like I am, you still hear sound, it's just not enough. It's maddeningly soft, tinny, skewed. Sometimes I wish I heard nothing at all so I wouldn't constantly be reminded of everything I didn't.

Though I've always been a quiet person, I never thought I'd love the sound of silence as much as I do now. Silence is a relief, a break from the constant torture of straining and trying to catch any scrap of discernible noise that I can.

That silence doesn't last long.

"You and Sutter get anywhere with your project plan?" Aiden asks me the moment we tumble to the grass at the end of the trail and start stretching our legs.

I shake my head, then pull out my phone and type, *I just started talking to you again after you put us together. You really want to bring this up?*

Aiden laughs, and his light-blue eyes twinkle with sick amusement. I really had to restrain myself from throttling him over the first family dinner we had after he paired us off.

"She giving you a hard time about communicating?"

I pause, my jaw ticking as type, *No. She signs a little. Talks slowly and clearly. Texts with me mostly. Doesn't act like I'm ruining her life by being paired with the deaf dude.*

"Well, that says a lot about her right there, in my book. She's doing what all people should but many don't."

His point lands where he meant it to, right in my sternum.

Aiden straightens, then switches to stretching his other

leg. "You could try popping on both of the hearing aids, talking to her a little bit."

I roll my eyes and chuck my phone away. Conversation over.

My phone buzzes, and I begrudgingly read his text. *Ryder, why are you doing this? I don't understand.*

I cut a hand through the air. *Enough.* I grip my phone harder, anger tightening my breath to short, painful bursts as I type. *You have no clue what this is like. And not that I owe you an explanation, but I'll humor you. The hearing aids are really fucking complicated, especially with my more damaged ear. What's loud is even louder, what's quiet still isn't audible. That impacts how well I hear others and myself, and how comfortable I am with trying to hold a conversation.*

"Ry—"

I stand, palm up, as I type one-handed, *Leave it or I'll drop the class.*

"Now, wait a minute." Aiden springs up from the grass. "You need that class."

I nod. *But I need you to leave me alone about this more.*

His shoulders fall as he reads my message, then his eyes meet mine. "Okay. I'm sorry."

Thank you, I sign sarcastically, with a smack to my other hand.

I surprise myself by doing it because I rarely sign. When I realized my hearing loss was permanent, it was overwhelming to contemplate learning a new language, especially when I didn't have anyone to sign with. I bought a book, watched some videos. Learned a little in case I bumped into someone like me. Learning ASL is something I've thought about more often lately, another one of those equally daunting and compelling "what ifs" that have cropped up as I consider my future, my professional goals, the way I want to live, especially after college.

It was surprising and welcome when Willa signed *sorry* in class. And the next time I saw her, I took a chance. She understood my hodgepodge sign for telling her the food she was making smelled fucking incredible, and it made something in my chest twist with warmth. I liked being able to meet her eyes when I communicated with her, instead of having my head buried in my phone, waiting for her to turn away from me and read my words. It felt closer, more intimate.

Intimate? What the hell, Ryder?

I shake my head as I walk in silence with Aiden back to the car. I must be lightheaded from my run. Willa and I are collaborative partners, and maybe we have a few things in common—stubbornness, a background in soccer, a love of shrimp scampi—but that's it. We'd gouge each other's eyes out before we got *intimate*.

A tap to my shoulder draws me from my thoughts. "Want to go to her game?" Aiden says.

I text him back, *Are you insane?*

"Probably." He shrugs. "I feel like it's the least we can do after nearly sabotaging her eligibility—"

I smack his arm. *We?* Shaking my finger, I type one-handed, *Ohhh, no. This was all you.*

Aiden reads his phone, then grins. "Admit it. You like messing with her, even if you didn't mean to at the outset. Thing is, that's not going to get you far in teaming up this semester, so this can be your peace offering. You should come, show your project partner you're not a complete ass. Just fifty percent."

I shove him, sending him careening into the side of his car. But I don't say no, either.

———

IT'S SHOCKINGLY LOUD IN THE STADIUM. I SHOULD HAVE anticipated that. I stupidly pictured a women's soccer game being as poorly attended as they were when I was little. From a moral standpoint, I'm glad that I was wrong. For the sake of my ears, I'm cringing.

The stands are packed with families, coeds, and plenty of locals. Signs decorate the rows and those goddamn vuvuzelas blast from all corners of the stadium. It's dusk, and there's a hint of crisp coolness to the air that reminds me so much of fall in Washington, it nearly makes me smile.

I'd be lying if I said sitting here doesn't make me feel like someone slit my gut, took a fistful of my intestines, and drew them out. I'm shocked by the intensity of my reaction as it grips me—how wrong it feels for me to be on this side of that fence, the bone-deep sense that I belong on a field, the reliable defender in back.

It's been two years. I tell myself I've moved on, and most of the time, I feel like I have. I'm a practical person. Logically, rationally, I recognize that my life changed and with it, my relationship to the game I still love, and that's reality.

I thought I was past grieving what I lost, but maybe grief isn't linear. Maybe I can accept what I've lost *and* still mourn it. Maybe I always will.

My phone dings. Aiden.

She's good, right?

I shrug as I type, *Decent enough.*

Our eyes meet as he rolls his. *You're full of shit*, he texts.

Aiden's right, I am full of shit. Willa's not good. She's not decent. She's breathtaking. Her touches are fluid, her movement effortless. Her powerful quads flex as she jukes and spins and tricks every one of USC's defenders, blasting by them and bearing down on the goalie. She's had four goals, and she's not slowing down.

I barely recognized her at first, because she wasn't swimming in sweats and her hair wasn't in its normal pouf on top of her head. She wears a fitted jersey that hugs her lean torso and narrow shoulders, shorts that sit on her hips and cut off just a bit above the knee, revealing those defined quadricep muscles every real soccer player develops. But the shit kicker is her face, bare and clear, because her hair is French-braided severely down the back of her head.

It wasn't until the stadium lights bounced off her forehead, her cheekbones, those full lips, that I recognized her. Now, watching her score and smile, I swear I see her eyes light up from here. She's happy, and her eyes are sunshine bright, the luminous color of melted caramel.

Not that I ever expect to see that color up close. I'm expertly talented at earning that rich amber tinged furious ruby red. Pissing her off is easy, and for safe emotional distance, preferable.

But the competitive voice inside me itches to prove I could just as easily make Willa smile. That I could playfully poke and tease and sweet-talk her until her eyes turned toffee-colored sunshine again.

A vuvuzela blasts nearby, interrupting my thoughts and ringing in my ear. Almost instantly the tinnitus escalates painfully in my left ear. Freya must notice that I wince because she sets a hand on my neck and rubs gently. Some people might find my family's comfort with each other's bodies odd, but it's how we all are, and it makes sense, given half of us were raised by or were raising the other half. Freya's like a second mom—she rubbed my back while I puked and wiped my ass for a fresh diaper probably as much, if not more so, than my own mother.

My phone buzzes with a message from her. *We can go. Aiden forgets how painful loud environments are for you. You know he just loves you and wants you to be integrated, but he's an ass about it sometimes.*

I huff a silent laugh, replying, *It's okay. I like watching Willa. I'm just going to have a monster headache afterward.*

Freya's hands pause on my neck, then resume, after she types, *Do you *like* like her?*

Sighing, I shake my head. *I said I like watching her. She's good. That's it, Frey.*

At halftime, UCLA's up four-one, but twenty minutes into the second half, USC's managed to put three more past our goalie, who needs to have her eyes examined. The two teams are now tied, and they have no business being tied. UCLA's objectively better. They're just making sloppy mistakes.

Willa's defenders keep falling away from goal-side stance. The goalie's stepping too far out of the box. Willa's goddamn midfielder needs to push up and hold possession longer. Willa, though, she's technically flawless, incredibly fit. She balances possession and passing perfectly. She's no one-trick pony but instead has countless moves to keep her defenders tripping over her. She's been sprinting for sixty-five minutes, and she's not even starting to show fatigue.

Times flies as I watch her, the minutes of regulation play dwindling to only a few before stoppage kicks in. Willa isn't just a talented player, she's the kind of athlete that comes once in a generation. If anybody belongs on a professional field, it's her. An odd sensation of pride tightens my chest, which I immediately dismiss. Willa's not mine to be proud of. She's not even my friend. She's someone I can root for, though, even if she drives me nuts.

Just as I'm tying up my thoughts with that tidy concluding bow, Willa cuts a sick move around a defender, passing to a teammate I recognized earlier as her roommate, Rooney. Rooney one-times it back to her, and on her first touch, Willa rips it into the upper ninety, scoring again. She's secured the lead with less than a minute left in regulation.

Instinctively, I'm on my feet, clapping with all the UCLA fans. Without thinking, I lift my hands and set my fingers inside my lips, releasing a long, shrill, celebratory whistle that stuns Freya and Aiden. I feel their eyes on me, but I don't look at them. I look at Willa on the field and refuse to even begin to analyze what I just did.

Willa jumps into the arms of her teammates, who tug her braid and smack her ass. Her smile is wide as she floats down the field in their arms. When they drop her at the top of the center circle, Willa faces toward the stadium, hands on hips, gaze scouring the stands, like she's searching for something. I can't tell whether or not she's found what she was looking for before she turns back toward the field.

The oddest sensation settles beneath my ribs. My chest is tight, burning, tangled. I'm looking at Willa Sutter, the pain in my ass who goes from zero to ninety on the rage-o-meter, who smacks off my ball cap and scowls at me like *that*'s what she got a full ride for, not soccer. I'm here at her game, my rib cage constricting as my heart whispers scary, unwelcome feelings. I turn toward Freya and type, *Can we blow this popsicle stand? I've got a migraine brewing.*

Freya nods, failing to hide her smile. "Migraine, huh?"

I ignore that not-so-subtle hint and swing an arm over her shoulder. Just as we leave the stadium, the buzzer ends the game.

6

RYDER

Playlist: "The Universe Is Laughing," The Guggenheim Grotto

A NUDGE TO MY SHOULDER MAKES ME LOOK UP FROM MY SEAT in the lecture room's front row. Willa gives me a cautious, inspecting frown as she settles in next to me, this time on my right side. I feel myself stiffen as she opens her notebook, and her arm inadvertently brushes mine. Shutting my eyes, I take a deep, chill-the-fuck-out breath, but that just makes the situation even worse.

A soft scent hits my nose. Citrus and sunscreen, a wisp of flowers. Roses maybe? It's the same one that infused her apartment, until the mouthwatering aroma of what she'd been cooking eventually overwhelmed it. I take a cautious breath in again. She smells like summer, like a hike through fields of wildflowers. I picture it perfectly, Willa ripping the flesh of a California orange with her teeth, slathered in SPF that does nothing to stop the freckles that pepper her nose, a rose blossom tucked in her wild curls.

Lost in that mental image, my eyes are still shut, my mind lulled, but I can feel Willa staring at me. I'm too chickenshit to meet her eyes. I know if I stare right back, unlike previous stare-downs, this one will make my heart tumble in my chest, just how it did when I watched her at her game.

Willa pats my hand, before I hear, "Ryder?"

My eyes fly open as I startle so badly, I slam my knee into the desk. Willa's voice—it's the first time I've fully heard it. My pulse trips and thunders through my body. A flush of heat rushes up my throat, then floods my cheeks.

Her voice is liquid velvet, poured sunlight. It's smooth and low and soft around the edges. It's the clearest sound I've heard since I woke up in the hospital. It feels epically unjust. Why? Why did Willa have to sit on my right side, why did she have to have a voice that falls in that tiny window of wavelengths that I can still pick up?

Why did it have to be her?

When our eyes finally meet, hers glitter with curiosity. She taps my right shoulder lightly with one finger.

"You can hear better out of this one, huh?"

I can hear the quality of her voice but can't understand everything as she talks by sound alone. I have a splitting headache today, and the thought of wearing my hearing aid, enduring the grating amplified noise in the lecture hall, was too much. Thankfully, she still says it slowly, and I watch her full lips. Those soft, pouty lips.

Dammit.

I nod.

Slowly, she leans closer, setting her elbow on my desk. Our arms press against each other, as she stares at my mouth, then meets my eyes once more. "Why don't you talk, then, Ryder? If you can hear somewhat? Why don't you use hearing aids?"

My jaw ticks as I pull back. She sounds like Aiden, and it's aggravating. How does she know I don't use hearing aids? Because I'm not running my mouth like her? Most people don't seem to understand how complex hearing aids are, that they aren't magical fixes. Extracting my phone from my pocket, I type, *Hearing aids aren't a panacea. Speaking with them is not that simple.*

I watch her open up the message and frown. She pauses, staring at the words for a long minute, then types, *Panacea. Damn, Brawny, that's top-notch bookstore vocabulary right there.*

I glance up. Willa's smiling gently, and relief loosens the tension in my shoulders. She's giving me an out, not pushing me to explain myself.

If I didn't think it would lead to world devastation, I would hug her for it. Instead, I text her back. *Bookstore vocabulary?*

Willa nods. "Summer job. Worked at a bookstore. You learn big words."

Favorite book, I type.

She exhales heavily. *I don't know where to begin. I have too many.*

Pick one.

She shoves me. "You're so bossy."

I smirk.

Willa taps her mouth. As I watch her, I find myself oddly thinking how satisfying it would be to drag that full bottom lip of hers right between my teeth. *Shit.* Bad train of thought. I need to get laid. I'm daydreaming about biting the crazy-haired thorn in my side.

My phone buzzes. *Jane Eyre.*

I scrunch my nose and type, *Rochester is such a dick.*

He's a Byronic hero, Willa fires back. *Tortured, moody, sexually intense. Like Darcy in Pride and Prejudice.*

Except Darcy proves to be a decent guy, I write, *and Rochester is a two-timing liar.*

Willa bites her lip and nods, conceding that point. *Jane is the real star anyway. She's strong and unapologetically independent.*

I smile at her response as I get that weird feeling in my sternum, just like when Willa scored at her game and I watched her eyes light up like sunshine. The feeling that made my mind spin and unease tighten my stomach.

"Ryder."

I can't quite suppress my shiver when I hear her say my name again.

Her head's tipped to the side. With her frizzy, untamed hair, her wide-set brown eyes catching the lecture room's warm lights, she looks young and innocent. That is until she traps the corner of that full bottom lip between her teeth.

I lift my shoulders quickly. *What?* I mouth.

Willa leans in closer and pokes my chest. I reel, frowning from my body to her hand. Her familiar scowl is back. When she pokes me again, this time I swat her away. She picks up her phone and texts me, *When were you planning on admitting you showed up to my game?*

I open my mouth, then shut it, turning toward my phone. *What's the big deal? I was just curious to see what all the hype was about.*

Her face freezes as she reads my message then types, *And what's the verdict?*

My thumbs hover. I should shut this down right now. Say something bland and disinterested, nothing of the smack-talking banter that we constantly volley. But instead, my thumbs type, *You'll do.*

A smile brightens her profile before she schools her face. Typing quickly, she then turns over her phone as Aiden starts the lecture.

My phone buzzes. *Asshole lumberjack. I could see your plaid from three miles away. Thanks for coming.*

The rest of the class, I studiously avoid her, our attention ahead on Aiden's lecture. It's hard to concentrate, thinking about how my name sounded, the memory of her voice. More than once, I bite my cheek, pinch my skin. Anything to bring back my focus. Spending my thoughts on Willa, our interactions and verbal sparring, paying her attention and back-handed compliments, is playing with fire.

But maybe just this once it would be worth it to get burned.

————

MY HANDS SHAKE. I STIR THE MEATBALLS ONE MORE TIME, then toss the noodles in butter and parsley. My heart's somewhere down in my stomach, banging around and ruining my appetite. I'll be lucky if I don't barf the moment Willa walks in the door.

It's become a bit of a habit to have dinner while we work on the final. Often, I arrive right after Willa's out of the shower from practice. She's always starving, so she shoves a protein bar in her mouth while whipping up something quick. A few times I've helped her, to speed up meal prep, but we bickered so badly while we did it, she demoted me to setting the table. She's cooked every time, and last week my mother's voice started lecturing me in my head, asking where her feminist son had gotten to, that he was comfortable letting a full-time female student athlete feed his fifteen-credit, lazy ass twice a week.

So, last time, I offered to host at my place, take a turn making dinner, and Willa accepted.

I'm nervous to have her here. I'm nervous to host her and

feed her and have a woman in my space as I never have. Because the girls I dated and brought home in high school were just that—girls. The few I've shared casual sex with thus far in college, much the same.

But Willa? Willa's a ball-busting, fire-breathing, hell-raising *woman*.

That's not the only reason I'm tense. It's probably not even the predominant reason. I'm shaking in my actual boots because I did something I've been putting off for so long, I started to think I'd never even do it: I went to the audiologist, and took them up on their standing offer to try a new model. I only had them adjust for my right ear, even though they encouraged me to adjust the left one, too, because I've had such terrible results so far with the hearing aid in that ear. It amplifies too much harsh noise, shrieks with feedback, and exacerbates my tinnitus.

The thought of giving my left ear another chance at responding well to a hearing aid—even a new one—hoping *this* time it wouldn't make me cringe when I turned it on and realized how little it was going to help, for how miserable it would make me, I couldn't handle the thought of weathering that kind of disappointment again.

To their credit, the audiologist respected my decision and focused on adjusting the right ear's hearing aid. The difference, even after one appointment, the first of a few, at least, to optimize it, is noticeable and exciting and a little terrifying. Because it makes more of those "what ifs" flood my thoughts —questions like what's next and how it might be possible. But with "what ifs" also comes hope. And with hope comes the possibility of disappointment. It's scary to hope and dream.

My hair's down, and thankfully it tends to fall parted to that side, covering my right ear and the hearing aid tucked behind it. I'm hiding it on purpose. Because if no one knows it's there, there's no pressure to talk, no expectation to hear perfectly. Maybe that seems to defeat the purpose of the hearing aid, but it doesn't. The hearing aid is for *me*, not for others' convenience.

Tucker, one of my roommates, walks in. "Smells good." He's facing me, favoring my right side, and I hear him the best I have in years. It brings an unexpected smile to my face that I manage to tamp down before he notices.

When he leans across me and tries to stick a finger in the meatballs, I smack him off.

"Geez, Ry. Can't a man eat?"

Tucker's my height but has even more muscle on him. Dark, glowing skin and an afro he's committed to growing bigger and bigger, he loves giving people shit when they ask how he could possibly head the ball with "all that hair," which he obviously can. One of the many reasons we get along is because we both similarly enjoy trolling ignorant humans.

We also went to high school together and lost our collective shit when we were both admitted to UCLA and signed onto the soccer team. We were roommates, already moved into the athlete's dorm, but when everything went south for me during summer training and I left the team, Tucker insisted on us still living together. We got a place right off-campus and haven't stopped being roommates since.

Becks walks in next, scratching his stomach before his hand disappears down his pants to adjust himself. He's an oddball I met in a freshman humanities gen ed. He's weird and funny, and he makes my six-foot-three height look dainty. While he doesn't play any sports for UCLA, the guy's a beast to have on your rec-league volleyball team. He's also slovenly, evidenced by the junk groping, especially as he advances on the food.

I lift a hand to signal he needs to stop.

"What?" he asks.

My finger points from his groin to his hand, followed by a colorful expression he knows by now means, *Get the* fuck *out of here.*

Becks groans. "But it smells so good."

I make a shooing motion, then shove Becks and kick him playfully in the ass when he won't leave the kitchen. Both he and Tucker flop onto the sofa, which takes up the far end of the combined living room and dining room in the house we rent. I clap my hands twice at them, earning their attention. *Get out*, I mouth.

"Hell no." Tucker throws his feet up on the coffee table as he picks up his phone and texts our group chat, *I am one hundred percent staying for this.*

I shake my head, typing, *No you're not. Get out. She'll be here any minute.*

Becks peers down to his phone, swiping open to join the conversation. *Duh. That's why we're here. I bet she's hot as hell. Twenty-five bucks says she's got a bubble butt. Ryder's weakness is a woman with an ass.*

Tucker snorts. *Twenty-five bucks says that our boy Ryder's bit by the love bug. He never cooks Mama Bergman's homemade meatballs for *us*.*

Tucker's laugh quickly turns into a howl of pain as I wrench his nipple in a violent twist. I pick up Becks's hacky sack and very accurately launch it at his nuts, earning his groan.

Every noise stops when a loud knock on the door draws our attention.

"I'll get it!" yells Tucker. He flies by me, shoving me out of the way.

A stifled growl rumbles in my throat as I reach Tucker, just in time to shove him back from twisting the doorknob.

When I open the door, it's not quite the welcome I was hoping to offer Willa. Her eyes widen as she takes in the scene. Becks still rolls on the couch cupping himself. Tucker climbs up the wall from where I threw him into it.

Willa tugs her lip between her teeth and cocks her head. Her hair's wet and twisted tight in a bun. All I see are those big brown eyes dancing with amusement, the shine of her cheekbones. "Sounded like a gladiator battle was happening inside."

I shrug, fighting the grin pulling at my mouth. Her voice sounds even better than I hoped it would. I hear its honey warmth in the middle and a scratchy note on the bottom, which has to be from shouting and exercise. It makes a filthy thought snag in my brain. What else makes her voice raspy and breathless? My dick swells and things start to get tight inside my jeans. I clear my throat as embarrassment heats my cheeks.

A quick visual of when I walked in on Becks taking a shit does what I need it to. My jeans are no longer uncomfortable, and I wave her in.

When she's inside, I have to reach past Willa to shut the door behind her, placing our bodies close. She smiles up at me and draws in a deep breath.

Our eyes lock. Carefully, I reach for my phone, swipe to open it and type, *Hope you're inhaling the aroma of Swedish meatballs, not me, Sunshine.*

Her eyes widen as she reads it, then pokes my stomach. "I am *not* a Sunshine."

I huff a laugh that's all air. It slipped out, calling her that.

It's the color of her eyes in the rare moments she's not livid, the sound of her voice, filling my ear. But I can't tell her that.

Ever heard of sarcasm, Sutter? I type.

She reads the text, and her eyes darken with irritation, the irises switching from rich coffee brown to murderous copper. It's intoxicatingly fun to coax reactions from her.

I tap a finger on her nose. She smacks my hand away and then shoves me. I don't even budge which just makes her scowl deepen. I try and fail to hide my grin. So easily provoked.

Taking her by the elbow, straight to the table, I pull out a chair, lift Willa's bag off her shoulder and set it on the surface. I pat the seat gently. *Sit. Get comfy.*

She drops down, that scowl still tightening her face.

Both the guys have recovered enough to silkily drop into their chairs at the table. I take one look at both of them, then type in our group chat, *Say hi, then be scarce.*

They read their phones and then obediently both stand.

"Hi," Becks says. "I'm the tall, dark, and handsome roommate—"

Tucker facepalms him. "That's actually my description. Tucker Wellington at your service, and that's Becks. Do me a favor—don't shake his hand."

Willa bites her lip again as she boots up her laptop, her eyes dancing between them. Something funny happens in my stomach when I see she gives them both only a perfunctory glance. Neither of my roommates are bad-looking dudes. Willa, it seems, could care less.

"Hi," she says, finally. "Willa Sutter. Nice to meet you both."

After I give them another death glare, the guys finally make their exit. As they back away behind Willa, Becks mimes the bang action with his hips, while Tucker flashes both hands. *Ten out of ten*, he mouths.

I flick them off and mouth, *Go!*

I thought Willa's speaking voice was the best sound I'd heard, but then once again she proves me wrong. Her laughter settles like windchimes in my ear. For the first time in years, I want to laugh right along.

———

AT SOME POINT, I SHOULD HAVE CONSIDERED THE MURKY ethics of telling someone I'm deaf and then neglecting to inform them when I augment my hearing.

I didn't want Willa to know about my hearing aid, because I don't want anyone to know I'm still trying to figure out hearing and speaking again. Because I know what comes next. Pressure. Pressure to get back to aural processing, pressure to use my voice. And that hasn't worked so far. It's just not happening. Not yet, at least.

Thing is, I didn't realize up to this point that Willa talks to herself *constantly*. I don't think she knows she does it, at least not right away, maybe not at all. Perversely, I'm enjoying this little window into that hotheaded, fast-moving brain of hers.

"Asshole lumberjack," she grumbles. "Shooting down another one of my ideas that I only spent—oh, ya know —*hours* researching." She drops her voice, imitating how she must imagine I sound. It's gruff and surly. "Hah. What a *stupid* idea, Willa. We can't offer a sliding scale of payment. What is this, communist Russia? Small-brained woman."

I open my mouth, about to defend myself when I remember that will reveal I've been inadvertently eavesdropping on her, thanks to my tuned-up hearing aid.

For a moment, I debate telling her. But then I think better of it. Willa's got a temper like no one else. I can see her getting pissed if I told her I actually *can* hear the evidence that she apparently has no filter between her brain and her mouth. As much as I like ruffling Willa's feathers, I'm not sure I'm prepared to see her *that* angry.

Carefully, I type a response, based on where we left off at our conversational impasse. *How about this: we take your concept of making the business financially accessible, but instead of offering a sliding scale, we offer service trades, like a co-op. Then, maybe we can do some sponsored ads with willing brands in exchange for them comping us gear that we can gift to people in extenuating circumstances. How's that?*

Willa frowns, her hands flying over the keys. *You're serious? You're actually considering a compromise?*

I scowl, typing back, *It's not uncommon. A couple of places I used to buy gear from allowed you to do that.*

Where'd you buy gear, Lumberjack? she writes. *Shredding black diamonds. Mounting summits. Wrestling grizzly bears.* She bats her eyelashes.

I scowl at her. My torn feelings about eavesdropping are quickly offset by her ribbing.

It was mountain lions, mostly, I write.

That earns her smirk.

Washington State, where I grew up. I hesitate, my fingers hovering over the keys, before I finally give in. *I want to run my own store up that way after graduation. Offer rentals and for-sale, stock accessible gear, too. Build an inclusive team that offers guided outdoors experiences to anyone who wants them—hiking, kayaking, climbing, that kind of thing.*

Our eyes meet. Her grin is wide and genuine. "That's badass, Bergman."

I shrug and move us past it before I can internally lose my

shit. I can't believe I just admitted that to her, and worse, that her response filled my chest with warm satisfaction.

You want to play professionally? I type.

She nods. *As long as these old bones will let me.*

I write back, *I'm sure you will.*

Shockingly, it doesn't hurt to wish her well on the journey that I wanted to be mine. Willa's a hard worker, a brutally determined and gifted athlete. All I can be is happy for her.

Setting her elbows on the table, Willa rests a cheek in her hand. She blinks slowly, looking owlish as she yawns, then types, *So the great outdoors, eh, Brawny?*

I text her immediately. *Brawny?*

She shrugs, then texts back, *Like the paper towel stud. Muscles. Flannel. Brawny. So why the wilderness life? Come from an active, outdoorsy family?*

I nod. Thankfully my beard hides the blush that crops up at her indirect compliment.

Willa yawns again. I glance at the clock to see it's after eleven already. She has to be exhausted.

"I have to go," she says sleepily.

I nod in recognition. When she stands, she sways. I lunge around the table, my arm wrapping around her waist to steady her.

Jesus.

I mean, I saw Willa in her uniform at the game. I know abstractly that she's strong and fit, but feeling those washboard abs under her hoodie, the narrow dip of her hips, nearly knocks the wind out of me.

I dig out my phone and text her. *It's late. I'll walk you home.*

"No," she whines, making sure her face is tipped toward mine, so I can read her lips. "I'm too sleepy."

A sigh puffs out of me. I type, *I'll give you a piggyback, Sunshine.*

She shakes her head and signs *bad*. "That's a bad idea."

Why? I sign, but she doesn't answer.

Slowly, she steps out of my grip and wobbles toward the sofa. "I'll just nap here for a bit, then I'll walk home when the sun's up. Once I'm not so…"

I think the word I miss is *tired*, which she mumbles as she collapses onto the cushions.

Tugging my hair, I stomp toward her. Before I can text her again, her eyes drift shut. By the time I'm crouching down at the sofa, she's snoring.

I'm not leaving her out here on the sofa. It doesn't feel right. Carefully I scoop her up and carry her into my room. I tuck her into my bed and set her alarm for six thirty, placing her phone on the pillow, near her head. I figure that gives her enough time before the earliest a class runs on campus, which is eight in the morning. Thankfully, I'm fastidiously neat and I just changed my sheets last night, so everything's clean and fresh in my room. She should sleep well enough.

After I do my last few tasks and lock up for the night, I set an alarm for six. Throwing myself onto the couch with a blanket, I try not to think about Willa Sutter sleeping in my bed.

It takes me a very long time to fall asleep.

WILLA

Playlist: "One Way Or Another," Blondie

I STIR FROM SLEEP GROGGILY, MOANING IN PLEASURE. THE scent surrounding me is obscenely arousing. I'm dreaming about misty pine forests and a blond-haired guy in flannel who has to start slowly unbuttoning his shirt when it comes time to fell a tree.

Wrenching awake, I sit up and realize I am neither in my bed nor in my apartment. If I go by the spruce and cedar scent infusing the air, the extreme tidiness of my surroundings, I'm in Ryder's bedroom, tangled in his sheets. His naked body has slept here.

Not that I've tried to picture Ryder's naked body or anything. Not that I'm doing that vividly now.

Don't. Just don't, brain. Don't go there. Don't think about it, about the solid slab I've felt beneath his shirt every time I poked his stomach, about how much I'd probably enjoy dragging my fingers through his dirty-blond bedhead hair. *Definitely* don't think about those bulging biceps, always straining as he moves. Don't think about them flexing while he braces himself above me, thrusting—

"Whoa!" I tumble off the mattress, scrambling upright. I have to get out of here. I'm drowning in hormones from my sexy lumberjack dream, and this room is quicksand. The longer I stay, the harder it will be to escape its tug.

I hustle through straightening his bed, then quietly tiptoe out and scoop up my bag. A crisp pile of papers sits on the table, along with a note in his tidy scrawl.

The semester's notes. All yours. Take the container with your name on it in the fridge.

– Ryder

My heart turns gooey and slinks down to my stomach. He printed the notes for me. A huge wave of relief that I finally have everything I need for this class is quickly replaced by suspicion. I'm not used to genuinely nice gestures from the lumberjack. I should run a little quality assurance on these bad boys in case this is his jackass idea of a funny prank. I flip through each page carefully, waiting for them to switch to hieroglyphs, but they prove to be in English and organized in chronological order.

First the delicious meal, then the hospitality of his bed, now these notes. The lumberjack is full of surprises.

Carefully, I slip the papers into my bag, sweeping up his note once again. *Take the container with your name on it.* "Bossy," I grumble. He might be bossy, but this time I'm doing what he says because those were some damn good Swedish meatballs and twisty noodles he made.

Container in hand, I pad softly toward the door, stepping into my tennis shoes, when I steal a glance toward the couch. Ryder snores softly, one hand draped off the edge of the sofa. What does he look like, asleep? When his defenses are down, is he just as maddening to stare at?

Don't do it, Willa.

I'm at a fork in the road, and I know it. It's that moment in many of the books I've read, with two paths before the heroine. One is shadowy. An owl hoots. Leaves rustle. The other is sunlit. Birds twitter. The path is wide and well trod.

A snort of self-amusement sneaks out of me. *Well trod.* I may be a tad overdramatizing this.

Still, a sinister breeze whispers on the shadowy path I can't stop eyeballing. *This way danger lies.* It's the truth. I can feel in my bones that nothing safe will come from what I'm tempted to do. Problem is, I'm me: I tend to do what I want first, then regret it later.

"Eh, fuck it."

Ignoring my own warnings, I walk back toward the couch and bend down, inspecting Ryder's features. I don't really mind the idea of a beard, but his frustrates me. I want to see all of his face, to know if he has dimples or soft lips. I want to see when he blushes and watch his throat bob as he swallows.

His hair's in his eyes. Carefully, I brush it back, then freeze when I see something curled around his ear. His right ear. His *better hearing* ear.

A hearing aid?

Shock tightens my stomach. Has he always had it? I rack my brain. Unfortunately, I pay a little too close attention to Ryder's features. So much so, that I can confirm I've never noticed this hooked around his ear before. Unless he's kept it hidden beneath his hair.

"You son of a bitch," I whisper.

I think about my brain's terrible habit of sending its most intense thoughts straight to my mouth, how it's worse when I'm stressed and freaking out. I don't know why I do it, why I can't keep the words locked inside my head. I already feel bad about it, because I know that's not right, muttering around a person who relies on texts and clear speech for lipreading to communicate, but shit, I am trying to keep those thoughts locked up tight—I don't *want* them to be communicated with anyone, let alone the guy who'll take any material I throw his way and undoubtedly use it against me.

For all he sets my teeth on edge and raises my hackles, I've taken a little comfort that, with Ryder, if I embarrassed myself with an exposing mumbled confession of one kind or another, he wouldn't catch it, or he'd kick my shin and tell me to unlock my damn jaw and speak clearly. Then I'd get time to cover my humiliating tracks by telling him something less painfully vulnerable and poured straight from my most private thoughts. Maybe that's cowardly. Maybe I'm a shitty person. Maybe I'm really fucking scared as I process how much of me Ryder potentially has in his grip, now that I realize I have no idea just how and when he's worn that hearing aid.

And there is nothing that turns me into my worst, clawing, scratching, hissing self than feeling exposed. Goddammit. All last night that trickster was eavesdropping on my verbal diarrhea freak-out about this class, acting all chivalrous, feeding me dinner and pulling out my chair, leaving me to sleep alone in his bed and preserve my dignity.

And it was all a ruse. Anger churns my stomach. Embarrassment heats my cheeks. That *asshole.* That tall, sandy-haired, smirking, flannel-wearing, asshole lumberjack son of a bitch.

"Oh, it's war now, Bergman. It's war."

———

CONVENIENTLY, RYDER AND I HAVE CLASS TOGETHER TODAY. I have thirty minutes between my morning literature recitation and Mac's lecture. Just enough time to set retribution number one in place.

I've had some time to think through plausible explanations for why Ryder wore his hearing aid last night and didn't tell me. I have to say, I'm quite proud of myself. I managed to coax my temper from explosive rage to a simmering level of irate, thus clearing my head enough to do some logical deducing.

Ryder's better hearing ear is his right ear. The first time I sat on his right side in class, and we talked, he acted...differently. His eyes followed my lips as usual, but they also roamed me curiously. His whole face lit up as he leaned in. Maybe he *liked* hearing my voice and hadn't exactly known what to do with that except explore it further.

He said in his terse-texting way that hearing aids aren't a cure-all, and they don't make speaking easy for him. His response, and many other moments I have thus far, unfortunately, had to endure with him, have led me to a hunch: Ryder Bergman, beneath all his formidable, silent intensity, is shy.

And if he's shy about being deaf and not speaking, why wouldn't he also be shy about when he tries to wear his frustrating hearing aids, too?

That still doesn't answer the question of why he wore the hearing aid around *me*. Why me? I've thought of two possible motivations for his behavior:

One, he wants dirt on me, and he's a sick jerk with no qualms about how he gains that material. Pretty grim option, but not outside the realm of possibility. He *is* an asshole lumberjack, after all.

Two, he's shy about his hearing aids, which he's implied are complicated for him, but he does use them, and he uses them to hear me better.

But why would he want *that*?

I have no idea what Ryder thinks of me, but I know that in his surly way, he doesn't *always* seem to find me a ball-busting nuisance. I know that he got a little gruff and shooed away his flirtatiously curious friends last night. I know that he might have pissed me off to high heaven as we discussed the final project specifics, but he took care making our meal, brewed herbal tea after dinner, and served tiny Swedish thumbprint cookies that I blissfully over-consumed.

Sure, he's a prickly type. As my fellow wild-haired woman and general feminist badass Hermione Granger would say, he routinely demonstrates "the emotional range of a teaspoon." But at the end of the day, I'd bet my cleat collection Ryder would run into a burning building to save a kitten.

Between my two options for his driving motivation to wear that hearing aid in stealth last night, I'm going with door number two. I think, just maybe, Ryder Bergman doesn't *totally* hate me.

And frankly, even though he pisses me the hell off at least half the time I'm with him, I think I might not totally hate Ryder Bergman, either. At least, enough not to bicker constantly, but instead, fifty percent of the time. At least enough to smile a little more at each other, back off the unrelenting, busting one-liners. Enough to maybe share an exploratory kiss if he wanted to shave that wild animal covering the lower half of his face.

Simply for exploratory purposes of course. Nothing serious. Certainly nothing emotional.

Because if I were to act on my emotions, I'd slap him first. Maybe yank his beard a little before I kissed that surly mouth. Remind him that spying on people who have jack crap for a brain-to-mouth filter and dearly wish they did—even if it's because you're intrigued by them—is invasive bullshit.

I could be truly wrathful in my revenge, but at some point, violence gets boring.

This tactic is way more fun.

My arrival to class is prompt for once, and I drop in the seat that I'm starting to suspect Ryder actually saves for me. Once again, it's on his right, and when I sit and softly clear my throat, it earns his attention immediately.

Carefully, I unravel the knit scarf I wore so nobody on campus got a Hooters hello as I walked to class. When I peel away the last spool of fabric, Ryder's eyes widen, before a furious blush peeks from the top of his scruffy beard. He blinks rapidly as his eyes struggle not to dip as they did at first. I can hardly blame him. With her blessing for my retributive tactic, I'm wearing one of Rooney's wrap tops in a saffron yellow that makes my eyes glow. Significant detail: Rooney is two cup sizes smaller than me. This shirt barely covers my nipples.

Ryder's mouth works, before he's pulling out his phone, typing furiously. *Sutter, what the fuck are you wearing?*

I unlock my phone. *Clothes*, I write. *Why do you ask, Lumberjack?*

His angry huff as he types sends a frisson of delight up my spine. *You know what I mean.*

I really don't, I type back.

I give him a once-over. Yet another flannel from the rotation. Very autumnal. It would look absurd on most guys I know. Annoyingly, Ryder wears it like a hot-as-hell L.L. Bean model. Don't even give me that attitude and try to deny it—you know you're not looking for slippers when you open that catalog. You ogle those sexy DILFs in the L.L. Bean men's section, too.

The flannel of the day is burgundy-and-navy-blue plaid, with a faint gold line woven through that matches my shirt. I take a deep breath, get my libido locked down, and type, *Hey look! We match.*

Ryder huffs again as he stares at me. He's exasperated, which is incredibly gratifying. There's an intense and delicious upside to our little tiffs. Always has been. Every time we start bickering, electricity crackles, generating a surging tug between us. Our circuitry keeps intensifying, and after last night, I feel like we're one high-voltage spat away from blowing a massive fuse.

Ryder's eyes are on my lips, but it feels like they're everywhere, absorbing so much more of me than just the words I say. It's always like that with him. When I'm with Ryder, I never question whether he's present or listening intently. I never doubt that he's taking pains to understand me, that he's observing everything I do and say, even if it's pissing him off. The irony is not lost on me, that he's the first man who's ever truly made me feel heard in my life and he can't hear a word I'm saying.

Or so I thought, Mr. Rogue Hearing Aid.

On a third angry huff, Ryder's eyes dart my way, then back to his phone. *Your tits are one millimeter away from telling the classroom good morning.*

His eyes go to my mouth, and I smile. "Tits don't talk, Bergman."

He pinches the bridge of his nose and takes a long, slow breath. When his hand falls, and I feel his eyes on me again, I peer down, playfully sliding my finger along the edge of my shirt. Ryder swallows so loudly, the students in back can hear him.

I glance up at him and watch his eyes dip to my mouth. "Besides, they're fine. I have boob tape that keeps them stuck." My finger still idles along my shirt, not far from my rapidly hardening nipple. This is getting a little out of hand.

Ryder's breaths are deep, husky tugs of air. I take a shuddering inhale, and I sound just as twisted up as him. Clearing my throat, I remind myself of the point of this.

Pausing, I flip the edge of the fabric, showing Ryder a peek of the double-stick adherent and probably a sliver of nip, if I'm being honest. Not like I care. I'm an athlete. Spend ten minutes in a pregame locker room, and you'll get it—I've been consensually stripping down in front of others for a solid decade at this point. It makes no difference to me.

Apparently, it makes a difference to Ryder. His jaw drops. I have to turn away so he doesn't catch the gigantic grin of satisfaction painting my face. It's just too good to pass up, so I open my phone and type. *Bonus of this sticky stuff? I don't even need a bra.*

Ryder's head drops as his fist lands heavy on the desk.

For once, when Mac starts the lecture, it's me who's studiously noting away. Ryder's a stone statue to my left. I'm not even sure he recovers his senses enough to absorb the lecture. But when the lights go up and class ends, I sure as heck don't stick around to find out.

———

THE FOLLOWING FORTY-EIGHT HOURS PROVE BENEFICIAL FOR both parties involved. I remember that the last thing I have time for in my life is seducing surly mountain men, and Ryder probably remembers why he prefers me in head-to-toe sweatpants.

I don't really know what I was thinking, wearing that revealing shirt, except that my temper is its own living, breathing thing inside my brain. It just kept telling me that trying to make the guy's eyeballs fall out of his head was an infinitely more proportional response than, say, dropping a laxative in his giant stainless-steel water canteen or, I don't know, dousing his boxers with pepper spray. By comparison, a well-timed titty tease felt practically docile.

But now, with a few days to cool off, I realize that if Ryder upped the ante with the hearing aid stealth move, I just went all in with my little peep show. As I wait for him to arrive at my apartment, I'm left wondering, *Now what?*

I don't have time to think any longer, because there's a knock at the door. When I open it, I'm met with Ryder, holding a hand over his eyes. My phone dings.

You wearing actual clothes this time?

I smack his stomach. It earns a soft *oof* from Ryder, as his hand falls. His green eyes are dark with mischief, and he tips the brim of his ball cap in greeting, then walks past me.

As I spin on my heel, my eyes narrowed. He's up to something. I can feel it. Perhaps I didn't consider my strategy as longitudinally as I should have. I didn't really think that Ryder would take my sartorial provocation and be vindictive —there's some bookstore vocabulary for you—I kind of expected him to choke on his tongue in class and leave it at that.

I think I may have miscalculated.

Ryder slowly lifts his messenger bag off his shoulder and sets it on the table. I watch his hands as they unbuckle the latch and slide out his computer. It's like weird IT soft porn, watching the way the laptop slips out of his bag, how Ryder's hands curl around the screen as he sets it upright.

A flush crawls up my chest and warms my neck. My cheeks pink. Shit, it's hot in here.

"Right." I clear my throat.

Ryder glances up and gives me a once-over. With his finger, he outlines my sweats-from-head-to-toe appearance then mimes applause. *Thank you*, he signs.

"Please." I roll my eyes, then text him, *Don't act like you didn't like what you saw.*

Removing his phone from his pocket, he types quickly. His jaw is tense, his eyes laser-focused on his screen. *I didn't say I didn't.*

My fingers tighten around my phone, as my gaze drifts up to his. Our eyes lock in the world's longest stare. That is until Ryder's face tightens with concern as he scrunches his nose and sniffs.

I whip a glance over my shoulder to the kitchen. "Crap!"

Rushing to the stove, I pull the soup off the burner, then scrape the wooden spoon across the bottom of the pot, searching for scorched spots. Thankfully I don't find any. "It's not burned…"

My voice dies off. Ryder is standing right behind me, heat pouring off his body. I close my eyes and can't help but picture my back to a roaring fire, the snap of its flames jolting me with surprise. I'm assaulted by the pungent fragrance of evergreens. He smells like a Christmas tree, the faint ghost of snow still on its branches.

Ryder leans in, then grasps my hand that holds the spoon. My eyes pop open as my body snaps to attention. With his other hand, he sets his palm on the counter. I'm caged in.

I glance up, so he can see my mouth when I speak, but before I can say a word, I freeze. His eyes are on me, his pupils blown wide, barely a ring of forest green surrounding them. Our mouths are inches away, our breaths faster and rougher than they should be.

"S-sorry," I tell him. My tongue darts out to wet my lips. Ryder's eyes dip, following its path. "I forgot to turn down the heat. It's not burned, though."

Ryder releases my wrist and brings his hand to my face. I

flinch, expecting some teasing flick or tug, any one of his many provoking touches. He pauses and frowns.

I would never hurt you.

He doesn't say it. Doesn't sign it. Doesn't text it. But the words hang in the air, as invisible yet substantial as the crackling atmosphere between us. Slowly, his fingers drift against my curls, gently tucking them behind my ear. His thumb traces the shell of my ear, down my neck.

Oxygen doesn't fill the air anymore. Or, if it does, I can't find it. Goose bumps dance across my skin as every neglected corner of my body roars to life. My heart beats in unfamiliar places. My fingertips and toes. Low in my stomach. Right between my legs.

Ryder's thumb settles at the hollow of my throat. His eyes lock with mine, reminding me how much he says with his eyes, how expressive they are. His lashes are thick, and while I thought they were black, now I see they're sable, a rich, smoky brown. They don't blink as Ryder leans toward me. Time suspends. My lips part as his grow closer.

He freezes, a breath away from my mouth. I'm doused in the haze of pine trees and manliness. My entire front is scorched by the heat of his body. Just as I begin to lean in, breaching the tiny remaining gap between us, Rooney barges through the door.

She stops as she sees Ryder and me leap apart so violently, I nearly fall into the sink. Her eyes bounce between us as a slow, satisfied grin lifts her mouth. "Am I interrupting something?"

Ryder shakes his head, lifting his ball cap and raking a hand through his hair, before he replaces it and tugs it low over his eyes.

"Nope," I manage. My voice couldn't be any huskier.

Clearing my throat, I turn back to the soup. "Dinner's ready if you're hungry."

Ryder clears his throat, too, and moves to the silverware drawer, getting spoons. Rooney's eyes flick once more between us as her grin widens. "Thanks, I'm not hungry just yet. I'll take a rain check."

The moment she turns the corner for her room, our shoulders drop with relief.

8

WILLA

IT HASN'T BEEN CONSUMING MY BRAIN EVERY SPARE MINUTE I have, which isn't that many spare minutes, between all the fretting I do about Mama, soccer, my grades, my career, the question of eternity, and the point of my existence.

Okay, it's been a little consuming my brain. *Was* Ryder going to kiss me?

Listen, I am a tough chick. I am a Bad. Ass. Feminist. I don't need a man to make me happy, and I sure as shit don't need one to validate my worth.

But maybe, just *maybe*, I want a man who's not only a penis to get off on, but an actual friend who knows and likes me. A big, warm body to wrap around me at night, to hold my hand and kill spiders, and if I'm really lucky, tiddle my tulip and actually coax an orgasm from it. A man has yet to do it, and I've been told I'm high-maintenance in that department. Apparently, I'm the one to blame for that track record.

Is it so wrong to want someone who knows how to bust me just as well as how to rub my back? Maybe I'm a little tired of being big, brave Willa, who juggles it all. Maybe, just *maybe* Ryder Bergman wants to be that guy who catches a ball or two for me.

I can't tell. Like, I really, really can't tell. Sure, he pays me attention. He knows my schedule, and we see each other most days of the week and text during all others, but Mac smooshed us together like peanut butter and jelly on the shitty Wonder Bread that is this hellacious course I enrolled in. We're practically dissolved into each other at this point, for all the work we have to do jointly.

He was probably just fucking with me, how I fucked with him in Business Math. But that seems like dangerous territory, to *pretend* to flirt with each other, to *feign* seduction. Doesn't it get tricky, when you're sparking and colliding, constantly circling each other, two hungry, horny animals, to differentiate what's fact and what's fiction?

Currently, Ryder types a million miles an hour, like some Pentagon techie who took too many uppers and washed them down with taurine-laced coffee. The man puts the *tense* in intense.

"Ryder?"

I sit to his right. He's at the long side of the table because the guy man-spreads like no other, while I'm at the short end of the table. He should be able to hear me.

His fingers peck brutally at the keys. He will break those keys to submission. He will subdue them to his typing will.

His eyes are narrowed in focus. I poke his arm. Ryder continues typing, but his keystrokes slow, a monsoon tapering to a steady drizzle.

"You okay, there, Sasquatch?"

Slowly, he swivels his head my way. I get one single nod, before he turns back.

We're working on separate parts of the final project right now, but frankly, I'm more concerned about the testing portion. If it's remotely similar to the midterm we just took and I barely squeaked a B minus from, then I need to up my game. When I told Ryder as much via text yesterday, he agreed we could study together, but since I got to his place and we ate in bizarrely banter-free silence, he's been at his computer like a cracked-up hacktivist.

"Are we going to study, Ryder?"

His typing slows even further. Now it's a lingering drip. Those green eyes swivel to my face and down to my mouth, then back up. Standing abruptly, he reaches into his bag, pulls out a massive pile of notecards, then walks over to his couch.

"O...kay?" I glance over my shoulder. Ryder's spreading the cards on his coffee table in some system I have no understanding of. I try not to stare but fail. He's unfortunately mesmerizing, mountain-man forearms poking out of his flannel. Tonight it's white with hunter green, gold, and blue plaid. It makes his hair blonder, his eyes greener, and his worn blue jeans pop as they hug his muscly legs.

Tonight, unfortunately, he's not just an asshole lumberjack. He's a sexy, strong-and-silent-type lumberjack, and he's driving me up the goddamn wall with this shutdown act. I miss the zingers, the banter, the repartee. He's just...quiet. And in a way, yes, technically Ryder's always quiet, but tonight, it's like he's not even here.

What's up with you? I text him.

Frowning, Ryder pulls out his phone, reads my message, then responds.

Nothing, Willa. We just have a shit ton of work to do. Are we studying or not?

I stand, sweeping up my phone and my notebook before I walk his way. I don't miss how he averts his eyes rather than holding mine, like usual. I don't miss how he falls into the sofa with a soft but not inaudible sigh.

I tap his shoulder gently, earning his eyes, then sign, *What's up?*

His groan is a hoarse crack in his throat as he scrubs his face. When his hands fall, I see what I missed earlier. Dark smudges under his eyes. A pale cast to his skin. Kneeling gently onto the sofa next to him, I sit back on my heels.

"Do you feel okay?" I ask.

He starts by nodding, but when his eyes lock with mine, he stops. The nod becomes a shake.

No, he mouths.

Worry drops like a stone in my gut. "What's wrong, Lumberjack?"

He rubs his eyes with the heel of his hands, then pulls out his phone and types, *Headache. It happens sometimes. No big deal.* As soon as it sends, he shuts his eyes like the dim light from the nearby lamp is offensive.

Scooching closer to him, I pat his hand. He opens one eye and looks me over.

What? he signs.

"Sit on the floor, in front of me."

His brow furrows. He signs, *Why?*

"I'll rub your neck and temples. My—" I catch myself before I blurt the truth. My *mom*, I almost said, gets horrible headaches and nausea from her cancer treatment. I scoured the internet when nothing the hospital gave her worked. I read about homeopathy and peppermint's role in alleviating nausea, tension, and headaches. I've since learned the art of peppermint diffused in a carrier oil, rubbed on her stomach. For her headaches, I dab it right on her temples. I've mastered massaging all the right spots to give her relief.

Clearing my throat, I shrug, then pull out my phone to text him. *I'm well-acquainted with headaches.* It's not a lie. I am well-acquainted with headaches, just not mine. *I use peppermint oil to work out the kinks.*

Ryder's eyebrows wiggle, and I smack his shoulder. "Pervert."

He glances down at his phone as he types. *We're supposed to be studying. And I don't have peppermint oil.*

"That's okay. I do." Springing up, I jog over to my bag. I keep a vial in there for when I visit Mama in the hospital. A few of the nurses think it's hocus-pocus and confiscate it when I leave it there, so now I keep it on my person at all times.

Ryder stares at me with a look I can't read. Is he repulsed by the idea of my touch if it's not pokes or smacks but gentleness? Is the thought of a friendly gesture instead of biting off his head so terrible? Jesus. If so, he's worse than me when it comes to being vulnerable with others.

It's just a head rub, Brawny, I text him. *Chill. I need your brain sharp for this project.*

Something in his expression relaxes as he reads my text. I don't exactly know how to take that, so like all disquieting thoughts I have, I shelve it to obsess over at a later date. "Sit on the floor, Ryder."

A long-suffering sigh leaves him as he slips to the ground and leans his back against the sofa. I settle behind him and straddle his shoulders. Gently coaxing his head back, I pour a drop of peppermint on each pointer, then rub the oil into his temples, staring down at his damn perfect nose. Straight and long, it's practically elegant, something you'd see in a sculpture. His cheekbones catch the light and on a soft groan. His head's weight increases in my hands. He's actually relaxing.

"See? That's not so hard. You're uptight, Mountain Man."

He sighs again, a long, weary exhale. A few minutes of silence pass between us as I study Ryder from above, listening, observing what unknots a tense point and what makes him wince. Pausing me, he pulls away, sweeps the cards together and gathers them into his hands. When he leans back again, he lifts one. It's an equation. A handwritten equation.

I tap him to earn his eyes. "What is that, Ryder?"

He gives me a look like, *Are you serious?*

I pinch his shoulder, making him scowl. "You know what I mean. You *wrote* these? All of these?"

He shrugs, then turns back to his lap and opens up his phone. *How else would I quiz you? I can't exactly ask you out loud.*

"Ryder…" My voice falters. He had to have spent *hours* on these. There are at least a hundred.

He ignores me. Tapping the equation, he stares at his phone, waiting for my answer.

That's the break-even point formula, I write. *Fixed costs over the difference between sales price per unit and variable costs per unit.*

He pats my foot, then squeezes. Somehow I know it means *good job*. He flips over the card, showing me my answer was right.

We continue in that same vein—me unknotting his muscles, Ryder holding those cards high for me to see. When I get it right, I earn a soft squeeze to the foot, when it's wrong, a finger jabs the notecard. After I get quite a few right and Ryder's head doesn't seem like it's locked in a vise anymore, I pause with my fingers tangled in his hair.

Why aren't I quizzing you? I text him. Ryder lifts a hand and guides mine to keep massaging. "Greedy asshole."

Picking up his phone, he writes, *You're not quizzing me because I know this shit, and my time's much better spent getting my head rubbed than repeating what I know.*

I tug his hair but feel a smile pulling at my lips. There's the cranky lumberjack I know.

I text him back, *Twenty bucks says you don't know this quite so well as you're boasting, Ryder.*

He cocks his eyebrows while shuffling the cards in his hands. When he has a card, he pauses and picks up his phone.

Twenty bucks says I'll get this right AND you owe me head massages every time we study.

I scowl. That's a rough one. But I don't back down from bets. I blame my competitive nature.

A thought springs into my head. Ryder's still looking at me, as I slide my fingers through his hair, but this time, I make it different. This time, I scrape my nails along his scalp.

It's like a flipped switch. His eyelids droop before snapping wide again, as if he's been hit by a tranq dart and is trying to stay alert. I graze my fingertips down the side of his neck and sweep them to his collarbones. His breath hitches, and I watch his hands grip the carpet. I drift one single finger from the base of his skull, down his neck, and watch his lips part.

Sure, Bergman, I text him one-handed. *Answer it right now, and you've got yourself a bet.*

I lift the card, hold it in front of his face and watch his eyes try to focus through a dazed expression. Leaning in, I place my lips to the shell of his right ear, careful to be as quiet as I can while loud enough to be heard. "Ten seconds, then you lose. Ten, nine…"

I whisper the countdown in his ear, my tits smashed into his back, my curls sweeping against his face. He takes a stuttering breath as his eyes narrow at me. He knows what I'm doing. Sitting up, Ryder rips the card out of my hand, but I just lean in closer as he stares at it. His chest heaves and I slide forward, basically hitching myself on his back. I rub his neck, sweep my fingers once more along his clavicles.

"Three...two..."

He smacks the floor.

"One."

Ryder whips his head my way, fury sparking in his eyes. We're nose to nose as I smile a slow, satisfied grin. "Class dismissed, Mr. Bergman."

———

"OH, WILLA, YOU'RE TERRIBLE!" MAMA CACKLES AND THEN fights a cough.

I wipe my eyes, my stomach aching from laughter. "You shoulda seen his face, Mama."

She shakes her head. "Aw, honey. I think he likes you."

My laughter dies off. "I don't think so. He teases and yanks me around a lot. If he does like me, he has a funny way of showing it."

Tucking a loose curl behind my ear, Mama smiles. "Maybe he's scared. It's quite human to lash out when we're afraid."

"What's he have to be scared of?"

If anyone has cause to be afraid, it's yours truly. I don't date. I don't trust men. Generally, I don't even *like* them.

"Well, Willa, he's deaf, and he doesn't talk, doesn't sign much. That has to be isolating, anxiety-inducing, at least sometimes. Have you ever tried living without all the auditory clues the world offers us to keep us safe, let alone being unable to express yourself to those around you?"

"No." I frown. "Have you?"

Mama nods. "Years ago, one of my deployments, an explosion went off. My ears rang so badly, it was all I could hear for two days. I almost got myself hit twice by jeeps moving through base. I missed people calling my name. Forty-eight hours, and by the time I went to bed that second night, Willa, I was a nervous wreck, exhausted and frustrated."

My heart feels like it's being squeezed in a fist so brutally tight, it's about to pop from pressure and liquify. I've spent most of my time being angry or annoyed with Ryder. Not once have I really thought about what life must be like for him. I see him as capable and independent, adapted to his life. Beyond the consideration to text and speak clearly so he can understand me, I don't treat Ryder differently than I would any other cranky, muscly, bristly-bearded, flannel fanatic.

But that's not exactly the same as empathizing, is it?

"No, sweetheart," Mama says. "It's not."

I sigh. "I said that out loud."

"Yes, you did. You've always been a verbal processor." Patting my hand, then holding it, Mama smiles gently. "It's one of my favorite things about you, how you wear your heart on your sleeve—"

"Do not." I playfully brush her hand away. Mama clasps it again, her grip strong.

"You do. Your anger *and* your affection. Your love is as hairpin-trigger as your temper, Willa Rose. You love selectively and passionately. You fight only the wars that are close to your heart."

After a beat of silence, I meet her eyes. "I don't know what to do, Mama."

She tips her head to the side. "About what?"

I shrug as tears well in my eyes. "Everything. The team, my grades, my future...him."

It feels like an avalanche of emotions—all the pressure, the overwhelming anxiety, and expectation, collapsing my chest. I fall into Mama's arms and cry silently. I let myself pretend I'm a kid again, whose life is so much simpler, safe in her mother's embrace as she rubs my back and soothes me.

"Thanks, Mama." I swallow my tears finally. "I'll be fine, I just get—"

"Tired," she finishes for me. "It's okay to be tired, you know."

Something shifts behind her eyes when she says that. It makes me worried. I'm about to push that point when a knock precedes Dr. B walking in.

The guy's such a dish. I get why Mama blushes around him. Tall, lean, he has a full head of wavy ginger-blond hair that reminds me of the roaring twenties, like a silver screen hunk. He has bright green eyes that I've always thought warm and genuine, and he's clean-shaven as ever, smelling like minty aftershave and antibacterial soap.

I haven't caught the guy in a while, so I take my chance while I have it. "Dr. Bezoozywhatsa-a-*achoo*!"

"God bless you," Mama deadpans.

Dr. B pumps the hand sanitizer and gives me an unimpressed cock of his eyebrow. His actual last name is a European tongue twister. *Bezuidenhout*. Its pronunciation is *not* phonetic. I still don't know how to say it. The first time I tried to read his name on her chart, Mama genuinely thought I'd sneezed. Now it's our running joke.

"Wilhelmina." He knows that's not my name. It's just his payback. Grinning, he offers me a fist bump which I meet. "Joy Sutter, looking joyous today," he says to Mama.

Mama winks at me as she straightens her robe over her hospital gown. "Who wouldn't be, when her daughter's here for a visit?"

I slide off the bed, making space for Dr. B. When he steps closer, he turns toward me and kindly says, "Miss Willa, would you excuse us, oh-so-briefly? I have a confidential matter to discuss with your mother. We'll only be a minute."

My eyes narrow at Mama. She smiles brightly and waves her hand. "Go on. Buy me one of those sweet peach teas they never want me to drink."

"Pure sugar!" Dr. B says playfully. "It'll go straight to your hips, Joy."

Only an oncologist and a veteran cancer patient could find humor in her sickly weight loss. I step out, shut the door behind me, and feel dread roll up my spine. I can't think of any reason a parent kicks their kid out of their hospital room unless the news in that room is the kind you never want them to hear.

She's dying.

I feel myself start to shake, fear clawing up my throat.

Inside the room behind me, both my mother's and Dr. B's laughter echoes. Who would laugh about death? About palliative care and end-of-life choices. Maybe Mama isn't in danger after all?

Dr. B throws open the door, an easy smile on his face. "Have yourself a nice evening, Ms. Willa," he says.

"You too, Dr. B."

I know better than to ask him for answers. *"Talk with your mother, Miss Willa,"* he's told me countless times. *"It's her prerogative."*

"What was that about?" I ask her. Mama's tongue is stuck out, her eyes focused on her crossword.

"Oh," she says on a sigh. "Some plans for a new experimental drug. Because it's still in clinical trials, he can't discuss it with other people in the room—blah, blah, blah. You know. Now come here and help your old lady with a few of these words, Willa."

I do my best to concentrate as I answer Mama and peel

our orange, but I can feel it churning inside me. Anxiety. Fear. I'm terrified she's dying and lying to me. I'm desperate to hope everything's as fine as it seems—Mama doing her crossword, Dr. B strolling out breezily.

It's chaos in my head, a hurricane in my heart. Emotions collide, intensifying into frantic energy. I'm a building storm, the first bolt of singeing electricity about to touch down.

There are two proven methods to diffuse Willa Sutter when she's about to erupt: long, excruciating runs and getting shit-faced. Both work the same way. They wreak havoc on my system until that furious energy is grounded and drained. Until I'm empty, so numb and dissociated that I crumple into unconsciousness.

I know. I didn't say they were *healthy* coping mechanisms, just that they were proven effective.

My body's spent from practice today. If I try to run, my legs will collapse from underneath me long before I'm adequately wrung out. Running won't work. Which means tonight's a night to pickle my liver.

Swiping open my phone, I find Rooney's number and text her. Neither of us party, but in a rare crisis, we're there for each other, prepared to do what's necessary, even if that includes alcohol. I don't drink much, and I never do it without paying the price, but we have a rare rest day tomorrow, so I can spend it hungover and recovering.

Maybe during my lazy day tomorrow, I'll figure out how to retaliate after Ryder's latest trickery. He got me back for sexually torturing him during notecard studying and costing him twenty bucks. His mature response was a whoopie cushion he set on my chair in Business Math. As usual, I was a little late. After a sprint right to my seat, I dropped down, shattering the silence held for Mac's lecture with an echoing "fart."

It took Mac ten minutes to get the class in order.

That motherfucker. Ryder had to turn and hide his face in his arm those whole ten minutes before he could look me in the eye and not fall into hysterics. His eyes glittered with tears from laughing so hard, and beneath all that beard, I caught a wide smile. If his prank hadn't been beyond humiliating as well as annoyingly clever, I would have been almost happy that I put such a giddy look on that smartass tree-hugger's face. *Almost*.

In summary: I owe him. Big. Time.

Maybe it's because I'm still stewing about the whoopie cushion, as I make plans with Rooney, but a brilliant thought comes to me. At some point after I met Ryder's two room-mates, I told Rooney about them. She made the small-world connection that she and Becks have chemistry together. Did not see that one coming. Becks strikes me as lots of things, sciencey *not* being one of them.

I text Rooney my sinister plan. It's a stretch because I'm not sure how friendly she and Becks are beyond being lab mates.

She responds immediately. *I'll text him. He'll know where to go. Be there in thirty. Is it a little red dress night?*

I stare at my phone, debating. Bad, bad things happen in the little red dress, *dress* being a generous term for that garment. It's more like an extended tube top. But tonight, I want to forget about being responsible and self-respecting. I want to be stupid and careless and not worried about biopsies and GPA and my average goals per game. I want to be twenty-one and carefree and reckless. I want to dance with my friend and sexually punish a certain overly bearded vengeful lumberjack.

Yes, I type back. *And bring my fuck-me-shoes while you're at it.*

9

RYDER

Playlist: "Sugar on My Tongue," Talking Heads

WILLA'S TRYING TO KILL ME. IT'S THE ONLY EXPLANATION for what's been going on between us the past few weeks, since she showed up in that shirt in Business Math. I've never seen a woman wear that color and not look like her kidneys were failing, but yellow made Willa light up like a ray of sunshine.

Her hair was combed out and wild. Thick, wavy tendrils that coiled around each other fell down her shoulders, faint wisps teasing along all that cleavage.

I can't figure out what prompted her to do it, what could possibly make her dress herself up like that. That's not Willa, not the Willa I know. Even though I was confused by her behavior, even though I missed those oversized sweatpants and her frizzy bun, I had a hard time not responding to the seductive appearance of her body, and she damn well knew it.

I might have come back with a vengeance the next time I was at her place. At first, when she was fretting over the soup, I had the irrational need to soothe her, to tell her I didn't give a shit if dinner was a little scorched. But I resisted and stuck to my plan. I cornered her, leaned in, touched her until she was a lusty mess in my arms. I wasn't planning on kissing her, not really. I planned to get so close, so very close, until our lips almost met—

My phone buzzes, snapping me out of my thoughts. I drop the loaded-up barbell I'm lifting in our makeshift basement gym in the house and swipe it open.

It's a video from Becks. It's hard to see at first, so I tilt it to avoid glare and increase my screen brightness. Dark shadows, strobe lights. It's obviously a club, which isn't surprising. That's where Becks lives most nights. Two women dance, writhing against each other. One's tall, legs for miles, a sheet of blonde hair drifting down her back. The other's shorter, more compact, light striking the defined muscles of her thighs that trail down to strong calves and sky-high black stilettos. She wears a short red dress. Jesus, is that even a dress? Her hair's wild, misbehaved curls, caramel brown under the lights.

Wait.

Before I can text him, Becks sends another message. *Isn't that Willa? She's wrecked, man.*

I swear mentally, sprint up the steps and take the fastest shower of my life. *Where are you?* I text him while I hop into jeans, madly running a hand through my wet hair.

He answers immediately, *Club Folle.*

Shit. That's a nice one. I take a quick look at my beard and try to comb it. I should probably trim the thing at some point. No time now. Scrounging around in the closet, I find a wrinkle-free button-up and throw it on. Keys, phone, wallet, then I'm in the Explorer, flying down the 405 for Culver City. It's not far, but it feels eternal, driving to find her.

Willa hasn't been herself the past few weeks, and I'm worried. I know she's under a lot of pressure with grades and the team. I certainly don't make her life easier. Working with her on our project, though, I've tried to lighten up, to present my issues with gentler language. I served her cookies and tea. I finally gave her the entire semester's notes. I've tried not to be an absolute dick. I know I can be a bit rough around the edges, and I can see Willa has a lot on her plate. Besides the admittedly juvenile sabotaging one-upmanship we've been dabbling in the past two weeks, I've tried to be decent to her.

Was the whoopie cushion taking it too far? I mean, I owed her. She made me look like a horndog fool with those notecards, scrambling my brain with sensual touches so I couldn't even recall the inventory shrinkage formula. Nothing on *me* was shrinking when she pulled that stunt.

And in retaliation, I embarrassed her in front of like... four hundred people.

Maybe not a reasonable response.

Before I can think about it any further, I pull up to the club, tossing the valet my keys and jogging to the entrance. I'm waved in because this is Becks's kingdom and if you're in with Becks, you're in at Club Folle.

Places like this are my worst nightmare. Immediately, sound smacks my ears and what's normally a persistent tinny ring ratchets up to excruciatingly loud steel drums. I squint, trying to minimize the overwhelming impact of the strobe lights as I slip through the crowd. Thankfully, it's easy to see. I'm taller than virtually everybody else.

I spot Rooney first, doing the kinds of moves my mom would ground my sisters for even trying. When she spins, there's Willa, and now Rooney's dancing looks like a Puritan shuffle by comparison.

Willa's ass swings in mesmerizing circles, her powerful quads sustaining her body as she grinds to the floor, then snaps up. Her hands are in the air, revealing defined shoulders and a peek of cleavage not dissimilar to the morning of the yellow shirt that shall live in infamy.

A loud sigh leaves me, swallowed up in the sounds of the club.

Rooney spins, then freezes as her eyes start at my feet and trail appreciatively up my body. When her gaze settles on my face and she recognizes me, her features shift from interest to wide-eyed fear.

"Oh *shit*." She says it emphatically, with a bright blue strobe light shining on her face. Otherwise, I'd have no idea what she just said.

Willa's oblivious, bumping her butt against Rooney's thigh, making Rooney bounce in rhythm with Willa's movement. Rooney stares at me in horror as she sways. I step around her and crouch until Willa and I are eye level.

Willa's eyes are shut, her plump bottom lip pinned between her teeth. Sweat beads her neck and chest. Rooney manages to bump her enough that Willa opens her eyes and immediately locks them with mine. They narrow coyly as she checks me out. As realization dawns, they widen, and she stands up. "Ryder!"

Standing turns to swaying. Before Willa can fall and concuss herself, I sweep her into my arms, carrying her toward the back exit I pegged the moment I entered. Shoving open the door, I set her down carefully in the night air, and press her up against the brick wall. Bracing my hands over her head, I face her, making sure she doesn't collapse as I try to calm my anxious anger.

She's plastered, in a napkin of a dress. There are shitty men in this club, creeps who would gladly take advantage of her vulnerability. What if I hadn't gotten here? What if someone had used and hurt her?

Willa's panting, her eyes wide. Slowly, her gaze travels

down my body. Her head tips to the side, in that way she has when she's thinking something through.

Drawing her head back up, her eyes look different tonight. A color I can't quite describe. Then it comes to me. Molten lava.

"You look weird without the flannel." My left ear's ringing sharply, but in the quiet air outside, my right ear catches her voice, my brain marrying it with her lips' movement. She hiccups. "Very un-lumberjack-y."

Her hands slip along my chest, setting a fire beneath my skin, heat surging through my veins. I push them off instinctively and step back.

Willa's shocked, by the look of her widening eyes, which begin to shift. I watch their transformation as her jaw hardens, her molten-lava eyes narrow and turn volcanic. She's pissed at me, but maybe not lethally pissed. She's still sure to tip her face in full light and speak clearly so I can read her lips as I listen to her. "What are you doing here, Ryder?"

I pull out my phone, wiggling it at her. She shakes her head. "I don't have it."

An angry huff of air leaves me. If she doesn't have her phone, I can't talk to her.

"Sometimes I wonder if you're ever not angry, Sasquatch."

I balk, my eyes searching hers. What can I say? How can I explain all the twisted, knotted things I feel and think about her, especially when we can't even communicate?

"Do you hate me?" Her eyes are wet with unshed tears.

When I was in elementary school, my older siblings were big fans of a brutal comic series that I had no business sticking my nose in. I remember snooping through it, turning the page to a gruesome full-length spread in which the villain had just been slit from nose to navel. I had nightmares for days and couldn't unsee it for weeks. I feel like that villain and the boy who saw him, all at once. Viciously gutted, scarred by that look in her eyes.

Some kind of pained noise leaves me, and Willa's head snaps back. I clasp her jaw, turning her face so she watches my mouth say the words silently. She has to understand this. *Willa, no. I could never hate you. Never.*

Her eyes squint. "I can't, Ryder. I can't read lips like you." She hiccups again. "I can't…" Her speech slurs, and now I'm the one who can't understand. I smack a hand over the wall, frustration building that I can't talk to her or understand what she needs to say.

I pull out my phone and open the notepad. *Go home?* I write.

She squints, her tongue stuck out as if she's relying on that for better concentration.

Nodding, Willa tries to type *yes*, I'm guessing, but it ends up being *urd*. When I glance up, I see her color fading and recognize the warning just in time. Spinning out of the way, I clear her hair from her face as Willa bends and vomits, emptying her stomach.

She hacks and sputters. Refastening my grip on her hair, I dig in my jeans for a hankie. Yes, a hankie. Cloth over Kleenex gives Mother Nature a hug. I wipe her mouth when her body finally stops spasming and help her stand upright.

Willa's bleary-eyed, her lips trembling. Then her eyes roll back in her head, and she drops in my arms.

———

"RYDER," SHE MUMBLES BLEARILY. I HEAR IT ONLY BECAUSE I brought her home with me and—safe from the booming noise of the club—immediately shoved that hearing aid on my right ear. Now certain sounds are too loud. Others, too quiet. I barely caught Willa saying my name, but I can hear a microwave beep through the wall connecting us to our neighbor's house.

Now Willa's singing to herself as I kick the front door shut and head for my room, something about lakes of stew and candy mountains. We're here because Willa said she wanted to leave the club but didn't want to cut Rooney's fun short, and this resulted in an argument via my phone's notepad involving lots of drunk typos before an agreement was reached that we would leave first, then text Rooney later, on the condition that I bring Willa home. I was nervous to leave her alone in case she got sick again in her sleep.

Carefully, I lay her on my bed.

"Ah yes." She hiccups. "The room of evergreen seduction."

I want to respond to her, but Willa still can't find her phone so I can't. Frustration surges inside me, beating inside my lungs and volleying up my throat. Remembering what I did at the club, I pull out my phone, then type in the notepad, *Evergreen seduction?*

She squints as she reads, then she flops back onto my bed. "Yes."

That's all I get. *Yes.*

I roll my eyes. Willa flails in my bed until she's wrapped up in my comforter like a burrito. Watching her, I unbutton my shirt, which smells faintly of vomit and sweaty bodies. I throw it in the laundry hamper, then turn toward the dresser to pull out a T-shirt, when I catch a strangled noise coming from the bed.

Two dark eyes peek over the comforter.

As I drag the V-neck undershirt over my head and torso, I sign, *What?*

Slowly, she gropes for my phone on the bed, types, then lobs it my way. I'm equally annoyed and anxious as it arcs through the air, but thankfully I catch it. After giving her a disapproving glare, I read what she wrote in my phone's notepad: *Ryder, Keeper of Notes. Asshole lumberjack of Los Angeles County, you have a fantastic upper body.*

A laugh leaves me. An actual laugh. I feel it bubble out of my belly, soar through my throat, and reverberate in the air.

Willa sits up, throwing back the blankets. "You just laughed! I just made you laugh!"

My heart pounds with nerves. My skin crawls with dread. I'm waiting for the inevitable. For her to say I sound weird or terrible.

But she just throws her hands up and crows, "*Wooohoooo!*"

I cover both of my ears instinctively before the hearing aid squeaks feedback. Willa climbs out of the bed, tripping over her feet until she runs smack into my torso and wraps her arms around me. Muffled sound lands somewhere between my pecs before Willa seems to remember to unsmoosh her face. Setting her chin on my sternum, she peers up at me. "I made you laugh, Lumberjack."

I try not to smile but fail, grinning as I nod.

Slowly, her fingers trail up my chest, leaving a wake of sparks simmering beneath my skin. Her fingers skate up my throat and drift through my beard. They rest over my lips, parting my facial hair as she squints at my mouth. "This squirrel tail is a problem."

My eyebrows lift. My beard isn't *that* scraggly.

…Is it?

"I can't see your mouth. And I'm suspicious that it's a pretty mouth. Like one of those mouths that a man with eyelashes like yours has no business having."

She sways slightly in my arms, her eyes drifting shut as she sighs sleepily and says, "Ry."

My hands go to her waist, to steady myself as much to right her wavering posture. My grip tightens as the sound of my nickname on her warm, husky voice hits my bones and echoes.

Fear creeps up my spine. I feel its exact journey, icy fingers climbing each vertebra until it clutches my throat. It's getting harder and harder to lie to myself when Willa Sutter's around. To tell myself my heart doesn't trip when I look at her, that need doesn't torture my body. That I don't daydream about sliding my hands under those baggy hoodies she always wears, feeling the silky skin along her ribs, the soft handfuls of her tits. That I don't fantasize about hearing her voice and mine, not perfectly, but well enough to drive down the road, holding hands affectionately while still lobbing jabs and busting bullshit. Willa would slide her hand up my thigh as she gave me hell, and I'd pull over, then kiss her until that mouth finally stopped running at me long enough for me to give it all the attention it deserved.

Willa as my nemesis is safe. As my antagonizing quasi-friend, a manageable risk. Or so I thought. But now I see that anything more than that, and nothing remotely manageable comes of it. Nothing at all.

I'm brought from my thoughts as her hair whispers over my skin. Those untamed tendrils are the same rich brown as her eyes, streaked crimson and gold from hours spent daily in the California sun. They tickle my arms and chest as Willa sways in my grasp, her eyes shut as she smiles.

Carefully, I hold her to me and give myself this one moment that I can only hope she won't remember, even though it's one I never want to forget. I press my nose to her hair, a long, deep breath as I commit her gentle scent to memory—orange zest and sunscreen at the ocean, the pure softness of roses. One soft kiss to her temple—

Shit.

I pull back. It might be the barest touch of my lips to her forehead, but I'm kissing my drunk project partner, and I don't have her consent.

"Shut up your head," she says. "I want you just fine, now kiss me again."

Freaky mind reader. Her lips sear the skin exposed above my shirt, where she presses a soft, wet kiss.

Willa's hands link around my neck, her fingers slide along my scalp, making some kind of desperate groan rumble out of me. Willa shoves herself even tighter to my front, and we stumble until we bump against the wall. My hand dips down to her waist as she hitches her leg around my hip. I wrap my hand around her iron-solid thigh and try to take a steady breath.

Her gasp is a soft burst across my neck. Her nails sink harder into my scalp as she presses on tiptoe, those soft, full lips inches from mine.

"Ryder," she says. "I demand to be kissed."

Gently, I clasp her jaw and my thumb traces her mouth. If I do this, who knows what will happen, what kind of damage control this would require tomorrow? She's half-asleep, half-drunk. If and when I kiss Willa Sutter, I want her to remember it.

I press my lips to her temple again and feel a heavy sigh leave her. Her mouth slides, wet and hot along my collarbone. I suck in a breath, leaning my cheek against her wild hair, my fingers sinking into its chaos. Her tongue swirls at the hollow of my throat. My lips sweep the shell of her ear.

Willa and I aren't even kissing, not on the lips, but we're moving, rolling against each other, and that has to stop. What we're doing only leads to one thing. One thing that absolutely cannot happen right now.

When I pull away, Willa does too, her features tightening. "Why did you stop?"

I tug at my hair. My hand falls, and I shake my head. Fatigue from the day makes my thoughts fuzzy. I don't even know what I'd try to sign to her, what words I'd write in my notepad.

"You don't want to anymore?" she asks faintly.

Her eyes are getting heavier, and I think this time, there won't be any waking her. Before Willa can argue anymore, before she can demand a kiss or ask for one step further, her eyes fall shut and she drops, a dead weight in my arms.

"Sleep," she says.

Nodding, I scoop her up. For once, Willa Sutter and I agree on something.

WILLA

Playlist: "Surround Me," LÉON

"Oh, God." Blinking hurts. Thinking hurts. I shift and bump into something solid and immovable. Whatever it is, it smells like sex in an evergreen forest. Cedar. Pine. Spruce. I'm warm, with one tree limb draped around me, another poking my butt. Wait—

Startling, I spin inside the tree limb that I realize is an arm. It's so damn heavy, it might as well be timber. Ryder's out cold, his mouth open softly in sleep. There are smudges under his eyes which I'm sure have everything to do with the fact that he went driving to some ritzy club Rooney and Becks picked at God knows what hour of the night. That plan backfired a little bit. I know loud environments are night-marish for his hearing. I didn't mean to lure Ryder there. Becks was just supposed to send a picture of me being obnox-iously sexy. In the name of retribution and all.

But instead of rolling his eyes and saying he was worried for the male population of Club Folle, Ryder showed up incensed and swept me away before I passed out and some-body took advantage of that.

Last thing I remember is vomiting in the alley. A few

patchy moments of rubbing myself all over Ryder like a cat in heat.

Oh, Lordy. I rubbed *all* over him. I remember that vividly now.

I mean, his arm's wrapped around me, we're spooning in his bed, though there's his chivalry again: he's sleeping on top of the blankets that my body is practically swaddled in. He can't mind that I was treating him like my personal dance pole *that* much, can he?

Racking my brain, I try to piece together the night. I remember jumping him like a kitten on catnip. I scaled him and scratched my way through his surprisingly silky hair. I remember kisses that weren't kisses but decadent tastes of each other's skin. They felt more sexual and intimate than any kind of physicality I've ever experienced.

I remember when that bliss faded, how his hips stilled against mine, his strong hand tightened around my waist. It didn't go any further than that. I don't remember, but I know, because I was a puking, twerking, drunk-as-a-skunk mess and Ryder Bergman might be a surly son of a bitch, but he's also a gentleman.

Three cheers for that. Because let me tell you, last night, I would have kissed him stupid with my vomit breath and happily jammed on that lumberjack's log if he'd have let me.

An involuntary groan leaves Ryder. It might have some-thing to do with the fact that I've been unconsciously shim-mying myself, like a little tree-abiding forest creature, against the piece of wood that extends rather prominently from his sweatpants toward me.

That groan brings another part of the night to my memory. His laugh. I made him laugh, and it was *beautiful*.

Ryder's hand flexes as it meets my waist. One eye cracks open, greeting me with grass-green irises and thick lashes. It's followed by a slow, sexy smile. I'm hopeful it's here to stay, but I'm not counting on it. He's dazedly half-awake, in that pliant, relaxed place I was a few weeks ago, in my sexy lumberjack-about-to-fell-a-tree dream.

He gropes overhead, never breaking eye contact with me. On a soft sigh through his nose, he swipes open his phone and types, spinning it so I can read the notebook.

You snore.

I smack his shoulder as embarrassment reddens my cheeks. I'm aware of this, but like hell am I admitting it. "Do not."

He nods, mouthing, *Do.*

Our eyes hold, and because I'm a self-sabotaging, punishing hothead, I shove down the blankets and lean closer to him. Ryder's grip never leaves my waist, and the heat of his palm seeps through my dress. His hand flattens on my back and pulls me even closer, making Ryder hiss under his breath when I press my pelvis to his. I watch his jaw clench, his eyes scrunch shut before they open again.

Gently, he uses his arm underneath my neck to pull me until I'm tucked into him. My head is on his shoulder, in a cloud of cedar-and-spruce nirvana. I stare up at the notepad as he types furiously.

What's been going on? The past few weeks you've been... different. Why were you dressed like that, out at a club?

I glance up at him, brushing my fingers against his now rather bushy beard. How do I explain what I've been doing without laying all my cards on the table? Without telling him I know about the hearing aid, and I wanted to get back at him. That I got carried away in my vengeance—we both did—and now I don't even recognize where we are anymore. I can't admit any of that, because that would leave me exposed and ridiculously vulnerable. So, like the big wuss that I am, I change the subject, taking the phone and typing, *Sleeping next to this thing felt like having a cuddling threesome with a forest creature.*

Ryder sputters. A hoarse cough of a laugh leaves him.

"Not that I'd know! About threesomes, that is…" My cheeks darken. I'm beet red. I stop talking before more nonsense falls out of my mouth. Burrowing deeper in his arms, I hide my face and soak up every tiny noise of amusement that leaves him.

Ryder's laughter finally fades on a breathy sigh. He uses a thumb to wipe a tear out of the corner of his eye, and then takes his phone from me and types again, arms extending so that the phone is held over my head. It gives me a very exclusive look at all the burly muscles and tendons that make up the lumberjack's arms.

You don't like the beard?

I peer up and tip my face so he can read my lips. "I'm…" Combing my fingers through that soft blond hair, I tease the pad of my pointer along his lips. "Curious. If it tickles. What's beneath it…"

His eyes grow darker, his breath faster. Unexpectedly, he sets his teeth on either side of my finger and dances his tongue against the tip.

Something like *unghh* leaves me as I shamelessly rub myself against him. Ryder's eyes drift shut. And we're zero to one hundred in three seconds flat. He's panting, I'm rocking against him, and now my wet finger's trailing down his throat, down, down the V-neck of his shirt, until I pull it aside and swipe the damp, chilly tip around his nipple.

Somewhere between a groan and a gasp bursts from his mouth, more faint sounds that I soak up hungrily. We lock eyes, sharing a long, unbroken study of each other, jagged, shared bursts of air as we move. His hand slides down my back and cups my butt, easily hiking my leg over his hip.

We pick up right where I'm pretty sure we left off last night, and it's dizzying. My toes curl. My back arches. I'm so close, I don't even want to breathe. But then the door bursts open, making me shriek.

Becks stands ten feet away in tighty-whities, and it's burned into my retinas. I'm still shrieking as Ryder spins off the bed, whipping the comforter over me so that I'm covered in one smooth motion. His echoing double clap and a few gestures that clearly don't mean nice things shoo Becks out. I watch with an unresolved heaviness between my thighs as he strolls out of the room, black sweatpants low on his hips, that white V-neck clinging to every long, defined muscle of his back and arms.

Falling back onto the bed, I huff a desperate sigh. I'm right on the edge, torturously close. One sweep of my finger, and I'd tumble. I could come so easily.

But I want more than an orgasm at my fingertips, fueled by the sight of a beautiful man. I want Ryder to send me over. For it to happen when it's more than just two bodies getting off on each other. That's a problem, that I want to have not just part of Ryder Bergman. I don't do that. I don't want *more* from someone. I don't set myself up for heartbreak and disappointment. I take what I want, I shield my heart, and I move right along. Ryder seems to operate just as guardedly.

What is wrong with me? I sigh shakily and chalk it up to hormones. Lust. Hate-crazed sexual attraction. My hand splays across my belly. I don't move. I lie still until the torturous pulse between my thighs subsides and I'm thinking straight again. My heart locks tight, the key turns with a click that rings in my ears.

Safe and secure once more.

W<small>HILE</small> R<small>YDER'S</small> <small>STILL</small> <small>OUT</small> <small>IN</small> <small>THE</small> <small>HALLWAY,</small> <small>RIPPING</small> B<small>ECKS</small> a new asshole, I use my finger and his toothpaste to brush my teeth. Next, I swipe one of his hair ties to pull back my Bride of Frankenstein hair—seriously, how did he even *look* at me this morning?—before I realize that this red dress needs to be burned into the shameful annals of deplorable dress history.

I peer at my backside and am horrified by what little is left to the imagination. There is no way in hell I'm waltzing past Becks, probably Tucker, and definitely Ryder in this getup. So, hastily, I riffle through Ryder's drawers, huffing the incredible pine-forest scent as I look. Finally, I find a black shirt that's so long and big, it works as a shirt dress. That will go best with the fuck-me-shoes.

Throwing open the door confidently, my red napkin dress folded under my arm, I stroll into the living room and am promptly met with three pairs of male eyes.

Tucker's widen, then dance away. Becks squints like he's seeing double of me and trying not to. But Ryder's gaze starts at my hooker shoes, then slowly drags up. A long single sigh leaves him. His expression is a portrait, titled, *Why the* fuck *didn't I hit that last night?*

I'll be damned if I know what's going on between us right now, but his undeniable lust puts a small triumphant smile on my face. I add another scratch to the mental tally I've been keeping since Hearing Aid Gate. Point for Willa.

Tucking a rogue curl back into my bun, I smile at the guys. "Good morning, fellas."

I pause next to Ryder, whose gaze is locked on my mouth. "I have to find my phone, but I have my laptop, okay?"

He nods slowly. *Okay*, he signs.

I take his hand in mine, squeeze it tight, then leave.

After an Uber ride of shame home, I shower and line my liquor-singed stomach with toast and a cup of weak tea. I wish I could tolerate coffee, but after a night of that kind of drinking, I'll puke. When the carbohydrates and paltry caffeine hit my bloodstream, I feel conscious enough to search for my phone. Eventually, I discover it in the laundry basket, shoved into the pocket of my jeans I wore to the hospital yesterday evening.

Found it, I text Ryder immediately.

My phone pings. *Good. How are you feeling?*

As bad as I deserve to. Sorry I was such a mess. Needed to blow off some steam.

You were fine, he writes back. *Besides the vomiting. And the snoring. And your death grip on my arm all night.*

"Such an asshole," I mutter. *Well, drunk goggles, and all.*

Ouch, he responds. *Touché.*

He has to know how full of shit I am. I was practically scaling Mount Ryder this morning, chasing a stunning view. You don't do that stone-cold sober with bedhead and puke breath after making a fool of yourself the night before unless you're desperate for someone. He has to intuit this, right? That I'm despicably sexually attracted to him. *Just* sexually.

The way he was looking at me before I left, I'm thinking Ryder's hurting for it as much as I am. And when he figures it out, when we have to acknowledge this animal, sextacular thing between us? Then what?

He texts again, breaking me from my thoughts.

Did you check your email?

No, I type. *Why?*

I'm going to murder my brother-in-law.

When I open my email and read what Professor MacCormack has to say for himself, I have to restrain myself from throwing my freshly recovered phone at the wall. If I survive this semester without having committed assault, it will be a Christmas-break miracle.

———

Your proposal is solid. MacCormack paces his office, phone in hand, texting us in a group chat. *Really, it's good. My issue is this—I'm sensing a lot of tension between you two, and I can't grade an unrealistic business model. Business partners need to be tight, trusting, on the same page. Now, take heart. You two aren't the only pair I'm concerned about.*

Ryder death-grips his phone and sucks in a breath. He leans, elbows on his knees, and even with the beard, I can see a scowl tugging at his expression. His ball cap's back on, tugged low. The lumberjack flannel stretches across his broad shoulders. Today it's a classic black watch—hunter green and ink-black plaid. It's dangerous looking. A little sinister.

Every remotely erogenous part of my body, from my traitorously hard nipples to my aching choo-cha, voice their demand to be plundered by the plaid-wearing rogue.

Jeebus Christmas, I need to get a handle on myself.

I wiggle on my seat and fold my arms across my chest.

I'm assigning you two a team-building day, Mac texts.

I sputter as my hands fly unhelpfully in the air. This can't be real. It has to be a joke. "Are you serious, Mac?"

MacCormack nods fervently while texting back. *I need to see increased camaraderie, or when due date comes, I won't be able to grade your project as a practicable business plan. This course is professionally oriented. It's not theory. It's application.*

"Okay, I get that, but—"

My phone dings, as does MacCormack's.

Ryder's message says, *In case you forgot, Willa's a D-1 student athlete. She barely has time to sleep and eat meals as it is, Aiden. We can't go backpacking and bonding over sunsets. You're being a dick.*

I stifle a snort that dies off when MacCormack's icy blue eyes land on mine. He swivels, throwing a finger at Ryder before he texts back. *I'm not your brother-in-law right now. I'm your hard-ass professor who's here to tell you, figure it out. I need to see camaraderie. You two have more common interests than you think.* He gives me a pointed look. *So find some time to set aside classwork and bond. I'll have you two back here individually to account for your experience.*

Ryder's eyes are burning holes into Mac's head. Common interests? I mean what does Mac know of me beside the fact that I live and breathe soccer? If that's what Mac's implying, does Ryder play? He's never mentioned it.

MacCormack pushes off his desk and taps his watch, which is his version of *Get the hell out of my office.* He can hardly move us out of the room fast enough, shooing us like chickens from the coop. Our phones buzz and ding. *You've got one week. Learn about each other, get on the same page, or your project's in jeopardy, got it?*

Before either Ryder or I can answer, the door is slammed in our faces. Ryder pounds his fist once against the door, an angry twitch to his jaw telling me if he was speaking, he'd be ionizing the air.

A solitary thud answers, followed by a new message from Mac. *Get over it. One week.*

My phone pings with a message from Ryder: *I told you. I'm going to kill him.*

WILLA

Playlist: "Billie Jean," The Civil Wars

I WISH I COULD SAY RYDER AND I MANAGE TO CONVINCE Mac that he's smoking some terrible human-resources-laced strain of hashish, but he proves unflappable and only gives us stony glances when we corner him after the next class.

Between Ryder's course load and my studies, practice, and game schedule, then dashing over to the hospital in the evenings to see Mama, who looks a little perkier since that experimental drug got thrown in her pharmacopeia, we barely manage to keep up with assignments while pulling together a day to "bond."

Ryder performs a magic trick and convinces Mac to give us an excused absence from class, seeing as it's the only day with my practice and game schedule that we can make work. We agree to leave at nine in the morning for our day hike, but before that, Rooney and I traipse over to the practice fields early in the morning to pass the ball and shoot around.

We have a favorite field that we often use but someone else was there, so we continue our walk to a more secluded, less-maintained field that's normally used for rec-league games.

As I walk with Rooney, I try to breathe deeply, to release the anxiety that's knotting my stomach. I'm nervous for today, but I don't actually know what exactly I'm apprehensive about. It's just that since my wild night out, things feel tense with Ryder, in some unnamable but palpable sense. Yes, there's obvious sexual tension, but something more is going on. I just can't put my finger on it.

He's been a bit surlier than normal. I've been busier. While I could talk to him about what happened, that would be...well, that would be wildly uncomfortable. I don't do that. I'd hive and choke on my words. It would also be trying, and if there's one thing Willa Rose Sutter doesn't do with a man—friend or foe—it's try.

In part it's because of the man who bequeathed fifty percent of my DNA, then headed for the hills. I'm sickened by the thought that the guy I fall for could reject me just like the sperm donor. Then there's my mother's perspective on men. As I was growing up, Mama didn't say it often, how untrustworthy she found men. I think, in her way, she wanted me to form my own opinion about the opposite sex. But she showed me that men were something you use and lose, hit and quit. Anything more was just an invitation for disappointment.

That's why this thing with Ryder lately has me panicking: I have never spent this much mental energy on one infuriating man, and I have no idea how to change that.

Walking with Rooney, half-listening to her prattle on about some chemistry assignment I'll never wrap my head around—why, I have asked, does a pre-law student need a chemistry degree? Because she's a masochistic dork who wants to be a *biomedical lawyer*, that's why—I find myself wondering why I'm so hung up on my dynamic with Ryder.

We're project partners. We banter well. There's sexual tension. Fine. What's the big deal?

I've tried shelving it, but I can't stop thinking that in all these hours together with my nemesis-turned-forced-ally, somewhere along the way, we became friends. Yes, friends who routinely bust and burn each other so bad, we're a little singed around the edges. Okay, so maybe we're more frenemies than friends, but that's more than straight, vehement opposition. Even then, so what? Can't a man and woman be frenemies? Especially when both of them have shown themselves to be totally allergic to maintaining anything more?

"Man, this bag is heavy," Rooney huffs, the only break in her chemistry soliloquy. "How many balls did you pack?"

I take the bag from her and hike it high up on my shoulder. I always pack too many balls, but you can never have too many, especially with how often Rooney shanks them.

"Rude!" She shoves me.

Seems I said that out loud. "Sorry," I tell her sheepishly.

As we round the bend to the rec-league fields, Rooney back to bitching about chemistry, I freeze and slap a hand against her chest.

A man stands far down the field, juggling the ball, his head bent in that easy way you have when you're effortlessly screwing around, juggling when you could do it in your sleep. His hair's tugged back in a small bun at the base of his neck. His blond facial hair catches the sunlight when he flicks the ball and lands it on his back, steadying it easily between his shoulder blades. The ball hovers seamlessly until he bounces it off his shoulder. On a scissor kick while the ball is mid-air, he cracks it straight into the goal.

Rooney's whistle cuts the silence. "Well, hi, and who ordered him from the hot stranger vending machine?"

I smack her chest again. My heart is racing. "Rooney, I

think a ball pump fell out of the bag. You better double back and check."

"What?" She frowns. "How could I have possibly dropped tha—"

"Rooney?"

She finally notices the brittle edge in my voice. Staring out to the field, Rooney narrows her eyes and takes a longer look. "Wait, is that…holy shit. *Holy. Shit.*"

I can't even manage a nod of agreement.

"Okay, I'm going to, uh…I'm going to go check my ingrown toenail. I'll hang back here."

"Thanks," I mutter.

I'm so distracted, I walk off with the gigantic bag still hanging on my shoulder and trudge through the gate onto the field.

As I walk, a searing pain knifes through my sternum. It's heartburn but a hundred times worse. Now he rainbows it, flicking the ball around as easily as a puppy lobs a toy and artfully, consistently catches it. I'm close enough to recognize that mangy beard. That perfect nose. It's him. It's Ryder.

It's hard to appreciate the way his shorts sit on his hips, how he wears tall soccer socks the way all hot soccer dudes who are too badass for shin guards always have, crinkled at his ankles. His cleats are beat to shit, which means they're perfectly comfy. Your cleats always finally get comfortable right before it's time to retire them. His muscles press against his T-shirt, which he lifts to dab his face, revealing the narrow taper of his waist, a stretch of tan skin and divots right above his shorts. The asshole soccer jock has butt dimples. Of course, he does.

I don't exactly know why tears prick my eyes, or why an overwhelming sense of betrayal surges up my throat, constricting it painfully.

Suddenly, Ryder whips around, eyes widening as they take me in.

Instinctively, Ryder abandons the ball, then jogs up to me, yanking the massive bag effortlessly off my shoulder and transferring it to his. He cocks his head, fumbling for his phone from his pocket, then texts me, *What are you doing here?*

I read his message and exhale a long, jagged breath. Sharp blades of confused emotion etch their marks in my throat as I try to swallow, then text back, *Just came to shoot a little bit.*

Ryder studies me, then his eyes drop to his phone. *Why do you look upset?*

I have two choices. I can tell him what this means to me. Pour out my guts. Confess my shocking hurt that he didn't trust me to see past his surly lumberjack surface, that I can't wrap my head around why he's so good and why he doesn't play. Demand his explanation for knowing what the game means to me and keeping his own deep connection to it such a closely held secret.

Or, I can do what I've always done. Repress the pain, bypass the uncomfortable truth, and move right along.

"I'm fine, Ryder."

He squints and clenches his jaw. He's about to get feisty with me and call bullshit. I don't think I can handle any pushy demands or singeing banter this morning, so I stop him, holding his wrist.

Once his eyes settle on my mouth, I tell him, "I'll see you in a few hours, okay?"

Before he can answer, I rip the bag off his shoulder and carry it back toward the other end of the field. When I dump the balls and wave at Rooney, showing her the coast is clear, I feel Ryder's eyes on me.

I tell myself I couldn't care less what Ryder Bergman does, let alone that he's watching me. I don't want his trust, and I particularly don't want to know *him*.

It's a lie. Luckily, if you tell yourself a lie enough times, eventually it becomes a truth.

———

FOLLOWING AN AWKWARD REUNION TWO HOURS LATER, Ryder and I pass the forty-five-minute drive along 1-North onto the Pacific Coast Highway in silence. Silence was a given anyway since Ryder can't text and drive. Since I sit on his right, he could have worn the hearing aid and I could have talked his ear off, I suppose, but I'm not supposed to know about that. Another facet of his obvious distrust in me.

So he doesn't trust you. He doesn't tell you much. You're the same way. You hold your cards close, too. What do you care?

I don't know. It's an infuriating refrain in my head: *I don't know, I don't know, I don't know.* God, I'm so confused.

My forehead's smooshed against the glass, taking in the views until we blur by a sea of parked-in cars. Ryder seems to know some secret place, because he confidently speeds by the masses and rolls down the road. All I've heard is Escondido Falls is a dreamy view but a nightmare when it comes to parking. When he brings the car to a stop under a shady nondescript grove, Ryder pulls out his phone.

You were quiet. Did my driving make you nervous?

I glance at the message, then text back, *No, Ryder. You drove fine. I was quiet because we can't talk while you drive.*

He fusses with his keys, then he drops them in his lap and types, *Some people aren't comfortable with a deaf driver. I should have asked you.*

My stomach sours, anger on his behalf surging through me as the words rush out. *Well, those people are assholes, Bergman. I know I can be a salty bitch, but I don't see you as any less capable or safe because your ears don't work the way they used to, okay?*

I can't handle the look on his face or the way the car suddenly feels like a sauna. Throwing open my door, backpack in hand, I escape the car and stare up at the trail before me.

I did my homework before I agreed to this hike, lest the mountain man decide on torturing me with some horrifyingly technical trail. Seems Ryder was looking out for me. The hike to Escondido Falls is only four miles round trip, beginning just off the Pacific Coast Highway and reaching its apex at a dramatic waterfall. Our journey starts on asphalt, below a cluster of swanky Malibu homes. The online guide I read promised it soon transitions to coastal wilderness, and that the rugged, lush beauty of the falls is a well-worth-it reward for dealing with the oddly residential beginning.

My phone dings. *Have your water?*

I meet his eyes. "Yes. And my eighteen granola bars you insisted I bring."

He smirks as he types. *You are not a woman to be crossed while hangry. Consider it a personal insurance measure.*

Rolling my eyes, I turn back toward the trail. I feel Ryder's attention on me again but ignore it. Hiking my bag higher on both my shoulders, I begin walking.

After a few hundred feet of ascent, we pass the houses and leave the paved part of the trail. A sign reads *Escondido Canyon Park*, and a nearby dirt path bears another marker: *Edward Albert Escondido Canyon Trail and Waterfall*.

I turn over my shoulder for direction from Ryder. He nods toward the dirt path.

We walk in silence that starts off chilly, thanks to me and my bottled-up feelings. But as we ascend and the sun moves higher in the sky, our frigidity thaws in the growing heat to companionable quiet. After trekking a field of fragrant mustard and fennel, we cross a creek that flows through an open thicket. Ryder takes my elbow, pointing left, so that we continue upstream into Escondido Canyon.

The path broadens. It's level and packed dirt, a safe trail to take that isn't likely to make me twist an ankle or tweak my knee. If Coach knew I was hiking, she'd murder me. Twice.

At some point, my five-six frame starts to fall short of Ryder's long, steady strides, and he takes the lead. Shade buys us relief from the still-strong November sun as we walk under a canopy of trees. But soon we're out in the open again, traipsing through fields of dying wildflowers. There's something haunting about them, a sea of husks and pods, the last lingering petal on a dry, cracked stem.

It reminds me of what Grandma Rose always said as we winterized the garden, as we ripped out plants and pruned bushes and buried bulbs. *Life begets death begets life. The only thing we can do is honor the beauty and dependability of that cycle.*

I can't say that I see the beauty just yet, especially in its dependability. I'd prefer it if death weren't dependable at all.

We come to a creek crossing that immediately I can tell I won't be able to manage on my own. The water is high, and to get past it will involve hopping several rocks that my legs won't span before the level drops low enough to trudge through.

Ryder throws his backpack onto his front, and for a second, I fight a laugh. He looks like he's pregnant and very proud of it. He squints at me from beneath his ball cap as his mouth twitches. Maybe he's trying not to laugh, too. Crouching down, he pats his back. *Get on,* he mouths.

"No." I say it nice and loud, showing him my mouth so he'll understand me. "Absolutely not. I'm too heavy with our gear."

Ryder makes some noise close to a snort. Glancing over his shoulder, his eyes lock with mine. There's an intensity I haven't seen in them before, an urgency. I sense his meaning like a rumble of thunder in the air, vibrating through my bones.

Willa Sutter. Get. On.

My legs move without my direction. My hands wrap around his neck. Effortlessly, Ryder stands, his broad hands grasping my thighs. We're two live wires that meet, making electricity flow freely between us. Sparks dance on my skin at every point of contact.

Ryder's shirt is plastered with sweat. I lean into it, hungry for everything about him that isn't tidy and cool and perfectly controlled. He smells heavenly. Like a lumberjack that just felled a tree, his muscles are coiled tight, his skin damp. I inhale cedar and pine and something undeniably *Ryder*. Pressing my chest into him, I almost moan. My boobs feel heavy, my nipples pebbled through layers of clothing as they scrape against the muscles of his back. He's hot and perspiration drips down his neck. I have the weirdest impulse to drag my tongue along his skin and taste him.

Squeezing my thighs, Ryder's dropping some kind of hint. I take it as a cue to hold on tighter, so I increase my grip around his neck and press my front to his back. I'm glued to his skin. His fingers dig into my legs as he pulls me even closer.

I knew Ryder was strong—mountain manly, feller of trees, climber of trails—but I didn't quite anticipate *this*. He steps evenly, long reaches from rock to rock with a solid-muscled woman on his back and two bags of gear. He's not even winded when we make it to the other side of the water, and I slide down his body.

The air's thick, not just with the heat of an unseasonably warm November day, but with something I can't name. Ryder's eyes hold mine as he straightens my gear on my shoulders. He steps closer, bringing our boots toe to toe. The sun beats down on us and makes every blond hair on his body glow golden. His chest rises and falls heavily, while his hands hold my shoulders, then slowly slide up my collarbones to my neck. Crickets sing in the grass and a hawk casts its shadow on us as it flies overhead. My pulse slams in my throat beneath Ryder's thumb. His eyes are on my mouth, his head bending.

Suddenly something slithers through grass close by, and I scream so violently, a chorus of finches shoots out of a nearby tree. Without thinking, I launch myself at Ryder, a petrified monkey, plastered to his body. His hands cup my ass as he watches the grass protectively, and I almost orgasm on the spot.

Goddamn, that guy looks hot in his mountain-man element. I'm all safe up in the stratosphere, watching his eyes dart across the grass. He'd murder that snake for me in a heartbeat. Then he'd spear it on a twig and roast it for me over the fire just to spite the amphibious abomination.

"Is it gone?" I whisper.

His eyes meet mine again. He tips his head.

"Is it gone?" I ask louder.

He nods. Our eyes search each other. The moment we almost had, another *almost* kiss hangs in the air between us. Unless…unless he wasn't going to do it. Unless I had dirt on my face or a booger.

Oh, shit. What if I'm imagining all of this?

Ryder easily holds me one-armed and reaches for his phone in his pocket. I'll admit it: I'm terrified of what he's going to say. Is he about to set me straight? Tell me to quit making sexy eyes at his mouth and rubbing myself on him like a koala in heat?

I'm a pathological avoidant, I know this, but for me, facing painful emotions is like fear of heights—the moment I'm too close to a potentially fatal drop, I scramble back and bolt.

I slink out of Ryder's arms and brush by him. Pushing forward, I can hear the faint din of the falls, and a sulfurous odor tinges the air. It's a sobering scent, breaking the heavy sweetness of what we just did. It reminds me why I'm here, to hike and check off a box for asshole MacCormack. If I lose sight of that, there's more than one way that I could fall off course. None of those ways are remotely safe.

The next mile is a gradual ascent, maybe another 150 to 200 feet, that brings us to the Lower Escondido Falls. It's a fifty-foot cascade, its pool of water flanked by moss-covered rocks and dewy ferns. The sulfur smell is stronger here and plenty of people seem to be happy ending their trip at this peaceful spot. Ryder told me we could easily call this our halfway point. Sit and relax, enjoy the view for a while, then turn back.

But I'm competitive. I love a good challenge, and I've never been one for taking the easy road, at least when it comes to making demands on my body. What I read when I did my recon for this mission was that if you're willing to work for it, Upper Escondido Falls is only three times higher than the lower falls, but it's infinitely more beautiful.

To get there, our next step on the trek is a treacherous wall of limestone to the right of the falls. It looks like it will be challenging to ascend and downright terrifying to scale on the way back, but we're both wearing hiking boots, and Ryder said it's intuitive. *Grab on tight and enjoy the ride down, Sunshine.*

It's by far the hardest part, a gain of nearly 200 feet over less than a quarter of a mile. We grapple for roots, rely on a length of rope afforded us for a stretch. At one point, Ryder has to reach down and yank me up to him, until the climb finally flattens, bringing us to land at the base of the upper falls.

The path veers left, and we trudge through massive, old roots, crawl between and over equally ancient boulders. Then, suddenly my breath is ripped from me.

Water roars, spilling past a fortress of moss-slicked stones. I've heard it's not the best flow this time of year, but the waterfall's power is still tangible. Its steady pound resonates in my chest, as it pours down the rocks and lands in a wide glassy pool.

This breathtaking view was worth the work.

As I stare up at the water, movement snags my peripheral vision. I turn, only to see Ryder yanking off his shirt. I swallow a choked sound as my body incinerates, my every sense tripping like a wall of breakers. All those muscles I've gripped and poked beneath his shirt, muscles I saw for one fleeting moment in a drunken haze and wanted to punch myself for not being sober enough to remember. There they are. And shit. Ryder's bigger than I thought he was.

He has a lean grace to his body. His clothes drape off his frame, suggesting a narrow build, but those flannel shirts have been lying. Ryder's shoulders are powerful and rounded, his pecs cut and shifting under taut skin as he tosses his shirt. His waist is solid, his every abdominal defined. Lots of guys in college still have boy bodies.

Not the lumberjack. The lumberjack's a man. And I'm a woman. Whose body is molten hot and bothered looking at him.

Next go his shorts.

Boxer briefs. Thank you, Lord Jesus, boxer briefs. Powerful quads that I recognize. Soccer quads. A scar across his knee. Long, solid calves. My eyes are stuck somewhere around the soles of his feet when Ryder shifts, jerking my attention upward again.

There's a shallow overhang behind the falls that he stares at, hands on hips. Slowly, his head tips my way, his eyes trailing my body. One eyebrow lifts. *You coming, or what, Sunshine?*

Dammit, it's like he's infiltrated my brain. With only a tip of his head, a tilt of his brow, I know exactly what he wants from me.

"Fine," I huff, ripping off my shirt. I'm down to a sports bra, as I bend over, then toe off my boots, peel off my socks. My shorts go last, and when I glance up at Ryder, his eyes are dark, his gaze traveling my body. Slowly. Patiently. How I imagine his hands would. Calloused palms that would sprawl across my skin, slide up my calves, then my thighs. A hard grip that would spread my legs wide and pin my hips roughly.

I swallow. "Hell of a team-building exercise, huh?"

Ryder's eyes finally meet mine. His grin is slow. But it's warm and genuine. And somehow, I know it's all for me.

12

RYDER

Playlist: "Set Fire To The Rain," Noah Guthrie

SURROUNDED BY THE ROAR OF THE FALLS, WE CLIMB OUR WAY to the overhang. My body's in hell. Not because of our hike, but because Willa's wearing sporty black panties, a simple bikini cut that wraps around her magnificent ass, which is unsurprisingly perfect—muscular, soft, round.

I try to avert my eyes, but she slips once, and I have no choice but to brace a hand on her backside and shove her ahead of me. My palm burns from touching her, just how it felt when she leaped into my arms and almost pissed herself at a little garden snake. Jesus, her body, molded around mine as I carried her. Her tits smashed to my back, the heat between her thighs flush against my waist. My fingers still buzz from gripping her strong legs, feeling that smooth, warm skin.

Finally, we make it onto the ledge behind the waterfall, and Willa drops down, immediately leaning against the mossy wall of the overhang. Water sprays in a fine mist, dampening her hair against her neck and her cheekbones. Her eyes hold mine, her chest heaving with exertion from the climb. My own chest rises and falls harshly. My lungs tug for air they can't seem to get enough of. I feel lightheaded, and it's not because of the climb.

Willa tears her gaze away, reaches inside her sports bra and pulls out her phone, wiping the front clear of residual water. *Right,* she texts. *Time for this godforsaken 'getting to know you' questionnaire.*

I groan in agreement, ripping my phone out of my armband case as I read her message. Willa sighs and crosses her legs at the ankles, swiping through the list. *First things first,* she texts. *Full name.*

Ryder Stellan Bergman, I answer.

Her phone dings, and she taps the message. Her face brightens with a grin as she texts back, *Could you be any more Scandinavian, Lumberjack?*

I shrug, typing, *My mom is Swedish. First-generation.*

She frowns as she texts me back. *But your last name sounds Swedish, too. Your dad isn't?*

A grin slips out because I know Willa will appreciate this. *My dad took my mom's last name. Well, legally, it's hyphenated to his family name since that was tied to his degree, but he goes by Bergman. His was an awful mouthful, and he liked hers better. She said it was the least he could do, for all the kids he wanted her to pop out.*

Willa snorts. *That's badass.*

Quiet falls, but for the roar of the water creating a curtain between us and the outside world. *Sutter's a good name,* I write. *I think you could find a guy who'd take it.*

She reads it and taps her phone, thinking. *Maybe. I won't have all those kids to justify it, though, at least for a while, maybe ever.*

My question is out of my fingers into her phone before I can help it. *Why?*

Can't play pro with a baby bump.

I nod. Of course. Willa's going to have a professional athlete's life. She's going to travel the world for the National Team. She'll make the Olympic Team next time they compete. Her life is going to be so different from mine.

I'll admit it, I was fucking *livid* with Aiden after he pulled this couple's therapy shit. I know my brother-in-law. I know exactly what he's doing, and I've resented him this entire semester for pushing us together, over and over. I drive Willa nuts with my blunt delivery, my pragmatic outlook, my dry, needling teases. And Willa's a temperamental pain in my ass. She makes fun of my flannel shirts. She provokes me almost *constantly*. She ribs me for my gruffness, then jabs me the moment I show her my soft side.

Yet, despite all that, she's important to me, and I've come to realize she needs a kind of gentle handling she won't admit. Underneath that tough exterior and irascible temper is someone just trying to protect herself from getting hurt. That clarity first came to me when I picked her up from the club. The way she looked at me so trustingly, how she leaned into me like I was somebody she could count on, someone strong enough to take her being human and a little needy. It was a rare window into her vulnerability. Seeing it felt like a gift.

But she was also shit-faced and exhausted, and she woke up the next morning just as feisty and playfully combative as always, teasing her body against mine, coaxing whatever reaction she could, just to get a rise out of me. And, so help me, for just a minute, I took the bait.

The moment she left, then texted me from her apartment, we were right back to what we always were. Enemies who can tolerate each other, friends who drive each other nuts. One of those. Both of them.

Who fucking knows. God, I have a headache.

The point is, her behavior that night and the next morning

was an anomaly, not the norm. Reading any more into that night is delusional, and this reminder, this sobering reminder that a world-class athlete, the next great female soccer star of at least the US, if not the world, does not have room in her world for someone like me, is exactly what I needed. Because even if Willa Sutter did feel anything for me besides contemptuous amusement, I'm the least compatible partner for someone like her. I'm a guy who wants to live a quiet life in the woods, who wants to take walks among the trees and build campfires and learn how to create a place where anyone, kids and adults, disabled or not, can enjoy being in nature.

"Bergman."

At least I think that's what she says. My head snaps up. *What?* I sign.

My phone buzzes, and I realize I felt it a moment ago but didn't process it, lost in my thoughts. *Where'd you go?* her message says.

Shaking my head, I sit straighter. *Sorry. Your turn. Full name. Cough it up, Sunshine.*

My phone buzzes in my hands again. *Willa Rose Sutter. Don't you dare make some crack about a cutesy middle name for a hellion like me. It's my grandma's name and I'll throat punch you.*

I stare down at those words, saying them inside my head. Willa. Rose. Sutter.

That's beautiful, I type.

Willa startles, as if I caught her off guard by complimenting her. Am I that terrible to her? I say nice things about her, don't I?

No, you ass, you don't. Because that's dangerous territory. We don't go there.

True, subconscious. Very, very true.

Willa finally breaks away from staring at me in bewilderment and lowers her eyes to her phone. *Favorite food.*

Spinach, I type.

She scrunches her nose. *You would, Mountain Man.*

I roll my eyes. *Healthier than yours. Double-stack cheeseburger and a root beer float. You and Rooney get it after two-a-days and rough games. You're secretly worried Rooney's going to confess your breach in strict diet to Coach because she has a guilt complex that typically prevents her from being able to lie at all.*

Willa's jaw drops, her eyes narrowing as they flick up and meet mine, then return to her phone screen. *Have you been following me, Bergman?*

A slow grin pulls at my mouth. *No. But you talk, Willa, and I listen. I know you, better than you think.*

Her face falls as she types. *Then why do I know almost nothing about you?* My body tenses as I read her words. *Why don't I know you're a badass soccer player? Why do you know my favorite food and post-game ritual, and I don't even know how you spend your weekends, or what you do for fun? How's that fair?*

I narrow my eyes at her, then type, *Fair?*

She throws up her hands, then grabs her phone and types furiously. *Yes, fair! Why do I run my mouth around you, why do I tell you anything about my life, just for you to use it against me, to throw it in my face and tease me left and right? Then there's you. What do I have to work with? A closed-off, cold, contained Abominable Snowman.*

Now back up, I type. *I tell you things. You met my friends, my roommates, I brought you to my house—I never do that. You know my schedule. You know I hate peanut butter cups.*

Because that's weird to hate peanut butter cups, she texts. *Because you deserve shame for hating peanut butter cups.*

And I only came to your house and met Tucker and Becks because we had to do this project together.

Because that's the only thing that ever brought us together, Willa! Your world is not my world. I hit send and watch her face shift as she reads.

Suddenly, Willa looks up at me, her eyes tight. Her stare is unblinking and so intense, I can't hold it. Recklessly, indulgently, my eyes roam her body. Water rushes around us, the mist plastering her scant clothes closer to her body, tightening the curls in her hair. God, she's perfect. Muscular and fit, and still the faint curves of a woman. I felt those strong thighs in my grip, her high breasts smashed to my back. Shutting my eyes, I try to scrub the image from my brain, to erase the desire staining my system.

I sense movement, and my eyes jerk open. Willa's gaze glows as she leans onto all fours, then crawls my way. My heart pounds in my ears, heat floods my stomach and lower. I'm keyed up and cornered, and I have no idea what Willa's about to do.

She straddles my legs, and I involuntarily hold my breath. Reaching past me, she yanks the stem off a plant, then sits back on her haunches, right on my thighs. My nails claw ineffectually into the slate beneath my palms. My pulse thunders, watching her rip off a leaf and set it to my lips.

"Mint," her mouth says. I can't hear her voice at all over the falls.

I sniff it, giving her a suspicious look that makes her grin.

Pulling out her phone, she texts me, *I'm not poisoning you, Lumberjack, see?* She stuffs a leaf in her mouth and chews happily. *You more than anyone should know what this is. Mint.*

I open my mouth, feeling the warmth between her legs slide over my thigh. Putting down her phone, she leans closer.

When she sets the leaf on my tongue, air finally rushes out of me.

Pungent mint bursts inside my mouth. The leaf tickles as I chew and watch Willa mirroring my movements. Her throat works as she swallows, and hunger coils tight inside me. Willa's hands clasp mine, then skate up my arms. I can't hear my breath, but I can feel it. I can feel each violent tug of air, the pound of my pulse along my length. Need soars up my chest, tightens my throat.

I stare at her lips. It takes considerable effort not to bite them.

"What do you want, Ryder?" her mouth says.

What do I want? That's not the question. The question is what do I get? Do I want Willa? Hell, yes. Can I have her?

She leans closer. "What do you want?"

I've spent weeks restraining myself. Weeks trying not to picture her every time I close my eyes at night or pass a soccer field or taste oranges or smell roses. I haven't touched myself once to the thought of her. I've shut it down every step of the way.

I could lie to her, text her some stinging jab, politely set her off my lap. But I don't want to. What do I want? I want her. So. Fucking. Badly.

Her eyes are luminous, sunlight pale and wide, as they flick to my mouth. My shoulders flex as Willa's fingers wrap around them.

She arches forward, making her breasts slide against my bare chest. My fingers sink into her hair and grab hold, nothing gentlemanly in my touch. I feel primal. Desperate. I fist her hair tight and watch her mouth fall open. Those lips. I've watched them for what feels like eternity, tortured by how full and soft they look, dying to taste them. I sit straight and cup her neck. My mouth lowers toward hers, controlled, slow.

One moment we're separate, the next we're fused.

Boom.

Velvet-soft, decadent. The feel of her sweet mouth is so much better than I imagined. I gasp for air and steal hers. She tastes like mint leaves and something sweet that must simply be Willa. I haul her tighter to me, wrap her in my arms, as my hands feel everything I've barely let myself imagine touching. The dip and swell of her backbone, the jut of her hips, the curve of her waist. Every single rib.

When I part her lips and tease her tongue, she moans. I want to throw her down, rip off what's left of her clothes and rut into her like an animal, but if I've learned anything in my life, it's patience, it's the long game. So I'm gentle, exploratory. Our tongues tangle, a seeking kiss that starts whisper soft and ends in an open-mouthed beg for more. It becomes hungrier tastes, wet and hot, slow and lazy. Breathing is an obligation, and I resent its interference in the best kiss of my life.

Willa's arms curl around my neck. She presses herself into me, her warmth seated over my lap, where I'm hard as fucking stone for her. She sighs as she feels it, and her fingers scrape through my hair. I can't help but groan and sense my voice filling her mouth. It's so impossibly sexy to feel her sounds, to give her mine.

Willa's lips open wider over mine, her tongue a teasing flick that taunts mine to find hers again and dance. Slide, then nip, a kiss that pretends to be delicate before it builds in rhythm like a wave swelling to the point of collapse. Willa writhes over me, her movement so natural, her fit so perfect, we were made to do this. Her thighs lock around my waist, her elbows prop on my shoulders as she slides her fingers through my hair, and my world telescopes to this tiny breadth of space in which we touch and kiss and feel.

She grinds on me, and I roll my hips beneath hers, panting against her mouth, knowing if I do much more of this, it's game over.

My hands find her shoulders and squeeze. Breaking apart, breathing heavily, I press my forehead to hers. Willa leans in for more, but I pull away just enough for our eyes to meet.

I'm beyond overwhelmed. My brain is scrambled, my senses confused.

When Willa sits back, her eyes search mine. She must read my torn expression, my shock. I watch her eyes cool and her walls go up. Clasping her hand, I rack my brain for the right words, wishing I were clear-headed or brave enough to make her tell me why she asked me what I want, why we're kissing when the drive up here was stony silence.

All we've done for weeks is banter and snap, prank and poke until this game ratcheted up to a dangerous realm of sexual tease. That damn yellow top started it all, and since then we've been brutally amping up each other's libidos, taunting each other's bodies.

Is this just the final move? Is this checkmate in our one-upmanship, and now all that's left is to knock every piece away, to wipe away the history of each lost battle and victory from the board, now that she's come out the winner? If so, I lost. She got me to kiss her. She undid me. I was putty in her arms. Willa fucking won.

Our eyes hold for a long moment, hers cooling even more as she crawls off my lap and leans against the wall. Willa gives me a halfhearted smile, then texts me, *Come on, Mountain Man. Back to reality.*

After more obligatory questions and more obligatory answers, our assignment is done and regret is a boulder in my chest. I know her favorite food, her twenty-year plan, her earliest memory, and the last state she lived in, but I still don't know why she asked me what I wanted, why we just kissed and touched like the world was ending. I still don't know what Willa Sutter wants from *me*.

Our descent's silent, light still high in the sky as we walk to my car. Our clothes are sun warm, our skin sticky from sweat and the falls. Willa leans her temple against the window and stares out at the Pacific Coast Highway as I drive and rack my brain for how I can gain some clarity, some insight into what the *hell* is happening.

Just then I drive by a billboard featuring a father, his arm wrapped around his son, and it hits me. *Dad.*

I don't often take advantage of the fact that my dad's a physician who practices minutes from campus. In fact, I never do. Mostly, it's because I'm conditioned not to need him too much. My whole life, many other people's need of him was more time-sensitive than mine, and I don't mean that to sound like a martyr—it's just the truth. Dad's an oncologist, a father of seven, a husband who loves his wife and prioritizes time with her. He's on the boards of too many things to count and even works with fellow veterans in his nonexistent spare time.

He's a busy guy. I'm the middle child of his seven kids, so even when it came to family time, big agenda items like baby fevers and periods and first steps and failed tests were way more pressing than Ryder waiting with a book under his arm to read with Dad.

I learned how to be patient. I learned how to find those slivers of time when Dad was mine. I'd get up early to watch him shave and tell him about my day. I crawled into bed after he got home late from work and had showered off. Just five minutes cuddling in his arms before he started snoring, that was all I needed.

So now, as an adult man with his education underway and a practical life plan ahead of him, I tell myself I shouldn't need my father at all. Except I should, and I do.

I *really* need my dad.

Dropping off Willa at her apartment, I watch her slowly walk up the pathway. She turns and gives me a tired, half-hearted wave before she steps inside and closes the door behind her. Confused and torn, worried I've hurt her and terrified she's played me, I feel the last emotional stilt collapse from under me. I pull out my phone, texting Dad, *Got 10 minutes for your favorite son today, old man?*

His response is almost immediate. *I always have 10 minutes for you, Ry. Bring your old man a sandwich and an iced tea. Then we're talking favorites.*

13

WILLA

Playlist: "Sunscreen," Ira Wolf

WHAT THE *FUCK* JUST HAPPENED?

Tears prick my eyes. I slam the door behind me, feeling the urge to do a quick sketch of Ryder's face and throw darts at it. That's followed by an oppositional tug to run after him, yank him by that overgrown beard, and drag him to my bed, where I'd take one punishing orgasm from him after another.

When he said *your world is not my world*, all I could think was how wrong he was. Ryder's a big part of my world, for better and for worse. He's my nemesis, my antagonist, my provocateur—perfect bookstore word for a moment like this —but he's not just someone as cut and dried or as extreme as my enemy. He really is my frenemy. Someone I can count on to soak up every little thing I say, find its one weak spot, and tease me for it. The person who'll notice when I have a booger on my nose, take a picture just to fuck with me, then wipe it away with his bare hand. The guy that knows I eat three helpings of Swedish meatballs and has my practice schedule memorized so he can harass me with texts while I'm sprinting, late to our class.

So, I called his bluff. Bullshit, my world's not his. I sat on his lap, got right up in his face, and pretty much dared him to kiss me. It was the only way I could think to express all of those icky, sticky, mushy, impossible-to-verbalize feelings I have about him. To make Ryder Stellan Bergman understand how much his world *is* mine.

Provoking him to a make-out session is how you tell him that? Great logic, Sutter. Crystal clear communication, right there.

"Oh, shut it," I mumble to myself.

I can't stop remembering those kisses. Every one of them is branded on my lips. Kissing him and being kissed, the confident way he tilted my head and cradled the nape of my neck in his rough, warm hand. I can still feel his tongue dancing with mine. Patient, steady strokes that indicate the tall, green-eyed, asshole lumberjack might have a trick or five up his pine-scented flannel sleeve when it comes to the sexy times.

Not that we're going there. Nope. People who torture and prank and provoke each other don't want sexy times together. They don't want to kiss until they pass out from lack of oxygen. They don't want to wrap themselves around each other until every incinerating square inch of their skin burns and smokes.

What the hell are Ryder and I playing at?

One minute I'm riding on his back at his chivalrous insistence, the next, he's giving me hell for my cheeseburger weak spot. One moment we're kissing, his hands gripping my waist with a desperation I have *never* felt in a man, the next, we're staring at each other like the other person is about to pull the cord to the trapdoor beneath our feet.

Is he fucking with me? Is this just more retribution, another move in his vengeance long game, for the absurdity I started with the yellow shirt?

I drop off my gear, change clothes, and nab a protein bar. Leaving, I shut the door with unnecessary force and almost snap the key locking it.

Shaking my head, I try to snap out of this nonsense. I'm going to see my mom—I want to be focused on her, not my trivial college drama. Rain begins to drop from darkening clouds overhead as I walk to the hospital. I tip my face to the sky, begging it to wash my brain clean. To erase all this worry and preoccupation over a fucking man.

I tamp down a fresh swell of confusing tears and palm my eyes despite rain painting my cheeks. I don't even know what I *am* feeling, just that I'm feeling too damn much. Whatever emotion it is, it's a hot, stinging ache that incinerates the path from my throat to my stomach. It reminds me of the time I gulped scalding tea, and rather than spit it out like a reasonable human being, I sealed my lips and swallowed. Except this burn doesn't dissipate. It's a living thing, a scorching, consuming fire that I have no clue how to quell.

My walk to the hospital doesn't take long, which is good since the drizzle accelerates to pouring rain. I squeak down the hall, water squelching out of my tennis shoes, as I round quietly into Mama's room. I don't want to wake her if she's sleeping.

Her eyes dart across the book she has propped on a pillow in her lap.

"*My Ántonia* again?"

She glances up at the sound of my voice and does a double take. "Willa!" Taking in my appearance, her eyes widen. "What the hell happened to you?"

After a long, slow breath to try to lock down my emotions, I wash my hands, then walk over to her bed. "I got caught in the rain on my way over."

Mama gives me one of her piercing once-overs. "I can

tell. But that's not what I meant. You look upset, Willa Rose. What's going on?"

Don't cry. Don't cry. Don't cry.

"You remember that guy from class I told you about? My project partner, who pulled the stealth tactics with his hearing aid?"

"The asshole lumberjack." She shifts in her bed. "Yes. What did he do to you? Do I have to go beat some Brawny boy's butt for making my Willa cry?"

It makes me laugh. "No. We just...things are getting confusing, more intense. The stakes keep raising, and now I'm not even sure what I'm betting on or what I'm trying to win."

She tips her head. "Oh?"

"I'm frustrated. The whole situation's annoyingly distracting. I don't want to be spending all this time spinning my tires about it. Men are a waste of time anyway, as we both agree."

Mama cocks an eyebrow. "I don't exactly remember saying *that*. I've taught you to be cautious with men. That many are disappointments. But also that some are good, rare gems in their species. The hard—and for me, deterring—part is that it's difficult to know which are which at first, sometimes for a long while." Her eyes search mine. "You want to talk about it?"

"Nah." I wave my hand and swallow the lump of tears thickening my throat. "Like I said, I don't want to think about him anymore. How are *you* feeling today, Mama?"

Her smile is a little forced, like mine. "Oh. So-so."

An unsettlingly evasive answer from a woman with aggressive cancer.

Fear pinches my stomach and twists it into a knot. "What's Dr. B have to say about things these days?"

Mama's pause is too long. My hands fist my wet shorts, creating a fresh puddle of water on the tiles at my feet. "Mama?"

Her sigh is heavy. It's the one that typically precedes her telling me something I won't like. "Willa, there's something I haven't told you that I should have. Come here." She pats the mattress.

I glance up and down my drenched body. "I shouldn't. I'm soaking wet."

"Nonsense." Mama waves her hand. "I have a shower coming up here soon anyway. That'll warm me, and they'll change my bed then. Now, come here, Willa Rose."

Obediently, I scoot onto the mattress and tuck myself against Mama.

She glances over at me. "Ready?"

"Yes, Mama. Please just tell me."

"Okay, so it's about Dr. B."

I pick my head up. "What about him?"

Mama bites her lip.

What does she have to be coy about? "Are you two..." I wiggle my eyebrows. "You know?"

Mama laughs, and it's a laugh I want to remember. It doesn't sound like a sick laugh. It sounds like her old laugh, clear and bell-like. Her smile is wide as her head tips back, and she *laughs*.

My laugh is quiet at first. But soon it's not. It's loud, and not unlike hers, and pretty soon we're laughing so hard, we're crying, and Mama's turning, hiding her head in the pillow as it becomes a racking cough. Her cough settles before we earn a nurse's attention, and Mama nestles back in her pillow, wiping her eyes.

"Oh, Willa, you have a way of saying things. Phew." She

sighs happily. "Now, where was I? Oh, right. No, we are not...*you know*."

I wipe my eyes, too, and return my head to her shoulder. "Okay, so what is it, then?"

"You can't tell anyone, Willa, because it's skirting a breach of ethics. It could cost Alex everything if word gets out."

"What?"

Mama's eyes search mine as her voice lowers. "Dr. B— Alex, rather—we go way back. We served together on a few deployments, then we bumped into each other again at a veterans' function five years ago. When we realized we were both living in Los Angeles, we agreed to stay in touch, just as friends, mind you. You ever see or speak to his wife, and you'll understand why."

I frown. "Mama, you're a total catch, inside and out. You're still smokin'."

Mama chuckles and gently cups my cheek. "Thank you, honey. I think I had a few pretty nice decades, but the point is the medical ethics board would argue Alex shouldn't be my doctor since we have history. They'd say it would be easy for him to let emotion get in the way of his care—"

"That's the last thing I want to hear about your cancer doctor, Mama, is that he's not fit to take care of you." *Has* his judgment been clouded? "Why are...what were you think-ing?" I hiss.

"He is completely capable of compartmentalizing. We don't know each other *well*. He's very sensible, very honest with me. I'm telling you it would *look* bad, not that it *is*. Trust me, I'm doing the right thing, letting him be my care provider. Alex is the best at this, Willa. I know it's a little murky, but he needed to do this for me, and I wasn't going to say no, given his credentials."

"Why did he need to do this?"

Mama's eyes leave mine as her hand fiddles with the blanket draped over her bony knees. "I saved his life on our last tour together."

My mouth drops. "You saved his life? How?"

Mama bites her full bottom lip, the original to the replica she gave me. "I don't like to think about it often. It was an awful day."

I squeeze her hand. "I don't want to pressure you." Mama doesn't talk much about her deployments, but I know it's taken years of therapy to help her cope with many PTSD triggers.

"It's okay, Willa. I just need a minute." Dropping her head back on her pillow, Mama stares up at the ceiling. "I think you know enough about the military by now to understand that a combat medic, being part of a medevac team, is a dangerous, nerve-wracking job. You fly into conflict zones, perform life-saving medical care on the ground. Bullets whirring past you, explosions, screams. If you make it back out, you're in a chopper with critically traumatized bodies, possibly fatal injuries, working with what you have until you're back on base with everything you need.

"Alex and I were a pair who worked well in the field. We were both exceptionally cool-headed, excellent compartmentalizers, we worked fast together and had this odd ability to communicate without words. Alex was holding…" Her eyes squeeze shut. "Alex was trying to save a soldier's life when he took a bullet to the leg. It shattered his femur, severing his femoral artery, not that I knew specifically at the time. I saw him take the hit, and then I saw lots of blood."

I suck in a breath. Mama's one of those medical types who loved raising her daughter to understand her body. We spent nights nerding out over anatomy books with me inside her arms while she taught me the Latin names for my bones and body parts. It led to my first social faux pas when I lifted my shirt in kindergarten, pointed to my belly button and told the class, *It's my umbilicus!*

All that to say, I know the significance of what she's saying. I know that an artery carries blood from your heart to the rest of your body, except when it's severed—then, it's pumping your life source right out of you, faster as your panic increases and your heart rate accelerates. It's a fatal injury and a swift death unless drastic measures are taken.

"Shit, Mama."

She nods. "Everyone was already crawling back to the chopper. Alex was the last man out there, holding Williams, who was gone by that point. The captain was screaming at me to get in, but I couldn't leave Alex, so I ran out, ripped off the bottom of my shirt, and tied the world's fastest tourniquet around his upper thigh, then dragged his ass back to the chopper."

She slides her gown off her shoulder, pointing to the nasty scar on her shoulder blade. "Took a bullet that lodged nicely in my scapular, but I got us to safety, otherwise unscathed."

Stars dance around the edges of my vision, alerting me to the fact that I've been holding my breath, listening to this story. My exhale is one big gust of air. "What happened?"

"We both received treatment. Alex went in for surgery. I did too, but not urgently. I got off easy, but Alex lost his leg from the mid-thigh down. He was lucky he survived at all."

A shaky exhale leaves me as tears prick my eyes. I know my mama's brave. I've always been proud to say on Veterans Day that my mother served her country in places so many people are afraid to go. But this is a new depth of understanding. It's the most specific she's *ever* been with me.

"Mama." I palm away my tears. "I don't think I tell you enough how much I admire you. You're badass. And brave."

She wraps her hand around mine and squeezes. "You've told me plenty, Willa. I know you're proud of me, and I know being the only child of a single military mom wasn't easy, but you were always such a trooper. New schools, new homes, new neighbors. You always bounced back from another change with that wide smile and your wild hair, walking up to kids' doors with a soccer ball on your hip, banging on the windows, inviting them to come play."

Her free hand tucks a loose curl behind my ear as she smiles at me. "Soccer's always helped you cope. It's what connected you to people, it's how you grew into yourself, your confidence and grace. It's such a vital part of you."

It's true. Soccer isn't just something I'm good at. It's as integral to my existence as my most basic needs.

I shift on the bed, sitting straighter so that we're eye to eye. "Why are you telling me this now, about you and Dr. B?"

Mama's eyes leave mine and dance away to the window, watching rain pelt the glass and trickle out of view. "Money, Willa. Money's not flowing. You and I were always modest spenders. We're not materialistic people, and we're simple women, but still. Breast cancer was expensive, leukemia is even more so. Alex has worked tirelessly with my insurance to cover everything they could, but he's also been encouraging me to consider getting out of the hospital, where it will be significantly less costly. Taking my care home."

I reel. I haven't been to our apartment in two months. Mama hasn't either. The place needs a deep clean. She'll need round-the-clock care. "But how would that work?"

Mama sighs. "Well, I should begin by telling you, I've

sublet the apartment, Willa. What valuables you didn't take to your and Rooney's place are in storage, and mine are, too."

"What? Why?"

Finally, she turns away from the window and meets my eyes again. "Because there was no point in paying for a place neither of us was living in."

I swallow my shock and try to focus on the pressing matter. "So where will you go?"

Mama squeezes my hand reassuringly. "Alex and his wife, Elin, want me to stay with them. They have a big family, and all but two of their kids are out of the house. They're nearempty nesters with more space than they know what to do with.

"Alex said since his injury, he's wished he could thank me in a way that feels adequate, in gratitude for his life. I don't see him as owing me anything—I just did my job—but this is what he wants to give me, and, Willa, I'm inclined to let him."

It bristles. It scares me. Mama and I have only ever lived alone, the two of us, except for seasons when Grandma Rose came to stay. When I was little, I had babysitters and Grandma Rose, and eventually went to daycare, but our life, our routines, our home—it was only ever ours. Now, when-ever I want to see my mom, I have to go to some stranger's house? Will she have privacy? Will I be able to stay with her over the summer?

Mama's hand patting mine breaks my thoughts. "My dear verbal processor."

"I said that out loud," I say on a resigned sigh.

She chuckles. "I knew it would unnerve you, but I hoped that explaining our history would help you feel more comfort-able with it. That's mostly why I told you. Because I figured you'd see that I've earned this. I did right by a friend and saved his life. Now he's trying to make mine a little more comfortable.

"I will have privacy. They have a few first-floor bedrooms, one of which has a separate entrance. You won't be under any obligation to see anyone but me, and I'll have a nurse tending to my needs. Alex and Elin will live their lives independently from me, though Alex will, of course, still oversee my care."

A heavy sigh leaves me as I stare down at my hands. "Sorry. I feel selfish, my first thoughts being what they were."

"Hardly, Willa." Mama grasps my cheeks gently and turns my face her way. "It's different. It's not easy. But I also know you understand, and you'll support whatever I need to be comfortable and have peace about our finances."

I nod, my face still resting in her hand. "I do. I want whatever makes you happy and feeling good, Mama."

Her eyes twinkle as she smiles at me. "I know, honey. You don't even have to tell me. I knew you'd understand." Slowly, she pulls me to her, until my head rests against her chest. Her fingers drift through my hair, another vain attempt to tame its wildness.

"I love you, Mama," I whisper. I count her heartbeats. I feel gratitude for each of them.

She presses her lips to my hair, a soft kiss that's as comforting as her strong hugs. "I love you, too, my Willa Rose."

RYDER

Playlist: "Snaggletooth," Vance Joy

DAD'S OFFICE IS MESSY. I'M PRETTY SURE IT'S BECAUSE THE man doesn't have so much as a stray necktie or fountain pen in our house. Mom requires a home as neat and minimalist as the one she lived in until she met Dad and then moved to the States.

"Ryder!" Dad stands with arms outstretched. I set down our food and let him hug me, hugging him back. Dad's American, but he's absorbed a lot of Swedish parenting philosophies from Mom, who's a nurturing force of nature. He took a long paternity leave when each of us was born, got down on the ground to play with us whenever he could. Our family's affectionate, and masculinity doesn't require gruff back slaps or avoiding kisses. Point in case, Dad presses a kiss to my hair, then squeezes my shoulder. He's as tall as me, so we're eye to eye when he speaks. It makes reading his lips easy, but I also wore the hearing aid, thinking I'd test how it handles the noise levels of the hospital.

As he rounds his desk, he gives me a once-over. "You look good, minus the Bigfoot beard."

I roll my eyes. Dad's never had a beard. He hates the feel

of them and spent long enough in the military to get used to the daily discipline of a full shave.

"You taking care?" he asks. Sitting, he pulls the sandwich bag his way and opens it up.

I take out my phone and type, *Pretty much. Classes aren't too stressful. I'm exercising, sleeping decently. Same old.*

He slides his glasses down from his head to read his phone. I watch his eyes dart left–right, then flick up to mine. "Same old, you say?" Raising his eyebrows, he takes a bite of sandwich and chews, then swallows and texts me back. *Things are so "same old," you came to see your dad when you'll see him next week for Thanksgiving?*

I shrug, tugging my sandwich bag my way and uncurling the folded paper. My hand hovers over my phone, debating. Finally, I go for it.

How did you know you loved Mom?

Dad picks up his phone, reads it, then sets it down. His eyes meet mine. Sharp green eyes he passed on to Axel and me and Ziggy. "Why do you ask?"

I shrug, then type a lie. *An assignment for a class in History and Philosophy of Human Civilization.*

Dad's eyes crinkle, and his mouth twitches. "That so?" When I don't respond, Dad sits back and gives me a once-over before he focuses on texting me. *Well funny enough, your mom and I didn't get along too well at first. We practically hated each other's guts.*

My stomach drops. The paper bag I'm gripping crumples in my hand.

Dad doesn't seem to notice. *I was on R and R, went up with some buddies to the northern part of Sweden, which, as I'm sure you remember from when we visited when you were little, is much less populous than the south. There are no major cities. It's quite rural and spread out. It's good for skiing and getting snowed in, if you know what I mean.*

I tip my head and give him the *don't-gross-me-out* look.

He laughs. *I'll keep it G-rated, I promise.* Then he pauses, glancing up at me. "I see that right ear's hearing aid. Can you hear me well enough like this, or should I keep texting?"

I can actually hear him fairly well. It's extremely quiet in his office, which helps. I'm also benefiting from additional adjustments to my hearing aid the past few weeks while building up how many hours per day I wear it, which helps my sound processing. Dad's a slower speaker, too, so watching his lips as I listen brings it together.

I feel an aching excitement as bittersweet hope swells inside my chest. Bringing a hand to my frustrating left ear, I curve it around the empty shell where a hearing aid sits on my right. Could I give that ear another chance?

Filing that away to explore when I have the mental and emotional energy, I clear my throat and text him, *Speaking is fine for now. I'll let you know if I need you to switch to text.*

He nods. "Sounds good. So, after a long day of skiing, we stopped in at this tiny hole-in-the-wall mountain restaurant to warm up and eat our weight in food. Your mom was there. Her family owned it, as you know, and she more or less ran the place at that point."

He gets a look in his eyes as he swivels in his chair and slides his glasses back up onto his head. "She spoke civilly, but she looked at me like I was a stray dog someone had made her take in and feed. That just needled me. She wasn't the first haughty European I'd encountered with a sour opinion of American soldiers. So I ribbed her back. I understood enough about Swedish culture that I knew plenty of ways to offend her. I purposefully committed every faux pas I could think of. Came on too strong, bragged, didn't say thank you enough, made too much small talk. Said *hi* every time I saw her. I drove her nuts."

A silent chuckle slips through my throat.

"But then we got snowed in." Dad smirks. "There was no going anywhere. I was stuck there for four days, and the first two, I was pretty sure she was going to poison my morning coffee. I wasn't unconvinced I didn't want to spit in hers either. I kept up with the torture, late to every meal, asking for all kinds of extras to dump in my coffee and tea, botching my Swedish. I left a mess everywhere I went, smiled too much."

What I can hear of his laugh is deep and tinged with nostalgia.

"But at some point on the third night, we were up late. Got a little drunk, and she invited—not challenged, of course, too much aggressiveness in that for a Swede—she politely *invited* me to a game of chess."

He takes a sip of iced tea, then folds his hands across his stomach. "She kicked my ass, crowed with victory. Now *she* was the one committing the faux pas. She'd not only made her guest lose a game but eviscerated him, and celebrated in his face, which is against every code of hospitality and humility in their culture. She was embarrassed, and rather than let it go, I just kept talking about her win, teasing her for her hotdogging.

"She got madder and madder as I got nicer and nicer. The angrier she got, the calmer I was, and before I knew it, she'd smacked the chess game off the table, climbed it, and was kissing me senseless."

My jaw drops. This is not the meet-cute story I've heard told at family functions, but then again, this anecdote would have scandalized plenty of our family and made my Swedish grandmother faint.

I'm blushing. I press a hand to my cheek to cool it, and it makes Dad laugh.

"Your mother." He sighs. "I knew it right then: I loved her. I mean, I didn't *know* that I knew right then, if that makes sense. I was still too twisted up in my frustration with her. But when I look back…" His shoulder lifts as he sips his iced tea again. "That was it."

Why? I text him. *How does that make sense to you? How do you look back and know?*

Setting down his drink, Dad rests his arms on his desk. "Hate, enmity, rivalry are all passionate responses. My personal theory is that they are incomplete expressions of one core human emotion: love. It's like that parable about the men who felt different parts of an elephant and each mistook it for something else. Love is a many-faceted feeling. It's anything but one-dimensional. Sometimes when someone's in love, certain emotions and behaviors, more than others, present themselves first."

I swipe open my phone and type, *That logic is terrifying.*

He leans in. "But it *is* logical. Think about it. We don't bother with people we're indifferent to. We provoke and prank and tease those who get under our skin and make us *feel*, people who incite our passion.

"That's why, when it came to your mother, I can look back and see I was doing everything I could to provoke her, not because I liked to tease her—"

I cock an eyebrow which earns his chuckle.

"Okay, I like to tease her *a little*. But back then, it was because I felt passion for Elin. And no, it wasn't clear at first *why* that was the case—just because we butt heads with someone, doesn't mean we're in love with them—but when I came back a few months later, and she was still there, I had perspective. All those unresolved, convoluted feelings of exasperation and tension were no longer partial and incomplete. Affection, protectiveness, the impulse to drop my defenses and soften up, completed the picture, so I could see the truth: I *liked* her.

"Being around her made me wake up and sit straighter. Simply existing in her sphere made my blood run hot, my heart beat hard. After that, we still needled and teased, but we stopped denying that we were attracted to each other. We listened to our intuition and gave the other person a chance to be someone we could love. Turned out we were right."

My appetite is nonexistent. I slide the paper bag aside and tug my ball cap lower, hoping my dad doesn't see written on my face how upsetting this information is.

Dad taps my hand, earning my attention. "You okay? You seem upset."

I nod, try to smile reassuringly, and rip back open my sandwich bag, forcing myself to attack my food with a singular focus. I can't sit here and brood. It will raise his suspicions, if they aren't raised already. I force down bite after bite, trying not to think too hard about the abundant parallels between my parents' rocky beginning and the rough start Willa and I got off to. The shift at some point when I looked *forward* to her snarky comments about my lumberjack flannel, when I started growing hungry to find out not only what made her irises burn angry ruby red, but also glow satisfied toffee, sweet with a lick of bite. When I started wanting to sweep her up and protect her from everything—garden snakes, club creeps, asshole professors who take things too academically far, anything that makes her eyes dim and that fiery spark extinguish inside her.

We finish our food while Dad prods me for more information about school, about my friends. He taps his ear, then mouth, looking at me sternly. "Still no hearing aid on that left ear?"

I scowl at him for a long moment. It's one thing for me to mull over what to do about my left ear. It's another thing entirely to have a conversation about it when I'm not sure what comes next.

Dipping my head to type and change the subject, I ask how Oliver and Ziggy—my littlest brother and sister, the last ones at home—are doing. I ask about Mom and her Thanksgiving cooking preparations for the cast of thousands to come. We bullshit as much as you can for ten minutes, and when I stand and start to clean up our mess, I inadvertently knock my water over all his haphazardly placed files. We're both quick, yanking the manila folders off the polished wood surface and dropping them to the carpet. Once I've dried off the table, I turn and crouch down, focusing on wiping away the excess water left on top of the files.

I'm a doctor's son. I know about patient-physician confidentiality, and I'm not a snoop. I honestly try not to think about all the sick people my dad cares for each day. Cancer's depressing, and selfishly, I'm absorbed enough in my own body's struggles not to want to think about other ways our bodies are vulnerable. So it's not like I'm looking or even noticing labels until a last name practically screams itself at me.

Sutter.

Sutter, Joy is a patient of my dad's, and according to the basic information page that fell out of her folder as if the universe insisted I see it, she's in Room 337. I stand abruptly, feeling the room swim.

Sutter. It's a common enough last name. LA's a huge place. It's probably no particular connection to Willa. But it doesn't *feel* like that. It feels like something I'm supposed to know.

Dad taps my shoulder gently, and I spin.

"You all right?" he asks.

I nod. *Hot*, I mouth, pulling my shirt from my chest as if cooling myself.

Dad seems satisfied with that. I let him hug me goodbye, hard, once more before he sends me off. I walk the hallway, counting tiles, telling myself not to look at door numbers, to not even think about them. Even if this Joy Sutter is someone to Willa, who am I to know? It's not like Willa told me.

Her voice storms my head as the memory of her anger, her frustration, floods my thoughts.

"Why do I know almost nothing about you?"

If this person is Willa's and means something to her, Willa has some balls to give me shit for holding my cards close, when she's been silently carrying a much heavier burden. As I'm walking and working my way through those thoughts, I hear a familiar sound. It carries faintly and distorted, an auditory mirage in the distance.

I freeze in place, turning on my heel when I catch the noise again.

That's Willa.

My body instinctively takes me toward the sound. I bypass rolling computer carts, sidestep a nurse, until I'm outside a door that's cracked open. I don't let myself see the room number, not yet. Instead, I see two feet tucked up on a bed. A pair of water-logged sneakers I watched walk away from my car just a few hours ago.

Willa.

Then I hear her voice in a way I hear no one else's. Not perfectly, not exactly how I want to, but with a clarity otherwise foreign to me since my ears went to hell.

There's her laugh again. Then another word. One that lands like a knife in my heart.

Mama.

———

I sit in my usual seat, waiting for Willa in our first Business Math class since everything got hot and heavy and superbly confusing on that damn hike. The room fills up quickly because Aiden's known for being a hard-ass who starts class on time and doesn't take kindly to late arrivals. The minute hand ticks closer to the hour. Nervousness is a weight wrapped around my body, compressing my muscles, tightening my throat. It's dread, not just nervousness. What is Willa thinking, after what happened? What if things are going to be stilted and uncomfortable now?

My eyes scan the back of the room. Maybe she's sitting there. I could see her making a point of creating distance. As I squint, craning my neck, I hear a voice from my right.

"Looking for someone, Lumberjack?"

I startle, once again smacking my knee against the desk, this time truly nailing my patella. On a groan, I drop my head to the wood surface. Willa's hand lands warm on my back, two gentle pats. My phone buzzes, and I unlock it to read her message. *You've got reflexes like a coked-out monkey.*

I sit up slowly, turning toward her as I type back, *Where do you even come up with that?*

She glances down at her screen, then up to me, and shrugs. "Who knows."

Our gazes hold, and I steal a chance to examine them for whatever insight they can give me. I see the pinch at the corner of her chocolate-brown eyes. I catch the faint smudge of purple under her lower lashes. She looks tired. Worried.

I start to type, but Willa texts first, *The hike was...weird.*

I nod, warring with words begging to be said. *Good weird? Bad weird? Never-again weird? I-want-to-jump-your-bones-and-do-it-forever weird?*

Willa offers her hand, as if we're meeting for the first time. "Frenemies still?"

I stare at her, trying to process what she said. *Frenemies?* I mouth.

She nods, hand unmoving. "As we were. Nothing changed."

My stomach drops. I don't know why, but it doesn't sit right. *Nothing changed?* Bullshit. It's different between us, and Willa wants to pretend it's not. Worse, maybe she's not pretending. Maybe, to her, that difference is nonexistent. Well then, I'll just have to show her.

I wrap my hand around hers and watch her breath hitch, her spine straighten. My heart pounds a violent tattoo against my ribs. My thumb skates along the satin skin of her wrist, over her pulse which trips beneath my touch. Dad's words weave through my mind.

Being around her made me wake up and sit straighter. Simply existing in her sphere made my blood run hot, my heart beat hard.

Willa's ramrod straight, her pupils blown wide. Her pulse flies beneath my thumb. There it is. Confirmation.

Nothing changed, my ass.

Willa pulls away first.

I need time to figure out how the hell we're going to talk about this because we are damn well going to talk about it. For now, I need to know. I need to know about today and tomorrow and if she's okay. I have to see if she'll open up and let me in, even just a sliver of truth about what's going on in her life. I've been worried about her since I heard her in the hospital. I can't imagine what it's like, what she's feeling and going through. Her mom is sick. Really sick.

I clear my throat, unlocking my phone, and writing, *Plans for Thanksgiving?*

Her face tightens in profile before she schools her expression and texts, *No. Just spending some downtime with my mom.*

Where do you guys live? I ask.

Willa drums her fingers on the desk and bites her lip. *LA*, she writes.

LA's a pretty big place, Sunshine. Where?

Slowly, her eyes slip up to mine. She clears her throat and swallows thickly, then types. *Just a few minutes from campus, if you can believe it.*

My jaw ticks. Damn hypocritical firecracker of a woman. Busting my balls for not spilling my guts and entire life history, when she can't even tell me her mother's seriously ill.

Willa just shook my hand, reclaiming our twisted, back-handed frenemyship, and lied by omission. It rankles me. I want her to trust me, to confide in me that instead of turkey and stuffing over a home gathering, she's going to eat shitty Salisbury steak and Jell-O with her mom. That, rather than hang out on the couch and moan about full bellies, they'll watch the Turkey Bowl from a narrow hospital bed until Willa's mom falls asleep.

I know how this goes because my dad's mom was sick with cancer in the last few years of her life. I spent a lot of time with her since I was still too young for school when Dad set her up at home and took care of her. I snuggled on Nana's lap, read her my favorite board books, and listened to her tell me about my dad when he was little. Every lunch, Nana would sigh with delight that she wasn't eating that hospital garbage anymore but instead Elin's delicious meals.

I'm about to do something, even if I don't know exactly what, to shake Willa out of this double-standard, infuriating mindset of hers. But before I can, Aiden's presence—not for the first time—messes things up and interrupts me.

Slamming his briefcase on the desk, Aiden clips on his microphone, turns to the class, and smiles, a sinister glint shining through his nerd glasses. "Pop quiz!"

15

WILLA

Playlist: "Fall," Lisa Hannigan

I DIDN'T LIE TO RYDER, BUT I DIDN'T EXACTLY TELL HIM THE truth either. It's just that talking about your sick-with-cancer mom is about as uncomfortable a conversation topic as I can think of, and as I've admitted, squidgy dialogues aren't my speed. So, I told him generally where we "live" for the time being and that I'd be spending Turkey Day with my mom. It wasn't a lie. The goddamn oncology wing at RRMC is, indeed, not far from campus. On Thanksgiving, I'll be snuggling up to Joy Sutter's bony ass, trying not to dwell on thoughts like whether this is the last one and just how thankful I am that I still have a mom to hug.

Given our unfinished soccer conversation and how little I understand about Ryder's secret relationship with the sport, I wasn't about to spill my guts about my own secrets when it comes to soccer. I didn't mention that I'd also be practicing plenty and mentally preparing myself for arguably the most important game of my career thus far, the NCAA Quarterfinals. I didn't tell him I was sick-to-my-stomach nervous, that I feel like I'm carrying not only my own success and future on my shoulders, but everyone else's on my team. I didn't tell him that I'm petrified every time I leave for an away game that I'll come back motherless. I didn't tell him that my fear is a tsunami building in its power, and I'm not sure I'll stay intact when it finally crashes into my heart.

I didn't tell him any of that. But I wanted to.

"Sutter!" Coach jogs over and drops her voice, giving me *the look*. The *what-the-hell's-gotten-into-you* look. "Talk to me."

I meet her eyes and swallow the lump in my throat, rolling my shoulders back and plastering what I hope is a determined smile on my face. "I'm sorry, Coach. Won't happen again."

She scowls. "My door's open, Sutter, and frankly I can't afford to have you not take advantage of that if it's going to compromise your play—"

"It won't." I step closer, hands up. It's a plea, a reassurance. "I promise, I'm fine."

Rooney's a few yards off, arms folded across her chest. When we meet eyes, she lifts two fingers, pointing them from her face to mine. *I'm watching you.*

Yeah, I've been avoiding Rooney, because she's my ride or die, and when shit's hard, she makes me face and feel it, which I just don't want to. The rest of the team, I like plenty. We have fun, but I'm not close with any of them, not a mile-wide, inch-deep friend. Rooney's basically my person, and I know when I dump all this stuff on her, it's going to be extensive and ugly.

Coach claps my back, snapping me out of my thoughts.

"Come on, then!" Her voice rings in the practice field. "Another half hour of keep-away, then we're done here. Tomorrow's the big day. I want everyone well slept, focused, and energized, got it?"

A resounding chorus of *Yes, Coach* echoes across the

grass. Even though it's deep into fall, it's swampy in Florida. Sweat drips down my face, and I'm dying for a cool shower and a long night of sleep.

Another half an hour of tiny spaces jammed with players, forcing my immediate first touch, my constant awareness of the shifting landscape between the ball, my team, and my opponent as I pass and shoot, then we're finally done. Drenched in sweat, wiped out, we walk off the field, guzzling Gatorade and stumbling onto the bus that will take us back to the hotel.

I sigh as air conditioning greets us on the bus. Seated, I press my forehead to the cool window glass and let my eyes slip shut. Rooney drops into the seat next to me. Her gentle nudge draws me back from thoughts of dozing off.

Her hazel eyes are tight with worry as she wraps her arm around my shoulders, then pulls me to her. I don't say a word, because, with Rooney, I don't always have to. I just let my mind empty and wander, lulled by the hum of a bus on the highway.

Once we're back at the hotel, I call Mama. She picks up after the second ring.

"Willa Rose, long time no talk."

I might have gotten my temper from my grandmother, but I got my sass from my mom. "Dang, Mama. Just wanted to check in."

There's a wet cough in the background, the rustling of fabric indicating she tried her best to muffle it. "I'm okay, Willa. You need to relax, honey. I'm not going anywhere just yet."

Just yet. Tears fill my eyes. When I blink, they wet my lashes and spill down my cheeks. "It's hard playing on the holidays. I just want to be home with you. I want our Chinese takeout and crappy nineties sitcom marathon."

"I know." Mama sighs. "But the fact is, life is full of change. You like the *idea* of doing that, but, Willa, the last few years we did, we were both bored halfway through *Clueless* and ended up playing Words with Friends, which I won, by the way."

"The hell you did."

Mama laughs, and it doesn't end in a horrible cough. It makes me smile.

"Willa, on your first day of preschool, you white-knuckled my shirt and screamed when it was time for me to go, even though countless times before that, I left you with Grandma Rose or with your sitters."

"I remember," I whisper.

"At first, I couldn't figure it out. You were always happy for a new sitter friend to come and play at our house, always glad for Grandma Rose to watch you while I was gone, but this...this was different. Because my leaving meant you had to join that classroom. You had to meet the unfamiliar and try new things. It wasn't so much *me leaving* as *you going* that bothered you. It was what you had to do after goodbye that wigged you out, Willa. It's always wigged you out. You know why that is?"

I wipe my nose, blinking up at the ceiling. "No."

"Because then you have to face the scary unknown and want something from it. You have to live with arms wide open to new things. You have to risk trying and failing. You have to release the baggage from your past, so you have room to welcome your future."

Unease bolts through my veins. It makes me shiver. "I already want something from my future, Mama. I want to play professionally and be on the Women's National Team. I want to win the World Cup and be on the Olympic Team. I want to see the world and learn about it. But...I just don't want to have to let go of what I know or leave behind anyone that I love."

Mama coughs. "You have to. And when the time comes, you will. You'll pick yourself up, and you'll move on and live that beautiful life."

We're talking about it without talking about it. I hate it when we do this. Even though the words aren't being said, it still feels like knives spearing every gap in my ribs. It feels like my throat is scorched and my heart is dissolving in my chest. A world without my mom isn't a world I want to be in. I hate when she makes me think about it. I hate what I know she's about to say to me.

"Promise me, Willa Rose."

I nod as a tear slips down my cheek. "I promise."

———

"You snored again." Rooney stomps around the hotel room topless. She's a shameless nudie who would literally walk the world naked if it wouldn't get her arrested. The woman hates clothes like I hate real talk. It scarred me freshman year, but I've since desensitized and learned not to notice.

I yawn, trying to make my eyes focus as I check the time. "And? This is significant how? I always snore."

"*And* I forgot my earplugs."

I frown, both because there's a message on my phone I didn't expect and because Rooney under-slept is not what we need at today's game. As Coach said, she needs us well-rested and ready to go.

"I'm sorry, Roo."

She waves her hand, unearthing a sports bra from her bag and finally putting me out of my misery. As I said, I'm used to the nudity, but it's not my favorite pastime, talking to my best friend while her mosquito-bite tits accurately indicate exactly how low we turned the air conditioning last night.

"It's fine," she says. "I'll be fine. I just need coffee, and I don't give a *fuck* what Coach has to say about that."

"You do you, Roo. I support your caffeination, so long as you adequately hydrate."

"Thank you." Rooney drops to the bed, then flops on her back. "God, I'm an asshole friend. Here I am complaining about snoring and needing coffee when you're the one with actual shit going on in your life. You didn't invite me to the hospital yesterday, and I know that's because you're worried it's your last—"

"You want hotel coffee, or should I order Starbucks?" I interrupt.

This is what Rooney's infamous for. Talking heavy stuff like that's normal, like hard feelings are felt, not repressed and subsequently managed in periodic outbursts of sobbing profanity, fifteen-mile runs, and whiskey benders.

Rooney sighs. "This hotel crap's fine, thank you. Willa, talk to me. Get it out."

I crack open a bottle of water and pour half its contents into the tiny hotel room coffee pot. Next, I place a coffee pod in the little percolator dish and slide it shut. "I just don't have a good feeling, Roo." I clear my throat and swallow a lump of emotion. "She's been low energy. She's not perking up how she did when she went into remission last time. She's still sick."

Rooney sits up, as her eyes meet mine. "What does that mean? What do you do if you keep being sick with cancer?"

"You die." I wipe my nose. "Generally how it goes." On a long, steadying sigh, I find that ironclad box in my psyche that I still have the key to, thankfully. I shove my worries about Mama, my anticipatory grief, my anxiety, all of it, into that cold, unreachable place. Slamming the door shut, I twist the key and bury it deep. "Okay, I don't want to talk about it anymore right now. Today, I will score at least three goals."

Rooney stands, knowing the drill. "Hell yeah."

"Today, I will elevate my team's play and be a leader on the field."

"That's right!"

I lock eyes with my reflection. "Today, we win."

Rooney stands behind me and sets her hands on my shoulders. "You got this. We all do. Unless you don't move out of my way and let me have my shitty cup of coffee, Granger."

I give her a look. "Calling me Hermione Granger is not an insult."

Rooney tugs my hair affectionately. "I know. I wasn't trying to insult you. I was trying to make you smile. Besides —" She grins as she swipes up her cup of coffee and backs away. "Making you angry isn't my job anymore. Someone else stole that real estate."

A scowl tugs at my mouth. "It's not like that with us."

She snorts a laugh, then takes a tentative sip of her coffee. "Sure, sweetie. Keep telling yourself that."

My phone lights up again, reminding me of a message I got just a few minutes ago from the person Rooney was alluding to.

Ryder.

> *Sunshine's in the Sunshine State.*
> *Good luck today, Willa.*
> *You've got this.*

That was his first message, and it was nice. I traipse over

to my phone and scowl at the new one. I knew he couldn't stand to leave it on a friendly note.

First, there's a screenshot of a Google image. A very unflattering photo of me clotheslining a defender to get around her. My face looks like I'm in the throes of both an epic shit and a foot-cramping orgasm. It is the least flattering photo of me that I've ever seen.

> *Try not to blind too many people*
> *with your radiance on the field today.*

Growling, I unlock my phone and type.

Well good morning to you too, Bigfoot.
Try not to get too many Thanksgiving
tidbits stuck in that dead squirrel
wrapped around your mouth.

> *You like the beard. Admit it.*

I really, really don't.

> *It's distinguished.*

It's disgusting.

> *I'm hurt.*

You'd have to have a heart
to hurt, Brawny.

> *You know Brawny isn't an insult, right?*
> *You're telling me I'm bearded hotness.*

That I look buff AF, about to burst out
of my manly flannel.

I'm going to focus now on annihilating
some women on a soccer field.
Then I'm coming home and
shaving that monstrosity off your face.

Lay a hand to my facial hair, woman,
and I swear you won't be able to sit for days.

My eyes widen, my eyebrows shoot up, and I drop my phone. There's a drumbeat between my legs. My nipples are taut peaks spearing my tank top.

Rooney smirks over her coffee. "Talking to Ryder?"

"Hm?" Finally, I glance her way, folding my arms across my throbbing breasts. "What? No. Yes. I'm fine. I'm going to take a shower."

She's still laughing when I step under the icy water.

16

RYDER

Playlist: "A closeness," Dermot Kennedy

NOW I REMEMBER WHY I HATE THE HOLIDAYS. PURE, unadulterated chaos.

My family tries really hard, to text, to tap my shoulder, not to sneak up on me, but it's still challenging, with so many people in one space full of sounds that stab my ears—shrieks of laughter, scraping chairs, the TV blaring when it's unmuted. That's when hearing aids are out, even though I know I'm supposed to wear them consistently, and I'm caught off guard by impending bodies and movement.

Yesterday wasn't terrible. The meal was fairly subdued and then we went for a long hike, which, though peaceful and restorative to my sanity after all that noise, just made me miss our old home even more.

But today, we're all in the living room, on the astonishingly large couch that my mother had to custom order from some factory for families that have too many kids. It seats twenty people, easily. Which is good, seeing as five of my six siblings, my brother-in-law, my dad's two brothers, their wives, and *their* kids are in the living room, gearing up to watch Willa's game.

I mean, they don't think of it like that. To them, it's only UCLA's women's team in the quarterfinals. We're a huge soccer family, and while not everyone here went to UCLA, it's not hard to get behind the women's team doing our state proud.

I sit on the end of the sofa closest to the mammoth flat-screen TV mounted over the fireplace, my back pointedly to everyone else. My body language says what my voice doesn't: *don't talk to me, don't touch me, let me watch the game.*

Ren's traveling for a series of games—he plays later tonight, actually—but it's like he knows I just want to be left alone right now, meaning, of course, it's time for him to bug me.

My phone buzzes with his text. *Your lady looks ready to kick ass.*

She's not my lady, I type back.

That's her, though, isn't it? The one with the braid? The forward who scores all the goals? Hm. Sort of sounds like me. Impressive forward. Goal-scoring machine. If she's nothing to you, maybe I should ask her out.

I type back, *She's not nothing to me. She's MY friend, and she's off-limits.*

I can see his damn annoying smirk. He's lying down, getting massaged and iced and taped before his game, grinning that fucking know-it-all grin. *We're too old to stake claims like that. Date her or she's fair game.*

I come damn close to crushing my phone in my hand, but I settle for pocketing it and ignoring Ren's needling. Besides Willa, he knows best how to get under my skin.

Willa and her team disperse from their huddle, and I watch her compact body cross the field to the center circle. I can feel her nerves from here, or maybe I just simply remember what it's like. How your stomach tightens, the faint buzz in your limbs as you shake them out and adrenaline jolts your body to attention. The ringing in your ears, the blinding lights of the stadium.

The whistle blows, and Willa spins, efficiently passing deep to her defender. Then, she takes off down the field and finds her place at the top.

My senses tunnel-focus, as I track Willa throughout the first half. Florida State's all over her, but that doesn't mean much to Willa. Even with two people on her, her body finds that sliver of space between four defenders' feet and threads the needle. Inside touch, scissor step—a trick that as a defender, I always tried to anticipate, often apprehended, and other times got beat by. Her Maradona is lightning fast, a quick foot on the ball transferring to the other as she pivots, rolling it with her and taking advantage of her opponent's momentum.

Willa's the star, but she brings her teammates into her stratosphere. Their one-touches are flawless, the ball zipping from player to player, long balls sent to space that's fluidly filled by their offense. They're good, and Willa's excellent.

My phone buzzes. *Damn, son. Truly, if you don't go after that, I will.*

I pull up my phone's camera, glare into the screen and flip the middle finger. As soon as I hit send to Ren, a picture comes in from him. He's cross-eyed with his tongue stuck out.

Ren's full of shit. He's not chasing Willa. He can barely ask out a woman he's super comfortable with, let alone a virtual stranger. Ren's the king of sticking his foot in his mouth and unrequited love. Which is hilarious, because everywhere he goes, women trip over him. He's just clueless about what to do. I'd offer to help him with his game, but—

case in point—he pisses me off too much for me to be that nice.

You've been warned. Claim her, or she's fair game, he texts. *And remember, I am the better-looking one so...*

Before I can threaten violence to my brother, a gentle hand on my shoulder startles me and makes me glance up. My eyes drop to Mom's mouth.

"Is this seat taken?" she asks.

I stare down at the sliver of cushion that my wide-leg stance and broad body have left. Scooching over, I pat the sofa.

Mom smiles at me as she sits and sets a hand on my back. She lifts her phone. "Text or talk?"

I tug my hair back so she can see my hearing aid, then set my hand on her phone and lower it to her lap. Her smile softens as she smooths my hair and says, "I miss you, Ryder. You don't come home like you did last year."

I swipe open my phone and write, *I miss you, too. This semester was unexpectedly busy.* I jerk my head toward Aiden, who's doing some stealth groping of Freya that makes me almost throw up in my mouth. *Your favorite son-in-law has made my life hell.*

Mom laughs quietly, patting my back once again, then taking my hand in hers. "Is that really everything?"

I glance from the TV to Mom, because I'm trying not to miss a moment of the game, but I also don't want to be rude to my mother. I shrug and mouth, *Yeah.*

Mom's eyes drift toward the TV and watch with me for a minute, before she taps my arm so I'll give her my attention. But when she speaks, conversation around us has become too loud for me to hear her well enough to understand. I shake my head and point to her phone.

She picks it up and types, *She's very good, that one at the top. Very...feisty.*

Right when I glance back, the camera zooms in, catching Willa battling for possession near the box. Willa jukes, then spins, hopping over a defender. One final touch before she nails it into the far corner and scores. We all stand up, whistling and clapping.

Willa throws her hands back, chest out, glorying in the moment as her teammates jump her, then quickly disperse, four of them bending over halfway, locking arms, to form a flat surface. Rooney holds a hand over her ear and with the other mimes DJing at a turntable. Willa drops and pulls a few swirls of her hips that immediately tighten things beneath my zipper. Then she kneels, leans on her shoulder, and pulls a breakdance move.

Everyone in the living room cracks up except for Mom. Swedes *detest* hotdogging, any form of arrogance or pride, really. She cocks her head like she's trying to understand what could possibly motivate a human to behave how Willa is.

Interesting choice of celebration, Mom texts.

My laugh is breathy, straight through my nose. Taking my hand, Mom leverages herself to stand and cups my cheek, then writes, *Well, you might not be home as much, but you certainly are smiling more. Whatever's keeping you happier is a good thing in my eyes.* Her focus swivels to the TV, then back to me.

That immediately raises my suspicion. It's almost like Mom knows that I'm connected to Willa. As Mom walks off, I search the room for Aiden. He's the only one who's invested in me and Willa. If he's blabbing to Mom about her, over-stating the nature of our relationship, I might finally have to beat the shit out of him. It'll have been a long time coming.

Our eyes meet. His widen. They dance over to Mom who still has a coy smile on her face as she leaves the room, then they find mine once again. Slowly, Aiden disentangles himself from Freya on the couch and starts backing away.

I glance at the TV. The final seconds dwindle to halftime, so I won't miss a thing. Perfect time to pummel him. Aiden seems to realize this and sprints out of the room. I give him a second before I'm hurdling the couch, chasing after him. But it doesn't make a difference. The pain in my ass is finally going to pay.

————

How about this—if we win the championship, I get to shave your beard.

Willa pokes my arm. Since the hike, I have to make myself count to three before acknowledging her. It takes mental preparation to look at her without betraying that complex knot of feelings that tightens my chest. It also has the added benefit of pissing her off.

"I know you saw that text, Lumberjack."

Finally, I turn her way. Tipping my head, I feign thinking about it and then mouth, *No.*

"Come *onnnn*," she whines.

Aiden gives her a look. He sprung another pop quiz on the class. We both finished already, but not everyone's done.

I unlock my phone and type, *You do realize telling me that it would please you to see me beardless is all the incentive I need to grow this thing indefinitely, right?*

Willa rolls her eyes and types back, *Nothing about looking at you pleases me. I just want to stop having nightmares about Sasquatch and deranged blond-haired Vikings.*

Been dreaming about me, have you?

Willa's cheeks pink as she reads it. Clearing her throat, she straightens in her seat and types, *Yeah. They're my anti-spank-bank material. When I see a man so hot, I just want to jump him, I think of that gnarly animal tail on your face, and my libido shrivels up, just like that.*

I narrow my eyes at her, then type, *Who are these hot men you're borderline jumping?*

She smirks, idly twirls a curl of hair around her finger, and doesn't answer.

Willa.

Completely ignoring me, she writes, *We need to peer review our individual reports on our happy couple hike before we turn them in to Mac. I don't have a ton of time to go back and forth, so can we just meet at your place and go over them at the same time?*

I pinch the bridge of my nose, then type, *Fine. Tonight, or I can't until the weekend, which is your game, so…tonight.*

Perfect. Fair warning, Coach promised to make us wish we're dead at practice today, so I'll be cranky and ravenous. I'd like to submit a formal request for the Sulking Swede's famous meatballs.

I'm not sulking, I type. *You're just not answering my question.*

Aiden collects quizzes and starts discussing the reading assignment I already did. Willa pretends deep concentration in what he's saying before finally turning back toward me when Aiden finishes. Holding my eyes, she sweeps her books into her bag and zips it up. When she stands, I see her whole outfit for the first time and swallow thickly.

Dark jeans hug her muscular legs, sitting low on her hips. A sliver of tan skin peeks out beneath a tight tank top with tiny flowers in all the colors that make me think of Willa—gold, russet, crimson, caramel. Her cardigan's creamy white and slips off her toned shoulder. She's pulling that sexual teasing shit again. I scowl because it worked. I'm going to have to sit at this desk for a few minutes once she leaves to cool things down.

Smiling, she hikes her bag higher on her shoulder. "Bye, Mountain Man. Gotta run."

I stare after her and have to bite my cheek not to groan because Willa's got an ass and it is in its element in those jeans. Turning back to my desk, I scrub my face.

After a very important minute in which I visualize the most revolting thing I can think of—and with six prank-inclined and vindictive siblings, I have plenty of material—I stand without embarrassing myself, then leave.

I can't tell you why I cross the quad when I otherwise typically go straight home and eat lunch after this. I can't tell you why I wander toward the campus café that offers smoothies and decent coffee and fresh salads, the spot where I know Willa eats her lunch on this day because then she has Feminist Literature soon after and there's no time for her to go home and cook, and she hates soggy sandwiches—all packed lunch ingredients, actually—with the passion of a thousand blazing suns...

Not that I remember her telling me all that.

I can't tell you why I drop into the line when I see Willa four people ahead of me, biting those tempting full lips as she reads the menu.

Well, I can. But if I did, first I'd have to own the truth of what I'm up against. That since the hike, keeping Willa in the frenemy zone is harder than before. That my feelings for her have grown big and scary and serious. That my heart now does a twisty, unnerving summersault every time I look at Willa.

I'm looking at her now. Staring, honestly. Daydreaming

about running my fingers through her wild hair, a tangle of waves and tendrils, swirling chocolate brown and caramel streaks and raspberry ribbons, that catch the high-noon sun. Watching a tall, dark-haired, blue-eyed guy who's not butt-ugly walk up to her and wrap an arm around her shoulders.

My heart drops to my stomach. It's beyond stupid of me to have assumed that Willa wasn't interested in anyone. But all I've seen is that she never gives any guys who eye her up a second look. She's not boy crazy, she's never out on dates, and given her many anti-male diatribes that she weaves in our evenings together working on the final, I assumed Willa more or less truly hated men, except for me, basically, and maybe Tucker and Becks, who seem to have grown on her during our project nights at my place.

This guy seems to be the exception. He grins down at her and gives her hair a noogie. Asshole.

I can't tell you why I do it. Why I watch them when my heart corrodes in the acid of my jealousy. But I can't look away.

17

WILLA

Playlist: "Hot Knife," Fiona Apple

"WILLA SUTTER. LOOK AT YOU."

If his irritating voice weren't unforgettable, I'd have recognized him by his asshole move—giving me a noogie. Stepping out of his arm's grip around my shoulder, I peer up at Luke Masters, a creep of a jock I stupidly slept with last year. He's on the basketball team. We have a few events per year that bring the women's and men's athletics programs together, and since our hookup, in which he ditched before I even woke up and left the condom on the floor, I tolerated seeing him at those events and nothing more.

Until this past summer, when he and Rooney slept together. Rooney had no clue about our history since I'm me and I never told her Luke and I hooked up in the first place. It's weird but that's not even the worst part. After he pulled the same stunt on Rooney, he told everyone what—in his words—*a freak between the sheets* she is. Now, instead of tolerating him I downright hate his guts.

"Luke, the Duke of Douchery." I reach up and pinch his nipple, making him yelp and step back. "What brings you here, polluting the atmosphere with your existence?"

He rubs his nipple and looks me over. "Just saying hi to my favorite fellow star."

"Ah." Luke is...vain. He likes to be seen with the right people, to maintain a reputation of having the best connections, rubbing shoulders with people who he thinks make him look good.

I had an incredible game in the semifinals. A hat trick and a mind-blowing assist to Rooney. I was on fire. I've been in the news, and I gave an interview that's made the rounds. I've had nice publicity through the playoffs, and this last game took it to the next level. Like many men before him, Luke's here to ride the wave of a woman's blood, sweat, and tears, hoping he can coast on her momentum.

"How'd your last game go?" I ask, stepping forward as the person in front of me steps up, too, and places her order. "Ohhh, wait, that's right. You lost. Again."

Luke's face sours. "Damn, Willa. Have you always been this much of a bitch?"

There's a shuffling sound a few people behind me, but I don't look back to see what caused it. I've got a dick to emasculate. "Ever since you told everyone who'd listen about my friend and her sexuality, yes, Luke. Now—"

A warm body presses into my back, as the scent of a pine forest wraps around me. I turn back and have to glance up considerably to see Ryder. His jaw is tense, his eyes locked on Luke.

Luke glances from Ryder to me. "Who's this guy?"

I've never been in this situation with Ryder, in which people don't know how he communicates. I don't want to speak for him, but he clearly won't speak, either. The two are locked in a stare-down.

"This is Ryder Bergman, Luke. He doesn't hear well, and he doesn't speak but he lip-reads like a beast. I'm guessing he saw you call me a *bitch* and decided that if you say that again, your face is going to meet his lumberjack fist."

Ryder's mouth twitches like he's fighting a smile. He's wearing my favorite flannel, the blue-and-green one that makes his eyes pop. I *had* to throw in the lumberjack part.

Luke's eyes finally travel Ryder critically. "Deaf and mute. Sounds like the only kind of person who'd be your friend, Willa. He can't hear all the stupid shit you say, and he can't tell you what a *bitch* you are for saying it."

Ryder starts to launch past me, but I manage to step in his way, spinning and facing him. "Look at me, Ryder."

Ryder's jaw ticks, anger darkening his eyes.

"Ryder Bergman. Look. At. Me."

Finally, he lowers his eyes. His chest still heaves, his entire body poised to spring and beat the shit out of Luke. And it would be a shit beating. Luke's muscular but lanky compared to the lumberjack. He has nothing on Ryder's build.

Our eyes meet until his gaze dips to my mouth. I slowly interlace my hand with his. "Don't waste yourself on someone like that, okay? Especially not for me."

My back pointedly toward Luke, I squeeze Ryder's hand. His eyes dance between mine. His calloused, rough grip squeezes back, too.

I smile as relief loosens my tense shoulders. "Come on, Brawny. Lunch is on me."

———

I NEVER KNEW I HAD A SANDWICH KINK, BUT IT SEEMS I DO. Ryder eats a big-ass Italian submarine sandwich, sleeves rolled up his forearms, as the December sun beams down on him. It is straight-up pornographic. I can see every tendon and muscle flexing under that fine dusting of blond hair on his arms. His fingers are elegantly long but rough at the knuckles, and he's missing a bit from the pad of his left index finger. How did I never notice that? Even after our questionnaire at the falls, how are there still *so* many things I don't know about Ryder Bergman?

Okay, pot, and what the hell does the kettle know about you?

Shit. Those are advanced metaphors, even for me. My wily subconscious is one hundred percent right. I keep stuff from Ryder big-time. Barring the extensive effort that I make both to burn and bust him, I treat him like every other guy I know. I hold him at a distance, keeping him far from anything to do with my heart. Well, for the most part. There was that little slipup on the waterfall ledge. I might have let him a little closer then.

I watch him lick mayonnaise off this thumb and feel myself smile. His lashes fan over his cheekbones and despite the beard's growing volume, he at least combs it now, revealing the faintest hint of his cheekbones. When he leans for his water, I catch a glimpse down his flannel shirt, undone a sexy two buttons. I can see the shadow of his pecs, a faint glistening of hair. My mind wanders, imagining if I unbuttoned his shirt, shoved it off his shoulders, then pushed Ryder until he lay on his back. I'd straddle his waist and run my hands down the warm, taut skin of his stomach.

A cyclist whizzes by and startles me out of my filthy fantasy. My fists are clenched, my nipples scraping against the thin material of my bra. I'm painfully aware of every inch of Ryder's body, of how much I think about sex when I'm with him. It's probably just all this pent-up aggravation, like static energy that's snapped and sparked between us so long, it needs *somewhere* to go, *something* to ground it. We've tacitly agreed not to murder each other, so what other cathartic activity does that leave? What can exorcise this hellish energy pulsing between us?

Sex is the only answer.

If he knows I'm watching him, Ryder doesn't say anything. He's been quiet, even for him, since we ordered our food and sat down outside. He put a hand low on my back when we walked out and held the door for me. Before the door shut behind us, he gave Luke a death glare that made my knees wobble a little.

Setting down his sandwich, Ryder dusts off his hands and picks up his phone. Mine dings seconds later.

Who was that douche?

I unlock my phone and type, *An old unfortunate conquest.*

Ryder's hand tightens around his phone as he reads my message. His jaw clenches. He swallows like he's tasted something unpalatable, and warmth fizzes inside me. Is Ryder jealous?

Interesting.

I swipe open my phone again and type, *I have lots of those.*

Ryder reads the text. His knuckles turn white as he glances up at me and holds my eyes for a long minute. When he peers back down at his phone and types, my stomach knots with anticipation.

You're a terrible liar, Sunshine.

I bite my lip, trying to hide my smile. *Okay, so I haven't had that many, but the ones I did were unfortunate.*

Why unfortunate? he types.

I answer Ryder reflexively. *Because they were uneventful, if you catch my drift.*

My ears burn. A blush heats my cheeks. Why the hell did I just tell him that?

His body stills as he reads. Ryder's empty hand drums all five fingers along his thigh as he texts back. *Then they were imbeciles. Imbeciles who have no idea what they missed out on.*

An inexplicable wad of emotion catches in my throat. I clear it. Then for some idiotic reason, I type and send, *Apparently, I'm hard to please.*

Jesus Christ. Apparently, I'm also devoid of a filter. My blush darkens tenfold.

Ryder's brow furrows. A scowl tightens his face. *Bullshit.*

An indecorous snort slips out as I reply. *Nope. It's the party line of your gender when it comes to sexy times with Willa Sutter.*

Ryder shakes his head, his thumbs flying. *Guys say shit like that when they don't know the first fucking thing about pleasing a woman. All it takes is a little time and a willingness to learn. Believe me, Willa, it has nothing to do with you.*

I sniffle as I read his message. My grinch heart grows twice as large. But my evil grinch grin makes an appearance, too. If my hair could curl up in wicked delight like that Christmas-wrecking monster, it would. *I think I need proof,* I write. *I'm a skeptic at heart.*

Ryder's head snaps up, his eyes narrowing at me. Dropping his gaze, he sends a brief text. *Is this your ass-backward way of seducing me, Sunshine?*

Arrogant mountain man. I want to say yes, but now he just made me look like a sex-starved hussy, begging him to whip out that lumberjack wood and logjam me into next week.

That's because you are a sex-starved hussy, begging him

to whip out that lumberjack wood and logjam you into next week.

"Shut it, choo-cha." It's most certainly my choo-cha talking. She feels empty and tortured every time she's around Ryder. I will not be steered by my personified vagina.

I swipe open my phone. *Please*, I type. *I've heard lumberjacks are notoriously clumsy when they're out of the woods and in the bush.*

Ryder reads my message and rolls his eyes. He has the audacity to shove the rest of his sandwich in his mouth and chew, like some hypersexual hungry woodsman. My thighs rub instinctively. The wind picks up, and my already tight nipples pinch, poking into my shirt. Undeterred by layers of bra and tank top, they make themselves glaringly obvious. Ryder looks up from his sandwich and gives me a calculating once-over. His gaze snags on my chest, but he recovers quickly. Reaching into his crossbody bag, he pulls out a UCLA hoodie and tosses it at me.

Greedily, I tug it over my head and huff the delicious evergreen scent. I can feel the frizz his hoodie causes in my hair and do not give a shit.

Thank you, I sign.

He nods, his eyes locked on mine. His stare lasts longer than normal.

"Everything okay?" I ask.

He finally blinks, then sweeps up his phone and types in his rapid-fire way. *I'm wondering if after you wear that hoodie, I'm going to be cursed with hair as frizzy as yours.*

I lean across our food and punch his arm. When I sit back, I make a point of jamming my fingers into my crazy hair and only making it crazier.

Ryder's face breaks into one of those rare, wide grins, and my heart skips a beat. He lifts his hand to the air in front of his face, swirls his fingers until they're pinched together, then opens them as if releasing a burst of magic. It's sign for something that I don't know.

A shiver rolls up my spine, but it's not because of the breeze swirling across the grass, making leaves dance between us. Wind whispers through my hair and plasters Ryder's shirt to his body. Time suspends.

"What's that one mean?" I ask.

Balling up the empty paper from his sandwich and tidying our mess, Ryder slides his bag up his shoulder and stands. His fingers ruffle my hair as he smiles down at me. Then he walks off, leaving me in a haze of unanswered questions and cedar-scented air.

Damn mind-fucker of a lumberjack.

———

"BECKETT BECKERSON, GET YOUR RANK-ASS HANDS OUT OF the taco meat!" Tucker smacks Becks's fingers away, then shoves him, nearly sending Becks crashing into me as I close the front door.

"Sorry, Willa," Becks mumbles, straightening me out.

"Wilhelmina!" Tucker shouts.

I flick him off. "I requested Swedish meatballs."

Tucker shrugs. "Ryder didn't get home until fifteen minutes ago. He asked me to do him a solid and get taco meat cooking."

Huh. That's weird. I hate to admit it, but there's no point in denying I have Ryder's schedule memorized. He should have been home hours ago.

Becks goes to the fridge, pulling out taco fixings. "You like tacos, right?" he asks from inside the fridge.

I drop my bag on the table and wave my hand, already

making my way toward Ryder's room. "I love them. Thanks, guys."

"Cool." Tuck nods, jamming to some music he has playing quietly from his phone.

Knocking twice on Ryder's door, I let myself in. He's on his laptop, squinting at something with headphones on. He looks so intensely focused, I'm wildly curious to know what he's watching.

When I step closer, he does a double take, eyes widening as he rips off the headphones, slams his laptop shut, and practically sits on it.

Tipping my head to the side, I fold my arms over my chest. "Okay, Brawny?"

He nods and swallows loudly. Pushing off the desk, he grasps my elbow and steers me out of his room into the main living area and signs, *How are you? What's up?*

I've noticed him using a little more sign in the past few weeks. We still talk our texting way plenty, but it seems like sometimes he just wants to look at me and have some conversation that way, too.

"I kicked my Feminist Literature final paper's booty, that's what's up." He releases my elbow now that we're safely away from whatever's on that laptop that he doesn't want me to see.

He smiles, and signs, *Good!*

Becks is organizing tiny little bowls of all the toppings, Tucker warming up tortillas. I glance from the kitchen to Ryder. "Putting your minions to work, eh? What happened?"

Ryder's face slips slightly. *I'm sorry*, he signs. He hesitates, frustration pinching his face as he retrieves his phone from his back pocket and quickly types, *Forgot about a doctor's appointment. I cook them dinner nightly. They owe me. You love tacos though, right?*

Something melts a little inside me. He's right. I don't like tacos. I *love* them. They were, until his Swedish meatballs, my favorite food.

Yeah! I sign, then text him, *Everything okay at the doctor's?*

I try to ask it in a way that isn't invasive but shows I care, because I do. I can't pretend I'm not invested in Ryder's wellness. He gently tugs a curl of my hair, then steps past me, into the kitchen, typing as he goes. My phone dings.

Just some tests because science has yet to understand how I got so manly and shockingly lumberjacked. Nothing serious.

"Lumberjacked." I snort a laugh, derailed from my concern.

Dinner's served, and I enjoy the tacos as much as the volley of insults lobbed between Tucker and Becks and Ryder via catapulted food, texts in group chat, hands thrown in emphatic gesture.

I stare at Ryder, feeling weird, un-frenemy things. Which is so stupid. A pointless road to go down. I'm a frizzy-haired, foul-mouthed thorn in his side, not a woman he wants. I mean, we might have, half-asleep and half-drunkenly, dry-humped each other a little. We might have kissed because our brains misfired. We might have made out like goddamn prodigies under that waterfall until we broke apart and it felt all at once awkward and transformed and mysteriously the same.

Giant, dry-humored, snarky, insult aficionado asshole lumberjack has emerged as my type for down the line, but Ryder Bergman is nothing but my frenemy. Maybe a frenemy I could hate-bang if he were up for that kind of thing.

"Willa."

I jolt, and my mind is now back at the table. "Huh?"

"Want any more?" Becks holds the taco meat bowl out to me. I stare at it, feeling my appetite dwindle.

"No. No, thanks. I'm okay."

Ryder's eyes are on me. His hair is pulled back in a man bun so it doesn't get in all the taco goodness, but he has some salsa in the corner of his mouth. I white-knuckle my jeans as an impulse strikes me to push away from the table and straddle his lap. To kiss that salsa off Ryder's lips until our mouths burn for a very different reason besides habanero peppers.

His eyes darken as they hold mine and he slowly lowers his food.

"Here we go." Tucker drops his tortilla chips and wipes his hands on his jeans. "They're doing one of their stare-downs. Quick, get the timer."

Becks yanks out his phone, setting it. Ryder and I have, in the past, engaged in a few juvenile showdowns of unblinking stares. Becks and Tucker have historically placed bets both on duration and victor. But this is not one of those times. This is…something very different, even if I can't say just what.

His irises are pristine, glittering green. It's unfair. I stare into their depths, their shades of lush hillsides, soccer fields, dazzling emeralds. My eyes start to water from staying open for so long. Ryder's jaw tightens as his pupils dilate. A huff of air leaves him, and finally, he blinks.

"Woo!" Becks slaps the table, then sets his hand, palm up, for Tucker. Tucker grumbles and smacks a five-dollar bill into it.

I turn their way and lob a lime wedge at Becks's head. "I should inspire a higher bet than that, Beckerson. I'm insulted."

Ryder stands, collecting plates and stacking them. I help clear the table, then dry the plates Ryder washes in a daze, staring at the backsplash tiles. What is going on with my brain and body? And does Ryder feel the same way? Empty and full at the same time, like a balloon about to pop, a bubble that's grown too heavy. Something between us feels incomplete and unavoidable. *Something*'s coming. I just can't figure out what it is.

WILLA

Playlist: "Stay," Rihanna, Mikky Ekko

MY EARS RING. I STARE OUT AT THE FIELD, STUNNED. WE lost. We *lost*. People try to console me. Stupid platitudes and empty reassurances.

At least you're only a junior.

There's always next year.

Hell of an effort out there, Sutter.

You did everything you could.

Nothing makes it better. Nothing dulls the sharp pain of disappointment. We didn't just lose, we didn't play our game. Our defense fell apart. Poor Sam took so many shots on goal, I think she broke her personal record for saves in a single game.

Rooney and I were in sync, as always, but it felt like everyone else was passing ten yards behind me or right to my defender. Our only goal was a long shot I took. Rooney flew up the sideline, hit me with a gorgeous pass off the outside of her foot. I cut with it on my first touch and thanked God for my feet's relative ambidexterity because I cracked that shot with my left and watched it sail over the keeper's hands, rippling into the net.

And then I watched Stanford drop four goals over the remainder of the game. I saw Sam defending that gaping box like a woman facing a firing squad. And I was helpless. I was stuck at the top, useless except to try everything I could to put more past Stanford's keeper. I could barely get the ball, and when I did, they triple-teamed me. My teammates took shots, some on target, but none with enough power or finesse to sneak by their keeper.

That feeling of helplessness gnaws inside me. It does not diminish after Coach's consolation talk. Not as I pack up my gear and walk, head hanging to the bus. Not on the four-hour ride home. Not on the call with my mom the moment Rooney and I stumble inside.

"You did your best, Willa Rose. You should be so proud."

I sniffle as tears stream down my cheeks. "My best wasn't good enough."

"Your best is *always* good enough," Mama says. "Your best just doesn't always mean that things turn out how you want."

Wiping my cheeks, I exhale shakily. "I know. I just don't like that."

Mama's chuckle is hoarse yet familiar. "Well, at least you can admit it."

A beat of silence stretches over the phone. Something in the background beeps, and I hear the murmur of quiet voices.

"Can I come see you in the morning?"

"Willa, you never have to ask."

"Okay," I whisper. I bite my lip, stifling more tears, swallowing my words. Words that would tell her how much I wanted her there, whistling in the stands, her strong voice yelling and cheering, urging me on. How much I wish she were home at our apartment so I could crawl into her bed and feel her arms wrap around me, so I could smell her vanilla perfume and cry through all my disappointment.

But I can't. Because she wasn't well enough to leave, despite the fit she threw with Dr. B. Because we don't have a home anymore since cancer swallowed up my mother's hard-earned money.

"Willa?"

I jolt. "Sorry, Mama. I got lost in thought."

"Willa, take a hot shower, eat something nourishing, and go to sleep. Tomorrow's a new day, and soon you'll be practicing for next season, one step closer to your dreams. Your dreams are still right there, waiting for you to claim. Your team might have lost tonight, Willa, and you're allowed to be sad, but tonight you shone, my little star. You wowed them. Don't forget where you're headed, okay?"

A faint smile tugs at my mouth. "Thank you, Mama. See you in the morning. I love you."

"Good night, Willa Rose. I love you, too."

I hit the end button on my phone. Staring down at it, I watch tears splash on its surface.

A knock on the door jolts me. Who could that be? It's late. Like, really, *really* late. I shuffle over and peer through the peephole.

"Holy shit."

Yanking it open, I step back. Ryder stands in the cool night air, his ball cap pulled low, wearing the torturous blue-and-green plaid.

"Asshole had to wear my favorite flannel," I mutter, and then immediately scold myself for it.

Ryder tips his head and signs, *What?*

"Your flannel," I say clearly. "I like it."

He gives me a look that says he doesn't trust that. Which

is fair. Because if I were honest, I'd have told him that flannel looks so fine on him, my knees went weak.

I wave him in. As Ryder steps inside, he turns and faces me. I shove the door shut, then stare up at him, before my eyes drift slowly down his body. In one hand is a bag of peanut butter cups, in the other, a bottle of whiskey.

I scrunch my nose to fight the threatening sting of fresh tears and palm my eyes. There's a quiet rustle, the clink of candy and booze dropped on the table. Then warm arms wrap tight around me, pulling me close.

An ugly sob bursts from my throat as I fall into him. I sink into his hug and cry so hard, my chest aches. Ryder's grip strengthens, making the worn fabric of his sleeve brush my cheek. I press my nose to it, breathing in deep that comforting scent of evergreens and fresh air, something rich and clean and uniquely Ryder.

I tighten my grip around his waist and squeeze. Ryder's arms span my entire back, his hand tight on my shoulder until carefully, it drifts up to my hair. Just like Mama, his fingers sink through my tangled curls, teasing them loose. It makes me cry harder.

"I tried my best," I sob into his chest.

He nods, hands sliding through my hair. *I know.* That's what his touch says. That's what he tells me with the dip of his head until his cheek rests against the top of my head.

I can't tell you how long he sways me in his arms, how long it takes for my chest-racking sobs to become quiet hiccups. When he seems convinced I'm not going to explode with tears again, Ryder pulls back enough to wipe his thumbs under my eyes and extract one of those ever-present hankies from his pocket.

Blowing my nose, I glance up at him, then stash the

hankie in my hoodie. Trying for a deep breath and a smile that ends up wobbly, I meet his eyes. "Why are you here?"

He tips his head, his eyes searching mine. It's a long moment that our gaze holds. I'm scared to read into it. I'm frightened to admit what I feel when Ryder shows up with my comfort foods and open arms and that unspoken way of understanding me.

When he steps forward, I step back. My butt smooshes against the table's edge as Ryder leans closer, and my thighs part. He lifts his hand, and my eyes fall closed. I'm waiting for him to throw me on the table, then tear off my clothes, when the rustle and pop of plastic make my eyes snap open.

Ryder smirks as he unwraps foil covering a peanut butter cup and brings the chocolate to my pinched lips.

Tap. Tap.

He presses the peanut butter cup to my mouth once more before it opens, and he sets the chocolate inside. I chew, trying to maintain my irritation with his teasing games. It's a struggle. He brought me peanut butter cups, and now he's uncorking the whiskey with his teeth and spitting the cork into his palm. The hairs on my arms and neck prickle. He smells like sex in a forest, standing inside the gap of my thighs and hand-feeding me chocolate.

"You're here to make me feel better."

He nods, giving me the bottle. With his hand free, he gestures *a little*.

"Yeah." I throw back a swig and swallow, not flinching at the burn. "Well, a little better is better than nothing."

Pressing the bottle into his chest, I meet his eyes and sign, *Thank you*.

Ryder's eyes don't leave mine as he tips the bottle back and takes a long drink. It's the sexiest thing a man's ever done in front of me.

I take his hand and pull him with me, toward the sofa. With his formidable wingspan, he snatches the peanut butter cups and brings them, too. He sets down the goodies as I drop onto the sofa, then Ryder straightens, eyes on me, unbuttoning the cuffs of his sleeves and slowly rolling them up. It's hardly a striptease, but it's turned my nipples to drill bits beneath my hoodie. My panties are soaked. The urge to get naked is overwhelming.

With one long step past me, Ryder falls onto the corner of the sofa. Toeing off his boots, he spreads his legs and pats his chest.

My eyes are not that high up on his anatomy. I've never seen Ryder sit like that, and now I know that not only does he tuck it right, but Ryder is packing a flipping tailpipe in his pants.

A throat clear interrupts me. It's deep and gravelly. Goose bumps scatter on my skin and send an involuntary jolt through my limbs. When I finally peel my eyes up, Ryder lifts one eyebrow. He looks like he's working very hard not to laugh at me.

Pulling out my phone, I text him, *There are so many puns I could make about your log jammer, Lumberjack, but you brought me booze and peanut butter cups, so I'm going to take the high road.*

He rolls his eyes after reading the message and shakes his head. *Thank you*, he signs.

I crawl in between the space of his legs and lay my back to his front. The peanut butter cups land with a *thwack* on my lap, as Ryder brings the whiskey in his large hand to balance on one knee. With a sigh, I let my head fall against his chest. It's like sinking into a hot bath, that moment of bliss when the water's just high enough, the temperature just right. I take the whiskey from him, throw back another swig, then set it in his grip once more. Ryder corks it, one-handed. A long, slow exhale leaves him, and when I glance up, he's staring down at me.

Good? he signs.

I nod, then text, *So good. I need more frenemies if this is how they roll.*

That makes his head tip back with a faint chuckle. Watching him, I slide my palm along his thigh. His breath hitches.

Emotion hits me square in the chest. It feels like the time my bike clipped the gutter and hurtled me over the handle-bars. I'm breathless. Dazed. I feel that high of relief after a near-death experience, as I sit in his arms. Letting Ryder touch me, comfort me, I'm not terrified my heart's going to break because of it.

What *is* this?

Eyes still on me, Ryder pulls out his phone. A moment later, my pocket buzzes.

You should be proud, Sunshine. You were perfect out there.

I stare down at it, then back up to Ryder as I swallow more tears. "Thank you."

Ryder's fingers drift up my arm until they rest at the base of my throat. His hands are ballplayer big. I'm vulnerable, curled up against his body. With my despairing, distrustful attitude about men, I should be freaking out.

But as his thumb whispers over my windpipe, as it traces the hollow of my throat, I know with complete certainty I have never been safer than I am with Ryder Bergman.

He shifts and lowers his head, until our foreheads touch. The whiskey bottle drops with a liquid clunk on the sofa, freeing both hands to roam my body, up to my cheeks.

Our eyes hold, and I refuse to blink. I search Ryder's gaze

as his thumbs stroke my cheeks, as his legs tighten around me. My body turns, so I can slide my hand along his torso and earn his stuttered breath. Over his pecs, traveling his throat, my fingers test the soft, thick hair of his beard. It tickled last time, like I expected it would. What I hadn't expected was to like it so much.

Now, I'm prepared.

Ryder's mouth lowers to mine, a hair's breadth away. I know what he's doing. He's waiting for me. He's going to let me make the first move. Just like I made him last time.

Fair and square.

I slip my fingers through his silky hair, curling around the nape of his neck, and pull him to me. Those soft lips that I wish I could see, I feel, taste, and bite.

Our kiss is languid—a bookstore word for luxuriously slow, decadently savored. It's torture of the best variety. Ryder's groan fills my mouth, the clearest sound besides his laugh that he's ever given me. His fingers tighten in my curls, as I lean into him. His mouth opens, his tongue finding mine with soft, teasing strokes. I fist his hair and tug him closer. His hands tip my head, controlling the kiss, and I'm at the mercy of his touch, as his tongue spears my mouth. I hear the gasps that leave me, the pleading noises I'm making.

I make to turn fully, with every plan of straddling his lap, ripping open his buckle and taking this home, but Ryder stops my movements and pins me against him. One solid arm spans my collarbones as he leans over me, his kisses softening, the gradual taper of a windstorm to a gentle breeze.

I reach for his neck again in demand for more. I'm hungry for his kisses. I'm greedy. I want him, and I don't care if it makes everything weird tomorrow. Ryder resists my first tug, but I pull him stubbornly toward me. Giving in, he drags me closer as our kiss deepens. One arm anchored across my chest, Ryder drifts his free hand down my ribs, over my stomach. It's a gentling, comforting gesture, but I want so much more. I wrap my hand over his and guide it downward.

His eyes meet mine as I slip his hand beneath my shirt and whimper. I tell him so he knows.

Yes. Yes. Yes.

Ryder's eyes darken. His fingers drift lazily along the waistband of my sweats. Teasingly slow, they slip beneath the elastic, right over my panties. My thighs clench involuntarily, but Ryder grasps my leg, pulling it wide. My stance is splayed, my thigh stretched over him, pinned between his powerful body and the couch. It leaves me thrown open, motionless, as his fingers graze my panties. I'm despicably wet, and Ryder groans when he feels the effect of his touch.

Breath bursts from my lungs, double-time gasps as one calloused finger rubs along damp fabric and finds my clit, then lower, everywhere that I'm aching and empty, begging for more.

"Hmm." It's the faintest noise that rumbles in his throat, but it turns me molten hot.

Ryder's touch is measured, exploratory. He watches me, what makes me shiver, what makes my breath stick in my throat before it rushes out, and I'm saying it again.

Yes. Yes. Yes.

I kiss him as his touch drifts to the edge of my panties until warm skin finally meets warm skin. Both of our mouths fall open, as one long finger, then two, curl inside me, and his thumb swipes across my clit. Gentle, teasing flicks.

I can't believe it's happening. I mean, in some dim corner of my mind, my brain's saying *Duh, Willa. You dry-humped through bedsheets and nearly came like a train. He more or less told you he knew what it took to make you come. What did you expect?*

I've never orgasmed with a man before. And now I believe Ryder. It wasn't me. It was them. Other guys did it wrong. *They* were wrong. They weren't Ryder, so used to reading me for each tic and vulnerability, that observing my every move is second nature to him. They didn't tease me as if time was something they had no regard for, as if their pleasure was the last thing they were focused on. They didn't pause and wait for the slightest shift of my hips so I could chase *that* feeling, so I could climb and climb and—

"Ryder," I whisper.

Another quiet *hmm* leaves his throat, and I swallow it with my kisses. Current jolts through my system, white-hot light dancing in the tips of my breasts, the span of my pelvis, every square inch that he touches.

"I'm c-com—" I can't even finish my words as I arch into his touch. A shockwave bolts through my body as I buck into his chest, his powerful arm holding me tight. Wave after powerful wave, and it doesn't stop. Ryder's fingers tease gently inside me, his thumb sweeps, perfectly faint.

His kiss is reverent, and I feel the smile in his mouth as he pulls away. When he lifts his hands from my sweatpants, I expect another one of his gentlemanly hankies to appear. Instead, I have to scissor my legs, as Ryder locks eyes with me and licks each of his fingers clean.

"Jesus Christ." My voice is so husky, I sound like I smoked a pack of cigs. "You're a filthy lumberjack."

He lifts a shoulder, pulling out the last finger with a *pop*. I'm in a daze, and I startle when my phone buzzes again.

Come on, Sunshine. You're tired. Off to bed.

I fumble for my phone, relying heavily on autocorrect because post-orgasmic Willa can't type for shit. *My turn. It's only fair.*

Ryder frowns when he reads the text. His fingers slide

beneath my chin and tip my head up so that our eyes meet. *No*, he mouths.

"Then you're ahead!"

He rolls his eyes and types, *This isn't a competition, Sunshine.*

I type back, *Everything between us is a competition.*

I immediately regret saying it. Historically, it's true. We've been neck and neck, tit for tat. A brutal running tally of pranks, jokes, and barbs. Until something shifted along the way. What I said makes this and the waterfall sound tactical, calculated. Heartless. Much as I wish it was, I'm beginning to fear it isn't. That something is there between us, as much as it scares the shit out of me.

Ryder's expression shutters as he reads my words. When he looks up, it's as if the flame brightening his eyes was extinguished. He bends over his phone before mine buzzes.

You don't owe me anything. I wanted to.

I stare at the words: *I wanted to.*

Ryder extricates himself from behind my body, setting the whiskey and peanut butter cups carefully on the coffee table. I give him a big pouty frown, which he ignores, answering with one of his double claps before he points to my bedroom.

I fold my arms across my chest and scowl up at him, kicking my legs when he sweeps me into his arms. "Don't you go thinking just because you gave me my first manmade orgasm that you get to start bossing me around, Bergman. I'm an independent woman, and if you're under the impression I take orders—" A massive yawn interrupts me, somewhat diminishing the impact of my rant that I'm pretty sure he can't even hear. "You've got another thing coming to you."

Ryder grins as he whips back my sheets and sets me on the bed.

"I didn't shower," I whine.

He lifts off my hoodie and kisses my forehead.

"I stink."

Off come my sweatpants.

"I can't sleep like this," I groan through a yawn.

The blanket creeps up to my chin. The softest kiss yet presses to my hair as he breathes deep. My eyes won't stay open, and sleep swallows me up.

RYDER

Playlist: "Lost in The Light," Bahamas

MY VISIT TO WILLA'S WAS IMPULSIVE AND INSTINCTUAL. IT was also extremely unlike me. I'm cool-headed, methodical, analytical. I don't do shit I haven't exhaustively considered. Except when it comes to Willa.

I don't regret what I did. I told her I wanted to, and I fucking wanted to.

The thrill I experienced, touching her, feeling her, hearing what I could of her sounds and voice, echoed the shift inside me. That ache for what I barely allowed myself to want for so long, because the thought of another possible disappointment was simply too much, is now a determined demand.

I've had one appointment with the audiologist to start adjusting the new hearing aids for *both* ears—not just my somewhat-cooperative right ear, but my left ear, too. The one that's been such a maddening source of pain and frustration, I leaned into the relief of pain-free silence rather than endure pain in the effort to hear.

But now, with promises of better technology and better results, with time to heal from the past and prepare for the future, I'm ready to try again, and soon—I hope—I'm going to use my voice. Because while silence has healed me, while silence has always been my friend, and I will always need it, I want the choice to hear as much as I can, to speak when I want, to communicate in whatever way suits me best.

There's just one problem: my second audiologist appointment to make more adjustments for my left ear, the appointment I hoped might give me a sense of how this was going to go, was supposed to be an hour ago. And I'm not there. Instead, I've had my head in a toilet, a fever burning up my body. I've felt this once before—swift, brutal, and agonizing. Food poisoning.

Hugging the toilet like it's a life raft, I picture that chicken wrap I ate after I came home last night and immediately start to vomit again. No more chicken wraps. Ever again.

After that round is out of my system, I'm slumped on the cool bathroom floor tiles, fixating on my other derailed plans: the messages I should be sending Willa to do triage on how badly I went off-script last night with her. If I know her at all, there'll be aftershocks from my latest move, and now, I'm in no shape to brace for impact.

The old Ryder would have never done what I did last night. He would have instead sent Willa an empathic text about her loss and then gone right back to haranguing her the next time he saw her. This new, fearless Ryder knew what he was risking, going to her like that, and simply could not stand to leave her alone. Watching that game's outcome, knowing how heartbroken Willa would be, he couldn't even consider not seeing her.

I knew she'd be alone. With her mother sick in the hospital, unable to comfort her late at night, I knew Willa was going to go home with Rooney, who would be just as dejected as her. She'd have no one else, as she felt all those awful feelings and thought those terrible things you think when you put a ton of pressure on yourself and your team falls short.

I only made it to summer training before our freshman season started at UCLA. I never got to compete here, but I competed plenty in high school. I lost state championships. I blamed myself. But I always had a handful of family members hugging me, distracting me with affectionate teasing, badgering me into playing a game, serving my favorite homecooked meal.

Willa has none of that. And I might know better than anyone what pushes Willa Sutter's buttons, but I also know that she doesn't handle her feelings well. I knew a lumberjack hug, plus a little chocolate and whiskey, never hurt.

Platonic hugs and comfort foods turned into something much more substantial. I touched her, teased that silky skin, felt her clench like a vise around my fingers. I was rock hard, pressure building in my jeans, kissing her, watching her come apart under my touch.

I can't shake the memory of when she came. Her body shook softly, her sweet breath burst across my lips. She was so beautiful, and all I wanted to do was make her come a hundred times more.

It's as I stumble from the bathroom toward my bed that I'm hit with the realization: I dreamed about her last night— hot, delirious dreams of sinking into her and feeling her writhe over every inch of me, hearing her sweet, breathless sounds as she came undone. And now, as I crawl beneath the blankets, I have to grumpily admit I'm too exhausted to do a damn thing about any of this.

I fall asleep, this time, mercifully free of fever dreams. When I wake up, it's to a concerned, pinched expression on my parents' faces as they lean over me. Why are they here?

"*Älskling.*" *Darling.* Mom's voice is close enough that my right ear hears her Swedish endearment and knows what it means.

I lick my lips, taking inventory of my body. Dad pats my hand and squeezes, drawing my attention so I'll watch his lips. "Becks called, said you have food poisoning. He's worried about you."

Panic hits me. How long have I been sleeping? I planned to check in with Willa as soon as I wasn't so sick I couldn't even text.

Pointing to my wrist, where my watch usually is, I look at my Dad.

His brow furrows. "How long have you been out?"

I give him a thumbs-up. Mom's hand slips soothingly through my hair.

"Almost twenty-four hours," Dad says.

I slam my hand on the mattress. Shit. Fuck. Fuckety shit. Willa's going to take this all wrong, I know it already. She woke up yesterday morning, probably wondering if what we did was some kind of weird postgame delusion, then when she decided it wasn't, she had to expect I'd reach out. It's a fair assumption. She knows me. Typically, I would.

And I've been radio silent for a day.

Phone, I mouth, miming the action, too.

"Easy, Ryder." Dad pats my hand again. "You look like hell, son."

I shake my head and immediately regret it. My fever's gone, I think, but my head hurts like a bitch.

Please, I mouth, then sign.

"Alexander," Mom says, "let him have his phone. It's how he talks. You're silencing him."

I sigh in relief as Dad hands my phone to me from my nightstand. Spinning it my way, I squint. Not a single message from Willa. I don't know whether to be disappointed or relieved.

"*Sötnos?*" *Sweetheart,* Mom asks. "Everything all right?"

No, I type in a group thread to my parents, who pull out their phones. *I missed my appointment with the audiologist.*

Mom frowns and types, *We'll get you another one, right away. I promise. I'll take you myself.*

Don't forget we're bringing Joy to the house tomorrow, Dad texts. *Need to work around that.*

A pained noise catches in my throat and earns my parents' attention.

What? I mouth.

Dad brings the chair at my desk next to my bed and sits. Mom's fingers stay in my hair. She's quieter, like me, but her touch says plenty. *I'm here. You're okay.*

I grope around for my hearing aid in its case on my nightstand, then pop it on. *You can speak,* I type in my chat with them. *I'll let you know if I need you to text.*

Dad reads my message, then glances up and says, "Joy's from my military days. You remember what I've said about my last mission when the injury to my leg happened?"

I glance down at Dad's thigh. When he stands, his titanium prosthesis is less noticeable beneath his sharp khakis, but sitting, the point at which leg transitions from muscle to metal is obvious beneath the fabric.

I give him a thumbs-up. Nodding is out of the question. My head hurts too much.

"She's the one who saved me from bleeding out," he says.

Holy. Shit. Willa's mom saved my dad's life.

"Joy and I bumped into each other at a veterans' function five years ago. We caught up and promised to stay in touch. Mom and I met her a few times to share a meal, but other than that, I didn't hear much from Joy. Not until she ended up right in my oncology wing. After kicking breast cancer's ass, she was diagnosed with acute myeloid leukemia. It happens sometimes after treatment, unfortunately, which is why it's dubbed therapy-related leukemia."

Jesus. My sadness for this woman and for Willa, whose mom has been so sick, wells inside me.

"Oh, Ryder…" Mom wipes my eyes and strokes my cheek. "Such a tender heart. You've always been that way. Papa's taking care of her, don't you worry." Her sympathetic glance morphs into a wry smile as she fusses with my beard. I'm sure it looks like hell at the moment, like the rest of me. She gives my facial hair a playful tug. "You wouldn't know you're such a sweetheart. This beard, *sötnos*, is quite the deterrent."

I stick my tongue out at her, and it makes her laugh. Looking at Dad, I try to show him I'm still following.

"So," he continues, "I feel deep gratitude to Joy. She saved my life." My parents' eyes meet across the bed. "She's dying, Ryder. Her medical expenses are extensive, and she sublet her apartment to conserve costs and spare her daughter debt once she passes. I want her last days to be spent in the comfort and peacefulness of a home. I'll be overseeing her care. We have a hospice nurse hired, and we set up the guest room where Nana stayed. It's the right thing to do."

I text them my response, my hands shaking a bit. *Of course. This is just complicated.*

My dad frowns. "How?"

Willa, I type.

Dad scrunches his nose. "What about her daughter?" His eyes widen. "Wait, how do you know her name?"

"That's Ryder's friend," Mom says. "Isn't it?"

Dad's stunned. "You're friends with her, Ryder?"

"Rather more than friends, from what Aiden says." Mom

lifts her eyebrows. I reach up and tug a strand of her shoulder-length blonde hair, making her yelp and swat my hand. "Ryder Stellan, behave yourself."

I frown, typing, *Aiden's full of shit, whatever he told you. The only truth is that he's had his hand in trying to set us up all semester. We're just frenemies.*

Mom squints at her phone. "Frenemies." She looks to Dad, the person she relies on when she encounters a limitation in her understanding of English. That's pretty rare after decades living in the States, but it happens. "What does that mean?"

Dad stares at me for a long minute, a slow grin warming his face. "Frenemies are people who spend plenty of time together but pass most of it bickering. If they didn't quarrel so much, people would see them as close friends, maybe even something more…"

Dad chuckles. "I should have known. Joy was always a firecracker. Of course, her daughter is like her that way, isn't she?"

Mom leans her elbows on the bed, smiling down at me. "She was very spirited during the game we watched. Very intense. I wonder how that works with this quiet, dry-humored son of ours."

Dad rocks back on his seat. "I do wonder…"

I smack the bed, groping for a pillow to lift myself up a little and put me at their level. My jaw's clenched, my head's pounding, and they're both giving me these infuriating looks of sympathetic amusement.

Please don't say anything yet to Willa or her mom, I text them. *I don't want to upset Willa. She hasn't even told me her mom's sick.*

Dad reads my message. "Ah, that does make it trickier. Perhaps it's wise to wait until she's ready for you to know."

What if she's never ready? I write. *How can I come home and avoid her?*

Dad sighs and rubs his forehead. "Perhaps the right time will show itself to you. I personally think the sooner you two get honest with each other, the better. After you get some rest of course."

Mom nods, her eyes narrowed critically at my beard. "And after you shave, too."

———

I TEXT WILLA THE MOMENT MY PARENTS GIVE ME A MINUTE alone.

Sunshine. This is truly not an excuse,
but I came down with something
yesterday morning,
and I've been out of it.
I wanted to talk, considering the other night.
This is the first opportunity I've had.

I watch my phone, waiting for the read receipt and the three little dots, but nothing comes. While I finished my finals earlier this week, it's the tail end of testing week at school for everyone else, and Willa missed a few exams, including our class, for her game and the travel it required. Maybe she's still in finals.

No response comes as I email the audiologist's office and explain why I missed my appointment. I throw in a beg for a new appointment, because now that I know I'm ready to try, waiting is torture.

Mom and Dad have left me lots of homemade meals stashed in my fridge. Now that he's sure I'm not dying, Becks is on his way home for holiday break, too, and Tucker's home already. I have the place to myself, and I use it to sit in my boxers, eating soup in silence, checking my email every five minutes. I take a hot shower that feels like heaven, and crumple back into bed.

And then I fall asleep, knocked out by a level of exhaustion not unlike when I came down with meningitis. It's not until undefined hours later that I wake up to the faint melody of a voice I know.

Willa.

She strolls in, my apartment key that I never gave her and am suddenly suspicious one of my roommates provided, dangling on her finger. She gives me a concerned once-over, a frown on her face as she texts, *Well, hi there, Lumberjack. You're looking swell.*

I drag a pillow over my face to hide, but soon it lifts at the corner, one big brown eye blinking slowly as it watches me. Willa moves the pillow and sits close on the edge of my bed so I can hear her and read her lips.

"Sorry you're sick."

I groan and shove my forehead into her thigh. Her hand sits heavy on my back, then starts to swirl in a lulling figure eight. She opens her phone and texts, *Need me to pick up a prescription? Spit in your chicken soup? Stick a laxative in your ice cream to deal with constipation?*

I glare up at her.

"Not constipated?" she asks, a twinkle in her eye.

My glare deepens.

I'm not making a very good case for myself, am I? she texts.

No, I mouth.

Her eyes hold mine, as slowly, carefully Willa slips her

fingers through my hair. It feels so good, a wave of warmth rolls down my spine, and I shudder.

"Need anything?"

No thank you, I type. *It was food poisoning, and I think it ran its course. I'm feeling relatively better.*

As I hit send on my text, a new email notification pops up. It's from the audiologist. I gasp and sit up, scrolling as I read. They have an appointment for me tomorrow afternoon.

What is it? she texts.

I missed an appointment with the audiologist because I was sick, but they have an opening for me tomorrow.

Willa tips her head, a coy grin on her face. *What's the audiologist for?* she writes.

I glance up and meet her eyes, searching them. Willa's smart. I think she knows what the audiologist is for, especially since I've told her I have a complicated relationship with hearing aids.

Suspicion dawns inside me. Does she know? Has she known this whole time when I've worn them?

I blink and, for just a moment, remember how she laid in my arms the other night, how she watched me—trusted me— to touch her and make her feel good in a way she blatantly admitted other men have made her feel like shit for. That took courage. And even though I'm not ready to tell her every-thing, I want to be courageous, too.

The audiologist is setting me up with new hearing aids, I text her. *I was having a hard time for a while and limited my use of them, but I'm working on giving them more of a chance, seeing how it goes.*

I almost tell her how much I've already been giving them a chance, the depth of my hope that if I can make them work, I can feel comfortable enough to speak, too, but I'm scared. Scared to set that fragile dream in someone else's hands, when it could shatter before I've even had the chance to truly hold it myself.

She smiles wide and infectiously bright as she reads my message. At that moment she completely lives up to my nickname for her. *Sunshine.*

That's exciting! she texts. *Though that will pretty much shoot your sex appeal. You work the strong, silent angle way too well.*

This is what has killed me about Willa since day one. She jokes and teases me, she gives me shit, and she's never acted like how I am, how I communicate, is something to be "fixed" or changed. Meeting me with whatever means necessary to land that next zinging barb, the perfectly placed needling jab, she's seen me in a way so few have.

Tamping down the swell of warmth inside my chest, I grasp my phone, then type. *Our final? How did it go?*

"Final?" Her eyes widen. "What final?"

I wrap a hand around her thigh and squeeze. I'm ninety-five percent sure she's joking, but you never know with Willa, and unlike her, I need a good GPA to help secure my future. If she missed her portion of our test, I'm fucked.

Oh, cool your tits, tree-feller, she types. *I took it and kicked its butt, mostly because your notecards are neurotically thorough. So thank you for that.*

I shift in bed. After expending the energy required for eating and showering, now I feel heavy-limbed, achy, and weak. Watching my attempt at moving, Willa tugs those full lips between her teeth. She looks like she's trying hard not to laugh at me.

Aw, you're like a sleepy little pill bug, she texts. *Let me help you.*

If I had the energy to grumble, I would. Willa stands from the bed, grips my waist and leverages me up with surprising ease for such a compact woman. And if that wasn't enough to twist my heart, she cups the back of my head and eases me down, quickly shoving another pillow behind me.

"See? There." She backs up and curtsies. "Nurse Ratchet, at your service."

I give her a look that makes her laugh.

Thank you, I sign.

A small smile on her face, she signs back, *You're welcome.*

I'm tired. My eyelids droop, but I don't want another minute to pass before I talk to Willa about everything from the other night at her apartment, to this painful reality wherein her mom is about to be a patient in my parents' home.

Does Willa know the severity of her mom's prognosis? My gut says no. I've seen Willa's face light up when her mom calls, when the screen brightens with a picture of a woman whose smile and eyes are identical to hers. If she knew her mother was actively dying, Willa would not be functioning like this.

I search the sheets for my phone, which got lost in the rotation. Willa leans over, searching the bed with me, and decks me with that soft, addicting fragrance of hers. I'm about to press my nose to her hair, but she straightens with my phone before I can.

"Aha!"

Taking it from her, I start to type. I'm not even halfway through when Willa's phone blares from her pocket, and she pulls it out to read the screen. Her face falls as her eyes dance left–right.

Terror pools in my stomach. It doesn't look like good news. I pat the bed and earn her attention, making her eyes snap up to mine.

"Sorry…" She glances down at her phone and types, *My mom's doctor just messaged me about tomorrow. It's her moving day.*

Willa drags her fingers through her hair, sending mad spirals popping in their wake, then texts, *Sorry, Ry, I have to go now. Are you okay?*

Am I okay? What do I do? When do I tell her? *How* do I tell her? I can't not go home for Christmas, but I don't want to bump into Willa and blindside her. Something tells me Willa does not do well being blindsided.

I can barely stay awake. Fatigue's dragging me under. Willa takes my hand, squeezing before she lets go. She looks torn, like she wants to say as many things to me as I want to say to her. But when our fingers untangle from each other's until our hands drop, it feels final. It feels like goodbye.

How do I tell Willa I want this to be just the beginning?

20

RYDER

Playlist: "Hearts Don't Break Around Here," Guitar Tribute Players

WILLA'S BEEN AVOIDING ME AS MUCH AS I KNEW SHE WOULD. I've known her for a few months now. I know how she copes with difficult things. She avoids them. She's checked in with me via text a few times, but only her usual nonsense teasing and banter. It's driving me nuts. I want to rip out my hair and scream, beyond frustrated at the yawning gap in our communication.

I can't tell her via text what's going on. The subject matter is too sensitive, the context too bizarre. This is a face-to-face conversation. Problem is, I can't talk to her on the phone or get her to see me in person.

One week away from Christmas, my mom's having a coronary that I'm not home yet. Willa has yet to be available to see me and has been incapable of saying one serious thing in days. I unlock my phone and send her the message I should have sent her the day after she left my place. *We need to talk.*

Three dots appear almost immediately, then, *Brawny, are you breaking up with me?*

Goddammit, this woman. I rub my eyes and breathe deeply. My phone buzzes again.

*You're doing that thing where
you rub your eyes and take deep
centering breaths so you don't commit
homicide on the world's next
soccer star, aren't you?*

A begrudging grin tugs at my mouth.

*I can neither confirm nor
deny these allegations.*

*Knew it.
I have to come down to my
apartment and grab some
things for the holidays.
I'll be around until midday tomorrow.
Want to do dinner?
You can cook me meatballs.*

I roll my eyes, but before I can respond, a new text message pops up. Mom.

*Ryder Stellan Bergman,
I ask one thing of you. One.
To be home for Christmas holiday.
Where are you?*

A growl leaves me. The women in my life are going to make me go insane.

*Mom, I'm sorry.
I'm trying to figure out this
situation with Willa.*

She won't see me to talk.

Mom's dots appear.

Make her.

Jesus. I'm my mother's son. It's part Swedish culture, part disposition—she thinks everyone should be as blunt and direct as she and I are. No bullshit, no games.

That's not how Willa works, Mom.

I've guessed as much. I just miss you.
Home isn't the same without my Ryder.

Lay on the guilt a little thicker. My phone buzzes again.

Can you at least come for dinner tonight?
Just Ren, Viggo, Oliver, and Sigrid.

So basically everyone.
Except Ax, Freya, and
her despicable other half.

I suppose you could see it that way.

Okay, but I'm coming back
here afterward.
I'll be back in time for
Christmas, promise.

Your terms are acceptable.
See you in an hour.

An hour? I toss my phone away, then remember I need to text Willa back.

My mom's going to murder me
if I don't show up for family dinner.
Can't cook for you after all.
Breakfast tomorrow?

> *Jerk.*
> *Make me those cinnamon rolls*
> *and fresh coffee,*
> *and you've got a deal.*

I want to be pissed at her presumption that I'll get up and make her smart mouth fresh pastries. But we both know I'm going to do it.

Deal. Bright and early, Sunshine.

> *Can't wait.*

A stupid smile pulls at my lips. I don't type it, but it's on the tip of my tongue. *Can't wait, either.*

———

I'M PINCHING MYSELF. AFTER THREE ADJUSTMENTS IN THE past two weeks, my left ear's hearing aid works better than it ever has. Not perfectly, not as well as the right ear's, but better than before. I give my left ear breaks because my tinnitus is still aggravated after too much use, and it's going to take time for my brain to adjust to input after so much sound deprivation. But when I slip it on and my left ear's not ringing, the complexity of sound I experience is both staggering and beautiful.

I soak up the sounds of my family. My parents' laughter. Ren and Sigrid—Ziggy as we call her—who are incapable of talking without it being a happy yell. Viggo and Oliver, practically twins they're so close in age, who thrive on loud, incessant bickering. All that's missing is Freya's smoky voice, Aiden's smooth baritone, and my oldest brother Axel's bone-dry delivery.

And yet, I still have my limits and crave spates of silence. Sneaking away from the chaos briefly before dinner, I take the stairs up to my old bedroom that's frozen in time from high school and drop onto the twin bed.

Sighing with relief at the blissful quiet, I close my eyes. As I'm falling asleep, I find myself picturing a cabin in the woods, at the foot of some snowy mountain. A fire roaring, some kind of stew bubbling in the pot over it. I'm sitting in a worn armchair, listening to that soothing crack and pop of firewood as it catches and bursts into flames. Breathing deeply, I smell woodsmoke and evergreens, herby stew and that damp mustiness of a cabin. But then a new scent punctures it all. Roses. Citrus. Sunscreen.

Willa.

She slips her hand along my neck and her fingers massage my scalp as she slides onto my lap. My breath leaves me in one long pained hiss as her ass wiggles right over me, and she tucks her feet up on the couch.

Hi, she says.

I can hear her. I hear her voice, and it's liquid gold in my ears. It's a soft, low purr. Her eyes look like a jungle cat's in the hearth's glow, butterscotch and amber as the firelight dances in her irises. Her hair's wild. It looks how I picture it might after she's been in bed, tumbling around.

Everything thickens beneath the fly of my jeans, need tightens low in my stomach. Dream Willa shifts again, her hands cupping my face. Her lips are a breath away, her eyes locked with mine. She inches closer, closer—

A bang on the door makes me jerk awake. I glance down. My dick's raging hard, straining against my zipper. I'm obviously, painfully aroused. Scrambling up off the bed, I pull open the door just enough to hide behind it and see Dad on the other side.

What? I sign.

I'm not ready to talk yet. I want to be, but every time I try, I freeze, panicked. It's been so long since I spoke. How will I sound to my changed ears? How will it feel to speak and hear myself differently?

Dad looks apologetic. "The boys ran an errand for Mom, and Ziggy's too small to help me. Joy wants me to move her bed so she faces out toward the glass doors, but to do that, I need to move Nana's dresser."

I groan. That thing weighs tons. I swear it's lined with lead or has some secret safe with bricks of gold hidden in it. That's not the biggest deterrent, though. Willa and I haven't talked. Meeting her mom before we have seems like a terrible idea.

Pulling out my phone, I type, *Can it wait?*

What happens if her mom says something to Willa? Willa will kill me for not talking to her about it, even though I've tried everything I can think of. I can hear her saying it. *I'm gonna kill you, Brawny, I'm gonna kill you dead.*

Dad gives me that disappointed-in-my-son look. I'm sure he assumes I have balls enough to have somehow strong-armed Willa into talking about all of this. He'd be wrong. I appreciate his faith in me, even if it's misplaced.

I wave my hand, finally giving in. *Okay.* Talking about

Nana and looking at my father has done wonders for the discomfort inside my jeans, so I open up the door, close it behind me, and follow Dad downstairs.

Walking down the hallway to meet Willa's mom, dread tightens my throat. I'm sweating, on the verge of panic.

Dad greets her in his upbeat doctor pitch as we enter the room. A smoky voice that's a little hard to make out answers Dad with what I'm pretty sure is a tired *Hello*.

Dad takes me by the arm, stands on my better hearing side and drags me next to him. "Joy," he says clearly. "This is my son—well, one of my sons—Ryder. Ryder, this is Joy Sutter, Willa's mom."

I elbow Dad.

Joy looks like her photo on Willa's phone. She looks like Willa, but painfully thin, with a headscarf and a couple of decades to her.

I wave hello, and feel guilt twist my stomach. Willa should know about this. I want her to know.

Dad turns so I can read his lips as I listen to him speaking to Willa's mom. "Ryder's deaf, Joy. He came down with meningitis a few years ago which damaged both his ears. He wears hearing aids, but he'll follow what you're saying best if he can also read your lips while you talk, and you speak slowly and clearly. He communicates via texting generally, so I'll send you his number."

I swallow a strangled noise as I watch Dad send Willa's mom my cell. Joy just smiles, hands in her lap, her phone sitting on the side table. She looks like the cat that ate the canary.

"Ryder," she says clearly. "Nice to meet you."

I nod.

"Well." Dad glances over his shoulder at the ancient dresser. "Let's do this, son."

It's hell moving it, but we do, before carefully unlocking the breaks on Joy's hospital bed and spinning her. I can see why she wanted the change. There's a cheery view through the glass doors to the backyard this way. It might be December, but it's still sunny out, plenty of plants thriving. A soccer net sits toward the edge of her view. I wonder if Willa's used it at all.

"Thank you, gentlemen," she says.

"Anything you need, Joy?" Dad steps up to her and sets a gentle hand on her frail shoulder. "Patty will be in soon for your meds and such, but if I can do anything to make you more comfortable right now, just say the word."

Joy's staring at me. "I'd just like a minute with Ryder if that's all right."

I lock eyes pleadingly with Dad. He glances between us as a grin brightens his face. He squeezes Joy's shoulder once more, then walks up to me. "Good luck."

With a smack of my back, he leaves and closes the door behind him.

"Ryder," Joy gestures to the chair near her bed. "Please join me, won't you?"

I walk up to her slowly, sitting cautiously as she watches me.

"So you're the asshole lumberjack."

My eyebrows fly up.

Lifting one hand, she gestures me closer. I lean obediently. "Mind if I touch your throat?" she asks.

I frown, confused. Why would she want to touch my throat? Curious enough to find out, I shrug and offer her my neck.

Her hands go to my beard, down to my throat. "Can you make a noise?"

After a moment's hesitation, I hum. She holds her hand to

my throat, her eyes tight with concentration. When her hand falls away, she tips her head, the gesture so like Willa. "Voice box works. So you voluntarily don't talk."

I hesitate for a moment, then nod.

"Why?" she asks.

She's not the first person to ask this, but unlike others, I don't hear judgment, only a question. Maybe it's because she reminds me of my physician father and his unending anatomical curiosity, which is so familiar to me. While I don't *owe* her an explanation, I don't mind filling her in briefly via text.

I pull out my phone, but Joy's hand rests on my arm. "My eyesight's shot, son. Nice side effect of the latest cancer treatment. I can't text with you."

Any smartphone out there these days has the capacity to read aloud her messages. Doesn't she know? Doesn't Willa, who in a heartbeat would have made sure her mother understood the accessibility tools on her phone? Then again, I've only ever observed Willa stepping out to *call* her mom. Maybe Willa doesn't even know her mother's dealing with this. Maybe Joy hasn't known how or felt ready to ask for help when she realized she couldn't read her messages anymore. Maybe she's been scared to do something that makes her fully face what's changed. I know something about that.

She may perceive this as overstepping, but I can at least show her the tools she has at her disposal, then it's her choice what to do with them. My gaze travels to her phone. I point to it, then hold out my hand.

Joy frowns between me and her phone. "You want my phone?"

I nod.

"Go ahead," she says, a puzzled look on her face.

Picking it up, I swipe across the screen, then hold it in

front of her, like a mirror. I imagine if she can't see well, she doesn't use a security code. Sure enough, Face ID unlocks her phone. Angling myself over her hospital bed so that, to whatever degree she can see, she can observe me, I access her settings, then the accessibility features.

"Well I'll be damned," she says. Slowly, Joy takes the phone from me, bringing the screen close to her face. I watch her finger move across its surface as she starts to explore the Spoken Content settings. Feeling like maybe I'm encroaching, I stand up, walk to the glass doors, and peer outside, to give her some privacy.

Minutes pass, and then suddenly my phone buzzes in my pocket. I have a text from a number I don't recognize. *Touché, Lumberjack*, it says.

I grin, typing a brief response to keep things simple. *Glad to be of service.*

Turning, I hit send and face Joy. She gets my message and a little tentatively, swipes her phone down the screen with two fingers. I don't hear it very well, but I can tell my message is being read aloud to her.

She smiles up at me and signs, *Thank you.*

You're welcome, I sign back.

But then her smile slips suddenly. Her jaw tightens. Joy shuts her eyes and leans back in her bed. Pain. It's etched in every one of her features.

Slowly, I walk closer to the bed, wishing there was something I could do. Joy offers a forced smile that's more of a grimace than anything. "I'm fine."

I want to ask what I can do, but I'm not going to text her and force her to use her phone right now. Not when her eyes are scrunched shut, her hands white-knuckling the sheets. Silence hangs between us as I sit in the chair beside her bed. My eyes drift to her nightstand. A cup of water with a straw poking out of the lid. Peppermint oil. Lip balm. A pill container divided into daily medications. Is there something she can take? Something I can offer her? That's when my gaze snags on a book, hidden beneath the pill box and a box of tissues. A copy of *Pride and Prejudice*.

Joy opens her eyes wearily, then glances my way. "Willa's been reading it to me in the evenings. *Pride and Prejudice.* The original enemies-to-lovers romance. Well, maybe except for Shakespeare's *Much Ado*." Grimacing again, she settles into her pillow and pulls up her blanket. "You like to read?" she asks.

I nod. But her eyes are scrunched shut, an involuntary response to the pain she's obviously experiencing. So I clear my throat and manage a rough "Mhmm."

Her jaw ticks. "Me, too."

Sadness jabs my heart. It was one thing to hear my father tell me Joy is dying. It's another thing to see firsthand what she's going through. Willa's going to...I don't know what Willa's going to do. Her mom sounds like her world. I feel sick to my stomach. I hate cancer. I hate that she's suffering. I hate that it feels like nothing can be done for her.

Except...

Staring at the book, I lift it off the nightstand and softly flip through the pages. Something about the moment triggers old memories—the sounds of medical equipment, the sight of a hospital bed, a book, clasped in my hand. I remember Nana, who spent her final months here in this same room, years ago. I remember my small self, curled up with her, proudly reading to her from my board books. A strange, terrifying idea takes hold of my thoughts.

Carefully, I scoot closer to Joy's bed. Hands shaking, I open the book and turn to the earmarked page, Chapter 32. My breath catches in my throat when a gentle touch startles me. Joy's hand rests on my wrist as if she senses what I'm about to do.

"Take a deep breath," she says.

I do. A slow, long inhale.

"And out."

I release a steady exhale.

Silence stretches as I stare at the page. Then I shut my eyes, and for the first time in over two years, I try to speak. But my throat catches before I can. I clear it roughly, taking another deep breath. My stomach presses, air rushes up my throat, and the long-forgotten feeling of sound vibrating through my neck and head startles me as I say, "E-Elizabeth was sitting by he-herself, the next morning—"

Tears blur my vision as I hear my voice. Scratchy. A little wobbly. Quieter. Different than I remember. But still…mine. I palm my eyes before they can spill over.

My voice sticks as I begin to read again. I swallow and take another deep breath. Joy's hand squeezes mine encouragingly. I squeeze her hand back and hold it tight.

Joy settles deeper into her pillow and sighs. "Time to hear Lizzie shut down Darcy Proposal Number One."

I lean my elbows on her mattress and stumble through the words. I read aloud until my voice runs out, until Joy is sleeping. Her face is peaceful, her hand still clasped with mine. And while I know I gave her a gift, I know she gave me a gift, too. A hand to hold on the journey forward.

21

WILLA

Playlist: "hate u love u," Olivia O'Brien

"Slow down, Willa," Mama grumbles. Her hands tap the bedsheets, which is a tell for her discomfort. "You're rushing, and I can't understand. My gentleman reader is much more deliberate with his language."

I roll my eyes, letting *Pride and Prejudice* drop to my lap. Mama told me one of Dr. B's sons, who is home for the holidays, has been reading to her in the evenings that Mama mandatorily kicks me out so that I do things like eat a solid meal and keep up with my training and workouts. I have to admit that I felt my grinch heart go *lub-dub* when she told me about this. Some young guy spending his holiday evenings with a sick woman, reading her Austen, is about as sweet as it gets.

"Well, maybe your *gentleman reader* should read to you instead."

Mom sniffs. "He will. Our next date is tomorrow."

That makes me laugh. "A date, huh? You playing cougar, Mama?"

Mama's smile is faint but warm. "That would be something. He's handsome. Hard to tell since he's shy, always covered head-to-toe, but you can tell there's a real catch of a man hiding under all those protective layers."

That pricks my chest. It makes me think of Ryder. I've been awful. I bailed on coffee the morning after he canceled on dinner because I'm the wussiest wuss there is. I was terrified of what he was going to say. I have no idea where we go from here, since he came over after semifinals.

Actually, you're the one who came. Like. A. Train.

"Oh, for Pete's sake," I mutter to myself.

"What are you talking to yourself about now?"

"Nothing."

Mama hits the button to raise her hospital bed a little and slowly shifts to her side, looking as if moving hurts like hell. "How's your asshole lumberjack?"

"Still an asshole," I grumble.

It's all Ryder's fault. It's *his* brother-in-law who sent us on our team-building day that ended in the waterfall make-out. It's *Ryder* who seduced me with peanut butter cups and whiskey and the world's most glorious orgasm. Now we've crossed that invisible boundary and exist in some terrible limbo, far out of frenemy territory.

What if he wants to cross back over to how we were? I'll be stuck, pining for the guy who's ruined me for other men, while he's happy busting my chops and treating me like some platonic thorn in his side. I'm not doing that shit. But, on the other hand, if he wants to pursue whatever it was he started on my couch, I can't go there, either. I'm not cracking open my heart. I can't afford to. I'm stuck and miserable, and I miss him something fierce, which just makes me more miserable. I'm not supposed to miss Ryder. I'm supposed to miss *torturing* him.

"What are his holiday plans?" Mama asks tiredly.

I stand and hike the blanket over her shoulder, then gently

rub her back. "Just said he's staying at his childhood home, spending time with his parents and siblings."

"You're avoiding him."

I groan as I drop back into my chair. "Ma, can we not psychoanalyze me?"

"Did he try to get past friendship with you? Is that why you're freezing him out?"

"Joy Sutter, stop it. I'm not freezing him out, just letting things cool off a little bit. We're frenemies. There's sexual tension in spades. I drive him *nuts*, and he…he terrifies me."

Mama tips her head, her eyes pinched with concern. "Why does he terrify you?"

"Because I care about him. Because I don't want to lose our diabolical friendship. I'd rather stay frenemies than take the risk of trying to be something more, just to have all of it taken away. If I stay his frenemy, I only miss out on a hypothetical. But if I try with him, I could lose…everything."

"Damn, Rosie." That makes my heart twist. She called me that all the time as a little kid. "You've been doing some thinking."

I lob a peppermint at her playfully, making sure it comes up short and lands in front of her. "Not much else to do while I'm on break."

"Sounds pretty chickenshit to me."

My jaw tightens, my hackles rise. "Do not provoke me, Mother."

"Oooh, she *Mother*ed me. You're missing out. It's dumb logic. No, it's not even dumb logic, it's downright illogical. Have you ever considered that after you've spent months getting to know him, building trust and safety, finally your heart is giving you the green light? Now you're going to sit there, idling, and waste your one tank of gas."

Damn. I never thought of it like that.

Mama shifts in bed and tries to hide a grimace. It snaps me out of my thoughts. "What's going on, Mama?"

She sighs. "I just can't get comfortable."

Sadness, guilt, worry churn in my stomach. "What can I do?"

"Nothing." Mama burrows into her blanket and shakes her head. "Nothing to be done."

That's not okay. I glance at my phone. Her nurse is taking her break and isn't due back for another half hour. I'm not letting my mom shake with pain for thirty minutes. I'm fixing this. Now.

I pull out my phone and dial the number Dr. B gave me. He answers after the third ring.

"Everything all right?" he asks.

"Mama's hurting. Can you come down—"

"Be right there."

The line's dead before I can sigh in relief.

Dr. B's whipping open the door within thirty seconds, his attention on Mama. Just as he's shutting the door behind him, a shriek echoes from the hallway, followed by a man's laugh.

Chills soar up my spine. I know that sound. Dr. B freezes. Mama's attention darts from the door to me.

I eye the door that leads to Dr. B's home. I haven't once used it. I have no clue what the rest of the house looks like. A few times, I've heard the peal of laughter, the happy echo of voices in a kitchen. It sounds like a big family that sits at the dining room table and hangs out. The idea is completely foreign to me.

Mama sees me staring at the door. "Willa, what's the matter with you?"

"I just heard something."

There's that man's laugh again. The hair on my arms and neck stands on end.

I'm unaware of Mama and Dr. B as I rush out the door. My steps are soft down the hall that's dark and quiet, tucked away from the rest of the house. But with each step I take, noise grows and light sends long beams across the polished floors. With each step, I'm greeted by the fragrant smells of cooking and happy sounds. I stand on the edge of the wing, facing a large foyer, blinded by the beauty of their home. Airy white walls, clean lines. Natural wood, linen drapes, tall windows.

I'm dumbstruck, startled by a flame-colored blob flying past me, followed by a taller blob of straw yellow. On a delay, my brain processes that it's a redheaded girl and a blond boy, two teens whose feet tap a futsal ball, a small, weighted ball meant for practicing touches and control. It's pretty much perfect if you want to play soccer inside without breaking anything. The ball's too heavy to get up in the air.

They whip past me, not even noticing I'm there, and disappear into a large open room to the left. There's a long table with a few people seated at the far end, their hands around mugs of tea as they play a board game. A woman's silhouette is deeper in the room, tall, with shoulder-length blonde hair. She's lean and willowy, and when she turns in profile, my heart catches in my throat. I know that nose.

My brain's in denial. I heard his laugh. She has his nose. But that's impossible. It's a coincidence. Ryder's nose is just...well, it's a perfect nose. A gorgeous woman would have a perfect nose.

I walk timidly toward the echoing room, as my hands shake. One of the people at the table glances up. A man with dark brown hair and bright green eyes. This time, my heart's pounding in my ears. I know those eyes, too.

Yes, dummy, you do. They're Dr. B's eyes. This guy's most likely his son, anyway.

The man straightens in his seat, eyes locked on me while he calls, "Mom?"

The woman doesn't seem to hear him. Her hands and eyes are focused on a food task.

"Mom," the man says again. There's a bite to his voice that earns her attention.

Finally, she looks up. I stare at her as nausea churns my stomach. I know so many of those features. I know the tops of those cheekbones. That smooth, tall brow. Those wide-set eyes, except hers are quicksilver blue.

I have to be imagining things. There's no way, there's just…

The woman rushes toward me, the urgent set in her features reminding me even more of Ryder. I have to be hallucinating. It's because I miss him something stupid, because I'm stressed and lonely. I want his tree-branch arms wrapping me in a solid hug, his pine and cedar scent, the whisper of his flannel against my skin, the press of his lips to my crazy hair.

She practically drags me to a seat at the table and sits me down. "There now, *sötnos*," she murmurs.

I stare at her dazedly. "What did you say?"

She smiles softly. "It's just an endearment." Her voice is tinged with an accent I can't place. Her vowels are round and lilting, her consonants landing at the front of pursed lips. "Are you okay, Willa?"

I nod slowly as embarrassment burns my cheeks and reality sinks in. God, how embarrassing. I have no business being here. I'm hearing his laugh, seeing his features in these people. I'm imagining all these invisible connections to Ryder in a roomful of strangers who are trying not to stare at me curiously, but mostly failing.

Elin sets her hand over mine. This is the first I've met her, but I'm not surprised she knew who I was. I look just like Mama. I stare at her, dazed, noting that she's ridiculously beautiful.

"Can I get you anything?" she asks quietly.

A door shuts somewhere nearby, drawing her eyes. They widen, then flick back to me. Before I can answer her, she wraps an arm around me. "You look faint. Would you like to lie down? I have a room next to your mother's that—"

"No." I stand shakily but manage to stay upright. "I'll be okay. Thank you, though. I'm so sorry I barged in. I thought..." Mortification tightens my stomach. "I'm going to go."

I walk backward, knowing I'm being weird and rude. I'm intruding. I'm out of place and emotional. I need to go back to Mama's and my little cave.

Elin stands, her face pinched with worry. "Please, Willa, just sit here a moment."

"I can't." I start to spin away. "But thank—"

I bump viciously into a wall of very solid human, which knocks the wind out of me. As I stumble backward, a hand reaches out and steadies me.

Wait.

Evergreens, warm man, clean soap. It's Ryder's scent. I glance down at the man's feet. It's his knit socks he always wears. His worn jeans. My eyes travel higher. Flannel. My breath is flying, my heart racing. Higher. Higher. Squirrel-tail beard. Perfect nose. Green eyes.

Tears blur my vision. Ryder's eyes lock with mine, tight with concern.

"It was you," I whisper.

I stumble back, out of his grasp. Swinging around, I look at all of them. His *family.* Their faces resemble his. Guilt. Pity. Sadness. They all know. They've been in on this.

Turning back to Ryder, I blink rapidly, disbelief rushing through me like a numbing cold.

Peripherally, I hear his mother herd everyone away. There's a pocket door that she closes, leaving us alone in the entranceway. Even though it's humongous, the room feels painfully small, the space between us claustrophobic. I have to get out of here. I can't even begin to straighten this in my head.

As I back away, my hand fumbles for the front door handle. I wrench it open and sprint outside, running as fast as humanly possible. Humiliation, confusion, betrayal roar in my ears as I round the house. I've sat in Mama's room, staring out of its glass doors enough to know their backyard is flanked by a grove of trees I can disappear into.

I'm sprinting, but I hear footsteps pounding behind me, gaining on me. I'm almost to the trees, so close—

"Willa!"

I gasp, my toe catches in the earth, and I slam to the ground. Staring up at the dusky sky, I gulp like a fish out of water. I had to be imagining it. It couldn't…it can't…

Ryder drops over me, his hands whispering over my body, checking for damage. Tears stream down my face as I stare at him. I have never felt this many things at once. When his eyes meet mine again, they're brimming with emotion, too.

"Ryder?"

He makes a noise I've never heard before—a full, pained sound. His palms go to his eyes, wiping them furiously. I sit up and grasp his wrists, the tables somehow turned. Now *I'm* worried about *him.* "What is it?"

Ryder's hands drop, his eyes meet mine. "Beautiful," he says quietly. His voice is low and gravelly with disuse. It's velvet stretched across raw wood, hot tea poured over crackled ice. "Your voice, it's…" His voice gives out and he mouths, then signs it, the word I couldn't figure out that day we ate outside.

Beautiful.

He can hear me better. He's speaking.

My confused thoughts dissolve as a sob wrenches out of my chest because suddenly all I can do is feel—too many things to parse or name, except the need to touch him. The emotion in his voice is a mortar blast ripping through my ribs, wrecking my heart.

I grab his shirt and yank him toward me. It's not a kiss. It's a collision. It's the smash of one mouth into another, a demand for something I never believed I'd have, desperation for it to be mine. His groan is loud and uninhibited. It echoes in my mouth as his lips meet mine hungrily, as his fingers delve into my hair.

Roughly, Ryder shoves me down, his weight anchoring me against the grass. Elbows framing my shoulders, chest against mine. I push him off enough to gasp for air and grab his face. "Was that real? Did you—"

"Willa," he says immediately.

I yank him back to me. Another punishing kiss bruises our lips, clacks teeth. I suck his tongue, palm him through his jeans. I'm wild. I'm off the deep end. I need him. His hands fly up my shirt, as my fingers work his jean buttons loose. He pinches my nipples gently while he leans into my palm's grip. My eyes roll back in my head.

He breathes against my skin, "Willa."

It finally sinks in, every question that demands to be answered, ringing inside my head and heart. He's speaking. He's hearing me. He's *heard* me, even if to a lesser degree, for months now, since the night I first saw that hearing aid, while never letting on. He's kept so damn much from me. "Ryder, stop..." He leans back, staring at me in confusion.

"You…you, you lying asshole!" I screech, madly crawling out from underneath him and yanking down my shirt.

How did I end up underneath him, about to beg him to take me in the grass right here, under the stars? I got sidetracked. I got *a lot* sidetracked when that voice called my name. The voice made possible by the hearing aids that he's using, that he hasn't trusted me enough to fully know about. Just like I never knew his dad was an oncologist, that his dad was my *mom's* oncologist. He damn well better not have known either.

"Did you know?"

Ryder stands, buttoning his jeans, staring at me. I'm so used to his quiet, that the long moment that stretches between us doesn't faze me.

"Willa—"

"Answer me." I have to fight the shudder his voice sends through my body. It sinks through my ears, rolls down my spine and ignites between my legs. I have to ignore it. "Did you know he was my mom's doctor? Did you know about my mom?"

Ryder sighs. "It was an accident. I met him for lunch—" His voice catches. He clears his throat and swallows. "I met him for a meal and spilled water on his desk. Her file got wet."

The backyard swims. Ryder reaches to steady me by the elbow, but I drag myself out of his reach. "Why didn't you tell me?"

His mouth works. I watch his green eyes widen. "Tell you what? That I knew your mom was sick? That my dad was her doctor? Willa, you didn't tell me *anything*. I asked about your mom, your home life. You kept that from me."

"Don't you *dare* blame me!" I march up to him and jab a finger in his chest. "That's my private business—"

"So is my dad's medical practice!"

I tear at my hair. "When you knew we were coming to your home, why didn't you say anything?"

"I tried," Ryder groans. "You kept avoiding me. I couldn't text you that."

It's not enough. It's not okay. The depth of omission that's been between us is staggering. I feel like everything that made Ryder feel safe has been ripped away from me. How could he smile at me and talk to me and study with me, night after night, knowing all this? Not trusting me to know about the hearing aid. Hiding his history with the sport we both love. Keeping our parents' connection to himself. What the fuck *has* Ryder told me?

"Willa," Ryder pleads. "Slow down."

Seems I continue to verbal process. He steps toward me, but I back away. His eyes narrow, his jaw clenches. And before he can say one more thing, I turn and sprint into the trees.

RYDER

Playlist: "Bloodsport," Raleigh Ritchie

GODDAMN, THAT WOMAN IS FAST.

Willa bolts for the trees, her agile body slicing through the shadows. Thankfully, I've kept up on my speed-training too, and my legs are fifty percent longer than hers. Soon, I'm right behind her, hearing the sharp gasp of sobs as she runs. I hate that these are the first new sounds I'm hearing from her. I hate that this is how she found out. But I can't change the past, and I'm a practical man. All I can deal with is the present, and as much as possible, the future.

She hurdles a felled tree and falls funny, wobbling for a second before she takes off again. Glancing over her shoulder, she's wide-eyed, flaming with anger. Her head whips back around, and she picks up her speed. I'm at an advantage in that I know where and how my parents' property ends. Soon, she'll run right into a ten-foot-high privacy wall. She'll be cornered.

Willa's run slows as she spots the fence. Her head swings left, then right. When she spins and faces me, her eyes dart around, planning her escape.

"Enough, Willa. No more running away. We're going to talk about this."

Willa glares at me, wiping an unsteady hand under her nose. "No."

"Yes."

She shakes her head. Fine. I can be the bad guy. Piss her off a little bit. Not the first time I've done it. Two strides toward her before she even knew I was coming, I bend and toss her over my shoulder.

As predicted, she shrieks. I wince, recoiling at the shrill feedback stabbing my eardrums.

"Put me down, you lying, flannel-wearing, tree-limbed, lumberjack son of a bitch!" she hollers.

I just tighten my hold around her legs and hoist her higher on my shoulder. The entire walk across the lawn is punctuated by her yelling strings of expletives. She slams her fists on my back and jerks her strong legs under my grip. I just lock my arms around them.

When I swing open the front door, poor Ziggy's there, gaping at us. Ren slaps a hand over her eyes and drags her back into the kitchen. Willa seems to sense we're headed to my room because her panic picks up in the form of fists pummeling my back.

"Put." *Punch.* "Me." *Punch.* "Down."

After I slam my door shut, I let her slide down my body, and immediately earn a fist to the chest. Our eyes meet. She's shaking with anger or shock or maybe both, but she still pulls out her phone, her knuckles white around it. "Phone or speaking?" she says, her voice brittle and tight.

"Speaking." I swallow thickly. "Tell me what you're angry about."

"So you can talk your way out of it? So you can deceive me some other way as you cover your ass?"

I reel. "Willa, no. I...I never wanted to deceive you."

"Except for when you snuck your hearing aid on me. When you never told me you played soccer. When you figured out my mom's your dad's patient. When you learned she'd be living here. Explain to me how you've managed to do all that without *wanting* to deceive me."

"I wore the hearing aid because I wanted to hear your voice," I blurt. "Because when I heard you in Aiden's class, it wasn't enough."

Willa's jaw drops.

"I-I-I didn't know you mumble to yourself. I didn't know until it was happening, and I realized you don't mean to do it, Willa, that you barely catch how often you think out loud, and I didn't know how to say something without making you feel exposed and embarrassed. I didn't tell you about soccer because it felt pointlessly sad. I was trying to move on. I didn't talk about your mom because *you* never talked about your mom. I tried, Willa, but you don't make it easy. You push people away when they want to be close to you."

I pause as my throat tightens. Willa stares at me, her eyes widening. She looks scared, like a cornered wild animal.

"I know you're in shock," I tell her. "I know this is some twisted, small world, but, Willa, it's still me. No, we haven't been as open about some things, but we've been there when we needed each other—"

She stiffens. Her eyes tighten with panic. "I didn't need you."

Those words hit me like a physical blow. "Everybody needs someone, Willa."

"Not me." She leans in, locking eyes with me. "I. Don't. Need. *Anyone*. Except for Mama." She sniffs and wipes her nose roughly. "Who I'm going to go make sure is okay.

Mama's never lied to me. Can you say that much for yourself?"

I'm empty of words. No, I can't say I haven't lied by omission. No, I can't deny that I've withheld parts of my life. But Willa has, too. She's just scrounging for every bit of material she can and throwing it against me. Anything to keep her distance.

Willa draws her shoulders back, her jaw set as she interprets my silence exactly how she needs to. "That's what I thought."

She throws open my door and walks out, but this time, I don't chase her. This time, I slump to the floor and let those words settle in.

I didn't need you.

I don't need anyone.

"But, Sunshine," I mutter to the empty room, "what if I need you?"

———

"RYDER, DO YOU WANT MILK?"

Mom's voice snaps me out of my daydreaming. Her hand hovers over my coffee with a small pitcher.

"Oh, no, thanks, Mom."

She sets down the pitcher, then turns back to the fresh-baked bread she's slicing, glancing up at me analytically. "Honestly, Ryder, that beard. It's overtaken your handsome face."

"I vote the beard goes," Axel says, falling onto a neighboring stool.

"Good thing I didn't ask your opinion," I tell him cheerily.

"Morning, Axel." Mom gives him a soft smile, sliding a cup of coffee his way.

"So, your friend." Ax drops his voice and sips his coffee. "She's lovely."

I clench my jaw. "She's not yours for the taking. She's also, like...ten years younger than you."

"Six, if she's your age. Besides, I bet she'd appreciate a little maturity."

"Which rules you out," I say between clenched teeth. "Back off, old man."

Axel scowls.

Ren drops on the other side of me and reaches to the cutting board, nabbing a slice of raisin bread faster than Mom can swat away his hand. "Good morning," he says to me and Mom, before pointing with his bread in Axel's direction. "What's got Grumpy Gramps here frowning?"

"Fuck off, Søren," Ax grumbles into his coffee.

Ren's cheeks darken with an angry flush as he shoves the entire piece of bread into his mouth. He looks about to flip his shit. Ren hates his full name.

"*Boys.*" Mom raises her eyebrows. Something in the intensity of her frown oddly reminds me of Willa. My coffee curdles in my stomach. "I use that term, *boys*, deliberately. Do you see your younger brothers acting like this? Why am I lecturing the older ones?"

"Because they're still sleeping," Ren says around his mouthful. "Give Viggo and Ollie time to wake up and then ask them about what they did to the backyard."

Mom's eyes widen in alarm before they close, and she takes a centering breath. Those two put the first signs of aging on her forehead and near her eyes. "I'll deal with that later. The point is that it's *Julafton.* Christmas Eve. I'd like you to pretend for one day you don't have disgusting mouths, and that you somewhat like each other, *förstått*?"

It's the Swedish version of *Am I understood?* with the emphatic expectation to be damn well understood.

"Yes, Mom," we all mumble.

"Now. I want to discuss Willa and Joy." Mama resumes slicing the last of the bread and begins neatly setting it in the basket in front of her. "I think we should invite them to Christmas dinner tonight."

I choke on my coffee. Ax takes the opportunity to smack my back harder than necessary.

"Get off." I shove him so roughly, he nearly topples off his stool.

"Ryder?" Mom watches me, her head tipped.

"It's your home, Mom. Your decision. I wouldn't expect them to say yes, though. Willa's pissed at me."

Mom sips her coffee and drags a stool toward her side of the counter. She sits with a sigh. "Why?"

"She says that I kept a lot of myself from her, but she did, too. We were both playing the same game—"

Ren laughs. "The one where you pretended you hated each other, but all you really wanted to do was—"

I slap a hand over his mouth and raise my eyebrows, gesturing toward Mom. Mom smiles and sips her coffee. When I'm confident Ren isn't going to continue that train of thought, I drop my hand.

"We've been playing with fire for a while. I don't think Willa likes feeling as if she got burned and I didn't."

Mom nods and sets down her cup. "But you did, too, didn't you? Maybe you've even been burned the worst?"

Her eyes hold mine in understanding. It's hard to think about and impossible to say, how stealthily my feelings for Willa shifted. "She doesn't know that."

"She will if you tell her," Mom says softly.

I fiddle with my napkin. "I'm not sure she wants to hear it."

My brothers' eyes bore into the sides of my head as they realize what we're saying. Mom reaches for my hand and clasps it. "Be brave, *älskling*, and give her a chance. If you don't, I think you'll regret it for a long time."

Nodding, I manage a smile. Mom's idea is nice in theory. But she doesn't know Willa. She doesn't know all that I'm up against. "Thanks, Mom. I'll think about it."

My phone buzzes. After just a few days of practice, Joy has gotten the hang of the text accessibility features I showed her, and now my phone's blowing up hourly. Swiping open my phone, I read:

> *It's Darcy's visit to Longbourn today*
> *Get your ass down here and*
> *read me my happily ever after.*

A laugh I can't stop rumbles out of my chest.

At your service, milady.

> *Wrong century, squire.*

"Tough crowd," I mutter.

"What?" Mom asks.

Standing, I pocket my phone in my PJ pants. "Sorry, nothing." Rounding the counter, I give Mom a peck on the cheek. "Thanks for breakfast. I'll be back in a bit."

"Don't be too long!" Mom calls. "I need help with the *julskinka*."

"I won't, promise."

Jogging up to my room, I change into jeans and a flannel, of course. Willa's jokes about them echo in my head as I button my shirt. She can tease all she wants, but wearing a flannel shirt is like wearing a socially acceptable security blanket. Sue me, I like to be comfortable *and* comforted.

Once downstairs, I round the banister and stroll down the hall to Joy's room. Knocking twice, I wait for her voice.

"Enter," she says dramatically.

I smile as I walk in because I can't help it. I like Joy. She's a smartass, like Willa, with all the fun and a fraction of the bite. Unlike Willa, she's incredibly blunt, but I am too, so it works out fine. She's also whip-smart. Each time I read to her, Joy explains cultural contexts I never knew about in *Pride and Prejudice* and tells random funny anecdotes when something in the story jogs her memory. Not that Willa wouldn't love her for the fact alone that Joy's her mother, but I can see why Willa loves her *so* much. Joy Sutter is a good time.

"You're giving me that look again." She shifts in bed and sighs heavily.

"Am not." Sitting down, I sweep up *Pride and Prejudice*. I frown when I open the book. "This is where we left off."

"Willa was too tired to read last night. She just curled up on my bed and passed out."

Tired my ass. Willa was a wreck is what she was. Worry hits me like a kick to the stomach.

Joy reads me easily. "Willa's an emotional minefield, Lumberjack, which, to her credit, is with good reason." She sighs again and raises the bed. "Willa never had a dad. She grew up being carted all over the country for my military career. The only constants in her life have been the soccer ball at her feet, and her mom whistling for her from the stands."

Joy draws in a shuddering breath and betrays a rare window of emotion. "And she's about to lose one of those."

Reflexively, I wrap my hand around hers. Silence hangs between us as I search her eyes. "Does she know that?"

She shakes her head. "I can't."

"Ms. Sutter, you have to tell her."

Joy's hand grips mine hard as she blinks up at the ceiling. "I don't know how. I don't know how to break my daughter's heart. One promise I have always made Willa is that I will never leave her, that in this world she could count on her mama being there for her."

I stroke my thumb gently along her skin. "Due respect, you made a promise you could never keep. Parents always leave their children, unless horrifically their children leave them first. Willa knows this. She's going to grieve and struggle, but not because you failed her. You're not doing wrong by her, being sick, by…"

Tears paint her cheeks as she stares up at the ceiling. "By dying," Joy whispers.

I swallow around a lump in my throat.

Silence lapses again as the sun hides behind a cloud, bathing us in shadows. Joy squeezes my hand and tugs me closer. "Promise me something?" Her eyes lock with mine. "Don't give up on her, okay?"

I only nod, because I'm struggling for the right words. Joy releases my hand and lifts her pinkie. "I mean it, Bergman, or I'll haunt you."

I laugh through the thickness in my voice, blinking away tears as I lock fingers with her. "Deal."

"Now." Joy drops my finger and sits back, hands folded primly in her lap as her eyes drift shut. "Where were we?"

23

WILLA

With one ear pressed to a crack in the door, my eyes scrunched shut in concentration. That's the first time I hear the words spoken out loud. My mother is dying. I've refused to acknowledge it, but I've known. Subliminally, I knew why she was leaving the hospital, but hearing it, *thinking* it is so much more painful.

I must be in shock because I'm not crying. I'm not even breathing unsteadily. My heartbreak is a white-hot knife, slicing down my sternum. It rips open my chest, and I feel as if I'm watching my heart tilt, then flop out of my chest, where it lands with a splat on the hardwood floor. Next, it's as if my intestines unravel slowly, a steady, nonstop unwinding. There's a sad, sick parallel to how I spun that scarf off my neck and unveiled my body to torture Ryder.

Ryder.

I hear his voice on the other side of the door.

My body is distant from my consciousness. I'm floating away, staring down at myself, slumped to the floor in a fragmented pool of parts. My lungs are the next victim. They collapse in on themselves. They tighten and shrivel as I gasp for air.

I see myself, balled up on the floor.

My sobs are silent. I'm airless, carved out, breaking, until—

Laughter. Mama's belly laugh yanks me down to my body, jamming everything inside again, knitting me together. My lungs fill. My heart pounds safely inside my chest. My stomach tightens. Everything is where it should be, as I listen. The mood shifts in the room.

"Reread the first proposal, please," Mama says.

"'In vain I have struggled.'" Ryder's voice is deep and ragged. He reads Darcy's voice with suffering that's as believable as it is expressive.

He's her gentleman reader.

Oh, fuck.

Hot, fat, tears slide down my cheeks. That asshole. That infuriating asshole lumberjack is reading to my sick mom and putting Colin Firth to shame.

"'It will not do. My feelings will not be repressed. You must allow me to tell you how ardently I admire and love you...'"

I listen, rapt, my ear pressed tight to the door. The famous heated exchange as Darcy stupidly degrades Elizabeth's family, points out their every flaw. When he finishes, I hear Mama sigh heavily.

"I always wish Austen wouldn't have tortured us," she says before a wet cough stops her. Finally, she catches her breath. "All that longing at Pemberley, the misunderstandings over Jane and then Wickham. I wish Lizzie and Darcy told each other what was going on. Then they could have gone straight to happily ever after."

"I mean, in real life, I'm one hundred percent with you,"

Ryder says. "I see no point in anything but direct communication."

Mama coughs. "Amen. If everybody spoke their damn
truth, we'd all avoid a hell of a lot of drama."

"Agreed. But it seems like it's not that straightforward for
most people. Saying hard truths takes time and courage,
whereas for blunt, analytical people like you and me, it's our
hardwiring. It's not a virtue, it's just our nature.

"And of course, in the case of Lizzie and Darcy, this is
literature. It's *meant* to torture us, for lack of a better word, in
a pleasurable kind of way. That dragged-out tension, it's the
best part."

Ryder's voice is low and extra rough. He sounds like he
got maybe a cup of coffee in him before Mama was blowing
up his phone to read to her. "You have to slog through their
stilted ability to be vulnerable, their dogged fear of opening
up, which causes all those misunderstandings, before their
reconciliation. That's what makes it feel so gratifying and
meaningful," he says. "The sweetness of them admitting their
feelings is only powerful because they've gone through so
much to arrive at that understanding. They have to work past
their insecurities and assumptions, to fight their way to
uncover the truth. Then and only then do they realize what
they mean to each other."

Mama laughs quietly. "You talk like you have some
insight into this, young man."

I hear Ryder's body shift in the chair. His throat clears.
"It's…it's a good story. I've read it before, had to study it for
a class last year. Anyone would tell you what I'm saying."

"But perhaps not everyone would have felt it."

There's a long silence until Ryder's voice finally ruptures
it. "Perhaps."

"All right. I'll stop making you use your feeling words.

Thank you for rereading that. Now let's pick up at the good part."

"Right." Ryder clears his throat.

I sit there longer than I should, listening to Darcy and Lizzie clear up the confusion, to Darcy's second proposal. I eavesdrop, committing the very transgression I ripped Ryder a new asshole for, but I'm neck-deep in my hypocrisy, rooted to the spot. Ryder reads on, pausing for what sounds like a drink of water before he clears his throat. He reads through the Bennet family's surprise at their engagement, and my thoughts drift with the story. I'm lulled, content with this happy ending, until their dialogue, beginning with Lizzie's words to Darcy, sends a cold sweat trickling down my spine.

"'My behavior to you was at least always bordering on the uncivil, and I never spoke to you without rather wishing to give you pain than not. Now be sincere; did you admire me for my impertinence?'" Reading Darcy's reply, he says, "'For the liveliness of your mind, I did.'"

My heart beats double in my ears. Ringing drowns out all other sounds. It's like Austen's describing *us*.

Ryder reads on, but I don't hear it clearly until the ringing in my ears dies down, right as he reads Lizzie's line: "'Why, especially, when you called, did you look as if you did not care about me?'"

He reads Darcy's response with a stoic matter-of-factness that is Ryder to a T. "'Because you were grave and silent, and gave me no encouragement.'"

I've read this book too many times to count, so my lips mouth Lizzie's line automatically. "'But I was embarrassed.'"

"'And so was I,'" he reads.

The words fall silently from my mouth. "'You might have talked to me more when you came to dinner.'"

He pauses. Darcy's reply in Ryder's voice makes my heart skip. "'A man who had felt less, might.'"

I slump to the ground completely and stare up at the ceiling.

Scary thoughts bang around my head. I see our entire frenemyship in one sweeping montage. Misunderstandings. Weighted quiet. Long glances. Relentless debate. Playful touches, hair tugs, rib pokes.

Every. Single. Kiss.

Too many emotions tangle in my chest, pinching and tightening. It's harder to breathe again. One second, my heart's tugged toward my mom, the next, toward this slowly unfurling portrait of reality between Ryder and me.

Before I can think it over anymore, I'm jarred from my thoughts as Ryder's voice grows closer. I had to enter from their front door because the outside entrance to Mama's room was locked. I didn't want to risk waking her up when I realized I forgot my key. It was suck it up and take the main entrance through the house or wait until it was late enough to call my mom to have someone let me in.

Scrambling upright, I dive into the neighboring room and hide behind the door, hearing the click of Mama's door being shut, then Ryder's steady footfall as he strides down the hallway. He pauses for a fraction of a second outside the room I'm stowed in. His nose tips up. His eyes narrow. He looks like a jungle cat who's caught the scent of his prey. When his head drops down, I see his hearing aid nestled in that thick blond hair, curved around his ear.

I wonder where and why he does and doesn't wear them. Does he take them off in the shower? Does he wear them when he goes to bed at night? When he's in bed for other reasons?

Nope. Not going there. Do not think about Ryder in sexually suggestive settings.

Finally, he walks away. A long exhale leaves me.

Phew. Safe.

Carefully, I peek my head out and slink back into the hallway before I slip into Mama's room.

"Willa." She smiles up at me, patting the bed. "Guess what? We're invited to Christmas dinner."

A groan leaves me. Maybe not so safe after all.

————

MAMA AND I HAVE AN ARGUMENT. IT GROWS HEATED. I stomp out of her room and slam the door like a petulant child. It's my last Christmas with her, I'm not stupid. I don't want to share her with anyone else.

When I return, moderately cooled off, Mama jumps right back into it. She really would have loved to be paid to argue for a living. She lives for a good brawl.

"They're a kind family, Willa. You're friends with their son—"

"Frenemies," I correct.

Mama is undeterred. "You know Dr. B well. What's the big deal?" she asks hoarsely.

When she coughs into her arm, I just feel guilty. I know I'm being difficult and obstinate. Doesn't mean I can make myself stop. "Fine, they're a nice family, but they're not *my* family."

"But they could be a family to you."

Anger and hot tears choke my throat. "No you don't, Joy Sutter. You don't get to pass me off on them. You're not gone. Not yet."

"But I will be!" she yells, slamming her hands on the

blanket. "And you won't even let me do what I can to look out for you. To make sure you won't spend next Christmas alone…" Her shoulders shake as she covers her face. I immediately throw my arms around her.

"I'm sorry," I whisper.

"You're so damn stubborn, Willa." She wipes her eyes. "Having Christmas dinner with them won't usher in my death. Sitting here alone with me in this room won't slow it down, either."

"Okay," I say hurriedly, rubbing her back, feeling terrible for making her cry. Mama *never* cries. "I'm sorry. I'll do it. We can go whenever you're ready."

Mama sighs shakily and sits back. "Thank you."

After a nap snuggled together, which goes some way to restoring both our moods, I help her put on a warm knit sweater and a soft pair of sweatpants. We wrap her in a thick blanket when she slides off the bed into her wheelchair. I find her gold hoop earrings and hook them on because her hands are too shaky.

When I stand back, I look her over. "Smokin' as ever."

Mama smiles genuinely, smacking her lips as she caps her tinted lip balm. "Why, thank you. You, however, look like hell. Go shower, tame that bird's nest, and change out of that rag."

I glance down at my vintage Mia Hamm tee. "Excuse you."

She folds her hands in her lap. "I'm waiting."

A quick shower and some curl-controlling cream later, I throw on black yoga pants and a slouchy red sweater that tends to slide off my shoulder. It drives me nuts, but Mama says it's sophisticated.

"My bralette keeps showing."

Mama rolls her eyes. "Honestly, are you the twentysome-thing or am I? That's the point."

I give her a good glare. "I'm not going to Christmas dinner to seduce anyone, Joy Sutter."

She makes a noncommittal noise in her throat. "Come on, obstinate offspring. Time to watch you squirm."

"Mother!"

Cackling, Mama wheels herself ahead of me. I follow in her wake, pushing the wheelchair when her arms start to tire and she sets her hands in her lap. Like the first time I ventured down this hall, noise amplifies, light grows. Nerves tighten my stomach.

"I think I'm going to throw up," I mutter.

"Nonsense. Take a deep breath. It's Christmas dinner, not the Last Supper."

"Could have fooled me."

When we round the corner, my heart jumps into my throat. It's an explosion of Christmas. Fresh garland, candles burning on every possible surface. Acoustic guitar playing Christmas music is a soft backdrop to the starlit wall of glass windows and doors of their great room. A Christmas tree is covered in handmade ornaments and sparkling lights. People snuggle on a massive sofa in front of the fire, hands cupping steaming mugs, reaching for pieces of a board game, laugh-ing, talking, mingling.

It's sickeningly cheery.

But then, away from the cozy chaos, Ryder stands next to his mom in the kitchen, talking. She speaks in a language I can't understand, but Ryder seems to follow, nodding his head as she points to a massive ham on the counter. Following her instructions, Ryder is poised to cut into it. But then he sets down the knife.

I watch his hands grip and wipe the towel, then unbutton

his cuffs and slowly fold the fabric along his arms. It's another damn forearm striptease as he rolls up soft, worn flannel. This one's Christmas-tree green, checkered with white and wine red. It's festive as hell. He looks like a yuletide wet dream.

I swallow so loud, Santa hears me in the North Pole.

Ryder must hear it, too, because his eyes snap up and lock with mine. Those grass-green eyes crinkle with what seems like a smile, but who knows, the bushy beard hides it. When he picks up the towel again, I gulp, watching his hand work the fabric.

I need to get laid. This is not right. I'm eroticizing hand-drying.

"Hi," I manage.

Mama practically yanks herself out of my grip and wheels herself forward, as Dr. B guides her to a space at the table that they've cleared for her wheelchair.

Ryder steps close as he tucks the towel in his back pocket. Even that's hot. There's no mercy in this world.

"Hi," he says quietly. His eyes hold mine, and the room gets twice as hot. "Willa—"

Before he can say another word, I make a fist and set it over my heart in slow, steady circles. *I'm sorry.*

Holding my eyes, he signs the same message. We stand, mirrors of each other. *I'm sorry, too.*

Then Ryder softly taps my mouth with his finger, like he did that day in class, months ago. He's telling me to speak.

"I shouldn't have lost my shit," I tell him. "I have no place to criticize what you kept private." I should say more. I should own my part more fully, but I'm so overwhelmed, so lost in everything I'm feeling, I can barely talk.

Ryder sighs and drags a hand through his hair. His fingers snag on the strands, reminding him they're pulled back. I have to suffer through him retying his hair, watching those damn muscles bunch under his shirt, his long, calloused fingers pulling each blond streak back into a tight bun. "Looking back, I wish I would have told you more. But I was scared of what would happen if I laid it all out. Holding my cards close felt necessary because we were playing a pretty brutal game. The stakes were high."

I nod. "They really were."

Ryder doesn't seem to mind my paltry answer. He grins. "Forgiven?"

"Forgiven." I swallow thickly. "And me?"

He frowns and steps closer, then wraps his hand around my shoulder. "Of course."

His touch completes the circuit that I've missed. Electricity snaps and sparks between us. I sway toward him, then pull myself out of it.

"You look incredible." His hand gently seeks a curl of mine and winds it around his finger. "You and this color. Reminds me of the infamous red napkin."

I swat his hand away. "I don't remember you disliking that *napkin* at the time."

Ryder smirks, but his eyes bore into my skin. I feel their heat, their weight as they travel my body. "I never said I did."

"Your eyes are kind of scary, right now, Ryder." His pupils are so wide, I only know his eye color because I've seen it before. He bears that same thigh-clenching intensity as when I first met him.

He swallows and blinks, snapping himself out of it. "Sorry. Caveman moment."

A smile tugs at my mouth. "Caveman moment?"

"You're beautiful. I have four brothers about to see you. I'm feeling a little possessive."

Those words roll off his tongue and dance across my skin. "Oh," I say faintly.

Scrubbing his face, he then drops his hands. "Ignore me." His eyes hold mine for a long minute, before he leans and places a soft kiss to my temple. "Merry Christmas, Sunshine."

I stand in place after his lips leave me, after his steps fade away. I'm rooted to the spot, my eyes shut, the world condensed to the echo of his kiss, burning with significance.

24

WILLA

Playlist: "River," Joni Mitchell

MacCormack's on his best non-professorial behavior, and when he catches me after dinner, he looks like a dog with his tail between his legs.

"Willa, I want to apologize."

"What for, Mac?"

He clears his throat, his eyes sliding over to Freya, who sits nestled on the couch. She gives a tiny wave as her eyes glint menacingly at her husband. If I didn't find it such an admirable look in a fellow badass female, I'd be scared shitless for him.

"Well, it's come to my attention, after some thought and reflection, and of course, the very wise insight of my lovely wife—"

"Mac, I'm not going to go report to Freya about your behavior."

"Maybe not." He wipes his forehead. "But she's watching, trust me. She has ears everywhere."

I snort a laugh. "Dude, you are freaking out."

He clears his throat. "To the point: I blurred professional and personal lines. My intentions at the outset were good. I saw a struggling student and a spirited person in you, and a disciplined student and a despondent person in Ryder. I knew he'd be able to give you the help you needed academically, and you'd be persistent enough to pursue what you wanted and hopefully lurch him out of his rut. It seemed like a good character-building exercise."

"Oh, it built character, all right. Also shaved five years off of my life, *easily.*"

He nods. "Yeah, like I said, I let it get out of hand. I got invested in what I saw between you two. I saw your potential, and I…well, I played God a little bit, and I shouldn't have. I'm sorry. If you decide to take this to my superiors, I will completely understand."

"Mac." A grin tilts my mouth. "As much as I fantasized about many ways to murder you in your sleep, I'm grateful. After all is said and done, I did well in that class, much in thanks to Ryder and to the fact that working with him required I get my shit together. No, you weren't always nice or sane or professional, but you gave me what I needed."

My eyes drift to Ryder. He stands, arms crossed, talking to the youngest sons who seem so close in age, they could be twins, Viggo and Oliver. My heart flip-flops as I watch all three of them explode in laughter, as his head tips back with a smile. "I wouldn't change that for the world," I tell Mac.

Once Mac returns to Freya on the couch, she raises her glass to me. I cheers her in the air, and soak up the moment alone, taking stock of the evening. It's been stunningly pleasant. Ryder's family is beyond warm. His sisters are conversational and kind, Freya chatting with me about the women's soccer program at UCLA—she played, too, "a lifetime ago," as she said—and Ziggy fangirled over me because she wants to follow in her sister's and my footsteps.

The brothers…they all introduced themselves. But from

every single one of them, I had the distinct sense of cautious propriety, like they weren't really being themselves, but on their best, most dignified behavior. It's almost like Ryder told them to straighten up or else...

"That's because he did."

A voice close to Ryder's but not quite as rough, less baritone, cuts through my thoughts. I sigh. "I have a regrettable inability to not think out loud."

Ren smiles. "Ah, no worries. And trust me, be glad Ryder gave them a talking to. Axel's artist's eye homed in right on you, and the man cubs are still barely housebroken."

"But, I mean, eventually they won't act like that, right? They'll talk to me without looking like they're scared Ry's going to break their thumbs?"

Ren pats my shoulder gently. "Trust me, you'll get hazed soon enough. For now, you're under Ryder's protection." His gray-blue eyes twinkle. "He's wild about you. He'd break my kneecaps if he knew I told you that, but it's obvious. You're obviously wild about him, too. So what's the hold-up?"

I cross my arms over my chest. "Now, Renny Roo, we shouldn't insinuate ourselves in other people's business."

He wrinkles his nose. "Renny Roo? My name's Ren, Winifred."

"Stop it. That doesn't sound remotely like Willa."

"It was off-the-cuff. I'm not smooth like Ryder. Take it easy on me."

"I can't. I'm an antagonist at heart." I shrug and smirk as his eyes narrow in irritation. "Which is why I had to prod you about your name. Søren, isn't it? That is badass, and Ryder says you don't like it. Why?"

Ren's expression shutters slightly before he rallies with a grin and a coy look of amusement. "I'll answer to Ren, half-pint." He dodges my attempt to poke him viciously. "You should be more afraid to provoke me. I'm a giant ginger Viking who skates on knives for a living—"

"Hey." Ryder cuts in. He crosses himself. "We don't talk about the fall of the prodigal son." His voice is still new, yet somehow familiar. My stomach tightens, hearing its deep, gravelly notes.

Ren sighs wearily. "Hockey is not that terrible. I guarantee you Bergmans have been skating on ice much longer than they've been chasing a ball across a field of grass, looking like demented sheep."

Ryder shoves him. "You were good at soccer, too. That's what hurts."

"Wait, you *chose* hockey over soccer?" I lean in and lock eyes with Ren. "And they still acknowledge you as family?"

Ren throws up his hands. "I'm a professional hockey player, and you'd think I sold organs on the black market. Jesus. He didn't even tell you?"

"Nope." Ryder puts his arm around me and pulls me close before I shove him off. "I'm trying to protect her. She doesn't need to know about the sordid world of smelly hockey gloves and playoff beards and puck bunnies."

Dr. B calls Ren's name as he laughs. "Saved by the Big B. I can't take the persecution," Ren says wryly. "See ya, mini Mia."

"That's a compliment!" I call after him. The Mia Hamm part. Not the mini part. I am not mini. I'm five foot six, thank you very much.

My eyes travel from Ren, across the room, then land on Mama. She's nestled on the couch, playing a card game with Ryder's parents and Axel.

"Hey," Ryder says. I look up at him, and my heart beats double time.

When he steps close to me, I nearly tumble into the

Christmas tree. "Easy." His eyes drift over me in assessment. "Did you hit the glogg a little hard at dinner?"

I shove him. "I'm sober, Sasquatch."

"Doesn't look like it." His eyes on me are too much, so I turn and look at the tree.

"Little bit of national pride?" A hundred tiny Swedish flags pepper the branches. Gnomes, hard gingerbread cutouts, and braided straw designs. It's perfect.

Ryder smiles as he sips his steaming cup of spiced wine and doesn't say anything. I'm used to his quietness, but this feels different. This silence has a weight I'm uneasy with.

"Your house is the lovechild of West Elm and IKEA," I blurt. "Your siblings are funny and smart and welcoming. Your family looks like a Swedish Christmas card. Your mom cooked the best food I've ever eaten. She's a culinary genius and a supermodel. Julia Child meets Claudia Schiffer. I could slice cheese on her cheekbones."

Ryder chokes on his drink, then brings a hand to his lips and dabs them. "Jesus, Willa. Where do you come up with half the shit that flies out of your mouth?"

"Blurting nonsense is my spiritual gift, Mama says." My eyes search the tree, admiring it, as much as it tortures me. What a home they have, such close family. I know their abundance doesn't equate to my lack, but it feels like a quart of lemon juice dumped in an open wound.

Ryder grips my elbow, making my breath stutter in my throat.

"Willa, I want to talk. Can we go somewhere private?"

My head snaps his way. "Why?"

His hand smooths his beard, a new habit that sprang up as the infernal facial hair grew to survivalist-deep-in-the-woods length. "Well, if I told you, that would defeat the purpose of speaking in private."

"Then say it here and forget the private part."

Ryder sighs, his eyes drifting shut before slowly opening. Once again, his bright, grass-green irises aggravate me. They're too beautiful. This whole night is one big, beautiful, juxtaposition to my reality.

"Fine." He sets down his wine on a side table and steps closer, sliding his hands up my arms and locking them in when I try to back away. "I want a truce. A ceasefire."

"A what?"

"I don't want to be frenemies anymore."

"W-what do you want?" My voice is husky. I sound like my panties are drenched and the lace of my bralette is about to curl off my burning skin because them's the facts.

Ryder's hand cups my jaw, his thumb stroking along the bone. "I want you."

"You have me." I swallow. "I'm here."

Ryder shakes his head. "Not how it's been. I want more. I want everything."

"I-I don't do that."

His brow furrows. "Don't do what?"

"I don't do relationships. Dating's not for me. I have to focus on soccer and graduating, then going to whatever professional women's team wants me. Getting attached to someone here is a recipe for disaster..." My voice trails off, as his thumb circles the skin behind my ear. My eyes nearly cross as it slides down my neck.

"Hm." Ryder steps even closer, fusing our fronts. Every hard plane of his body, every dip and swell of mine. A small, pathetic noise squeaks out of me. The tailpipe's at half-mast already, knocking against my stomach. "Too bad," he says quietly.

He's going to step back, I can feel it. I fist his shirt before he can, twisting that soft material inside my fingers, wishing I was wrapped in it. I wish it were torn off his body, a blanket beneath us as he filled me. "B-but I might consider expanding the parameters of our frenemyship."

Ryder's body stills. "So, you'd just want me for...sex," he says quietly. "Just to fuck."

The words are simple, but his voice rattles my ribs and lands between my thighs with a resounding *boom*.

"Yes," I tell him.

His thumb's still at work, drifting along my exposed collarbone. I want him to bite it. I want him to throw me over his shoulder again and lock us in his room. I need him to tear off my clothes, pin me against the wall and pound into me with my leggings binding my knees. I want filthy depraved things from him.

Ryder's mouth dips to my ear, as my body changes states from solid to liquid. "What are you thinking about right now?"

I swallow loudly. "Dirty things. Things I shouldn't think about."

His quiet laugh vibrates across my skin. "The look on your face suggested that."

"Uh." It comes out breathy and weak. I'm searching for whatever it is that solidifies my molecular structure, whatever it is that normally sets my spine with steel and sends these soft, hazy feelings far from my mind. But I can't find it.

His hand curls over my shoulder and bumps down each vertebra of my spine. It feels obscenely sexual. "We're at an impasse, then."

"N-no, we're not. You want me, I want you." I lean into his touch, watching with satisfaction as he hisses a breath and tips his pelvis away. "I felt that."

"Doesn't mean he's getting what he wants."

"Okay, so we're talking about your tailpipe in the third person now—"

"Sutter, so help me." He pinches the bridge of his nose and breathes deeply.

"Come on. We can do this. We won't have class together anymore, won't see each other unless we make time to. We can be fuck buddies."

Ryder winces as I say it. I realize I said something he didn't want to hear, but it's all I have to say. I wish I thought I could give Ryder what he wants, but I can't. I can't set myself up for heartbreak. I can't be vulnerable when I'm about to go through the worst pain of my life as I say goodbye to Mama. I can't fracture my soul into another piece and give it to someone else, just to have to say goodbye to him, too.

"Lumberjack, if I gave it to anyone, it would be you. But I can't."

His face tightens. One large hand wraps around my waist. "Give me what?"

I press on tiptoe and kiss just above his beard, as I tell him, "Everything."

Cowardly. Willa, the cowardly lion. I slink away and join Mama on the couch, threading my arms through hers. She smells like peppermint oil and vanilla bean ice cream.

She pats my thigh softly. "How's my girl?"

I smile up at her and kiss her cheek. "Okay. How are you?"

Mama smiles, turning away long enough to lay down a card that seems to secure the victory. She throws her hand up in a celebratory fist, ushering in a sweeping memory of her presence in my soccer career. It hits my chest with the force of a sledgehammer. Mama screaming in the stands, her hands fisted high. That piercing whistle she'd send up into the evening air. I always heard it. I always knew she was there, cheering me on.

What will I do when I can't hear her anymore? How will I know she's still there?

"You'll always know, Willa," she whispers, tapping over my heart. "I'm right there, forever. Listen close enough, and you'll hear it. I promise."

———

MAMA DIED NEW YEAR'S DAY. THE NIGHT BEFORE, WE watched the ball drop from the TV in her room, curled around each other under a pile of blankets. She'd been quiet most of the day, staring out the window a lot. She held my hand and asked me to sing to her, lullabies she sang to me, growing up. I massaged her body with her favorite vanilla bean lotion, rubbed her feet when she said they were cold. She wasn't hungry. She licked her lips and wanted Chapstick, but didn't drink any time I tipped the straw her way. I knew it meant goodbye was getting closer. But I didn't know it was that close. I don't think anybody did.

I fell asleep, my arms wrapped around her tiny waist, my head buried in her neck. And when I woke up to chirping birds and the faint light of sunrise, I knew she was gone. The room felt empty. The world seemed dimmer.

It hasn't felt full or bright once since then.

I lay with her for hours and cried. I kissed her cool cheek and whispered all my fears about how I was going to live without her. I tangled my fingers in hers and promised I wouldn't forget a single moment, that everything she'd given me was locked safe in my heart. I looked at her beautiful face and told her she was brave, and if I was half of who she was,

I'd be proud of that. Then I kissed her one more time, as I whispered *goodbye* against her lips.

The moment Dr. B took over for me, I walked the room in a daze and swept up every trace of us into two duffel bags. My mom's life and mine, so easily contained in a few flimsy pieces of fabric. When I got back to my empty apartment, I threw them against the wall and screamed so loud, the windows shook.

I ignored Ryder's calls. I didn't have a funeral. Her ashes sit in a white ceramic urn on my dresser. I talk to her whenever I'm home, hiding from Rooney and Coach and Ryder and Tucker and Becks and my whole team. Anyone who cares has been shut out. Because my heart is vacuum-sealed. If I open it in the slightest, if one slip of air sneaks in, then my memories aren't safe, and my life moves forward.

I don't want a life without my mom. I don't *want* to move forward.

I've heard Rooney talking on the phone. I've heard Ryder walk into my apartment. I've picked at the food he leaves. I've seen the notes he scribbles. Once, when he dared to enter my room, I hid in bed, the blankets thrown over me. Ryder stood with a hand on my back for long minutes, until slowly, his fingers slid into my hair, trying to make order out of chaos.

Just like Mama.

Somehow, I held it in. For a desperate moment, I let myself pretend each soft stroke through my wild hair was her hands, the warm steady presence behind me, hers, after a long shift at the hospital. I shut my eyes and held my breath and bathed in that dream until his touch faded and the door clicked shut. Then I cried until sunrise blazed through my curtains.

I've made progress. I eat regularly now. I run and lift a

few times a week. I keep up with my drills at the field with Rooney. But I'm a shell of myself. I know that. I just don't know how to be anything else anymore.

"Hey, you." Rooney sets a warm hand on my back. "What are you hungry for?"

I stare down at my homework, knowing I need to memorize these equations but also knowing I'm too tired and hungry to get anything accomplished. On a heavy sigh, I drop my pen. "Anything. You pick."

Rooney sits slowly at the dining room table and clasps my hand. "Willa, I want to say something. I think…No. Let me start again. Willa, your grief is valid. Your pain is real."

I stare at her. "But?"

"But nothing." Rooney shifts in her chair, scooting closer. "*And* it's threatening your well-being. I think it's time to go talk to someone. Go to grief counseling. I don't know if they're suitable for this, but maybe also look into antidepressants. It's been months, and you're still struggling to function, Willa. There's no shame in grief. You'll grieve as long as you need to. There's just room for caution when it's compromising your well-being."

Rooney wipes tears from my cheeks that I didn't know were there. "I'm here to remind you of who you are and what you want, Willa. You will always be Joy Sutter's daughter. That's never going to change. But you won't always be a soccer powerhouse. You won't always have this free education. You won't always have a man waiting at your door to give you comfort. Some things are timeless—your mother's love, her mark on your life. But so much else, you have to find the strength to snatch them up before they're gone."

"Roo, I don't know how," I choke. She pulls me toward her, rocking me in her arms.

"I know. *Shhh*." Rooney kisses my hair. It makes me think

of Ryder and his kisses to my wild hair. I miss that spark and fire that used to crackle and roar between us. I miss his bushy beard and his butter-soft lumberjack flannel. I miss our loaded silences as much as his newfound, deep voice.

"First things first, okay?" Rooney says. "Let's get you set up with a university counselor. Get you feeling better rested and clear-headed. Get your grades back on track. Then we get the guy."

I laugh. "Yeah, that's still not happening. Not the way you think. I need friends, Roo. Nothing else."

Rooney pauses her rocking for just a moment and squeezes me tighter. "Okay, Willa. Okay."

25

RYDER

Playlist: "Do I Wanna Know?" Arctic Monkeys

"WHO DID IT!?" I ROAR.

Both Tucker and Becks have the wisdom to look terrified.

I kick an errant soccer ball right at them and watch with satisfaction as they scatter to avoid getting nailed. "You motherfuckers!" I lunge for Tucker, quickly wrestling him down to the ground. His back is pinned under my knee, and I have his arm twisted in a position that's hopefully excruciating.

"It was his idea!" Tuck howls.

I release Tucker with a lunge upright and bolt for Becks. He barely sidesteps me before he trips, then slams into the table and crumples to the floor.

"Please!" Becks holds up his hands. He looks like he's about to shit himself, and he should. My six foot three, two hundred pounds is south on both Becks's height and Tucker's weight, but it doesn't matter. I'm an angry, angry man, and when I'm pissed, my Viking blood roars through my veins, demanding violence.

"Give me one good reason I shouldn't break your goddamn arm, Beckett Beckerson."

Becks whimpers as I set my foot on his throat. "B-because you'll thank me once you shave that animal off your face and it knocks Willa on her ass."

I hiss in a breath because it hurts to hear her name. We don't talk about Willa. I got very drunk a few months ago, not long after Joy died and Willa shut me out, and I told them everything. Then I made them swear not to speak about Willa or torture me with anything related to her. They've been saints about it.

Until now.

"Why?" I growl.

Becks glances over to Tucker, then back to me. "Rooney said she's going to grief counseling and finally coming around. Before that, she was getting bad—"

"Don't." I can't hear it. I almost lost my mind at first, desperate to push myself on her when I knew how badly she was hurting. I tried everything I could think of, and still, she wouldn't look at me, talk to me, answer my texts or calls or notes.

I understood she needed to grieve, and that she'd grieve in her own way, which was obviously entirely alone. But for once, logically understanding something didn't make it hurt any less.

Taking a long, slow breath, I look between the two of them. "So because Willa's back on the grid, you two decided this was the best time to shave the middle of my fucking beard off my face."

Tucker has the dumbass audacity to giggle from the corner, where he cowers. I fake a lunge at him and earn a high-pitched yelp. "Fucker," I grumble.

Becks's throat is still stuck under my instep. I feel his Adam's apple roll under the arch of my foot when he swallows. "Okay, it was…a little aggressive. But I saw you take melatonin. That shit knocks you out—"

"Because I've had insomnia!" I yell. Since Willa stonewalled me, my mind was racing constantly at night. I kept having these horrible nightmares about her wading into the Pacific and drowning, hiking alone, getting lost and falling off cliffs. Dad told me melatonin was a gentle, non-habit-forming supplement that would help me fall asleep, but apparently I'm a lightweight. Melatonin doesn't just quiet my mind—it knocks me out.

"Okay." Becks swallows nervously. "Okay, so that was a little shitty, to prey on your drugged state. But the intent was noble."

"Noble." Scrubbing my face, I stare up at the ceiling, reminding myself murdering them will put a cramp in my outdoorsy lifestyle. Jail's claustrophobic as hell, I hear. Barely any time outside.

"Shave that thing all the way, man," Becks has the balls to say. "Look less like a doomsday woodsman and a bit more like a collegiate hottie."

Tucker snorts. "Hottie's a stretch."

"Please." Becks rolls his eyes. "We all know why Ryder grew the beard. Because he got too much attention clean-shaven, and when his ears went to shit, attention was the last thing he wanted."

"Damn. Okay, Dr. Phil." I let off Becks's throat and trudge back to my bathroom, eyeing the damage.

They're stupid enough to follow and stand behind me as I face the mirror. I tip my head from one angle to another, trying to figure out how to salvage this without shaving my entire beard.

There's no way.

"Unless you want mutton chops," Tucker offers. "But

considering I grew up next door to a creepy guy with mutton chops who always tried to offer me popsicles, I'd get very strong pedophilic vibes. Your facial hair would be triggering, so for my emotional safety, that only leaves fully shaving your face."

I stare at him in the mirror. "You have serious balls to shave a landing strip on my face, then make up emotional triggers *and* a pedophilic neighbor."

Tucker groans. "You're too hard to lie to."

"Nah. You're just a shit liar," Becks chimes in.

I throw up a hand, silencing them. "Both of you. *Out.*"

Tucker fist-pumps the air. "You're going to do it?"

I level him with a look that makes his hand drop slowly to his side. "Right. We're leaving."

"Sorry again," Becks says right before they shut the door.

Staring at my reflection, I heave a long sigh. When I pull open the vanity drawer, the hair scissors sit right in front, gleaming as if they've been waiting for me.

Joy's voice echoes in my head. "*Promise me something. Don't give up on her, okay?*"

"All right, Joy." I tug the first chunk of beard away from my face, then drag the scissors through it with an echoing *snip*. "This one's for you."

————

I FEEL NAKED. AS I WALK CAMPUS, IT'S JUST LIKE THOSE recurring dreams I had as a kid. The ones in which I showed up at school only wearing my parka. The moment the dream became a nightmare was when I began to unzip my coat, only to realize I had nothing on underneath. In my dream, I'd yank the zipper up and hide in the coat closet until Mom came to get me.

But this time, there's no zipper to secure me, no mother on her way to save the day. The beard is gone, only faint blond stubble lining my jaw. A warm wind drifts over my face, reminding me how little now protects me from the outside world.

I had no idea how much I hid behind that beard until it was abruptly taken from me. At least I still have my flannel shirts. This one's Willa's favorite. Blue-and-green plaid. Her eyes always lit up a little bit more when I wore it.

Becks, damn him, is not wrong about the attention my face gets without the beard. I feel more eyes on me as I walk. I don't want more eyes. I want Willa's. I tug my ball cap lower and check my phone when it buzzes. I still keep my phone on vibrate rather than ring, and I still hope it's Willa every time.

It's a text from the man who started this shit. *I spy a hottie.*

I growl. I'm going to kill Becks. Glancing around, I try to find his hiding place. As I'm distractedly searching for him, my head high over the sea of most others that I wander by, I suddenly slam right into a small, compact body.

"Jesus, watch where you're going…" Willa's voice dies off as she stares up at me, her eyes wide with disbelief. She sways alarmingly, so I grip her arm, frowning at how much less mass is there. She's thinner. An odd giggle bubbles out of her.

"Something funny?" I ask.

She shrieks and jumps back. "Who the *fuck* are you?"

I raise my eyebrows, tipping up the brim of my hat. "Sunshine, are you serious?"

Willa makes a small, pained noise. "What the hell, Ryder?"

Her eyes roam my face as she leans toward me and bites

that dangerously full bottom lip. When her eyes lock with mine, I drag my thumb along her mouth's soft fullness, tugging it free from her teeth.

Her eyes sparkle with what looks weirdly like tears. "The squirrel tail's gone. You're even beautifuller."

I laugh and roll my eyes. "Shut up, Sutter."

"No, I'm…" She groans, as her forehead hits my chest, then she pulls back and stares up at me. "Oh, dear."

"We had a whole Beauty and the Beast thing going. I had to make sure you liked me for my stunning personality, not my mom's cheekbones."

"Cheese," she mutters. "I could totally slice some Swiss on those puppies."

It makes me laugh again. I haven't laughed for months. Dipping my head until my mouth is close to her ear, I whisper, "Can I hug you?"

Willa nods, followed by a sniffle. Stepping closer, I wrap my arms tight around her shoulders and squeeze until she's flush against me, until I can feel her heart beating against my chest. God, it feels so good to hold her like this. She smells like sunscreen and fresh air and flowers, and I want to kiss her so badly, I can barely think about anything else.

Her hands creep tentatively around my waist and then lock at my back. "I missed you," she says.

I press a kiss to her hair, one hand slowly rubbing between her shoulder blades. "I missed you, too."

She mumbles something into my chest that I can't understand. I pull back enough to clasp her face, then tip it up so I can see her mouth and hear her better. "Say it again?"

A grimace tightens her features. "I said, I'm sorry. I'm sorry I disappeared." She blinks away tears cresting in her eyes. "My reasons for shutting everyone out felt undeniably necessary at the time, but my grief counselor has since explained that while understandable, it wasn't the healthiest choice I've made."

"You took the time you needed, Willa. I was always going to be here waiting."

She nods and sniffles again. "I know. I knew that. And that meant...a lot. Thanks for all the food, too. And the back rub. And playing with my hair like Mama—" Her voice catches.

"She did that for you?"

Willa nods. "She also whistled at my games, like you have."

"How did you know that was me?"

A soft smile plays on her lips. "You were the asshole lumberjack wearing an unmistakable flannel plaid shirt, whistling so loud, they heard you in Orange County. When I caught that sound, I knew rationally that Mama wasn't there, but it felt like she was. You made her feel close."

Willa's eyes search mine curiously. "Maybe you remind me of her a little. Is that weird?"

My heart aches. I knew Joy Sutter only a few insufficient weeks, and I miss her so much. I have no idea how much Willa's hurting, or how hard it must be to talk about her. I only know it's the highest compliment from Willa, to be told I remind her of her mother.

I rub her back some more and smile down at her. "It's not weird. We had a few things in common. Excellent whistlers. Blunt delivery. Impervious to your bullshit." My fingers slide through her untamed hair. "A deep appreciation of your crazy hair and your weird metaphors and the bizarre things that come out of your mouth."

Willa leans and bites softly into my shirt. It sends a shudder through my body as I tighten my grip on her back. "Behave yourself."

She smiles. "Now why would I start doing that, Mountain Man? You like me just the way I am."

———

THINGS AREN'T EASY OVERNIGHT, BUT WILLA DOESN'T disappear anymore, and she answers my texts. A few nights later, she agrees to have dinner with me, so long as the boys and Rooney are there too. She's still putting up every possible barrier between it being just the two of us, for as long as she can manage it.

I understand why. Everything she said at Christmas still stands. She's heading out of this place with the soccer world to take by storm, and as far as she knows, I'll be teaching canoe lessons in The Middle of Nowhere, Washington. Her heart's still tender, too. She's grieving. She's going to be grieving for a long time.

Right now, she needs a friend. I might be a friend who's about to die with the need to be more, but I'm her friend nonetheless. Or, more accurately, back in old, familiar territory: her frenemy.

"What the hell do you call this?"

I glance over my shoulder. Willa's poking the guacamole I made with a disdainful look on her face.

"It's guac, Sunshine. You need glasses or something?"

"I'm aware it's guacamole, Brawny. Or it was until you threw mango into it." She tosses down the mixing spoon in disgust. "What the *fuck*?"

"There's something wrong with you. Everybody loves jazzed-up guac."

"This here woman does not. Tucker? Becks? Rooney?"

Tucker and Rooney are playing FIFA on the Nintendo. Becks stares at their game. None of them answer her. Willa turns to me and shrugs. "Kids these days. Addicted to the tube."

I have one of those moments that's becoming harder to tamp down—the fierce urge to heft her by her fantastic ass, wrap her thighs around me, and kiss her senseless.

Willa's gaze flicks between my mouth and my eyes. "You look hungry."

"I am."

She swallows loudly. "O-okay. Well, tacos are pretty much ready. We can eat."

I turn away from her, willing my body to cool down. It doesn't work. Nothing stops making every inch of me burn for her. It's fucking torture. Platonic hugs and kisses to her forehead. Swaying her in my arms and keeping my breath steady. Every little brush of elbows and hips. The swish of her hair and its tempting scent that never leaves.

Hands slam down on my shoulders, interrupting my thoughts. I turn to face Becks as he releases his grip with a squeeze. "Smells great."

Tucker and Rooney trickle in, grabbing toppings and fixings. Once again, my eyes snag on Willa. We stand there as if life is in slow motion, our friends circling us in a blur.

"You guys?" Tucker pokes me. I finally whip my head his way, making him jump back. "Jesus, you're scary. You have psycho eyes. You need to go for a run or what?"

"That's exactly what I need—*or what*," I mumble.

Willa's cheeks pink. She holds the stack of plates and white-knuckles them. When I walk up to her, her chest is heaving, a flush darkening her neck and ears. "Can you stay after dinner?" I ask.

Her eyes bug out of her head. "Um, what?"

"Just stay after they leave. I want to put something to you."

Another one of her snort-giggles sneaks out. I've figured out it's her nervous laugh. "That sounded filthy, Bergman."

Raising an eyebrow, I take the plates from her. "Pervert. Sit your ass down, and eat some tacos."

She bites her lip, and for the first time in a long while, she smiles like the Willa I used to know. The one who had something in life to smile about.

Tucker and Becks are college guys, so they destroy a serious amount of food. Rooney's not far behind them, but it's Willa I watch, picking at her black beans, popping them into her mouth like she's willing herself to eat at all. My eyes lock on hers, as once again time and space fade to the periphery. I need everyone to leave so I can ask her. And then I need her to say yes.

Willa's eyes flick up and meet mine. First, they widen like, *whatcha looking at?* But as I hold her gaze, they narrow to irritated slits.

Becks pulls out his phone. "Timer."

"Bets," Tucker calls.

Rooney tosses down her taco in disgust. "Nope. I am not enabling this any longer. I'm sick of Mom and Dad fighting." Standing, she rips the phone out of Becks's hand, shoves Tuck's money into his shirt, and yanks both of them up by the arms. "Out. These two need to get the hell over this astronomical sexual tension and deal with it the old-fashioned way."

Willa's jaw drops as she looks over at Rooney.

"Seriously, Rooster?"

Rooney shakes her head. "I'm so over this. You two. Talk. Touch. Fuck. Please, God, just end the torture. I'm drowning in it. I'm contact-horny around you guys—"

"I can help with that," Tucker offers.

Becks smacks him upside the head. "Cut it out."

"I can handle myself fine, boys," Rooney says before she directs herself to Willa and me. "The point is this: It's enough. Work it out."

Rooney drags the guys with her out the front door and slams it behind her.

Willa tracks their movement, but eventually, her head turns back my way, disbelief tightening her features. She looks wildly uncomfortable, and when Willa Rose Sutter is uncomfortable, she does *not* talk about it. "Well, that was out of nowhere."

Correction. She'll talk about it if it accomplishes downplaying or denying.

"Not really, Willa." I stand and collect plates, stacking them until they're a tower of teetering leftovers.

Willa sputters while she jumps up and gathers the fixing plates, sweeping shredded cheese off the edge of the table and dashing in with her handful. "What the hell are you talking about?"

I round on her, dumping the plates in the sink with a clatter. Willa carefully shoves her arms' contents onto the counter, then turns to face me.

"I told you what I wanted at Christmas."

"Yeah," she snaps. "And then my mom died, forgive me."

"I didn't mean it like that." A sigh rushes out of me. "I'm saying Rooney's stating the obvious."

Willa's jaw clenches as her eyes spark furious copper. "It's not obvious. We're not obvious."

"Oh?" Slowly, I walk toward her. Willa steps back in sync with me, until her ass bumps the counter. I place my hands on its surface, bracing my arms so that she's caged inside my body. She has to crane her neck to look up at me. Her pulse slams at the base of her throat as color floods her cheeks. Her nipples are diamond bits beneath her threadbare Mia Hamm T-shirt, and she presses her thighs together.

"Head to toe, Sunshine, says you want me. Look at me and tell me you don't see the same thing."

She juts her chin up, her eyes meeting mine. No beard to hide my own blush or the way my throat sticks when I try to swallow. My shirt does nothing to cover my rapid breaths. My jeans are a lost cause. No possible material could hide that I'm rock hard for her. My fingers are white-knuckling the counter. We're a combustion reaction the moment before its elements meet.

I dip my head, sliding my lips along the shell of her ear. "Tell me you don't see it, Willa."

She shudders. "I see it."

"Because you want it," I whisper against her neck, trailing faint kisses down her throat.

"I don't want it…any more than you do."

A dry laugh leaves me. "What if I told you I want it so bad, I can't think straight?"

She swallows. "Well, then I'll admit I want it that bad, too, just not how you do."

"And how do I want it?" My lips graze her collarbone

She huffs a frustrated sigh but leans into my touch. "You know what I mean. You want warm fuzzies. And I just want sex."

"That's bullshit, Willa." I straighten and press my pelvis to hers. Willa whimpers. "You want more. You're just scared."

"Am not," she rasps.

"How about this. Come with me to the cabin up in Washington over spring break. Give me that time to show you there's nothing to be scared of. You. Me. The woods. Four days."

Willa bites her lip. "I should stay here and study."

I push away from the counter. Yanking a towel off the handlebar, I throw it over my shoulder. "Study at the cabin. Study naked. Study clothed. I don't care. I'll cook. You rest. You need some R and R."

She's staring at me. Her irises are nonexistent, her legs scissored shut. Her hair practically crackles with raw energy. Willa's warring with herself, battling over what she wants and how she's lived her whole life. They're mutually exclusive. You can't give yourself to someone and wall yourself off.

She's cornered, and she knows it. I've called us for what we are—two people who care so much more, want so much more than we've allowed ourselves to admit. First, we were both too pissed to see what was really there. Then as the heat of our tension began to boil over, and the real structure of our dynamic revealed itself, we were both too shocked and apprehensive to do anything about it.

That was then. This is now.

I've spent the last eight weeks without Willa in my life. I never want that to happen again. I'm done pretending this stilted frenemyship works. I can only hope Willa is ready to give up the act, too.

"You wussing out on me, Sunshine?"

Her eyes narrow and darken. "Bullshit, I am."

"Good." I turn toward the sink and run the water. "Then it's a plan."

I catch the sound of Willa's voice, but over the running water, the clank of dishes, I can't understand her. She seems aware of this because suddenly she's closed the distance between us and shut off the valve. Our eyes meet as the plate slips from my hand, into the soapy water with a heavy *plunk*.

"Ryder, I don't...It's not..." She sighs and throws her hands on her hips. "You need to understand that this is a lost cause. I am not girlfriend material. You are not going to change my mind. When you see sense, we're going to fuck like rabbits, but it'll be no strings, no commitment. Then I'll wreck you with one emotionless orgasm after another, for which I expect to be repaid in Swedish meatballs and those delicious mini-sausages you made at Christmas."

Slowly I turn to fully face her, leaning a hip against the counter. Willa's bravado fades a bit when she sees my eyes. "Willa, if anyone's getting *wrecked*, it will be you." Pushing off the counter's edge, I take a step toward her and wrap a curl of hers around my finger. "I've always played clean with you, Sunshine, but I don't have to."

Her legs clamp together. "Is that a threat?" she manages hoarsely.

"No, Willa. It's a promise."

Spinning away, I step back to the sink, then start scrubbing dishes. Her eyes are one hundred percent on my ass. I can feel her heart pounding from over here. It might take me a while, but I'll convince Willa Sutter she's safe to share everything with me, to take the leap and risk her heart, if it's the last thing I do.

"Pack warm," I say over my shoulder. "Washington's chilly in March."

26

WILLA

Playlist: "Not Over You," Guitar Tribute Players

"WILLA, RELAX."

I startle so hard, I spill half my coffee all over my lap. "Jesus, Bergman. A little warning."

Ryder's eyebrows lift over his sunglasses. "A little warning before I talk to you?"

Just…goddamn him. He was despicably lumbersexual to begin with, but now that he's only working that week-old beard, it's game over. His scratchy stubble does nothing to hide his soft lips which are, as I predicted, unfairly full while still masculine. Throw in the thick, smoky lashes, enviable cheekbones, a jaw you could cut glass with, and I'm ruined. I am a puddle of shameful lust.

Then there's, ya know, his whole personality. He's an asshole, in the right ways. He shoves back when I shove first, when he knows I'm looking for a harmless fight and I need our snap and sizzle. He finds weird ways to figure out my feelings and moods without making me feel like I just had another soul-draining chat on the shrink's sofa. He makes the best fucking Swedish food, and he knows exactly how to give a back rub. His hugs are life-affirming.

He'd be very easy to fall in love with. *If* I did that sort of thing. Which I don't. At least, when I'm able to keep up all my boundaries and walls and distancing mechanisms, most of which were ripped away from me the moment he stuffed me in his Explorer, then made us hop a flight to Seattle and drive the gorgeous terrain of Washington State.

And I voluntarily agreed to this bullshit.

I grumble something noncommittal and stare out the window, looking at my surroundings as we drive south on I-5. It's Ryder in topography. Evergreens and still waters running deep. It's intoxicatingly beautiful.

Ryder's barely touched me since we boarded. Our only physical contact was me falling asleep on his shoulder. To my horror, I drooled extensively. I only know this because when our plane landed roughly and I snorted awake, his entire shoulder was soaked. Ryder seemed unfazed, but I wanted to shrivel into my seat with mortification and disappear.

That's all. No easy hugs, no playing with my hair. No kisses to my forehead when I fall into his chest, which is the best target for my frustration with the world. The center console between us in the SUV feels both a mile wide and a millimeter thin. Too much. Not enough.

I'm losing my mind.

"I'm edgy," I finally manage.

He smirks like a sexy asshole. "Ya think?"

"Are we almost there?"

Ryder nods, checking his mirror before he takes a soft left turn. I stare at him, caught in one of those moments where I find it particularly surreal that I can both see his face and hear his voice. I liked him so much when I had neither of them. How can I resist him now?

"Where the hell are we?"

Ryder grins. "If I told you, I'd have to kill you."

"Not funny." I smack his arm and bruise my hand. "Jesus, Bergman. You been juicing on me?"

"Do you know me? Juicing is an environmental disgrace. It wastes valuable fibrous contents of fruits and vegetables— Ow!"

I found that special spot beneath his elbow and pinched. "You know what I mean. 'Roids. Juice."

His throat works as he swallows. I watch his Adam's apple bob and have to fold my arms across my rock-hard nipples. "Had to do something the past couple of months," he says.

"What's that mean?"

Ryder glances at me briefly, before his eyes travel back to the road. "I was worried about you, Sunshine. Kind of went crazy for a couple of weeks. Got drunk daily for a stretch, then realized working out compulsively was a better coping strategy."

My throat's a desert. My heart slams in my chest. "Oh."

Ryder clears his throat and points ahead of him. "That's it."

My jaw drops. A breathtaking A-frame greets us as we roll down the gravel path. Floor-to-ceiling glass perches between deep wood beams that triangulate the house. Everything's either rich brown, dark green, or cerulean blue. Spruce and pines, boundless sky, shining water not far off. A dense patch of woods surrounds the house, only cleared enough for a magnificent waterfront view.

"The property's private," Ryder says, throwing the car in park. "You can wander the woods topless, skinny-dip—" His swallow is thick. "It's yours for the using, I mean."

I'm flabbergasted. "Ryder, this is *crazy* nice."

He shrugs. "Dad invested well for a while and bought it. Wisely paid it off promptly. When the recession hit, he lost most of his investments, but at least this was paid for. The older siblings take turns throughout the year visiting and doing maintenance work. It's how we earn our use of it."

"You don't pay someone to maintain it?"

"No." He stares analytically at the house like he's itemizing a to-do list. "That kind of upkeep costs more than my parents can afford."

I roll my eyes. "You guys seem like you're fine financially."

"Well, Sunshine, sometimes looks are deceiving. Yes, Dad's a doctor, but there's seven of us, and most of us have gone to college and racked up tuition costs." He glances my way and smiles softly. "Come on, let's stretch our legs a little bit."

I follow him out of the car, heading for the trunk, but Ryder wraps his fingers around my wrist and tugs gently. "Leave it. First, I want to show you something."

He turns and walks toward a narrow dirt path in the woods.

"But I'm hungry," I whine. A granola bar flies over his shoulder and hits me. "Wow."

"I anticipated your hanger, Sutter. Eat and walk. Let's go."

"I need water." I'm not ready for this. Ryder's got something up his sleeve. It feels like the death of our relationship as I know and love it. Do I want more? Of flipping course, I do. But I'm terrified of the unknown, of the loss I could experience if I take that leap.

A canteen dangles off Ryder's finger as he raises it over his head, still not looking back. "Don't make me throw you over my shoulder again."

I growl, ripping off the granola wrapper and stomping after him. "Asshole lumberjack."

———

"HOLY SHIT." MY LUNGS TUG FOR AIR. THE HIKE DIDN'T wind me. It's the view that's to blame.

Ryder smiles over at me as I take in the vista. We're high up, staring down over the water beneath us, the surrounding land dotted with neat little triangles of trees. Clouds sweep and cut across the sun, dappling the world in patches of sunlight.

"It's…I don't even have words."

Ryder laughs quietly. "First time for everything."

I punch his shoulder, never breaking my stare. "How do you leave this?"

His exhale is heavy. "Not easily."

"I can imagine." His words sink, then settle heavy as a stone in my stomach. This is the place that makes him happy. Ryder's said this is where he wants to live. This is my problem. He says he wants me, but he can't possibly want the life I'll have. As much as I hate that he said it, I can't deny that in one sense, Ryder was right: his world is not my world, his ideal life does not align with mine. So what the *hell* are we pretending at, then?

Turning, I grab his shirt and tug him toward me. Ryder tumbles close, his hands landing on my hips. "Why are you doing this?" I ask him. "What do you want from me?"

Ryder's brow furrows. The jerk even looks gorgeous when he's totally confused. "What?"

I sigh in frustration. "Ryder, this is your happy place, it's where you want to be. We have one year of college left, and then I have *no* idea where I'll end up signing. Why should we go down a road that's only going to end up hurting both of us?"

He smiles. I resist the urge to slug him in the stomach for looking so composed. He's too fucking unflappable.

"What do you have to smile about?" I snap.

Shaking his head, Ryder slips his fingers through my hair and smooths the sweaty flyaways off my forehead. "You really think that once I had you, I'd ever let us end over something so inconsequential."

My heart twists. "Location and lifestyle are not inconsequential."

"I can be happy anywhere, Willa. As long as you're there, and there's earth and sky around me." His smile deepens. "But you don't want it to be that simple. Because you're scared of where it leads."

"Of course I'm scared. I'm four-alarm-fire freaking out."

Ryder's smile falls as his hands drift down to the sweaty nape of my neck. I know better than to try to pull away or worry it will gross him out. He steps even closer so our fronts brush. "Guess what?" he whispers.

I lick my lips and watch his head bend toward mine. "What?"

"I'm scared too, Sunshine. This is vulnerable shit." His mouth is a breath away from mine. "I just know I'd rather be afraid with you than fearless with anyone else."

He kisses me as he hasn't in months. Expertly, patiently. My body roars to life as my legs give out. I grasp Ryder like he's my anchor to the world as his hands cradle my head, and the impulse to cry hitches in my throat. His lips…without the beard, I feel so much more of them as they skate over mine, as they sweep over my cheeks. They're warm and soft, prodigies at teasing, claiming, taunting. His teeth scrape my bottom lip, sending a thunderbolt of need jolting down my body.

Our mouths open together, breath stealing breath, as his

hands drop and he wraps me in his arms. My fingers dive into his hair, savoring those thick, silky strands. My nails scrape down to his stubble. A shiver waves through my bones.

"Willa," he whispers. His hands are hungry. They're tugging my shirt, clawing over sensitive skin. Waist, stomach, ribs.

"Yes." I can't stop kissing him. I can't stop sinking into this man who holds me like I don't have to hold it all myself. I feel him, iron hard, pressing into my stomach through his jeans. "You've got a two-by-four down there. How's that gonna work?"

Ryder laughs against my lips, shaking his head. "It'll be okay. We'll fit."

"How do you know?"

"We will, Sunshine. We've always fit."

"What if you hurt me, Ryder?"

His whole body freezes. Ryder pulls away just enough so my gaze can fall headlong into those grass-green irises. The exact color of the trees that canopy us, the earth beneath our feet. "Willa Rose Sutter, I will do everything humanly possible with every breath I have *never* to hurt you."

A tear slips down my cheek, and Ryder thumbs it away.

"That said, I will mess up. I know I'm pretty damn perfect, but I *am* still human."

I grab his shirt, then shove him halfheartedly. His grin warms his face and makes his eyes twinkle.

"I want…" I scrape my lip between my teeth as I peer up at him. His smile is warm, his eyes patient. His hand wraps tight around my shoulder as he holds me close.

"You don't have to say anything, Sunshine, not until the words are real and right." Ryder kisses my temple and exhales slowly. "I'm not going anywhere. At least not for the next few days. Someone's got to keep the grizzlies away."

I gulp as he backs away and scoops up our canteen. "Are you…wait, Bergman, are you serious?"

Ryder's laugh echoes in the trees as he starts down the path. "If I tell you, where's the fun in that?"

I run at him, then lunge like a monkey onto his back. He doesn't so much as break his stride.

"The last known California grizzly bear, *Ursus arctos californicus*," Ryder says gently, hitching me higher in his grip, "a now-extinct subspecies of the grizzly bear, was killed roughly a century ago."

"Well, that's a relief. Aren't you just a little California wilderness encyclopedia."

Ryder squeezes my legs, his hands nearly wrapping around my thighs. "That said, we're in Washington, and there are grizzlies here."

"What?" I squawk.

"*Ursus arctos horribilis.* Contained exclusively to the Northern Cascades, which are nowhere close to us, by the way, where they are in serious danger of extirpation—being locally extinct."

"Good."

He snorts a laugh.

Dropping my head against his neck, I rest in that easy quiet we have and remember our hike to the falls. The clean, sharp scent of his sweat. Muscles shifting in his back. Once again, I feel them. I breathe in deep mountain air and Ryder's warm body. I press my lips to his skin how I was too afraid to last time. His grip tightens on my legs, and when he glances up at the path ahead, a smile warms his face.

Tree leaves whisper in the breeze. The sun slips lower in the sky. Ryder carries me the whole way down.

———

ADD COOKING TO FROWNING, OPENING LAPTOP BAGS, SLEEVE cuffing, and other mundane activities that Ryder Bergman magically makes pornographic. Any time I've eaten at his place, the cooking's pretty much done when I get there, which betrays deep wisdom on that man's part. I can only last about five hungry minutes around the smell of food before I *need* to eat. Before I turn into an angry food troll.

But tonight, the jerk had the audacity to set up a tray of fancy snacks, pour me a fat glass of red wine, and not only roll up his sleeves in front of me, but prepare our meal from scratch.

"Enjoying the show?" His eyes are on his hands as he finely chops an onion, but the smartass grin on his face is unmistakable.

I lob a cashew at his head. He pauses only long enough to pop it in his mouth and resume chopping while he chews. Jeebus Christmas, watching him chew and swallow is even disgustingly sexy.

"I'm enthralled," I answer drily. Ryder's smirk says he doesn't buy the sarcasm, but I take the high road because he *is* cooking for me. If I kicked his ass before dinner was finished, then what would I do? "Where'd this food come from anyway?"

"I ordered it, Sunshine. There's this modern marvel called online ordering and delivery of groceries."

"Bergman, you better watch that mouth. I'm a vengeful woman with a gift for nighttime pranks, and it won't be hard to find where you sleep tonight."

"Won't be hard at all. Seeing as we're staying in the same bed."

I choke on my wine. "We're *what*?"

"Well, we might start in separate rooms, but you're a

SoCal sissy who shivers when it dips below sixty degrees. Here, it's still low-thirties at night."

A pathetic noise escapes my throat. "That's fucking arctic."

Ryder snorts as he scrapes the chopped vegetables into the pan and dials up the heat. "To you, Willa, yes. Fifty bucks says you don't make it past midnight before you come crawling to me for body heat."

Right now, it only feels cool. I listened to Ryder for once and packed hoodies and long-sleeve shirts. I'm layered in clothing, topped off with oversized sweats and fuzzy socks. Very seductive. But at least I'm not freezing. Yet.

I let out a shaky breath. "Don't you have heat?"

"Woodburning." Ryder nods toward the hearth. "Fans send the fire's heat throughout the house."

I stare at it. The fireplace is cold and empty. "Are you going to light it, then?"

Ryder frowns, glancing up slowly from the chicken he started butterflying. "I wasn't planning on it, no."

"W-what?" I stammer as my eyes widen. "But I'll be cold."

He shrugs. "It's environmentally irresponsible to heat this entire place for two people. I won't do it, but if you can start that fire yourself, be my guest. Or you could consider doing your part to protect the dwindling polar ice caps, harbingers of impending climate-change catastrophe, and bedshare with a warm-blooded human. Your choice."

I throw an escaped sliver of chopped onion at his head. "Tree-hugging survivalist."

I don't know the first thing about Girl Scout shit like that, and Ryder knows it.

Once again I'm tempted to do him violence, but the food smells really good, and I'd like him to see it through to completion. Maybe then I'll get his balls in a twist and make him light the fire.

My stomach growls, so I shove a handful of English cheddar and dates in my mouth and chew, struggling to hate someone who can make a charcuterie board this damn tasty. "You're playing dirty, Bergman."

His smirk is almost imperceptible before he schools his face. "I warned you I wouldn't always play clean."

He's fucking with me, and that's what we've always done. He ribs me, I rib him. We take turns playing the roles of cat and mouse, provoking each other, nudging the other person until they're cornered where we want them before we take mercy and let them go.

But he's leaning in, applying more pressure. He's not just cornering me. Ryder's forcing my hand. Because while he knows I'd sleep with him at the drop of a hat—what woman in her right mind wouldn't?—Ryder doesn't want that. He wants me to want more than six foot three of muscles, handsome face, and just enough asshole to make him my kind of surly. He wants me to want *him*. He wants me to make the move that shows him that.

I sip my wine and stare at him, thinking about our hike earlier today. I felt brave back up on that mountaintop. I let myself think about terrifying possibilities with falls as precipitous as from that altitude. But our climb down was returning to reality—to what's scary, to how delicate my heart feels.

Fear tunnels through my body, and yet I want to push back on it. I'm scared shitless, but I also can't lie anymore. I can't say I don't want to try somehow to make sense of what this is between Ryder and me. How can I even begin to do that if I never take the first step on the path of possibility?

I need a solid first move. It can't be small. It can't be half-assed. This is me we're dealing with. The only thing I can think to do is what we've always done, to see Ryder's bet and raise him.

Standing, I set my wine on the counter and drag my hoodie off, over my head. Next my long-sleeve shirt. I'm wearing a white tank top and no bra. Ryder's hand holding the knife slows, then comes to a stop.

"What are you doing?" he croaks.

I bend to remove my sweatpants, then toe off my fuzzy socks. Now I'm down to panties and a tank. "Well, if I'm going to freeze all night long, I might as well warm up in that hot tub first. Looks mighty toasty."

Ryder makes a strangled noise.

Stepping away from the counter, I saunter toward the glass door and push it open. The hot tub's a mere five feet away, the sky a black dome dappled with bright stars, so far from city lights. With my back to Ryder, I stare over my shoulder. I hold his eyes as I peel off my tank top and let it fall to the floor.

Ryder's head drops. His hands brace themselves on the counter.

"I'll take my dinner outside, Brawny. Thanks."

27

RYDER

Playlist: "God is a Woman," Jamie McDell

MY HANDS SHAKE AS I SET THE CHICKEN IN THE PAN. THE skin snaps and pops when it hits the heat. It sounds how I feel, watching Willa lean her head back in the Jacuzzi. Hot, agitated.

Dangerously close to bursting into flames.

She's completely naked in there. I can see her panties and shirt puddled like spilled milk on the dark patio deck. Moonlight bathes her skin blue, and the curve of her breasts peeks above the tub's bubbling water.

I'm so hard, my dick's about to bust my zipper. I have to keep reminding myself to breathe so I don't pass out into a pan of seared chicken and add third-degree burns to my head's stunning repertoire.

I can't stop imagining what she looks like, and I'm dying to touch her. She stripped, all right, but I didn't see it happen, not fully. I averted my eyes when those thumbs hooked inside her panties. I couldn't. I couldn't let the first time I saw Willa naked be such an incomplete moment. When I see her, it's going to be on even ground, and she's going to be just as goddamn hungry for me as I am for her. This is one game I won't play under.

I'm nice enough to bring Willa her wine. She smiles up at me and shifts beneath the bubbles as she accepts the glass. She makes zero effort not to stare at the state of affairs in my jeans.

"Yikes, Lumberjack. That log looks uncomfortable."

I scowl at her, then storm back inside, aggravation mounting when I hear her throaty laugh. I add finishing touches to the food and then plate it for both of us. Double-checking the burners are off, dishes in hand, I tuck my beer under my arm and walk out to join her. Willa's staring at the stars, one arm stretched along the ledge of the tub, spinning her wine.

When her eyes meet mine, they're softer. Warm, chocolate brown, with flecks of caramel. Her glass is almost empty. Wine makes her a little pliant, and by the look in her eyes, a lot horny. Wine leads to horny eyes. You bet your ass I file that away for future use.

As I hand Willa her plate, she smiles up at me. "Thanks."

We eat in silence for a few bites, me on a neighboring Adirondack chair, Willa in the tub, her plate held over the bubbles. She uses her fingers to eat since she can't use her lap and cut with a knife and fork. First the chicken, then she slides a few green beans between her teeth and chews. "Damn, you can cook, Ry."

I make a noncommittal noise as I take a swig of my beer.

"Ryder."

I glance over at her. "Hm?"

Her eyes soften further. Her irises shift to pale, golden candlelight. "Come in here."

Our gaze holds for a long time. My finger taps my beer bottle.

"Why?" I finally manage.

Willa doesn't blink away. She just takes one long breath and sighs, shutting off the hot tub, bathing us in silence. "Because I want you."

I almost drop my beer. Setting down the bottle and my plate, I look at her once again. "I need more than that."

Willa bites her lip, then blinks away, staring into the dark horizon. "I want Ryder Stellan Bergman. Flannel king and fearless mountain man. I want my Business Math buddy. I want the guy who ruins guacamole and who knows how to touch my hair. I want the asshole who whistles at my games and hugs me so hard my lungs feel like they'll pop." She swallows. "I love that feeling when you're so close to pushing too hard, squeezing too tight, then you know exactly when to stop. You know when to battle and when to say sorry."

My breath comes out jagged. My heart is smashed in a vise of emotions that Willa's words only twist tighter.

"I want Ryder who read to my dying mother," she whispers. "I want Ryder who brought me whiskey and peanut butter cups and was the first man to ever slow down and hold me and help me feel safe enough to fall apart. I want the man who carried me down a mountain today. I want his quiet strength and his big heart. I want you."

I stand. Willa does too. And everything changes.

Air rushes out of me. She's so beautiful, there aren't words. There aren't words to describe what moonlight looks like on the lines of her muscles in her shoulders, her stomach, her legs. No words to capture the soft dip and swell of her hips, the curve of her breasts and her taut nipples, which tighten in the cold.

Her fingers dance by her side as she waits. I know I'm

breathing because I'm still alive, but it doesn't feel like it. I'm stunned.

"Ryder," she says quietly.

My eyes meet hers, and my heart burns with knowledge. I love her. I've known I loved her, but the truth bursts inside my chest, surges up my throat, and beats a violent tattoo inside my mind as I stare into her eyes.

"Come here," she says.

I step closer. Willa does too. She leans onto the ledge inside the tub, placing her at eye level. I hold her gaze as her hands settle on the first button of my shirt that's still done, working them open, one by one.

Halfway done with my buttons she pauses. She presses a kiss to my forehead and wobbles. My hands go to her hips, holding her steady as she resumes unbuttoning my shirt. Her skin is smooth and taut, hot from the water. When she presses my shirt off my shoulders, I shake it off and finally do what I can't avoid doing anymore.

I drag my mouth hungrily over her breast and taste her skin. Her nipple's hard, the most beautiful berry pink. I plump it in my hand and roll my tongue across its surface.

Her hands are in my hair, and air rushes out of her.

"Oh, God," she moans.

Willa drops to her knees in the water, furiously tugging at my buckle, yanking open the button. She drags down the zipper and shoves my jeans off my hips. I tug them down the rest of the way, shucking my boxers next.

Willa's eyes are wide as she stares at me. It's the hardest I've ever been, my length so tight and thick, it smacks into my belly button as it springs free.

A slow smile brightens her face. "Well?" she says. "What are you waiting for?"

Hot tubs are relaxing, but they're not great for this. I want to see her well. I want to take my time. I need my wits about me, and Willa's naked body all over mine in a Jacuzzi spells disaster for that. Not to mention, hot tubs are also terribly unhygienic for anything sex-related, not that I'm telling Willa that. She'll give me shit for my neurotic cleanliness.

My hands slide down her shoulders to her waist, as I hold her gaze. She yelps as I haul her out of the water, wrap her around my torso and step back through the door.

Willa's smile is infectious as she locks her arms around my neck and squeezes her thighs. I have to bite my cheek not to lose my senses because she's centimeters from sliding along my cock. "Where are we going?" she asks.

I shoulder open the door to the massive first-floor bathroom. A glass shower with a tiled bench and two waterfall spouts winks from the far end of the room.

Willa's eyes follow mine. "Wow," she says breathily.

I set her down and flip on the light switch. Turning on the water, I adjust it, then turn on the towel warmer, too. Willa shivers a little, and I drag her with me toward the echoing space.

She looks around, her hands running along my arms distractedly. "Why aren't you coming in?" Her eyes follow my hands as they reach into my hair, near my ears. "They have to come off."

I nod.

Willa hesitates, then steps closer, gripping my arm. "Do you want me to get out, so you don't have to—"

"No. I don't mind. Do you?"

Willa smiles, her hand cupping my cheek, smoothing back my hair. "Of course not."

I kiss her wrist, never letting my eyes leave hers. "I'll read your lips, and I can still hear you a little in my right ear. If you're close." I tug her against me. "Very close."

"Hm." Her smile widens. "That can be arranged."

Carefully, I remove my hearing aids and backtrack into the bedroom, setting them on the nearby dresser, safe from the moisture in the bathroom's steamy air.

As I reenter the bathroom, the world's sounds telescope once again. Gone are those many ambient noises I've already begun to unconsciously take for granted. I'm left with the tug of my breath, the husky whisper of Willa's. My heartbeat pounds in my ears.

"Come on, Willa." Slowly I lead her into the shower, letting water tumble over us.

Her eyes snap up and hold mine, surprise coloring her expression.

I know what it means to her, to talk, to say her name when I have very little sense of how it sounds. Before I revisited using both hearing aids, I never did that, not once. I was too unsure about the sound of my voice, the pressure, if I spoke, to also hear well enough to carry conversation that I wasn't confident I could sustain. But I want Willa to know that fear and hesitation aren't here between us anymore. I want to show her walls can come down, even after you've put time and energy into building them.

"Ryder." I see my name on her lips more than I hear it. I feel its sound vibrate across my chest, and settle in my heart.

She reaches up on tiptoe and gives me a kiss I'll always remember. It's not a wild clash of tongues and mouths. It's not a battle for control. It's gentle, and it's scared. Hopeful and fragile. Her lips are so impossibly full as they slide and press against mine. Tugs and bites, quiet puffs of air that dance over my face.

I cup her neck and lean between her legs. My thumbs gentle her cheeks as her hands wrap around my waist and pull me closer. I taste an indescribable sweetness that's just Willa, as I suck on her bottom lip and slide my tongue along its fullness.

Her moan dances over my skin and makes me shiver. One last kiss, before I pull her tight against me. She glances down between us, then back up to me with a massive raise of her eyebrows.

It makes me laugh quietly. I shake my head, lifting my hand, so she knows I plan to touch her this way, not take it home. Not yet. It's seamless, our jump back into our original dynamic—body language, eye contact, unspoken understanding.

Her breasts are full and soft, begging for my mouth. I kiss them, sucking her nipples roughly as I drift a hand down her waist and find her, warm and smooth. My fingers part impossibly silky skin, one finger, then two, sinking inside. Willa's hands clamp onto my shoulders. She falls into me, her chest smashed to mine, her mouth open against my neck.

My thumb finds her clit and swirls in a slow, featherlight circle. I feel each burst of hot air, the gift of her sound as she brings her mouth to my right ear and gasps against it. Willa's hand leaves my arm and wraps tight around the base of my cock.

I groan and throw my head back as she squeezes, then drags her grip up to the head. Her thumb sweeps over the tip of my cock as a sound leaves me that I couldn't care less about. Willa's mouth stays pressed to my ear, each desperate noise of hers mine to drown in. Her grip is perfect, her touch just slow enough to torture me. Her thighs begin to shake, her breath gets choppier.

My hips rock in her grip. My mouth turns and finds hers. We kiss and breathe against each other as we learn under the spray of water—fumbling and laughing a little, as we find that touch *there* that makes the other come undone. I hold her tight to me, my eyes glued to hers as her hips falter, as her nails dig into my skin.

Her eyelids flutter. A rosy flush sweeps up her chest, then pinks her cheeks. I watch her full lips say, "C-close," and curl my fingers tighter, rub inside her, harder, faster. Desperate heat soars up my legs and sizzles low in my spine. My body's taut as a wire, and her soft, small hands tight around my thick length makes me dizzy. Willa begins to tremble as her eyes widen, her mouth falls open. She comes around my hand, shaking as she moans into my kiss, and watching her go over sends me with her. One last thrust into her tight fist, then I spill for a small eternity against her stomach.

Willa leans into me, curling her arms fiercely around my neck. Her lips press to my ear, my cheeks, my mouth. Our foreheads rest against each other's before she steals one last kiss. She pulls back, flushed and breathtaking as a shaky smile brightens her eyes. Then, her hand sweeps over her face, before it pinches and flicks into the air.

She knows what it means now, and I can't help but smile back.

Beautiful.

————

I CAVED AND MADE A FIRE. SEEING AS WE CROSSED THE Rubicon back in the shower, I have a hunch Willa's going to let me big spoon her in bed in a few hours anyway. She lies stretched on the couch, her feet in my lap. Her toes wiggle as I slide my thumbs up the arch of her foot.

"Let's play a game," I tell her.

Willa turns from staring into the fire and faces me. "A game?"

I nod. "It's called fill in the blanks."

"Fill in the blanks of what?"

"Your life." Her foot starts to pull away, but I grasp it. "Willa."

Her eyes turn darker, boding anger. "What?"

"Talk to me. What upsets you about that?"

She sighs, her head dropping back to the sofa's arm. "I don't like talking about myself."

"Yes, but when the kids are older, who's going to explain to them why Mom always gets weird around corn dogs and tough conversations and grizzly bears?"

"Okay, I don't get *weird* around corn dogs. They're just gross. And grizzly bears—though extinct in the state of California and allegedly safely corralled in some nearby Washington State mountain range—are still terrifying."

"And tough conversations?"

Willa scowls. "I was going to take issue with the *kids* portion of that statement, next."

"You said you needed time, and I'll give you all the time you need, Sunshine. I'll wait until you're done winning Olympic golds, then, when you're ready, I want crazy-haired angry ankle-biters running around."

Willa's scowl deepens. "This isn't a joking matter."

"Completely agree." I tug her legs deeper onto my lap and switch to rubbing the other foot.

"Ryder…" She scrubs her face. "Ugh. Feelings. Talking."

I pause my massage of her foot and tap it so she'll look at me. "Baby steps, okay?"

Willa's expression wobbles. She looks so scared, my chest tightens in a protective reflex. I rub her heel and work my way up to massaging her Achilles tendon. Her eyes drift shut as she groans. "Where were you born?" I ask.

"Tulsa," she says quietly. "You?"

I smile. "Here."

Willa's head snaps up. She glances around, looking disturbed, as if evidence of a traumatic birth is still somewhere littered across the wood floor.

"The story goes, Mom said her back hurt, stood up from the sofa and made it halfway to the door before she sat down and pushed me out, right at the bottom of the steps."

Willa stares horrified at the landing. It makes a belly laugh tumble out of me. "I mean I was number four. It's kind of an automatic process by that point."

"Spoken like the half of our species that will never have to shove the next generation out of their vagina," Willa says flatly.

It makes me laugh harder. "I've traumatized you."

"Jesus. Okay." She shakes her head. "So. My turn." Her fingers tap her lips. "I want to know exactly what happened with your hearing."

It's like a bucket of ice water over my head, but I'm asking her to be brave. I have to be, too. "Bacterial meningitis. I was halfway through summer training for my freshman season at UCLA. I spiked a horrible fever, developed a headache that was so painful I couldn't open my eyes. My parents took me to the hospital. I dropped out of consciousness at some point, and when I came to, my hearing was like this."

Willa blinks away tears. "God. I'm sorry, Ryder."

I shrug. "It's okay."

"No it's not," she says urgently, sitting up straighter. "You lost something you loved."

"I know. But I grieved. Sometimes I still feel sad, but I moved on. There's nothing to be done now. Just life to live in this new direction."

She hesitates for a beat, her hands seeking my legs. She rubs up and down my shin bones like she's always done it.

Like we're used to tangling our legs together in front of a blistering fire, shacked up in the glorious middle of nowhere.

"What position?"

"Defense. Left-back. I'd have your number, Sunshine."

Her eyes spark. Feistiness crackles off the ends of her hair. "The hell you would."

I laugh into the mouth of my beer bottle before I take a drink. "I guarantee you."

"You're on."

Lowering the bottle, I meet her eyes. "Tomorrow, then. It'll be warm by midday. We'll head down to the field."

Willa gapes. "You have a field?"

"Well, we used to spend lots of time here. There are seven of us, and all of us play or, in my case, played…"

She smacks my shin. "You still play. Maybe not how you once did, but you still play."

I nod, my eyes holding hers. Silence stretches comfortably between us as Willa sips her wine. The fire pops intermittently and casts her face in a warm, blazing glow.

"I want to know about your dad."

Willa stiffens and her jaw sets. "My dad was a local who pumped and dumped my mom during a stretch of R and R. He didn't want anything to do with her pregnancy, and I've never known who he was."

I squeeze her leg. "I'm sorry."

She shrugs. "Whatever."

"Whatever? You never had a daddy, Sunshine."

"Yeah, thanks. Never figured that one out."

I sigh. "Willa, I'm just trying to empathize."

"Well, don't. I don't need pity." She tips her wine back and takes a hefty gulp.

"I don't pity you, and you know it."

She lifts a shoulder. "Okay, fine."

"You know it's okay to hate his guts for being the biggest idiot to miss out on your life, right?"

"Jesus." She throws my legs off hers and stands up. "I really don't need the shrink session."

"Willa, wait." I stand from the couch slowly. "I'm trying to talk to you about this. About the fact that the first man in your life was a complete disappointment and you're inclined to see most men that way. You've *said* that to me. I'm not putting words in your mouth."

Willa stares at me. "That's because most men I've met *are* complete disappointments. They're all pretty words and promises until real life hits. Then they're gone."

She spins away, dragging a blanket from the sofa with her as she heads for the stairs. "I'm tired, and I'm aware I'm being defensive. I want to talk more, but I can't, okay? Not right now. I'll say something I'll regret."

I stare at her, deciphering her face. She looks vulnerable and sad. She looks like she feels guilty, but she doesn't need to. She's telling me her limit. She's not running away. She's postponing.

"Okay. I'm sorry I pushed, Sunshine."

She looks at me with thinly veiled surprise. "You're not mad?"

"No, Willa. Not at all."

Her shoulders drop in relief. "Okay, well…I'm just going to bed, then." Wading toward me with the blanket swallowing her up, Willa presses a kiss to my sternum, then peers up at me. "Good night."

I watch her ascend the steps. She stops at the landing and pauses to look at me curiously before taking the stairs the rest of the way up.

Staring into the fire, I let my thoughts settle. I think about how much I want to curl around her in sleep tonight, but how much more important it is to show Willa that I can respect her process.

Baby steps, I told her. This is what I want her to see. That I won't bolt when she bristles, that I won't punish her when she tells me her boundaries. That I won't resent her when she says *this is all I can do*, especially when every word I read between the lines says, *but I want to do more.*

The hearth's flames dim, and Willa's footsteps quiet upstairs. I break up the embers, lock the doors, and trek upstairs. When I check on her, she's just how I found her months ago, after Joy died. Burrowed under blankets, pretending to be asleep. And just like last time, I hold my hand on her back, then slide my fingers through her hair. I keep my promise.

I don't give up on Willa. Just like Willa, even scared and scarred, has never given up on me.

28

WILLA

Playlist: "The Lotto," Ingrid Michaelson, AJR

"Good morning, Sunshine." His voice is raspy in the morning, and my nipples peak in response. *See?* they say. *That rough mouth could have been directed on us all night long. Licking, biting, sucking, whispering against us as he does that thing with his tongue—*

"Shut up, boobies."

Ryder stills on the other side of the counter. "Did you just talk to your tits?"

"Don't mind me. Coffee." I slide onto a stool at the breakfast bar and accept the mug he places in front of me with a weak smile.

"Thank you," I manage after the first sip. Peering into my cup, I realize it's exactly how I like it. "You know how I drink my coffee?"

"I value my life." Ryder tops off his mug and smiles at me. "I've seen you enough mornings to figure it out. Brewed strong. Splash of milk."

My belly does a summersault. "Ryder, about last night..." I slide my finger along the rim of the cup, staring into my coffee. Wouldn't it be nice if the words were spelled out in those swirls of milk? Talking about this stuff is so hard. "I'm sorry." I meet his eyes. They're warm and kind as always. He's so damn calm. Unshakable.

"Why are you sorry?"

I stare at him, willing the words to spill out with the same force that they leave my mouth when I *don't* want them to. But they stubbornly refuse to cooperate when I need them most. And then I peer down at my phone. Maybe it's because it's how we started, but I feel a swell of comfort, opening our text thread and seeing months of conversation scroll by as I slide my finger along the screen.

Maybe, even if I can't speak them, I can *write* these impossible words. Maybe I can talk to Ryder in our first, familiar way. I pick up my phone, showing it to him. "Is this...Can I tell you like this?"

He tips his head and searches my eyes. "Course, Sunshine."

Nervously, I stare down at my phone. And then I start to type. *I went thermonuclear on you. Yesterday and last night felt as fantastic as they did frightening. I've been trying to work through my emotions with the counselor, but my relationship and trust issues are deep-seated. It's about the anger and resentment I feel toward the sperm donor. It's about having a ton of upheaval throughout my childhood, constantly relocating, making friends, then losing them.*

I threw everything into loving my mom because where she went, I went. She was my mom, my dad, my best friend, my everything. Then, when she was sick, I spent years worried and stressed and heartbroken that I was going to lose the one person I had let myself love with all my heart.

I started to adopt this habit of never letting myself get attached so I could avoid getting hurt. That's not a behavior that's just going to disappear overnight.

Ryder reads the message, then glances up, meeting my eyes. "I know," he says quietly.

And like last night, another lock on my heart pops open and falls away. Like last night, he's not mad or impatient or unimpressed that this is the best that I can do for now.

My voice is thin, but I need to send the message home. I need him to understand what he's getting himself into. "Pretending like doing this kind of thing doesn't really, *really* scare me is impossible. I'm not good at it. I've never done it before."

Ryder stares at me. He sets his hand on the counter, palm up. I give it to him without hesitating, then sigh as his fingers softly stroke my hand. "That's tough stuff to say, Sunshine."

My eyes tear up as I nod.

"Thank you," he says quietly as he squeezes my hand.

I bite my lip and squeeze back. When he lets go, I cup my coffee to warm myself. Heat comes quickly enough, though. It shoots up my spine as I watch Ryder drink from his mug, and take in his whole adorable morning appearance. He has great bedhead and a distracting line of skin peeking between his shirt and his pajama bottoms.

"So." Ryder sips his coffee, then sets it down. "*This kind of thing. It.* What are we talking about?"

"Didn't I use enough feeling words this morning?"

Ryder just stares at me and smiles.

I swear under my breath and gulp some coffee. "You and me, Lumberjack. What we are."

He bends far enough to lean his elbows on the counter. He's wearing a gray thermal shirt that's worn and fitted in all the right places. It hugs the cut muscles of his shoulders and arms, running snug along his trim waist. I'm scared to see what's below that point. I'm pretty sure it's plaid flannel, and

I'm not sure I'm prepared for that much lumbersexual hotness.

"What we are," he repeats. "Which is…?"

I open my mouth, but no words come out. I want to be courageous, I want to say what Ryder means to me, what I want *us* to try to be, but my courage sticks somewhere between my throat and my tongue.

His phone shatters the silence as it buzzes, skittering along the quartz countertop. Ryder silences his cell without looking at it, but stupidly, my eyes travel to the screen. *Emma.*

Red tints my vision. *Emma*? Who the everloving fuck is Emma?

"No one important," Ryder says evenly.

My eyes snap up to his. "I said that out loud?"

"You did, Willa." Ryder smiles and gently brushes one of my curls off of my forehead. "Seriously, she's no one to me."

I stare at him, blinking rapidly. Very strange things are happening in my chest. It feels like someone beat it with a crowbar, cracks rapidly forming. My skin is hot, my head pounding. I think… I think I'm jealous?

Ryder slides the phone my way. "Don't believe me, see for yourself."

The phone screams at me to swipe it open, to deep-sea dive into Ryder's texts. Who else has been texting him? What other chicks with pretty, contemporary names instead of ones inspired by Prairie-obsessed twentieth-century authors are blowing up his phone?

I shut my eyes and exhale slowly. "I trust you."

"You can still look through it."

My eyes open and narrow at him. "Do you *want* me to?"

Ryder shrugs. "I don't care if you do. I'd be a little curious if some guy was blowing up your phone. I trust you implicitly, but I wouldn't mind knowing what he was saying, I think. Go ahead, Sunshine."

Swiping his coffee off the counter, Ryder backs away. Dammit, my worst fears are confirmed. Ryder Bergman wears flannel on his fantastic ass and mountain-man legs as well as he wears it over his tree-felling upper body. "I'm going to freshen up. Have at it."

He's gone without another word, leaving me with his phone burning in my hand.

I tap my fingers on the counter. The clock ticks. My coffee gets cold.

"Oh, what the hell." I swipe open his phone because yes, I know his password by now.

It starts off innocuous, this perusal of Ryder's cell. He texts his siblings a lot, and that warms my heart. I'm both jealous of and wildly happy for him, that he has such close family. He texts his mom every morning. That twists my gut. I deliberately avoid texts from Sadie, Emma, Haley, and Olivia.

Until I don't.

Fuckety fuckersons. These chicks are not subtle. Coffee invites, long-time-no-sees. *Let's grab dinner sometime.* Presumably, they're former conquests of his. One-night stands. Not girlfriends, because Ryder's been clear he hasn't dated since high school—why he was so emphatic about that, who knows. What I *do* know is all of these texts begin roughly around the time of the attack on Fort Ryder's Face, when Becks and Tucker forced his hand by shaving the middle of his beard.

I'm not surprised. I've always found Ryder hot, truly handsome. There's a quiet sexiness to a man who doesn't flaunt all he has to offer, and while I didn't realize it's my catnip, it clearly is. I might have wanted to throttle him from the first moment we met, but it didn't take me long to realize I also found him deeply attractive.

Without the beard, though, Ryder's, like...well, he's model material. He has classically beautiful features, roughened with enough masculinity and hard edges, the wear and tear of sunshine and years outside, to make him look mature and even older than he actually is. Ryder is a man among a sea of boys. When the beard got nixed, that fact went on full display.

My heart pounds. Ryder didn't respond to a single one of them. He left his read receipts on to make it clear he'd both seen them and was ignoring them. He sent a very clear message. But I'm still shaking with this new itchy feeling under my skin. I have the ridiculous impulse to sprint after and tackle him, to bite his warm, taut skin, head to toe, kiss him senseless, and then ride that lumberjack's wood all morning. I want every square inch of Ryder to say *Willa's*. I want everyone to know he's mine, I'm his, and we're the only one the other wants.

Holy shit. *Hooooly shit.*

Reality slaps me upside the head. If I saw him with any of those women, if he'd as much as agreed to get a cup of fucking tea, I'd have felt like my heart was ripped out of my chest.

It's not possessiveness. This isn't some petty female game I'm allowing myself to be sucked into. When I try to picture him with anybody else, another woman holding his hand, tugging his hair, another woman kissing or touching him, burrowing into his warm grasp, rubbing his head when a migraine hits, it feels like standing in front of one of those distorted mirrors at the funhouse. It's the wrong image. Instinctively, positively, I know it's not right. That's not how it should be, *ever*.

Why? The answer beats louder and louder inside me until the truth is jarring my bones, rattling the cage I locked it in. Because I lo—

"Sunshine?"

His voice echoes from upstairs. The affection and familiarity in my nickname is a warm blanket of reassurance, wrapping around me. It's the audible version of his hugs, those big arm squeezes that incite a feeling I've had for months. That when I'm with Ryder Bergman, I'm exactly where I'm supposed to be.

"What?"

"Rain looks like it's coming sooner rather than later. If I'm going to kick your ass on the field, we better get moving."

Sureness settles with a terrifying weight in my chest. It sinks into my stomach and lands heavy, solid, unquestionable. I can't believe what I'm about to do, and yet I'm determined to do it, now that I understand. Now that it's singing in my ears, filling my heart, demanding to be spoken.

"Coming!"

———

RYDER'S QUIET ON THE WALK DOWN THE WINDING PATH. Close to the bottom, my feet catch on loose stones. His hand juts out immediately, wrapping around my elbow.

"Yeesh, do you have eyes in the back of your head? You have freakish reflexes."

Ryder grins, his eyes ahead. "Reflexes you will soon see schooling you on the field."

I shove him playfully, and he doesn't even budge. He really did muscle up while I was hibernating in my grief cave.

"You're quiet, Brawny."

"I'm always quiet, Willa."

"No, you're not. I mean, sometimes you are but, generally, you talk to me plenty."

Ryder stops on the trail, making me bump into him. Slowly, he turns and peers down at me. "I guess I do. But that's different. That's only when it's us."

There's my grinch heart again, growing another size larger. *Only when it's us.*

I blink up at him. Ryder's eyes are deep, serene green, surrounded by the trees. His features are guarded, imbued with something bursting at the seams of his expression. I want to grab his arms and shake it loose, like a goodie jammed in the vending machine.

Two birds chitter in the tree above us and shatter our quiet when they shoot up into the sky. They arc and swoop, their flight a dancing chase and tease until finally they flatten on the wind and soar away in tandem.

"Only when it's us?"

Ryder stares at me. "Have you seen me speak to another woman besides my sisters or mother, since I met you?"

I shake my head slowly.

"Have I looked at one?"

I give my bottom lip a rough tug between my teeth. My heart rate trips and takes off at a dead sprint. "No," I whisper.

His eyes burn, and a flush crawls up his neck. "Since I got these"—he points to the hardware behind his ears—"has any of that changed?"

"N-no."

Ryder's jaw ticks. Without another word, he spins away, resuming our walk down the trail. I more or less tumble after him, catching up the moment we break through the woods into a clearing.

Turning, Ryder walks toward a shed, swiping the numbers

on a lock until it pops open. He disappears inside, then quickly drags out a mid-size net and a few balls. I pick up a ball, then a pump, and inflate it, watching Ryder from a distance as he straightens the net.

Dropping the ball, I touch it forward. Something about the brisk wind, the smell of mowed grass, reminds me of childhood. I'm transported to my first days with a soccer ball, that carefree happiness I felt, as autumn air sucked my shirt against my wiry body and sent the ball rolling just off course. I remember orange slices and secondhand cleats, Grandma Rose braiding my hair and Mama's mantra whispered over me as she rubbed sunscreen into my cheeks.

You are strong. You are brave. You can do anything you set your heart and mind to.

I still tell myself those words before every game I play. I'm telling myself those words right now.

Ryder glances up from the net and watches me as I dribble. I show off a little, flicking the ball easily in a rainbow and catching it on the top of my foot. I spin my foot around, never losing the ball, and scoop it up again, bracing it across my shoulder blades. Then I roll it to my shoulder and pop it off. It flies through the air and lands directly at Ryder's feet.

He struggles and fails to hide his amusement as he says, "Hotdogger."

There's so much pride and admiration in his expression, and my heart twists with that scary big feeling I almost said to myself in the kitchen.

"If you got it, flaunt it," I tell him.

"Did you just quote Beyoncé?"

I shoulder him and steal the ball from his feet, spinning so he can see my mouth clearly. "You say that like I should be embarrassed when you're the grown man who recognizes old-school 'Yoncé."

Ryder grins. "Two sisters, Sunshine. I went deaf too late in life."

I stop with the ball and feel a frown tug at my mouth. "That's not funny. I don't like it when you joke about it."

His grin falters. "Why?"

"Because…" I juggle the ball, hiding my feelings behind my movements. "I don't know. You're making fun of someone who means a lot to me. Tease me all you want, but don't joke at your own expense."

Ryder tips his head to the side. "One might almost think you liked me, Sunshine."

"One would be correct, Lumberjack." I send the ball into the air, then crack it with a bicycle kick into the net.

Ryder backtracks to retrieve it, then leverages the ball up and takes his turn showing off. Oh, hell. *Ohhhh,* freaking hell. His lips purse as he juggles, those sharp green eyes narrowed in focus. His lashes fan over his cheekbones, and his hair glitters in the sun. His body is long lines, grace, power. It looks effortless. I'm, at max, thirty minutes away from dying of sexual starvation. That fun in the shower last night was not enough. Not even close.

When his eyes meet mine, they widen. "Wow. You look…"

Sex-crazed. Hornier than humanly possible. Yes. Yes, I am.

I take a massive breath. "I'm ready to kick your ass. Now, let's go."

One-on-one is hard. Even the best player in the world gets exhausted working a field solo, never a teammate to pass the ball to and run for that give-and-go. It's just you and your foot skills, your speed and agility to throw off your opponent, then make it to the goal.

"You first." Ryder lofts the ball my way. I catch it on my

thigh, drop it immediately to the ground, then take off. "Shit, Sunshine!"

A laugh barrels out of me. Ryder drops, his insane quads flexing as his body takes a defensive stance. His legs are a little wide, so I try for a nutmeg, to thread the ball between them. He anticipates this, dropping his shin and catching it, then immediately pulling a Maradona that yanks it back from me.

"Asshole," I mutter.

"You thought you could 'meg me, Willa?"

I shove him. He doesn't budge.

"Keep it clean, Sunshine."

He's ribbing me. Provoking me. His feet hover over the ball. His stance is cocky and confident. I lunge for it, and he bypasses me, nailing a shot into the goal.

I stare at the net, then slowly swivel my gaze to him. "Beginner's luck."

His grin is wider than the field. "Whatever you say."

That does it. I leave the net with the ball, pulling it out to the top of what would be the box if it were painted on the grass. Ryder drops again, and this time I don't focus on his killer legs. I see the whole space, and I do something ballsy. I fake left, then lunge right, chipping the ball over his shoulder. Ryder's caught in the direction I faked him as I slice by, trapping the ball on my chest down to my thigh, where I boot it into the net.

Ryder's eyes dart from the net to me. "Damn. That was sexy."

I bite my lip to fight a smile. "And to think I'm just getting started."

We play for a long time. I get a few goals past him, but Ryder's formidable. He's fast, and he's physical. He also has nine inches and seventy-five pounds on me, which helps.

I'm tired. My thighs shake from exertion, and Ryder's drenched in sweat. Our play gets rougher, touches increase, and our bodies grow closer. I'm practically sitting on his lap, Ryder's large hand against my thigh as I hold the ball out, shielding it from his foot's reach.

Thunder rumbles a ways off. Ryder peers up to the sky, then down to me. "Last goal."

I whistle. It's my possession. We're tied. If I score this, I win. I shift slightly, and Ryder's right up against me, goal-side. Perfect defending. His body's low, his center of gravity exactly as it should be. He feels like a wall I'll never get past. Every time I've gotten by has felt miraculous. I can't even think about what tricks I have left.

"What's she going to do?" I say, peering at him over my shoulder. We're both dripping with sweat, Ryder's jaw's tight. "You called last goal, Bergman. What's it going to be?" His fist tightens on my shirt as I send my ass right into his groin.

"You tell me, Willa." He sends his hips back into me, making my eyes flutter for just a moment before they snap open. "It's your call, how this ends. I've done what I could."

Suddenly, air rushes out of my lungs as our eyes lock. We aren't talking about this little competition. We aren't talking about a friendly one-on-one game.

"No, we're not." His head dips closer. I can smell the perfect scent of his sweat. Heat pours off his body.

"I said that out loud," I say weakly.

He nods. "Do what you have to do, Willa, but please just do it already. Put me out of my misery."

Tears well in my eyes as I straighten my spine. Trailing the ball left, I lean into him. I lean so hard that if he pulled back, I'd fall on my ass, and he knows it. He could let me tumble in the grass, rip the ball off of me and score, no problem.

But he doesn't.

"You could let me bite it right now."

"I know," he grits out.

I shove into him again. "Why don't you?"

He shakes his head, his hands tightening around my waist. "Because it's a dirty move. There's trust. You lean into me, and I lean back."

I glance up at him and feel stupid tears spill down my cheeks.

His body stills. Rain sweeps across the grass, fine and warm. It dapples Ryder's cheeks, clumps his eyelashes. I kick the ball away and spin before my fists find his shirt, then squeeze tight. "I don't want the last word right now. I don't want to win. And that's not normal."

Ryder exhales shakily, his eyes searching mine.

"I want what you want," I tell him, loud and clear, slow and sure. I don't want him to miss a word I say. "All-in, fair and square. I want to be afraid with you rather than fearless and alone. Only when it's us."

Ryder's hands are vise grips on my waist.

"Because I love you, Ryder Bergman. I'm scared shitless to say it, but I love you. I love you, and I always will."

Air rushes out of his lungs as Ryder crushes me to him. "Willa," he mutters into my hair. One long kiss to my curls, as he breathes in, then sighs. "I love you."

I kiss over his heart, reach for his neck. Kisses there too. I want to kiss him everywhere. I want him to feel how much he means to me. I want to make up for so much lost time.

"I love you," he says again, his lips soft along my neck. "I have since you glared up at me and looked like you wanted to roast my skin for dinner."

A wet, gunky laugh bursts out of me, as the rain picks up. It's highly unromantic, how hellish I look. My hair's plastered to my head, snot dripping down my nose. My eyes are red. I'm an ugly crier.

"No, you're not." His hands smooth my hair off my face. "You're beautiful, always, and I love you endlessly, Willa Rose Sutter. I can't help it. I wish I could. I know this makes your life messier. I know I've tortured you. I know we piss each other off as much as we make each other happy. I know I want a quiet life and yours will be nothing but wildly exciting, as you deserve it to be.

"But I want your life to be my life, Sunshine. I'll do whatever it takes for your world to be mine."

"Ryder." I press my forehead to his chest. My ear rests over his heart. It's pounding, fast. It's this tiny reminder that the man holding me is just as fragile. He's just as easily wounded and broken. He's taking a risk, loving me.

Rain pelts down on us as we sway. Until one rough hand grasps my jaw and tips my face up.

Ryder's eyes search mine, a quiet, beautiful smile painting his face. "I love you, Willa Rose."

My smile is ridiculous. It's a comical, clown-at-the-circus, child-at-Christmas smile. "I love you, too, Ryder."

His kiss is soft and tender. It's a quiet press of his mouth, gently opening, unfurling into something warm and bone-deep satisfying. I flick my tongue and find his. I taste him, savor him, as our bodies lock tight. Hands find hair and fabric and skin, and tug, begging for more.

"More," I tell him. "I want it all."

His smile is soft against my lips, his sigh of contentment as warm as the breeze that surrounds us. "Me too, Sunshine."

WILLA

Playlist: "All Night," Beyoncé

I STAND IN A PUDDLE OF WATER AT MY FEET. THE RAIN PICKED up on our walk back. We're warm and soaked. Ryder stares at me, chest rising and falling like he's trying to quiet the storm inside himself. Thunderclouds darken the sky, casting the bedroom in sleepy shades of gray and taupe, rainwater blue.

Ryder steps closer and runs his hands down my arms. His lips press to my temple. Soft, warm kisses as his fingers curl around the hem of my shirt. It peels up my torso and catches on my wet hair before he tugs it resolutely off. Ryder sucks in a breath, the most beautiful expression on his face. Pained wonder. It's not even the first time he's seen me naked, but he looks undone.

Two shaking hands grip the zipper of my sports bra, the unfurling sound echoing in the room before he pushes it off my shoulders.

"God, Willa." He blinks rapidly and quickly wipes his eyes.

"Are you crying, Brawny?"

"Stop it," he mutters, kissing me quickly. "Say my name."

"Ryder," I whisper. His hands slide along my waist, to my shorts and panties, fingers hooking into the material and dragging them down. He kneels as he goes.

"Hold on," he orders quietly.

I grasp his shoulders as I step out of my clothes, but Ryder doesn't stand. His hands drift up my thighs, across my pelvis, then down—

"Willa." Ryder stares up at me, his fingers slowly teasing along impossibly sensitive skin.

A hum of pleasure slips out. "Yes?"

He smiles as he presses a kiss low on my hip. My eyes flutter shut. "I knew things felt smooth last night...but I did not see you being a waxer."

"Rooney said I should. Said if I didn't like your beard, I shouldn't make you deal with mine."

Ryder laughs against my skin.

Good grief, I need a filter. A hot flush surges to my cheeks. "I didn't mean to say all of that out loud."

His lips kiss their way down from my hip, along the tender skin inside my legs, before traveling upward again. "I would have been happy no matter what. Nothing would stop me from doing this."

"Ryder, I don't...historically, that is, this doesn't normally make me—*ohhh.*"

"Hush," he mutters against my skin. "We've already established that's not on you."

My grip tightens on his shoulders as Ryder gently splays me open. Air rushes over everywhere that's warm and wet and aching. I'm flushed, hot, and shivering. When his tongue sweeps over me again, teasingly slow, I buck into his mouth instinctively.

"Ryder," I whisper.

He grins against my skin. "Goddamn, you taste good, Willa. So, so good."

I blush spectacularly. "Really?"

"Hell, yes," he growls. His hands cup my ass and tug me closer.

Something he does with his tongue this time tickles, and I giggle reflexively. Embarrassment heats my cheeks. What if I offended him? Have I ruined the mood? Ryder pulls back and smiles up at me. Just smiles.

"Too soft?" he asks.

"I think so. It tickled."

He glances down at everything before him. He looks incredibly analytical for a second, just how he did when he was talking yesterday about troubleshooting the roof for a leak. Then a grin tugs at his mouth. "So beautiful. I get to see this, taste this, forever."

"Forever, huh?" I ask breathily, trying to sound flippant. Even though my heart's tripping at the weight and promise of his words. Ryder wants me. Forever.

"Yup," he says quietly in between kisses that tease and torture me, so close to where I'm dying for touch. "I'm like a...barn owl. One and done."

I snort and nearly fold over him as I laugh. "A barn owl?"

Ryder shrugs and kisses my belly as I straighten, his hands kneading my ass. "First monogamous species that came to mind. They pick one mate for life." He nuzzles my bare skin and licks gently, firmer this time. "Just be glad I didn't woo you with dead mice. You'd have to be very polite about it since you'd, of course, accept my offer."

His lips whisper over my pelvic bone. I feel a jolt of pleasure swirl in my belly and dance to my breasts. "A-and how would I accept this offer?"

"Well, if you were anything like a female barn owl, you'd make a croaking sound." He presses a kiss right above my clit. My knees buckle as some kind of ungodly noise leaves me.

"Pretty much like that." Ryder does it again. Another kiss right over the sensitive skin protecting where I'm wildly sensitive. I gasp and lean into it.

"Ahh," he murmurs. "She does like it. Noted."

I sigh as he kisses me just like *that* again and again, as his fingers slowly tease where I'm so wet, I'm starting to drip down my thighs. Which—I'd like the record to show—has never *ever* happened before. My hands go reflexively to his thick blond hair, half out of its bun. I tug out his hair tie and run my fingers through those soft, golden strands, fisting them.

It doesn't happen quickly, but Ryder doesn't seem to mind. I tangle my fingers deeper into his hair and find a rhythm against his mouth that feels incredible. It's a quiet, steady build, a candlewick catching, then slowly burning brighter, brighter—

"I'm close. Oh *God*," I yell so loudly, if there are people miles away, they heard it. I could not care less.

Ryder gently nods, a soft hum leaving his mouth. Tenderly, he lowers his lips to my clit and sucks, until my orgasm soars through my body, my toes, my fingers, my breasts, and settles heavily in the pulse between my thighs. More coaxing kisses and gentle words, then Ryder stands and sweeps me into his arms like it's choreography he had blocked out from step one.

"So beautiful," he whispers. I grasp his face and kiss him as he holds me. I taste myself and him, and I want him so badly I can't find air, I can't see the world around me. I just see and feel and want Ryder.

When he sets me on the bed, I sit up, tugging off his sopping clothes. Ryder shivers as I rub my hands up and down his arms, whipping back the sheets and thick comforter, then dragging him inside. Pausing, he unhooks his hearing aids and carefully sets them on the nightstand.

When he turns back toward me, he grins one of those rare, bright smiles of his. Better than the sun slipping out from behind a dark cloud, firelight glowing in midnight blackness. It knocks the air out of my lungs.

His eyes roam my body, following the path of his hand as it cups my breast, travels down my waist, wrapping tight around my backside and hauling me close. We both gasp when his erection presses between us. Instinctively, I grip him and slide my thumb along the sensitive underside of his length. I savor him how I savored him last night, delighting in the soft, velvety skin that moves gently with my hand, the thick rigidity of his cock, how it pulses as I stroke him.

Ryder's eyes slam shut when I slide his length along my soaked entrance. His head drops back as he falls onto the pillow. I'm doing that. I'm making him fall apart. When his eyes open, I sign *good. So good.*

He smiles gently and signs it back. Then I do something, sliding myself against him, that earns a pained sound of desperation. Grasping his arms, I pull Ryder over top of me. He drops his weight between my legs, making me cry out, and it feels incredible to be covered head to toe by his massive body, to feel pinned and held and consumed. Ryder's long, powerful frame, burning hot, so solid over mine, is blindingly sensual. It's comforting. Our gaze holds as he drifts over me, sliding the head of his erection right along my clit.

I ghost my hands over his fantastic backside, appreciating the gentle flex of his muscles as he moves against me. Eventually, my hands travel up his back to wrap around his neck. I bring him close and speak to his right ear. "I'm on the pill. I don't want anything between us."

His forehead drops to my shoulder as a groan leaves him, and when he picks up his head, his eyes are emerald flames. Molten gems, beautiful desire, as he leans back and guides himself until just the tip wedges inside me. He's slow, careful as he begins to ease in.

I grasp his wrist and squeeze to earn his attention. *More,* I sign.

An exhale rushes out of him, as our eyes lock, as with painstaking care and steadiness, Ryder fills me.

"Ry," I gasp.

It's overwhelming. I'm full and stretched, but so much more, I'm pinned by his stare, heart-struck as his mouth falls open the first time he drags back and thrusts into me.

"Okay?" he asks.

I nod furiously. "Yes." I cup his cheek, and he leans into it, turning to press a kiss in my palm.

On the next sure roll of his hips, sparks dance over my skin. Each time's easier, as my body relaxes, as I only get wetter. I'm drenched, and Ryder's gloriously hard. Somehow, we fit, just like he promised. Ryder drops to his elbows, and his hands cradle my head. His eyes hold mine, with each measured, sure thrust that sends air quietly rushing from my lungs.

I blink back tears which he thumbs away. He presses his lips to my ear and whispers, "Touch me."

My heart squeezes. He's nervous, too. Pulling him close in my arms, I kiss the crook of his neck and shoulder, rubbing his back, kneading his muscles. Ryder leans back enough to watch me again. He nudges my legs with his thighs and presses them wider, grinding his pelvis against mine. It rubs my clit, just how his tongue did before. Steady, soft circles as he swirls his hips.

His cock is thicker. His breathing is labored. Sweat beads his temple and a gust of air leaves him when I clench myself around his length. His rhythm falters when I do it again, but Ryder's eyes never leave mine.

Tender, aching need grows inside me, a tightening knot about to snap. It's harsh, urgent. Each time Ryder drifts out, then drives into me, I'm more desperate, more frantic. My toes curl, my hands groping the sheets. Anything to anchor myself.

Ryder dips his head and whispers in my ear, "Let go."

My body tightens, release impossibly close. I don't want this terrifying, beautiful bliss to end. Each stroke, my body coils harder, tension builds.

"Let go and fall, Willa." He grabs my hands and locks our fingers. "I'll catch you." His voice stutters as his movement grows quicker.

Tears stream down my face. My whole body shakes. It's the unsexiest thing, and somehow I still feel so beautiful as Ryder's eyes hold mine, as he dips and kisses me, never breaking eye contact. Seating himself inside my body, Ryder thrusts his hips into mine.

"I'm sorry," he mouths against my lips.

His brow pinches, his mouth falls open as he spills, hot and long inside me. I watch his face tighten, his arms tremor, but his eyes never leave mine. I know he didn't want to come before me, but it's what I need. Once again, Ryder bravely goes ahead, showing me it's safe so I know I can trust to follow him.

I cry his name as the first crushing wave hits me. I'm

clawing at Ryder, gasping for air. The next wave crests, and I scream. His hips roll into mine, he thrusts deeper, giving me the still-powerful feel of his length inside me. Another wave, then another. I shake and sob, arching into him as I smash onto shore, obliterated.

It's the most frightening, stunning, raw moment of my life. I wish it never had to end.

With one last tender roll of his hips, Ryder falls over me, then to the side, his arms scooping me to him and cradling me against his chest. Our breaths are ragged and loud. Our bodies heave. My hands are everywhere. His hair, his cheeks, his jaw, his arms. I kiss him wherever I can, making him laugh quietly.

Soon Ryder's hands caress my body, kneading and stroking until they find my thigh. With one swift motion, my leg's thrown over his hip and I'm being poked in the stomach by—

"Already?" My eyes widen as he slides the hard tip of his length between my thighs.

Ryder laughs. "Yeah, Willa. Already." Another shiver of happiness whispers through me. "I just came in, like, three minutes. That was the prequel. Now it's time for the main act."

I snuggle closer to him but still show him my face so he can read my lips. "It was perfect. I came fast, too."

Ryder grins as I kiss him. "True. But now I have to show off. Wow you with my stamina and lumberjacked moves."

"Oh, yes, please." Reaching past his waist, I cup his butt and squeeze it affectionately. Holy wonder buns. "I've wanted to do this for a lot of months."

Ryder slips inside me, and we both gasp. "Me, too, Sunshine."

My lips find his right ear and press the faintest kiss before I tell him, "I love you."

He sighs happily and nods. His hand tips his lips, a fist across his heart, to mine. *I love you.*

We don't leave that bed for a very, very long time.

30

RYDER

Playlist: "Coloring Outside The Lines," MisterWives

I'M ON THE ROOF, FINALLY GETTING AROUND TO REATTACHING the gutter where it pulled away. I already finished patching the chimney, which is where the leak was coming from.

I'm mid-swing when I hear it.

A shriek. A bloodcurdling, terrifying scream. I have never been so grateful for my hearing aids because there's no way in hell I would have heard her otherwise.

"Willa!" I bellow back. "You okay?" I'm scrambling, throwing everything in the tool bag I carried up the ladder. I climb halfway down the ladder, then leap off the rest of the way and sprint into the house. Willa stands frozen in the entranceway, staring at the ground.

"Willa," I call as I walk toward her. When she still doesn't answer, I wrap my arms around her, checking for broken bones, a hemorrhage. Anything to explain why she screamed like she was dying.

"Th-there," she tells me shakily.

I track her eyes' path and spot something small and dark scuttling across the floor.

"A spider."

"Shh. Don't. You'll summon it." She backs into me, and I can't help but smile at how damn adorable she is when facing the few things in the world that frighten Willa Rose Sutter. Bears. Snakes. Spiders. That's about it.

"It's a daddy longlegs, Willa."

"The hell, it is." She turns and climbs me like I'm a tree until she's wrapped around my waist. "Kill it."

I roll my eyes. "I'm not killing it. Spiders play an important role in the ecosystem—"

"Ryder. Stellan. Bergman." Willa grabs my jaw and looks me dead in the eye. "If you want to get laid tonight, you will kill that fucking spider."

"That's not fair. We agreed sexual threats weren't fair play."

She sighs and drops her forehead to the crook of my neck, before meeting my eyes again. "Fine. Please, just pretty please, kill it. If it's alive, I won't be able to sleep. Or eat. Or think about anything else."

"Willa." I press a kiss to her temple as I walk toward the spider and feel her cling tighter to me. "I'm not killing a harmless—"

I stop, staring closely at it. Willa glances at the floor, too, and shudders. "Okay, never mind." I hike her higher up. "That's a black widow."

Willa shrieks right as my boot lands on it.

Once my ear stops ringing, I deposit Willa on the floor and clean up the damage. When I straighten from that task, Willa's staring at me. Her eyes are chocolate brown turning butterscotch. I know those eyes now. Horny eyes.

I hold her gaze and fight the very real impulse to throw her over my shoulder and take her to bed *again*, but I still have to do my part on the A-frame upkeep while I'm here, and I didn't finish repairing the gutters. "I'm going to wrap up on the roof now."

Willa nods slowly. "Dinner's underway. Should be ready in about an hour."

"Perfect." I kiss her once, hard, on the lips. "I'll be done and cleaned up by then." She pulls me back for one more kiss, and when I break away, I instinctively give her an affectionate smack on the ass.

Willa hiccups and stares up at me, wide-eyed.

I stare back, then clear my throat. "Sorry. Don't exactly know where that came from."

"Like hell you don't," she says. Willa bites her lip and leans into me. "And don't be sorry. I didn't dislike it, for the record. I didn't dislike it at *all.*"

My unease dissipates, and I tug her close, kissing her slowly.

When we pull apart, her smile is warm, so impossibly trusting and affectionate. I can't get over watching those full lips part, that wide dazzling smile I've only ever seen her give me.

"Now get outta here, Slayer of Spiders." Willa swats my ass. "And come back hungry."

————

"Shit."

I suck my finger into my mouth. Second time I've stabbed myself with a paring knife in the last five minutes. That's what I get for trying to hull strawberries while watching Willa dance around in only one of my flannel shirts.

Fucking hell.

She bends over the dining room table, finishing setting it.

Proper silverware, big wine glasses. She even went on a walk for some wildflowers and stuck them in a vase.

"Everything looks and smells great, Willa."

Straightening, she turns and smiles at me. "Thank you. I wanted to make it nice, give you a big feast. All you've done is cook and take care of me." She walks my way and wraps her arms around my waist. "Now it's my turn."

I've liked taking care of Willa. Now I'm starting to not mind when she wants to take care of me, too. Though I'll always enjoy cooking for her, drawing her a hot bath, telling her to put her feet up and relax, it felt weirdly comfortable to finish my to-do list on the house earlier, then come inside to the view of her holding a bodice ripper in one hand while stirring *au jus* for the beef finishing in the oven.

Willa kisses me, and her wild hair tickles my arms. I pull her close and breathe her in. Sunscreen and flowers, a hint of herbs and red wine from cooking.

After one more kiss, I let her go. Willa sweeps up the bodice ripper off the counter which she took from the A-frame's hodgepodge library. I watch her walk the other side of the counter, turn a page and absently sip her wine. Her hair's the biggest it's ever been because I literally cannot keep my hands off her. I keep dragging her back to bed, shoving my fingers into those gorgeous curly waves, tugging, knotting, breathing them in.

Aaand I'm hard now.

I glance down at my dick insistently tenting my sweatpants. "Chill out, dude."

"You talking to your log jammer, Lumberjack?"

I startle and drop the paring knife before I stab myself again. A blush creeps up my cheeks. "Maybe."

Willa sashays around the rest of the island and drops onto a stool. The beef just has to rest in the oven. Dinner's ready.

I'm making dessert. Willa seems content to sit in the quiet of the kitchen and read. It makes my heart tumble as I watch her reading and a blush tingeing her cheeks.

"That is some vintage smut you found, Sunshine."

Willa snorts and drops the book just enough to meet my eyes. "It's so good. This duke is my kind of asshole."

"Isn't that stuff pretty misogynistic? Aren't they all damsels in distress, in need of a good plundering?" I toss the strawberries into a bowl and add the sambuca, Grand Marnier, and sugar. Willa loves peppered strawberries, so I'm making them happen.

"Some of it is, yeah. But others aren't. Like this one." Willa turns the page and takes a sip of her wine. "It's feminist, even though there's 'plundering,' because she *wants* to be plundered. It's feminist as hell, claiming your sexual preferences whether or not they include manhandling."

I freeze with the cream in my hand, spoon in the other. "P-pardon?" My voice breaks. Great. I sound like a blushing teenager.

Willa lowers the book again. Her cheeks are bright pink. "You smacked my ass earlier."

Jesus. "I did."

"And I liked it." Willa sips her wine and gives me a once-over. "You remember that text you sent?"

I pour cream over the strawberries and start stirring. "I've sent you a lot of texts, Willa."

She rolls her eyes. "When I was on the road for playoffs. I threatened to shave your beard when I got back, and you told me that if I laid a hand to your facial hair—"

"You wouldn't be able to sit for days." I clear my throat as heat floods my cheeks. "Yeah, that was inappropriate of me."

"But I liked that, too," she says quietly. "I practically

dropped my phone, I was so aroused. I felt like if I slid my hand inside my panties right then, I would have gone off like a firework."

Blood roars in my ears. I don't want to hurt Willa. In fact, I hate the idea of hurting her at all. I just like the idea of being intense. To hold her tight and fuck her hard, because it expresses how *much* she makes me feel, how deeply I want to be connected to her and her body. And, yes, I can admit some primal part of me gets turned on, swatting Willa's fine ass and watching that turn *her* on.

I haven't been rough at all because I'm not confident I can do it safely. What if I can't hear Willa saying no? What if I miss some quiet cue that I'm making her uncomfortable or hurting her?

I stare down at the strawberries and stir them slowly. "Before...before things changed, I would have been right there with you, Sunshine. But I don't know if I can do that now."

She sets down the book and reaches for my hand. I give it to her automatically and watch her small grip wrap around mine as best as it can. "Can you turn off the oven?"

My stomach twists. "Why?"

Willa grins shyly and releases my fingers. "I have something I want to try. Dinner can wait a little while."

I flip the knob to shut off the oven and circle the island. Willa takes my hand again and pulls me past the dining room into the sunken living room. I showed her how to start a fire the other night, and she has. There's a sea of blankets in front of the crackling hearth she built.

My stomach knots even tighter. "What is this?"

Willa squeezes my hand, then brings it to her lips for a kiss. "Hold on."

Stepping to the side of the bookshelf, she pulls out a

mirror that I recognize belongs to one of the bedrooms. It's an oversized rectangle that is usually propped against the wall to function like a full-body mirror. Willa drags it carefully, a blanket underneath its side. Then, she tips it and props it against the end of the sofa.

She turns and smiles at me. "I hope you don't find watching a turnoff. That was my solution. You'll watch. You can read my lips."

I cover my mouth with my hand and bite my palm. I feel stupidly close to crying. "God, Willa."

She rushes toward me. "What's wrong? Did I…Is it bad? Is it—"

I wrench her against me and kiss her roughly. Tongue, possessiveness. I bite the edge of her lip. "No. Not wrong. I love it."

Her smile is a mile wide. "Good." Her warm breath tickles my chest as she laces her hands behind my neck and pulls me down for a kiss.

"Sunshine. I'm so fucking addicted to you," I growl as I kiss her. "God, it's scary how much I love you."

"Ryder." Her voice cracks as she rips at my shirt, madly opening buttons. "Please. Now."

"Tell me." I pull at her buttons, too.

"You're mine, and I love you," she growls back, tugging me close for a rough kiss. "Forever. I don't fucking care what anyone says, what life brings. You are mine."

Heat blazes through my body. I shove Willa's shirt off her body and watch firelight bathe her every gorgeous curve. She yanks at my shirt, and I help her, tugging it over my head and throwing it aside. Kneeling, she shucks my sweats and boxers and takes me deep into her mouth. My hands go to her head as she pumps me, licking the sensitive tip. God, it feels good, but I'll come too soon if she keeps it up.

"Stop." My voice is low. Rough.

Willa shivers as she stands and wraps her arms around my neck. I hoist her up and hold her close, kissing her deeply. Walking to the blankets, I lay her down and run my hands along her ribs, kissing my way to that beautiful silky skin. I lick her, taste her. Soft, steady strokes, teasing kisses and bites. I want to take her a little harder, and there's no way I can do that comfortably without relaxing her body, giving her an orgasm. Plus, I love making her come. I'll never get over how hot it is to feel her come on my mouth, my fingers, my cock.

Only three days in, and I know just how to send her flying over the edge quickly. I lick, suck, curl my fingers and watch her shake into a fast, powerful release that sends a flush up her chest and throat.

I kiss her slowly, teasing bites followed by tongue as I crawl over her body. Then I flip her over and hear her gasp. I leave on the right ear's hearing aid but take off the left one, which is more sensitive to loud sound and being jostled, setting it on the coffee table. Turning back to Willa, I grab her by the hips and wrench them up. Our eyes meet in the mirror, and I could come right then.

Her eyes are hooded, her cheeks flushed. Her breasts sway beneath her, soft and full, her nipples tight little cherries I love to scrape between my teeth, then suck until she's swearing up a storm and demanding my cock.

Slowly, I splay my hand between her shoulder blades and press her chest to the ground. Our eyes hold as I drift my hand along her spine, down the seam of her ass and lower. I play with her, tease her tight bud and watch her bite her lip.

She wiggles, searching for satisfying touch, but I grab her hip and lock eyes with her. "Be still."

Willa swallows thickly and nods.

My hands squeeze her ass cheeks before I bend down and lick her. I go torturously slow. Long, light, swirling strokes. Never enough to satisfy her, only enough to make her smolder and beg.

Straightening, I lock eyes with her and slide my length over her wet skin. My grip is tight on her hips as I grind against her, and she bucks into me. I rub a hand softly over her ass and watch her lips fall open.

Please, her mouth says as she wiggles. I lift my hand and smack her ass.

"I said still, Willa."

She jumps, and her moan reverberates through her body to mine. Then she bucks her hips into me again. I smack and tease the other round cheek, bend and kiss, then bite, it. Then I watch her reflection as I spank it. She has this euphoric grin on her face.

"More," she mouths. "More, Ryder."

I lean over her and bite her ear, kiss my way down her neck. Long, tantalizing bites. I can feel her panting, how her body shakes as I tease her nipples with my fingers. My length slides perfectly through that hot, satin skin because we fit like we were made for each other. She's soaking wet, and my cock's covered in her.

"So beautiful," I whisper.

She turns for me to kiss her. I cup, then tease her breast again. I can't help but bite her lip as I kiss her. She nearly falls over, but I wrench her upright, seating her on my lap. We look in the mirror together as I hold her hips hard and nudge every throbbing inch against her wet heat. On one sure thrust, I seat myself fully inside her and watch her mouth fly open, her eyes scrunch shut in pleasure. I rub her gently and whisper in her ear. "Look at me."

Willa's eyes flutter open, then lock with mine. She bites

her lip as I stare at her, as my jaw clenches and my body tightens with need. Her body is so small inside mine, but she's powerful, her muscles, her compact strength. She wraps an arm around my neck, as her other hand drops and cups my balls while I drive into her. I rub her swollen clit, but with my free hand, clasp her throat and press my lips to her ear. "Don't hold back. I want to feel your sound."

I pump from beneath her and fill her to the hilt, feeling her moans resonate under my hand, as she cries my name again and again. Each drive inside her is velvet hot, so unbelievably tight around me as I unleash my body's force, as I give Willa everything she asks for, as she meets me thrust for thrust.

I taste her skin, kiss her, worship her. Stare at her in wonder because this is breathtakingly new and vulnerable and powerful. I thought Willa and I knew each other at every complicated layer of who we were, but now I know, this was what was left.

She screams, arching her chest, her body tightening, the rippling power of her orgasm tightening around my cock.

I call her name, not caring how I sound because I know Willa loves me, that no matter how it comes out, what matters to her isn't how I say her name, only that it's her name I'm calling. I kiss her, swallow her moans, feeling every sound under my palm. Lightning strikes my heart as Willa lifts her hand to my cheek and gentles it, turning her face to kiss me with impossible tenderness. The bolt of that touch surges through my system and makes me detonate deep inside her.

We crumple to the blankets, golden firelight scattering across us. Willa's eyes are soft, her body limp and warm against mine. I kiss her, a gentle tangle of tongues and searching lips.

"You okay?" I ask hoarsely.

"I feel shattered and put back together, all at once," she says. "Does that make any sense?"

I trace my fingers over her lips. "I think so. Kind of how I feel, too."

She takes my fingers gently in her mouth before releasing them with a smile. "I think that's what it means to love the way I love you. To love so much you feel broken open and at the same time healed. Maybe that's what it means to be vulnerable? Maybe that's intimacy? Whatever it is, whatever it means, I don't want it to ever end. I never want to stop feeling this kind of love for you. I want us to love each other this deeply, this powerfully, always. Promise me, Ryder."

I cup her cheek, bring her close for yet another gentle kiss. One of thousands and thousands I want from her for the rest of whatever time is given to us. "Promise, Sunshine. Always."

31

WILLA

Playlist: "Home," Edward Sharpe & The Magnetic Zeros

ONE YEAR LATER

"Willa, would you mind helping me?"

Elin gestures toward the sliding door that leads onto their home's patio. She holds a massive tray of snacks not unlike the ones Ryder built for me constantly over our four-day loveathon last year in the A-frame. Those snack boards came in handy when I wouldn't let him leave bed long enough to cook for us, when I was unendingly hungry only for him. When I made him spoon me and play hours of his game, *fill in the blanks.*

I rush over, yanking open the door for her and clearing space on the table.

"Thank you." She smiles as she straightens from setting down the tray. Over the past year, I've gotten to know and love Ryder's mom. She's quiet, like Ryder, and she's kind and affectionate but not over the top, which makes it manageable for me to receive. Ryder says that's very Swedish, that moderate, balanced approach to pretty much everything. Nothing too much. Just enough. *Lagom* it's called. I'm about as un-*lagom* as they come, but Ryder and his mom—his whole family—love me anyway.

Elin sighs and sets her hands on her hips. "Why don't we sit and have some wine, you and I? Ryder and Alex won't be back for a few more minutes from their errand."

I nod, swallowing nerves. Elin's in on my plan. It's the reason I asked her to keep it just the four of us tonight, knowing that was a big ask. Elin always wants all the kids together, and having spent a year's worth of birthdays and holidays with them, I get it. Yes, I need breaks and escapes to Ryder's room from the chaos, but the siblings are all pretty good to each other. They're kind and funny. They like board games and pickup soccer, and they make amazing food. They play old music and watch tear-jerker movies that make me feel my feelings. I understand why she loves having her family together.

But today, I need it to be just us.

Ryder and I graduated yesterday, him with honors, and me with enough honor that while I was not a top-marks student, I was proud of earning decent grades while busting my ass playing Division-1 sports. We're celebrating with his parents, as I sit on a daunting piece of information and an even more daunting question.

"I'll get the wine," I tell her. "Why don't you have a seat and relax?"

Elin smiles as she sits. "Thank you, Willa."

Slipping inside, I pull a chilled bottle of white from the refrigerator and grab two glasses. When I slide the door shut behind me, Elin is staring into the grove of trees, a sad look on her face.

"What's the matter?"

"Hm?" She turns back toward me. "Oh. I was thinking

about death and heartbreak. And I was thinking about your mother."

Air rushes out of me. I drop slowly into my seat.

Be careful what you ask a Swede, Ryder's told me. *They'll tell you exactly the truth, and nothing less. Job loss, dying relatives, affairs. I'm not kidding.*

I thought he was kidding.

Clearing my throat, I uncork the wine and pour her a glass, then me. "What about her?"

Elin tips her glass to mine in quiet cheers. "Life's balancing act, birth and death, the cycle of existence, is unavoidable of course. But it is sad, too. I grieve for you, and I'm sorry she's not here." After a beat, she says, "Joy would be very proud of you."

I blink away tears. Each day since Mama's death, I feel like I can breathe a little better, but the dull ache in my heart hasn't even begun to abate. Ryder holds me lots of nights in bed and lets me cry. I cry more now than I ever used to. Opening my heart to loving someone how I love Ryder means cracking open my heart to all other feelings. Ryder's never impatient, never resentful, even if it breaks up lovemaking, or interrupts dinner. He just holds me and stays right there with me in his quiet way.

"I hope so. I miss her."

Elin smiles gently. "I see so much of her in you. You always have her with you, Willa."

I smile back at her. "That's what she said, too."

Quiet descends between us for a minute as we sip our wine and the sun lowers in the sky. Their garden's an explosion of flowers, the grass as deep green as Ryder's eyes. Butterflies take flight in my stomach as I think about him. I'm still in that crazy-in-love phase. I'm not exactly sure I ever won't be. Every morning that I wake up next to him feels too good to be true.

Elin clasps my hand. "I have something to say to you."

"What about?"

She squeezes my hand, then sits back, her pale blue eyes locked with mine. "Ryder will die one day."

I choke on my wine. "Jesus, Elin."

"What?" She shrugs. "He will. He will also hurt your heart in tiny, very human ways, over the years. He might even break it."

"Well." I sit back and take a giant swill of wine. "The mystery of where Ryder gets his blunt streak is now solved."

Elin laughs. "Oh, Willa, I'm not explaining myself well. What I mean is…if you're going to do what I think you're going to do tonight, I hope you know that I support you two, not despite what life has already thrown at you both, but because of it. I've seen your love for each other. Your love is strong and tested, even stronger because life has already brought you both hardship."

Her words sink in. Old Willa would have never made it to this night with Ryder to hear that affirmation. She'd never be here, nodding, conceding how damn vulnerable loving him is, how open to heartache welcoming him deeper and deeper into her life has and will continue to make her. But New Willa, with over a year's worth of counseling, including several joint sessions with her boyfriend to work on building deeper trust and better communication, sits here, knowing that this scary, bottoming-out feeling in her stomach isn't something to fear—it's a measure of the depth of her love.

I take a slow breath and swirl my wine, focusing on the waves of liquid. "Thank you for saying you believe in us."

Elin's smile is gentle as her hand softly squeezes mine again. "I hope I didn't overstep. I want to encourage you, and yet I know I'm not your mother, and I can never replace her. But I am seven people's mama, and my arms are always open. My heart, too."

Meeting her smile, I squeeze her hand back. "Thank you."

"Hi, Sunshine." Ryder steps onto the porch, bending and kissing me immediately. It's as exciting as it is familiar, the way it always starts as an innocent press of lips and then opens to a gentle taste, a quiet reminder that want and hunger are never far away for him.

"Hi yourself," I say.

He straightens, squeezing my shoulder before he leans and kisses his mom's cheek. Plopping between us in a chair, Ryder riffles through the smorgasbord, pulling a few nuts, some dried fruit, and a hard salami slice into his palm. Elin's eyes meet mine over his head, and I nod.

She stands and pats Ryder's back. "I'm going to go help your father sort out the food you two picked up. I'll be back in a little."

Ryder's halfway standing. "You don't have to, Mom. I said I'd help Dad cook—"

"No." Elin presses him back in his seat. "I want a little time with him. He's been working a lot the past few days. You two relax. It's your celebration, remember, *sötnos*?"

Ryder's brows pinch. "Okay?"

Elin gives me a wink and disappears inside. The moment she's gone, Ryder scooches his chair closer and sets a hand high on my thigh. His eyes are on me, traveling my body.

"It looks even better on you than I thought it would, Willa."

I grin. Ryder surprised me with the dress I'm wearing. It's a saffron-yellow wrap style, not unlike the infamous shirt, with a sash at the waist as red as the napkin dress. I uncross, then switch my legs as Ryder's eyes darken.

"So, my lumberjack. What took so long? Did you and Papa B decide to fetch dinner from the river again? Slay any black bears or mountain lions on your way home?"

Ryder gives me a look as he pops more food in his mouth and crunches. "I didn't hear you complaining about my mountain manliness when you got us lost on that hike and *I* was able to navigate us back to the A-frame using the night stars."

I lob a cranberry at him which successfully drops down the front of his flannel. I raise a celebratory fist. "I did not get us lost. Getting lost would imply I knew where I was going in the first place."

Ryder snorts. "Fair. Hey, you have something—" He points to a spot over his sternum, mirroring where this alleged substance is on my body. "Right there."

"Sure. Never heard that one before." I refuse to glance down at my chest and get my nose bopped. Since we're not into severely torturing each other like we used to, we're reduced to harmless pranks like this that usually lead to making out and sex. Neither sex nor making out are happening right now, so I'm not taking the bait.

"I'm serious, Sunshine. It's fig jam, and it's about to drip onto your new dress."

"Nope."

Ryder sighs and glances over to the glass doors, peering at the kitchen where his parents are. "Fine," he grumbles.

I open my mouth to say something smart, but a gasp leaps out as he bends and his warm tongue slides along the swell of my breast. A tiny bite makes my thighs clamp together.

Ryder straightens and kisses me. "Stubborn woman," he mutters against my lips. I taste him. Warm, decadent Ryder. And…fig jam.

"Dammit."

He shrugs and smiles as he sits back. "Sometimes I'm not fucking with you, Sunshine. Sometimes."

I stare at him and feel my grinch heart grow bigger and bigger. It's almost like it's not even a grinch heart anymore, no frigid, rigid corners. Just a wide-open, safe, loved space. "Ryder."

"Hm?"

I interlace my fingers with his where they rest on my thigh, and take a long slow breath. "We need to talk about something."

Worry tightens his features. "Is everything okay?"

"Mhmm." I swallow emotion thickening my throat and blink away threatening tears.

He leans forward to gentle my cheek. "Then why are you crying?"

"I'm not," I whisper hoarsely.

A soft smile breaks across his face. "Sunshine, what is it?"

Clearing my throat, I reach behind me, inside my bag. There's a manila envelope, tied tight at the top. I set it on the table and slide it toward Ryder.

Ryder stares at it, his hand falling from my face.

"What is this, Willa?"

"Open it."

Ryder's eyes dance up to mine before they drop to the envelope once more.

"Go on," I tell him.

His hands grasp the twine and quickly unspool it. Carefully, he reaches inside and pulls out a hunk of papers, still warm from the printer. A noise catches in his throat when he sees the insignia on the top.

Reign FC.

"Willa," he whispers. A loud laugh of joy jumps out of

him as he sweeps me up and holds me in his arms. "You got signed, Sunshine!"

I nod, smiling ridiculously wide. His kiss is long and passionate, his hug the lung-squeezing, bone-crushing intensity I live for.

"Oh my God, Willa, I'm so proud of you. I'm *so* happy for you."

I slide my fingers through his hair and steal one more kiss before I wiggle, my cue for him to put me down. Our eyes hold as I steeple my fingers over the envelope. "Where's Reign based out of, Lumberjack?"

Ryder frowns in confusion. "Washington. Tacoma, Washington."

I tip my head and smile. "Huh. Tacoma, Washington, you say? Right on the water? Halfway between Olympia and Seattle? That Tacoma?"

Ryder's brow furrows deeper, but a small smile peeks out, too. "Yes, Willa."

"Hm." I tap my fingers on the envelope. "Well, I don't know my way around there. I was hoping I wouldn't be entirely on my own when I move up there next month."

Ryder's body stills.

My voice wobbles, but I catch it. "Would you mind checking that envelope further, seeing if there's anything that might give me some reassurance that I'll get settled how I hope to?"

Ryder gives me a cautious look as he reaches again for the envelope, slowly pressing his hand inside. His fingers search, he ducks his head. Then a deadly calm washes over him.

"Willa," he whispers.

"Yes, Ryder." My voice is thick with tears as I lose the

battle. My rare show of makeup is ruined, mascara running, blush smudged.

"Th-there's a key in there."

I nod. "I know."

Ryder's head snaps up. "What is this?"

I take one step closer to him, clasping his face inside my hands. "I was wondering, Ryder Bergman, lumberjack love of my life, if you wouldn't mind moving to Washington State with me. I found a bungalow for rent right near the water and a bunch of hiking grounds nearby. It's the perfect spot for a mountain man like you to hunker down and start his own outdoorsman business, don't you think?"

Ryder drops his head to my shoulder, and his hug is fierce. His lips press softly against my neck, my cheeks, my lips.

"Is that a yes?"

Ryder pulls away, his smile a thousand times more brilliant than the sunset behind it. "It's a hell yes, Willa. It's the best yes of my life."

Our kisses are unhurried, passionately tender, as the sun drifts below the horizon behind us. I cry and laugh and feel every single feeling I can. Because I want to remember this moment, even when our love is blissfully old and splendidly weathered. I want to close my eyes and feel the memory of the moment *only when it's us* became *only us, forever*.

THE END

Don't worry, Willa and Ryder's story is over, but this isn't the last time you'll see them! Ren's book is next, and you better believe the giant ginger hockey star's favorite brother and soon-to-be sister-in-law will make a significant appearance.

ACKNOWLEDGMENTS

Every romance novel is a story of growth, both individual and relational. Growth is born of curiosity, curiosity begets learning, learning begets healing, healing begets hope, and hope is what allows every romance to end in happily ever after.

Of course, growth isn't only the purview of romance novels—it is the very heartbeat of living. And growth is a big part of why this book exists, first in its original version that I published April 1, 2020, and this revised, expanded edition that I have republished this August 21, 2021. Growth enabled me to take a risk back in early 2020 and write the story I believed in and loved. Growth also enabled me to pursue republishing this story when I learned the ways I could make this story so much stronger.

Since beginning my author journey, I have grown in my knowledge of how best to write authentic representation. Where I am as an author now is not where I began, and when I learned that aspects of the late-deafened representation in this book fell short of the standard for authenticity that I strive for, I wanted to correct that through critique and resolution of those inaccuracies. Facing contractual obligations that I worried might prevent this, I pursued the help of my professional support system and we found a way to achieve what I'd hoped. I am so deeply grateful to my agent and agency for their help so we could do this, including re-record the audiobook.

Through growth, both personal and relational, the growth

I have experienced and the growth of a professional community, including a community of fellow authors and readers, *Only When It's Us* now reflects the consideration and authenticity I aspire to in all the books I write. I owe special thanks to A.K., my authenticity reader, for making this possible. A.K., I cannot thank you enough for all you did to make this story stronger, for all the ways you shared your heart and life and wisdom so that Ryder's journey and all the people who love him in *Only When It's Us* better reflected what I'd always hoped.

While no one character, let alone living person's, experience represents the totality of a disability, this story's portrayal is now, thanks to A.K., informed by a Deaf authenticity reader whose experience of being late-deafened echoes Ryder's. Thank you A.K., for seeing value in Willa and Ryder's story and diligently consulting with me to make this book its better self.

Today, as I republish this book, I am grateful for growth and the stories that thrive in its soil, blossoming with hope: romance novels that savor the joy of love in all its forms, celebrate the gift of intimacy, and affirm our worthiness of loving belonging, just as we are.

XO,

Chloe

EXCLUSIVE SNEAK PEEK: ALWAYS ONLY YOU

(Bergman Brothers #2)

CHAPTER 1: FRANKIE

Playlist: "Better By Myself," Hey Violet

Ren Bergman is too damn happy.

In the three years I've known him, I've seen him not smiling *twice*. Once, when he was unconscious on the ice, so I hardly think that counts, and the other time, when an extreme fan shoved her way through a crowd, yelling that she'd had his face tattooed on her lady bits because, and I quote: "A girl can dream."

But for those two uncharacteristically grim moments, Ren has been nothing but a ray of sunshine since the moment I met him. And whereas I myself am a little storm cloud, I recognize that Ren's Santa-on-uppers capacity for kindness makes my job easy.

As In-Game Social Media Coordinator for the Los Angeles Kings, I have my work cut out for me. Hockey players, you may have heard, are not always the most well-behaved humans. It inflates the ego, getting paid millions of dollars to play a game they love while tapping into their inner toddler. *Hit. Smash. Shove.*

With fortune comes fame and fawning females at their fingertips—those don't help matters, either. Yes, I'm aware that's a lot of "f" words. So, sue me, I like alliteration.

While the PR department has the delightful privilege of putting out public-image fires, I do the day-to-day groundwork of cultivating our team's social media presence. Glued to the team, iPhone in hand, I make the guys accessible to fans by implementing PR-sanctioned hype—informal interviews, jokes, tame pranks, photo ops, gifs, even the occasional viral meme.

I also document informal charitable outings geared toward our most underrepresented fans. It's not in my exact job description, but I'm a big believer in breaking down stigma around differences we tend to ostracize, so I wormed my way into the process. I don't just want to make our hockey team more accessible to its fans, I want us to be a team that leads its fans in advancing accessibility itself.

That makes me sound sweet, doesn't it? But the truth is nobody on the team would call me that. In fact, my reputation is quite the opposite: Frank the Crank. And while this bad rap is formed on partial truths and ample misunderstandings, I've taken the moniker and run with it. In the end, it makes everyone's lives easier.

I do my job with resting bitch face. I'm blunt, all business. I like my routines, I focus on my work, and I sure as shit don't get close with the players. Yes, we get along for the most part. But you have to have boundaries when you're a woman in the near-constant company of two-dozen testosterone-soaked male athletes—athletes who know I'm in their corner, but who also know Frankie is a thundercloud you don't get too close to, unless you want to get zapped.

Just like rainclouds and sunshine share the sky, Ren and I work well together. Whenever PR has a killer concept and I come up with a social media home run—pardon my mixing sports metaphors—Ren is my man.

Campy skit in the locker room to raise money for the

inner-city sports programs? There's Ren and his megawatt smile, delivering lines with effortless charm. Photoshoot for the local animal shelter's fundraiser? Ren's laughing as kitties claw up his massive shoulders and puppies whine for his attention, lapping his chin while he lavishes them with that wide, sunny grin.

Sometimes, it's practically stomach-turning. I still get queasy when I remember the time Ren sat with a young cancer patient. Turning white as a sheet, given his fear of needles, he told her the world's lamest knock-knock jokes while he donated blood and she had her bloodwork done. So they could be brave together.

Cue the collective female swoon.

I shouldn't complain. I shouldn't. Because, truly, the guy's a nonstop-scoring, smiling, six-foot-three hunk of happy, who makes my job much easier than it otherwise would be. But there's only so much sunshine that a grump like me can take. And for three years, Ren has been pushing my limit.

In the locker room, I scowl down at my phone, handling an asshole troll on the team's Twitter page, while I weave through the maze of half-naked men. I've seen it all a thousand times, and I could care less—

"*Oof*," I grunt as my face connects with a bare, solid chest.

"Sorry, Frankie." Strong hands steady me by my shoulders. It's the happy man himself, Ren Bergman. But this time, he's shirtless, which Ren never is. He's the most modest of the bunch.

I'm tallish, which places my gaze squarely in line with Ren's chiseled-from-stone pectoral muscles. And flat, dusky nipples, which tighten as the air chills his damp skin. I try to avert my eyes, but they have a mind of their own, drifting lower and lower to his six-, no eight-, no—dammit, his *a-lot-of*—pack.

My swallow is so loud it practically echoes in the room. "I-it's okay."

Well, hello there, husky, sexed-up escort voice.

I clear my throat and tear my eyes away from his body. "No worries," I tell him. "My fault." Lifting my phone, I wiggle it side to side. "Serves me right for traipsing around, nose-deep in Twitter."

Ren smiles which just spirals my mood even further south. The amount of dopamine that this guy's brain makes daily is probably my annual sum total.

Smoothing a hand over his playoff beard, he then brings it to the back of his neck and scratches, which I've learned over the past few years is his nervous tic. His bicep bunches, one rounded shoulder flexes, and I try not to stare at his massive lats, which give his upper body a powerful "V" shape, knitting themselves to his ribs, and a long, trim waist.

The visual feast results in a temporary short circuit, wiping my thoughts clean but for a two-word refrain.

Wowy. Muscles.

It must be because whereas the rest of the team are practically nudists, Ren always disappears for a shower and comes back rocking a fresh suit, crisp shirt, and tie. I've never seen this much Ren Bergman nakedness. Ever.

And I'm riveted…

Want to read more? Purchase ALWAYS ONLY YOU!

ABOUT THE AUTHOR

Chloe writes romances reflecting her belief that everyone deserves a love story. Her stories pack a punch of heat, heart, and humor, and often feature characters who are neurodivergent like herself. When not dreaming up her next book, Chloe spends her time wandering in nature, playing soccer, and most happily at home with her family and mischievous cats.

To sign up for Chloe's latest news, new releases, and special offers, please visit her website (www.chloeliese.com) and subscribe! Want to connect further? Find Chloe on the following platforms:

instagram.com/chloe_liese

tiktok.com/@chloe_liese

twitter.com/chloe_liese

facebook.com/chloeliese

goodreads.com/chloe_liese

amazon.com/author/chloeliese

bookbub.com/profile/chloe-liese

BOOKS BY CHLOE LIESE

The Bergman Brothers Novels

Only When It's Us (#1)

Always Only You (#2)

Ever After Always (#3)

With You Forever (#4)

Everything for You (#5)

If Only You (#6)

Only and Forever (#7)

Holiday Romance

The Mistletoe Motive